"By the horns of Kiri-Jolith, what is that?" roared Toron, suddenly gazing skyward. "It can't be a—"

But it was.

A dragon. A red dragon soaring high into the sky, burying itself in the clouds above.

They stood there, trying to make sense of it.

Next a smaller, sleeker dragon, gleaming silver, raced skyward. There was something on its back, something that Hecar was fairly certain was a rider.

"Silver and red," he whispered. He could never forget the battles he had watched in the sky during the war. "Deadly foes. They'll fight to the death. The rider . . ." It seemed a voice spoke in his head. He nodded to himself, not caring whether the others heard or not. "Yes, it is Kaz. It would have to be."

Saga

From the Creators of the DRAGONLANCE® Saga

THE LOST HISTORIES

The Kagonesti
Douglas Niles

The Irda
Linda P. Baker

The Dargonesti
Paul B. Thomson and Tonya Cook

Land of the Minotaurs
Richard A. Knaak

The Gully Dwarves
Dan Parkinson

The Dragons
Douglas Niles

**The Lost Histories
Volume 4**

Land of
the Minotaurs

Richard A. Knaak

DRAGONLANCE® Saga
The Lost Histories
Volume Four

LAND OF THE MINOTAURS

First Printing: January 1996
Printed in the United States of America.
Library of Congress Catalog Card Number: 95-62076

9 8 7 6 5 4 3 2

8371XXX1501

ISBN: 0-7869-0472-0

TSR, Inc.
201 Sheridan Springs Rd.
Lake Geneva WI 53147
U.S.A.

TSR Ltd.
120 Church End, Cherry Hinton
Cambridge CB1 3LB
United Kingdom

"We have been enslaved but have always thrown off our shackles. We have been driven back, but always returned to the fray stronger than before. We have risen to new heights when all other races have fallen into decay. We are the future of Krynn, the fated masters of the entire world. We are the children of destiny."

Ancient Minotaur Litany

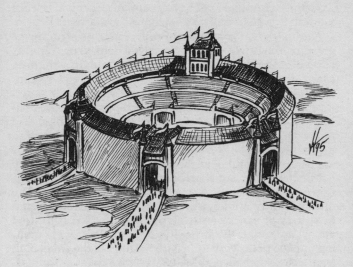

Chapter 1
A Balance to Maintain

Nethosak had obviously prospered in the past few years and yet to Hecar there was a hint of something poisonous in the air, as if the grand, imperial city of his people had somehow begun to spoil at the core.

Perhaps the stories are true, then, thought the tall minotaur. Perhaps the travelers were not exaggerating after all when they said that the empire had become corrupted, though even they had been at a loss to say exactly how.

The imperial capital of the minotaur empire had not only more than recovered in the eight years since the fall of the Dark Queen, it had swelled in both grandeur and might.

Even three years ago, when Hecar and his sister had last bid farewell to it, Nethosak had not looked so masterful.

Nethosak was a city of immense marble structures, great buildings whose entrances were flanked by columns carved in the shapes of triumphant minotaur warriors. Many of these were clan houses. The house of Orilg, to which Hecar belonged, was, fortunately for him, situated far on the other side of the city. The houses here were of lesser clans. Nearby were shops, trade buildings, and many smithies, for weaponry was in constant demand in an empire bent on expansion. All of the buildings appeared clean and new, though many were centuries old.

Minotaurs tall and short, dark and light, hurried along, ignoring the lone figure who stood to the side of the orderly, nearly unblemished street. The lane was covered in stone not unlike a pearly marble, so that it looked almost as though the structures around Hecar were melting into the path. Very little garbage littered the street and, even as he watched, a gully dwarf with a collar around his throat scurried to pick up what he could. Hecar's people had finally found a use for the dirty, childlike creatures.

The watcher's mouth curled into a sour smile. Such a wonderful folk his kind were. Three years away from them had made Hecar see the minotaurs as others did, and he was not pleased by this insight.

In the distance, other, taller buildings jutted toward the sky. The tall, wide edifice with the arched roof was the palace of the emperor. Up close, it very much resembled the clan houses, save for the great roof. Marble columns, a long series of wide steps, a few windows on the upper levels . . . and the same blank, colorless walls that marked nearly every building in Mithas and Kothas. Having lived in the woodlands, Hecar found his old home drab and emotionless in ways that had annoyed him only vaguely when he had resided in Nethosak.

Flanking the palace—but from a supposedly respectful distance—were two other large, even more utilitarian edifices. The rounded building was the central temple of the Holy Orders of the Stars, where the high priest of the state religion resided. Here acolytes were trained and clerics were given the word of Sargas, the Great Horned One. Humans continued to insist that the god was Sargonnas, the Dark Queen's consort, but even Hecar could not accept that. Whether true or false, he really did not care, for he was more inclined toward the smaller, less organized belief in Kiri-Jolith, the bison-headed god of just cause. The house of Orilg was that god's bastion, which oftimes meant trouble with the state priests.

On the other side was the plain, boxlike building that served as the central quarters of the Supreme Circle, the eight minotaurs who oversaw the administration of the empire. Each member of the circle claimed a great number of followers, subordinates, and personal guards. There were clans smaller than the numbers who obeyed the dictates of any one circle member. Even more important, all government workers, including the strong and ever-present State Guard, which policed not only Nethosak but the entire realm, acknowledged the superiority of the Supreme Circle. Of course, the circle and the priesthood were supposed to bow to the commands of the emperor, yet there were circumstances when both could not only bypass his authority, but dictate to him.

Overall, the system had always seemed a proper, efficient one to Hecar, until now. After hearing about the doubts and uncertainties of those who had departed the empire, he had to wonder.

A distant roar made him turn his gaze to the only structure in the distance that dwarfed even the palace.

The Great Circus.

It was as massive a colosseum as any built on the face of Ansalon, perhaps all of Krynn. Its architects had designed it with the thought that the entire minotaur race could be seated within, there to watch matters of justice and honor settled in hand-to-hand combat, as was the way of Hecar's kind. While the population had long ago outgrown the Great Circus, it still allowed a good portion of the imperial city's citizenry to enjoy the spectacles. There was no other building as important to minotaurs as the Great Circus, not even the palace, the central temple, or the headquarters of the Supreme Circle. The Great Circus was where the mightiest champions fought one another to prove their supremacy. It was where entire clans could be displaced from power.

It was where any minotaur who had proven himself worthy enough, who had risen in rank beyond all other champions, could challenge the present emperor and, if successful, succeed him as ruler. The imperial palace and everything within it would then belong to the victor. He or she would be the hand of the empire, guiding the race ever closer to its destiny. One day soon, so the priesthood kept proclaiming, a minotaur who would lead his people to dominate Krynn would sit upon the throne.

Hecar snorted. Of course, a challenger was just as likely to end up dead in the circus, killed by the emperor. Even when an emperor was replaced, which seemed to happen not very often these days, nothing much changed. The past few emperors, including the ones Hecar's father could recall, seemed interchangeably alike.

By the time we're finally ready to conquer the other races, he thought in some bitterness, the Last Day will have come and gone. We'll be masters of nothing.

From the distant, circular edifice came another roar of approval. There was a good match going on today, for which Hecar was grateful. That meant that a great many minotaurs he had no desire to see just yet would be at the circus, cheering and betting on the possible demise of their fellows. The traveler could go about his business and, with any luck, be gone from Nethosak before nightfall. Hecar did not want to stay even one night in the imperial capital. Simply setting foot in the city after three years of self-imposed exile was enough to make him realize how little he missed the politics and folly, both often intertwined in Nethosak, and how true had been the words of his sister Helati's mate, who had spoken to him just before his departure two weeks earlier. He had been warned that, having tasted freedom, neither he nor the other minotaurs living in the small settlement to the south would ever feel comfortable visiting the great city again. Hecar had laughed, recalling good memories, but those had paled even before the minotaur had reached the city gates.

What is it, though? Why do I feel so ill at ease?

The gully dwarf suddenly hustled to a spot just in front of him, the creature's gaze riveted by a small piece of refuse. The squat, ugly little figure, a male, snatched it up as if it were gold, then glanced up at the looming minotaur.

"Galump make clean, Master! Galump make clean!"

There was such fear in the gully dwarf's face that Hecar, taken aback, could think of nothing to say. Galump took the silence for approval and rushed off to snare another bit of garbage. Rather than laugh at the dwarf's desperation, something he might well have done long ago, Hecar felt disgusted. There was something dishonorable, he believed, about mistreating such a weak and helpless race. The gully dwarves were pathetic, but did that make the minotaurs admirable simply because they could dominate the simple creatures and force them to do such menial tasks?

It's because we've failed to conquer any other folk, Hecar thought. There, in the form of an ugly, weak thing with the mind of an infant, stands the sum total of our national ambition for conquest.

The gully dwarf was not even a slave actually taken in war. Galump's people had no real home, not even much in the way of leadership or combat skills. Hecar could picture in his mind what had probably happened. Someone had likely spotted one of the tribes wandering through the hills and sent a small force to round them up with nets. Catching a gully dwarf was easier than catching a legless rabbit. They generally froze in terror at the sight of a minotaur on horseback.

It was amazing that someone had managed to teach them how to pick up trash in so careful and thorough a manner. Hecar suspected that the gully dwarf's training had included torture of some sort.

With great effort, he tore himself from the familiar area he had so often frequented and headed deeper into the city. The streets were wide and the buildings tall, something that made him feel uncomfortable after so long in the woodlands. Hecar already found himself longing for the soft earth beneath his feet and the sweet, clean air that he had not breathed since coming within a day's journey of the overcrowded capital. He was welcomed not only by the smell of the sea, which, as a veteran sailor, he appreciated, but also a rancid odor prevalent in most minotaur cities, and especially so here.

Hecar's path took him closer to the docks, where the scent of the sea was stronger. The minotaur sniffed, recalling adventures from his younger days when he had sailed off on his first major expedition aboard the *Gladiator*. There were times he wished he had remained with the ship after his first two years, but if he had, he would have gone down with Master Ganth's vessel during the veteran captain's special mission for the empire. No one had seen or heard of the ship again, save for a few loose articles found by another vessel. For more reasons than one, Hecar missed Master Ganth. The captain had been a good teacher and a prime exponent of minotaur honor and strength. As a member of the same clan house as his first captain, Hecar always felt proud to recall that he had served with the stalwart minotaur.

All memory of his sailing days faded abruptly as he drank in the sight before him. It was not by chance that he had journeyed near the docks. Some of the news he and his companions had picked up from minotaurs who had recently departed Nethosak concerned a new fleet being built. What those newcomers had failed to emphasize was just how great a fleet had already been completed.

There were ships and ships and ships. All of them were obviously new, the oldest little more than three years. In all his life, Hecar could not recall so many fighting vessels docked at the capital. Nethosak had always been the busiest port in either kingdom, but it was clear that most of the vessels here were moored for some grand strategy. They were being saved for what had to be a substantial sea assault.

While the effort it must have taken the empire to build so many ships in the past few years was both astonishing and admirable, the fact that so much work had gone on since his departure disturbed Hecar. There had been some build-up of forces in the first five years after the minotaurs escaped the servitude of the Dark Lady, but the incredible rate of the last three years spoke of obsession.

It's far too soon to be thinking of conquest, Hecar thought, shaking his head at the sight, *far too soon. The empire will be heading for another downfall if this continues.* "What mad fool has become emperor since I left? What're the priesthood and the Supreme Circle doing?"

His questions had been muttered quietly. When a voice behind him responded, it took the visiting minotaur by surprise.

"You should be careful what you ask around here, Boy."

The owner of the voice was a scarred, light brown-furred, weatherworn minotaur with only half a right arm. He carried a heavy sack in the other one and was obviously a dockworker. His snout was long and wrinkled.

"Lost the arm to a shark I killed after my ship went down, Boy," remarked the elder, noting Hecar's glance. "Ended up eating *him* instead of the other way around." The older minotaur chuckled, then grew serious. "Talking out loud's not good sometimes."

"Just mouthing a few harmless thoughts, Elder." Why was this other so concerned about what he had said?

"Suit yourself." The other peered at him. "Been away for a while have you? Far away?"

"Far enough."

"Come in on a ship?"

He had not, but for some reason Hecar decided to nod. "Long voyage."

"Was it? Probably you had better luck on your voyage than I had on my last, Boy. . . . Which ship was that?"

"*Gladiator*," Hecar immediately replied, hoping his inquisitive companion did not know that the remains of that particular ship rotted away at the bottom of the sea. He shifted his weight, adding, "I've business to attend to,

Elder. May your ancestors guide you."

"And may yours guide you, Boy."

The old minotaur seemed innocent enough, but Hecar did not relax his guard. He had the distinct notion that he had been questioned for some reason. Perhaps he was just being paranoid. He had, after all, spent several days of travel worrying about the rumors and rumblings of the minotaurs who had joined the settlement.

Yet, more than ever, Hecar was certain that something was different in the empire, something that had not yet come to fruition but which held the potential for disaster.

His quickened pace brought him to his destination sooner than he expected. The dwelling was of the modest type that a minotaur who had reached a respectable status would choose. Like most minotaur dwellings, it was little more than a cube-shaped structure, two stories tall and surrounded in front by a stone wall about three feet high. A wooden plaque bore the sign of that minotaur's clan house and his own personal marks.

Modest though it was, it was still more extravagant than the sort of dwellings lower-ranking minotaurs inhabited. Those dwellings, deeper in the core of the city and generally near the smaller arenas, were, more often than not, squat, single-room apartments of an unremarkable gray stone. They were stacked six high in some places, more than a dozen per floor, and were not as immaculate as the rest of the city. The inhabitants, usually striving to achieve better status, rarely considered those places permanent homes.

Hecar was glad that he had chosen to live in the barracks of the great clan house. In return for three years' guard service, he had been given a clean, small abode. Granted some of his bedmates had not been the friendliest of comrades, but he still considered those years better spent than if he had been forced to abide in squalor. Of course, many minotaurs had no choice.

The marks on the wall were the same ones that he recalled from when he had last visited. Hecar was pleased that the one he sought still lived here, but oddly disappointed at the same time. Surely Jopfer could have raised his status in three years. While more studious than some minotaurs, Jopfer de-Teskos, youngest son of the master of the Teskos clan, had been a favorite of one member of the Supreme Circle. In fact, when last they had talked, Jopfer had hinted that his master intended to groom him for a position as one of his senior aides.

By this time you'd think Jopfer would have risen to be one of the Eight, Hecar thought. Certainly if he knew anyone who fit the criteria for becoming one of the eight minotaurs overseeing the administration of the empire, it was old Jopfer. Yet an aide to a member of the circle would certainly not choose to reside in a place such as this. Such status demanded something larger and more impressive, nearer his master's quarters.

"Only one way to find out," he grunted. Marching to the tall, wooden door, Hecar slammed his fist against it. The sound against the wood echoed loudly. Anyone within would have to acknowledge such a racket.

Yet there was no answer. Hecar slammed his fist against the door again. He waited for what he thought a reasonable time, then snorted in annoyance. Either Jopfer's entire household had departed or everyone within was ignoring visitors. His short time in Nethosak made Hecar seriously consider the latter. Was there some reason that Jopfer would fear visitors?

"Come on, you bookworm!" he growled under his breath. "Answer!"

Still no one came. Stubborn as he was, the minotaur finally tired of waiting. If his friend was not available, then Hecar's only recourse was to go to his own clan house. He was not certain how the clan would greet him after his and his sister's decision to stay away, but certainly, after all this time, they could not still be angry with the pair. The others of their party who had returned to Nethosak after that idiotic chase would have explained Hecar's and Helati's reasons for remaining behind. All except Scurn, of course, but then he would have returned in shame. No one would have listened much to him.

The sun was already dipping downward. Hecar grimaced, realizing that if he visited the House of Orilg, he would be required to stay the night. It would be a dishonor to the clan if he appeared after an absence so long, only to leave again an hour or two later. The patriarch would certainly think ill of him, something Hecar did not desire. Orilg could not boast of an emperor on the throne in some seven generations—a point of great aggravation—yet Orilg was still one of the strongest clans. Falling out of favor with the present patriarch would have repercussions, especially where Hecar's immediate family was concerned.

His thoughts entangled over the proper way to present himself to his lord, Hecar did not at first notice the small form darting by. Only when it collided with him did the minotaur take notice of the gully dwarf.

"Sorry, Great One! Galump is sorry!" The dwarf bowed quickly, then ran off, his litter bag falling to the ground as he rushed away in near panic.

"You! Come back here!" His cry went unheeded. Hecar watched as the gully dwarf disappeared into the shadows. He was one of the quickest of the short creatures the minotaur had ever seen.

Hecar had more important things to concern himself with than chasing a gully dwarf whose only crime was carelessness. The dwarf would likely be punished for losing his bag, and in the process littering the very streets he was supposed to clean. But despite the compassion for unfortunate creatures that Hecar had learned from his sister's mate, the minotaur could do nothing to help save pick up the bag and place it neatly to the side.

He was just in the process of doing that when he heard the clink of metal. Tensing, Hecar stretched his hands around toward his back. Most minotaurs favored heavy battle-axes and many, including Hecar, carried them in back harnesses. All he had to do was reach a few inches more, and the axe would be in his grasp, ready to taste the blood of any adversaries.

"May Sargas watch over you, Brother," intoned a voice.

Hecar lowered his hands as he turned. He knew the

imperious tone, as did all minotaurs. A cleric of the Holy Orders of the Stars. To humans, a minotaur cleric might seem a somewhat humorous sight, for, unlike Hecar and most of his kind, who wore kilts and armor but little else, a cleric was usually clad in a solemn black robe covering him or her from foot to head. The hood and shoulders of the robe were crimson. Both colors were said to be favored by Sargas himself.

Only the cleric's muzzle was visible, the rest of his face shadowed by the hood. His hands were clasped together and, as he walked toward Hecar, there was the faint clink of metal, indicating that under his garment the robed figure was both armed and armored.

Behind him trailed a pair of warriors with the look of the guard on their cold features. Members of the guard were generally recruited from the more fanatical warriors in the armies. This pair carried long swords as opposed to axes and looked ready to run Hecar through if he dared resist.

And what is it I'm supposed to resist? wondered the traveler. "May your ancestors guide you, Brother."

"You have business with Jopfer de-Teskos?"

"I sought out an old friend, Cleric. He wasn't home."

"So I know. How do *you* know him, Brother?" The cleric reached up and pulled back his hood. The cleric was surprisingly gaunt for a minotaur and much younger than Hecar would have guessed. However, the chill eyes warned that it would be a mistake to cross him.

"He's an old friend. I've just arrived here and thought I would visit since I was close by."

"Did you come by ship?"

A slight sound behind him warned Hecar that the three figures were not alone. He gave no sign that he had heard the others sneaking up behind him, but shifted so as to get his hands as close to his axe as he dared without giving his movements away. "Aye, I came from a ship. Been away for a while."

The cleric nodded, mouth set. He neither smiled nor frowned. "The *Gladiator*, wasn't it?"

Hecar twitched before he could control himself. He had

given the name to the old male on the dock, not long before. "Aye, *Gladiator*."

The cleric nodded, closed his eyes, and a moment later uttered, "The *Gladiator*, lost at sea more than a decade ago. Nearly all hands lost with it." He opened his eyes and stared without emotion at the tense Hecar. "Therefore, you could not have just arrived on it."

Hecar said nothing. His hands were close to the handle of his axe. Any nearer and he would be committing himself to battling a cleric of high standing in the orders, not to mention several members of the guard. Yet, what could he do? He was not as clever as Helati's mate. Not nearly as clever as Kaz.

"What is your name?"

He was still debating how he should answer when one of the warriors behind him announced, "His name's Hecar, of the clan Orilg, Holiness. I thought I recognized him earlier."

The voice was so familiar that Hecar dared peek over his shoulder. There were three minotaurs behind him, one with a sword and the other pair with axes. It was one of the latter who had spoken. The tall, scarred figure grinned at him.

"Your house, is it not, Captain Scurn?" the cleric asked.

"The guard is my clan now, Holiness."

"Scurn?" When last he had seen the disfigured minotaur, Scurn had been an object of pity, defeated in combat by Kaz. The other minotaurs had been forced to lead their companion by hand from Solamnia all the way back to the empire, so broken was he by his loss. This incarnation, however, did not look at all defeated. In fact, he looked even uglier and more vicious than Hecar could ever recall.

"We are always happy to welcome a lost one back into the fold," commented the cleric. "Come with us, Brother Hecar."

Scurn and the other minotaurs closed in.

Hecar reached for his axe . . . and found that something held it firmly in its harness. The minotaur pulled harder but, despite his great strength, the axe remained stuck fast.

The gully dwarf? He was the only one who had come within touching distance of Hecar. Had he done something to the harness when they had collided?

Hecar glanced around, judged the expressions on the guards, and decided that he was surrounded and defenseless.

What, he wondered, would Kaz do under these circumstances? Of course, being far more clever, Kaz would not have made such a journey in the first place. He had warned Hecar from doing it, but the latter had been too curious and headstrong.

What would Kaz do in his position? There was really only one choice. If Scurn was the captain of this lot, going voluntarily with them did not vouchsafe Hecar's continued well-being.

Snarling, he charged the cleric. The robed figure was surprisingly swift, so much so that he was easily able to dodge his attacker. The two guards beside the cleric moved in to seize Hecar, as did the three others. Hecar swung a fist wildly and succeeded in catching one guard on the underside of the jaw. His attacker stumbled backward, but did not fall. The other guard who had stood with the priest seized Hecar's arm and twisted it viciously.

Roaring in pain, Hecar still managed to keep his footing. He brought one foot up and struck his adversary in the back of the leg, just below the knee joint. The guard fell to his knees, losing his grip.

"Alive!" shouted Scurn. "Alive!"

A heavy foot caught Hecar in the small of the back. He fell forward. Something hard and flat struck him on the head just behind the horns. The world spun.

"Not too hard, Captain. Save something for the circus."

Darkness began to creep over Hecar. He shook his head in an attempt to clear it, thinking, What's happening? What by Kiri-Jolith's axe is responsible for this madness? I've done nothing!

Then he was struck hard again. Oddly, the last thing he heard was a voice, a calming voice, say, "There is a balance to maintain. I am sorry."

Chapter 2
Kaz's Mission

Still no word from Hecar, Kaz thought as he gazed over the small settlement. "Small" was perhaps not the proper word anymore, for there had to be at least sixty minotaurs in the vicinity and another thirty down by the river. What had started out as a home for Helati and him, with Hecar, her brother, deciding to remain nearby, had grown into a village. Most of the newcomers had only just arrived during the past year and a half, and the population increased every couple of weeks. Word had somehow gotten back to minotaurs disenchanted with the reborn empire that a free settlement existed. If things continued at this pace, the race could soon claim three kingdoms instead of two.

And they'll probably try to make me emperor at that point. He snorted, not so much out of the ridiculousness of the possibility but rather at the realization that he was already well on his way to becoming such a figurehead. Already the others looked to Kaz as their leader. His reputation, instead of being sullied by rebellion against his former masters, had earned him respect in the eyes of many. His past glories in the circus also lent him an air of strength, for he was the only one of his rank who had ever chosen retirement rather than demanding his right to challenge the emperor for the throne.

Kaz grunted. He knew he had to return to Helati and tell her that her brother had missed yet another rendezvous. Hecar should have returned from the capital long ago. There was no denying now that something must have happened. Paladine protect you, Hecar! Why couldn't you listen to me? Going back to Nethosak was asking for trouble!

The tall, dark-furred minotaur started back to the dwelling he shared with his mate of two years' standing. Perhaps it would have been better to remain in the icy south, but after the snow wraiths and dwarves of frozen Farahngrad, the warmer and quieter north had looked extremely inviting. More important, the time in the south had brought Kaz and Helati closer to one another in a shorter time than even he could have dreamt. Instead of journeying across all of Ansalon, the two had instead decided to settle in a quiet, wooded region far south of their homeland. Hecar, never one to abandon his sister, had decided to build a place there, too.

In settling down, Kaz had found a peace that had escaped him all his life. He had really known nothing but battle since he had been young enough to train, and now he realized that quiet solitude, combined with sharing that quiet with someone he loved, was preferable. He and Helati had made a home for themselves, acting in many ways more like humans than like minotaurs. Kaz saw nothing demeaning in that. Despite his race's obvious superiority in some matters, the minotaurs truly were deficient in most important aspects of life. Humans could appreciate things that most minotaurs, not understanding, would have scoffed at. Humans were not perfect, but they were admirable in some ways.

Of course, he had met one of the greatest humans, so perhaps, Kaz thought, his opinion was biased. Huma of the Lance, the now legendary hero of the war against Takhisis, the dark goddess, had been one of the bravest, most honorable warriors Kaz had ever known. It was a friendship that should not have thrived, but it had, ending only when the young knight had died vanquishing the Dragon Queen. Kaz had been there, a part of the epic battle. He had witnessed the humanity behind the hero, and the lesson had stayed with him, influencing his own decisions and behavior. Like Huma, he had come to want only peace and a quiet life.

But that never seems to be the way. He snorted. I try to live in peace and only end up mired in one battle after another. Not that I haven't purposely walked straight into a few.

The first newcomers arrived shortly after the trio had settled here. Once the first travelers arrived, it seemed to him as if half the minotaurs in the empire followed. Worse, they all seemed to know who he was . . . and had been. The past that Kaz had thought buried seemed more alive than ever.

I will not go back to Nethosak! he thought, snarling quietly. I will not go back there again!

Yet if Hecar was in danger, what else could Kaz do?

He found Helati exactly where he expected her to be, cradling the newly born twins and trying to sing them to sleep. For a minotaur, his mate's voice was surprisingly melodious. He had thought it pleasant from the very first time he had heard it. Then, Kaz had been a prisoner of a band of minotaurs, hunters sent to bring him back on a mission of honorable purpose. The leaders of the band did not have any intention of giving him the opportunity to defend his actions, but a few had believed in him. Helati and her brother had been among those. When the matter had been settled, they remained with him. He could not have been more pleased. She was still the most beautiful female he had ever seen, and a fine companion in battle as well.

Her features were refined, gentle. Standing, she was a bit shorter than he was. Helati's horns were about half as long as his own. None of this meant that she was weak. She had been a seasoned warrior when he first met her, and the tricks he had taught her since made her better than most larger and stronger warriors.

The twins shifted restlessly. Both the male and the female were fitful like Kaz, though in looks they favored their mother. He wondered if that would change as they grew older. He wondered if he would be around to witness the changes.

The dwelling he and Helati had built was simple, a stone-and-wood hut with three small rooms. Some of the newcomers had built larger homes, but Kaz wanted only what his family needed. He was not in competition for status. Perhaps that was why the other minotaurs looked to him for guidance. They knew he cared nothing about fighting for dominance; he intended to live simply, as he and Helati desired.

Helati looked up as he neared. His expression was all she needed to see. "You're going, aren't you?"

"I have to."

"Why?"

"Because if I don't, Helati, I know you will."

There was no denying that. "Hecar is my brother, Kaz. By rights, I should be the one to search for him."

"And if there was not something more important for you to deal with," he said, indicating the two squirming bundles, "then I might let you go." But he wouldn't, in any case. If it weren't for the children, Kaz still would have sought some excuse to prevent his mate from riding off to treacherous Nethosak.

She looked down at the pair. Kyris, the boy, had a broader face and tiny buds that would someday grow into horns as great in length as those of his father. His sister,

Sekra, was just a little smaller and more narrow, but darker-furred. The stubs where her horns would come in were barely noticeable, as a female's horns grew in later and to a lesser size than those of a male. Both children were, of course, perfect in the eyes of their parents.

"You could just as easily take care of them as I." Her tone was hesitant, however, caught as she was between her care for her brother and her love for her children.

"You know they cooperate with you much more than they do with me, Helati." She could not deny that. The infants loved their father, but their mother had what seemed a sort of magic touch. Where Kaz might take all night to coax them to sleep, Helati would need only an hour . . . or two. The twins shared his rebellious nature, all right. "And we can't take them with us, now can we? Not if something's amiss in Nethosak."

Looking up, she locked gazes with him. "You know it might be dangerous for you to go back."

"Go back where?" asked another voice.

A shorter, muscular minotaur with a mixture of black and brown fur and a long snout came trotting toward them. One broken horn spoke of his past in the Great Circus. Brogan never talked about his experience there, much the way Kaz never did. Brogan visited them often, possibly because he had no family in the settlement, not even distant kin.

Kaz saw no reason to hide the truth. The others would notice his absence. "I'm going back. Hecar hasn't returned from Nethosak. I'm going to find him."

Snorting, Brogan replied, "I'll gather the others. We'll be ready when you are."

"I'm going alone."

"Alone?" The other minotaur snorted again. His thick hands curled into fists. "Not alone! You don't know what it's like back there—"

"Brogan." Kaz's quiet tone commanded silence. "I can't very well go riding into the imperial capital with a conspicuous force behind me. A lone rider will make less disturbance than fifty. Besides, it's been over eight years. It's less likely someone will recognize me. The war and the time since then have made changes."

"We could follow you."

"You haven't been gone that long. People will spot you or the others more easily than they would me. Besides, I work better alone." That was not entirely true, but other than Helati or Hecar, there was no one he would trust to follow his lead. . . . Well, there was one more, but "trust" was not exactly the right word where a kender was concerned. "Desperately hope" to follow his lead was more accurate. Fortunately, the kender concerned was not here.

Brogan looked unconvinced. He turned to Helati, but she looked away. Helati, more than anyone else, knew how Kaz worked best. It was not to her liking, but Helati was aware that he had a better chance of success without others to betray his presence.

"Was there something you wanted, Brogan?"

Blinking, the short minotaur nodded. "Aye, but it'll wait. Just some of us wanting permission to put your mark on our places. I told 'em to wait until we knew it was fine with you. It can wait, though."

He turned and stalked away before Kaz could pull himself together to respond. Helati gazed up at her mate, seeing the consternation in his face.

"My mark on their homes? They're supposed to put their clan markings there."

"Perhaps they've decided they belong to a different clan now."

Kaz was uncomfortable with the image of his name carved into the simple structures. That was reserved for the clan name, which was the way by which minotaurs asked their ancestors to watch over a new home. By putting his mark on instead, they were acknowledging him as clan leader, much the way Orilg himself had been chosen.

Clan Kaziganthi . . . or rather Clan Kaz . . . since there was a tendency to shorten the title. At one time, Kaz would have felt honored. Now he was unnerved.

"I leave before dawn, Helati. That should let me escape

the others. I can't take them with me. You know that."

"I know." She rose, careful not to disturb the infants, who were still wakeful. "Would you like to hold them for a while?"

Kaz nodded, taking his children in his arms. To his surprise, they nestled in close to his chest and began to drift off into slumber. It was the first time they had ever fallen asleep so smoothly. He was almost disappointed. This might be the last time he saw them before he departed.

Helati turned toward their dwelling. "I've got some things I want to prepare for your journey. Do you want to put the children to bed or hold them a while longer?"

"I'll hold them until you're ready to take them."

She nodded, then went inside. The massive minotaur watched her disappear, then returned his gaze to the twins. At the moment, Kaz did not feel like a former champion of the circus, a veteran mariner, or a seasoned warrior. He felt like a proud father, and the feeling was a good one.

Enjoy it while you can, he suddenly reminded himself. It may be the last time you feel this way for days . . . or ever again.

Cradling the twins closer, Kaz looked north.

* * * * *

Dawn was still nearly two hours away when Kaz began the final preparations for departure. His great war-horse, a cherished gift from the Knights of Solamnia, was impatient to go. Kaz needed only one more item to complete his gear, something long mounted on one of the walls of his dwelling.

The battle-axe he pulled from the wall was one that had been given him by an elf named Sardal Crystalthorn, an elf who had been dead for more than three years now. Even in the dark, the long, double-edged weapon somehow gleamed, its mirror face able to catch even the slightest illumination. The unknown dwarf who had crafted it had created a masterpiece. The balance was perfect. It had saved Kaz's life many times.

The runes on the side spelled out its name: Honor's Face. It was a name with magical connotations, for the mirrorlike finish enabled the minotaur to see whether a person was or was not to be trusted. Those with honor reflected brightly in its finish; those who sought to betray showed no reflection at all.

There were other things Honor's Face could do, but Kaz had no time to reflect. He gripped the axe in one hand and swung it with practiced ease into the back harness he had strapped on. It was a strange yet comfortable sensation. He had not carried the axe with him in at least three months. For chopping wood he used a more mundane household axe, not a well-honed weapon.

Kaz did not doubt that he would have reason to wield the axe on his journey.

Helati was waiting for him by the entrance. The children slept, the first time they had made it through the night without waking. Kaz wondered if that was somehow prophetic. Did they sleep unconcerned because they knew their father would return unharmed, or was it an omen of a doomed mission?

He was glad he could not ask them.

"You are ready."

"As ready as I can be."

They were embracing when a commotion from the darkness made them turn. Kaz had the axe out and ready without thinking. The clink of metal and the thud of hooves, accompanied by the snorting of horses, warned him that an armed party was coming.

The newcomers were shadowy forms, but it was clear that they were all minotaurs. One of the nearest rode close enough so that Kaz could make out the one broken horn.

"Brogan! Paladine's sword! What's the meaning of this?"

"We're ready to go with you, Kaz." Behind Brogan rode at least a dozen or more minotaurs. The darkness made it nigh impossible to say how many or who each of them was.

He was warmed by their loyalty and concern, but angered by their disregard for his wishes. "I told you I needed to go alone. It'll be easier that way. A party like this will attract the notice of the guard miles before arriving at the city gates!"

"Nethosak is dangerous these days," insisted another faceless minotaur. "More dangerous than it has ever been."

To Kaz, who had faced fearsome dragons, rampaging soldiers, dark mages, and darker gods, Nethosak was no worse nor better than any other danger of the past. He knew it would be treacherous, but he also knew he had no right to endanger anyone's life but his own.

He propped Honor's Face shaft-down on the ground, giving all a good view of its mirror side. "Your loyalty and bravery are commendable," Kaz returned, playing on those traits the minotaur race respected most. "And I am honored by your actions. But this is a thing I have to do on my own. It must be done this way, for in crowded Nethosak, stealth will serve me better than an army." He dipped his head in gratitude. "I appreciate that you want to help, but I must reject the offer."

Brogan was not to be put off. "Kaz—"

Straightening to his full height, Kaz growled, "That is my command, Brogan."

The riders grew silent. Brogan finally nodded. "We will wait for you, then . . . but if you do not return after a reasonable time, we will come to help you." Others nodded or grunted their agreement. The one-horned minotaur raised a hand. "Victorious journey, Kaziganthi."

One by one, the other minotaurs followed suit until the entire band had saluted him. Kaz raised a hand in return. Then, with Brogan leading, the riders turned their mounts and rode off, heading for their dwellings.

"You realize now they won't stop at simply putting your mark on the entrance of their dwellings, don't you? You've started giving them outright commands. By doing so, you've acquiesced to being their leader . . . their *clan* leader."

Kaz almost dropped the axe. "I don't want that! I should go after them now and—"

"And do nothing." Helati sighed. "My love, you might not want to be clan leader, but I know you too well. You won't let others take a risk that you can take yourself. To our people, that is the sign of a true leader, not like those who rule our race now."

"Then our race consists of a bunch of fools—with me the biggest fool of all."

"And I am a bigger fool for loving you." She embraced him. "I wish there were another way. I don't want to lose both you and my brother."

Kaz snorted, trying to sound like the reckless warrior he had once been. "You won't lose us. I'll bring Hecar back. He's probably stopped to talk to every female in the kingdom, that's all."

Stepping away, the minotaur warrior swung the axe back into its harness. He mounted, purposely looking away from Helati as he did. The thought of leaving her was almost unbearable.

"May your father watch over you, Kaz."

He pictured Ganth, so tall in the memory of his son. It was Ganth's example that Kaz had followed all his life. At that moment, Kaz realized he had become more like his father since his encounter with Huma and the others. Would his father or his mother, Kyri, for whom he had named his son, have journeyed back to Nethosak on such an insane quest? Both of them had gone down with their vessel, *Gladiator*.

It doesn't really matter what anyone else would do, Kaz decided. I'm the one going.

"Kaz . . ."

He looked down at Helati. Even in the dark, he could see the set expression on her face.

"If you don't come back soon, I, too, will follow. Somehow I will."

"I'll be back."

Turning away, he prodded the horse. The animal started off at a fast trot. He did not look back. He did not dare to do so. If he had, the minotaur was certain he would have turned around and stayed home, never leaving the solace of his mate's side again.

Nothing else slowed him as he left the settlement. The other dwellings were dark, but Kaz knew that not only those who had tried to join him but also many who had not were peering from the shadows. He had never wanted to be a leader, not really, but he could not help feeling some pride.

Before long, there was nothing to give sign that anyone lived in the area at all. Kaz had initially chosen the location because of its remoteness. He cared little for visitors or passersby. While he had become resigned to the influx of new settlers, he was pleased that few others sojourned to this hard land. There had been the occasional trader and, once, a foolhardy band of robbers who had not understood what it meant to steal from a minotaur, but otherwise his people lived in peace. That would change someday, but hopefully not too soon.

Dawn came and went. The day was cool and a little overcast, fair traveling weather. Kaz paused only to deal with necessities, such as feeding and watering his mount. The empire city was far enough without wasting time. He prayed to Paladine and Kiri-Jolith that nothing terrible had happened to Helati's brother. If Hecar was harmed, however, Kaz would see to it that the perpetrator regretted his act for the short time he still lived. Kaz had not become so peaceful that he was above meting out justice in time-honored minotaur fashion.

By nightfall Kaz had to admit that it might be better to bed down than continue on. It was an oddly starless evening, so dark that he could barely see even the shadow of his hand in front of his face. He found a reasonable site, two intertwined trees that would give him some concealment and allow him room to fight if the need arose, then set about taking care of the horse and building a camp.

It had been a good day's journey. As he settled down by his small fire, Honor's Face beside him, Kaz hoped that for the next several days he would be able to make similar progress. Near the lands of the twin kingdoms the going would be slower, but he saw no reason why the trek to that point should not proceed smoothly. The landscape consisted mainly of wooded areas until the extensive mountain range running along the upper half of the eastern edge of Ansalon. Fortunately, one could ride on the east or the west slope and avoid having to cross the heights. Only when he reached the southern borders of his people's self-proclaimed empire would the peaks cause him some difficulty, but Kaz, like most minotaurs, knew the best paths.

Kaz only hoped Hecar was not in any immediate trouble. He stared at the fire, wondering what it would be like to return to the homeland.

When he started to doze, he could not say. It was only when he saw that the fire was about to go out that Kaz realized he had fallen asleep. His hand gripped the shaft of the axe, but there was no obvious sign of danger. Kaz snorted in annoyance at his own jumpiness and started to work on the fire.

He had just finished rekindling the fire when he heard a branch snap.

Kaz eased his way to Honor's Face, clutching the axe and slowly bringing it to hand. Having wandered for several years before settling down with Helati, the minotaur was more than familiar with night visitors. It was the best time for beasts and bandits to ply their trade, and he had met more than his share of both during his various travels. Once he had even faced a scaled abomination resembling a dragon, the result of a mad mage's effort to create the perfect warrior for the Dark Queen. That had been the worst of the lot, as far as Kaz was concerned.

Abomination or bandit, I've no time for such games anymore, Kaz thought as he peered into the darkness. If it won't come to me, I'll go to it.

He really had no evidence that it was anything more than an animal, but Kaz had discovered long ago that he had some sort of instinct, a sixth sense, that more often than not differentiated between what was simply a deer or raccoon and what was worse. It might not be a threat, but then again . . .

His horse, too, was alert, though from long training it did not budge. Kaz stepped away from the fire, trying to determine exactly from which direction the noise had come. To his left, he decided. Cautiously, the seasoned warrior started that way, moving with surprising silence for one of his bulk. Most assumed a minotaur relied on brute strength and was therefore neither swift nor cunning. Being underestimated by his adversaries had proven to Kaz's advantage more than once.

As he stepped between two trees, he heard another twig snap, this time from his right. Kaz immediately turned, holding the axe close in order to avoid snagging it on a branch. The woods were not too thick here, otherwise he would have resorted to his knife. Honor's Face was his weapon of choice, but Kaz was expert with blades long and short, thick and thin, not to mention a variety of other weapons that were all a part of his training.

The source of the noise had to be only a few feet from where he now stood. Kaz readied the axe, gauging the limitations created by the various trees and shrubs he could only vaguely make out in the darkness. It would be close quarters if it came to fighting, but not too close. He had made excellent use of the axe in cramped battle conditions before.

Another branch cracked . . . from behind him.

Paladine's sword! Is the creature that swift or am I surrounded? Kaz turned cautiously this time, not wanting to make the obvious move and leave himself open to an attack from behind as he shifted in the new direction.

No attack came. Exhaling quietly, Kaz moved again, heading back to his campsite. His heart beat faster as he wondered if he had been so naive as to have fallen for a ploy leading him away from the fire so that bandits could plunder his belongings. If so, they were about to learn what the fury of a minotaur was like . . . for the few seconds that remained of their foul lives.

Throwing caution to the wind, Kaz charged toward the

camp, the flickering flames his beacon.

In the light of the fire, he first noted the smaller mount tied not too far from his own. Then his gaze alighted on the short, cloaked figure squatting in the exact location the minotaur had vacated moments earlier. The hood of the other's travel cloak was pulled forward, obscuring any glimpse of the face within.

Positioned as the newcomer was, it was hard to tell the race. An elf, perhaps, albeit a fairly short one. Slim for a dwarf, but not for a gnome, though what a gnome would be doing here was beyond Kaz. A human was a likely bet, Kaz thought as he edged closer, axe gripped tight, but the size was more that of an adolescent, not an adult. That really left only one other race. . . .

No, it couldn't be . . .

From within the hood came a booming voice. "Greetings, O Great Warrior—" The voice broke off, then became a higher, merrier one unable to control itself. "That was a fun game, wasn't it?"

Slim, tapered fingers fit for a pickpocket reached up and pulled back the hood, revealing a dark-haired, handsome, yet childlike face. The figure stood, revealing that he was no more than an inch or two over four feet—tall for his kind, but unmistakably a member of the most annoying race ordained by the gods on Krynn.

A kender.

A kender named Delbin Knotwillow.

Chapter 3
Unwelcome Companions

"What are you doing here, Delbin?"

"I came to see you, Kaz." The kender flashed a smile.

Leaning the axe handle against his shoulder, the minotaur eyed his companion with suspicion. It looked like Delbin, but looks, as he knew from experience, could be deceiving. "You just happen to be here in the middle of nowhere waiting for me?"

The kender laughed. "Actually, I had to catch up with you because when I got to your home Helati said you'd gone off to some place called Nethosak, which I remembered was somewhere in the minotaur lands but a place

---
28

I'd never been to, so I thought I should tag along because—"

"Take a breath, Delbin." Kaz relaxed some. It was his companion of old, all right. There was no mistaking that voice whenever it ran on about everything under the sun. Delbin was part of a small sect of kender who had the fool notion of writing some history of modern Krynn, which would have been fine if he ever got around to it. Plus, almost every time Delbin reached into his pouch for his supposed book, he managed to pull out something that had once belonged to someone else.

Still, Kaz could not deny that the kender had proven a worthy comrade on occasion, even risking his life to save the minotaur's. He was not willing to admit it to anyone but Helati, but Kaz had grown fond of the small creature. That, of course, did not mean he wanted a kender's company on this journey.

"When morning comes, you'll go back to wherever you came from and stay there. What I have to do, I do alone."

"But, Kaz, I've never seen a whole empire of minotaurs, and Helati seemed so worried, which I couldn't blame her for, what with the dream I had—which is why I knew you'd be traveling in the first place, and since you're traveling, you need someone to go with you, which ought to be me, of course—"

Not for the first time Kaz wondered if the kender followed him because even his own race would not put up with his incessant talk. Then, a part of what Delbin had said caught his attention. "What's that about a dream you say you had?"

"I had a dream and—" Delbin hesitated when he saw the minotaur's expression. Speaking much slower, he continued. "It was about you, Kaz! You were riding toward a big place with a cheering crowd and other minotaurs fighting. Then something big, bigger than a bird, flew over, and—"

"That was it?"

"No, then you were fighting yourself in this place—I guess it was an arena—while a tall, really tall, minotaur in cleric robes looked down. Then he turned into a bird and flew away." Delbin smiled. "Wasn't that an interesting dream? Oh . . . I forgot about the gray man!"

"What gray man?" Kaz regretted asking the talkative kender to explain his dream. Of what possible use could such information be to the minotaur? Still, he listened.

"He was all gray, Kaz! Even his face and beard. He wore gray robes and carried a gray staff. I never saw a human so very, very, *very* gray."

The description sparked a vague memory. Someone else had told the minotaur about such a gray man long ago. Much to his regret, however, Kaz could not summon the wraithlike memory. "All gray, then?"

"Yes, and he said you were leaving soon, so I should hurry to find you, and when I woke up I knew I better go, even though it was a dream—I just knew that I *had* to go."

Rarely had the minotaur seen the kender so adamant. But to let Delbin come with him into the heart of the minotaur realm was to sign the creature's death warrant. Minotaurs were not tolerant, especially when it came to kender. Delbin's people were considered to be on a par with rats and other vermin.

"No. You can't go, Delbin. It's for your own good. You don't know what the empire, much less Nethosak, is like. They would have you executed simply for being yourself."

Delbin Knotwillow looked down at himself. "What's wrong with me? So I'm a little big for a kender!"

"It's not your height, and you know it, Delbin. Unlike me, most minotaurs aren't very tolerant where kender are concerned. Most minotaurs would just as soon cut a kender up into fish bait . . ." Kaz despised himself for talking so, but he wanted to frighten his friend into turning back. "Go back."

"The man in gray said I had to come." Delbin crossed his arms, putting together as severe and determined an expression as a kender could muster. "So I am."

"That was a dream."

"A big dream." Delbin cracked a smile. "So what's Nethosak like, Kaz? Are there a lot of minotaurs there?

Why are there two kingdoms called Mithas and Kothas, and do they look exactly the same?" Before Kaz could say another word, Delbin reached into a pouch at his side. "I need my book! I should write this all—gee, I wonder where this came from?"

The object in the kender's hand was hard to make out in the fire's flickering light. Kaz stepped closer, forgetting for the moment his anger and frustration. The object was vaguely familiar, a medallion of some sort.

At first Kaz had the strange notion it was the medallion of Paladine he had taken from the hand of Huma after Takhisis's defeat, but that medallion he had hung on a tree branch not far from the great knight's tomb. Besides, Huma's medallion showed the symbol of Paladine, while this one featured another god, one just as familiar to Kaz as Huma's deity, if not as respected by him as he once was.

Sargas. It did not look like a cleric's medallion, however.

"Let me see that, Delbin." The kender turned the round object over to him. Kaz held it near the flames. Memories began to wash over him as he at last recognized the medallion for what it was. Years ago, he had worn one exactly like it.

" 'Champion of all,' " Kaz muttered, reading the script that circled the edge. " 'Hero of the people.' Where did you get this, Delbin? Come on, now. Think hard."

The kender screwed up his face in concentration, then grinned. "I remember! The man in gray gave it to me!"

"A man in a dream gave it to you? You know that can't be."

"But he did! I remember! After he told me to go to you, he gave me the medallion. I think he said you lost it! Isn't that neat? That's what I mean about the dream. It's important. I've never had a dream like it before."

Kaz almost threw the medallion into the fire. He had indeed worn one that resembled it . . . until the day he decided that his life would not be lived—or lost—in the arena. Fighting as a slave-soldier under the human and ogre masters had seemed preferable to the insanity and hypocrisy of the circus.

This could not be the same medallion . . . could it?

"Do you know what it is, Kaz?" asked Delbin.

Kaz knew exactly what it was, a medallion given to the supreme champion of the games, the greatest warrior of any of the arenas, including, of course, the Great Circus. The supreme champion could challenge the emperor to single combat for the throne, and the emperor would have to agree to fight or lose face. When the two met, it was always to the death. Combatants did not leave their rivals alive to foment discord or challenge them again and perhaps win the next time.

The Great Circus made for glorious entertainment for the masses.

"No," Kaz finally replied, putting the medallion into a pouch attached to the belt of his kilt. His eyes watched the campfire's darting flames. "No, I don't."

He sat down, leaning his axe nearby. Delbin watched him solemnly, wisely saying nothing. Kaz had forgotten about the kender. The dancing tentacles of the fire resurrected images of past opponents locked in duels. Kaz watched himself wrestle to the ground a reddish black minotaur taller than him, but then that adversary became a shorter but more muscular one carrying an axe longer than Honor's Face. Kaz deflected the blow with an axe of his own, then countered with a bone-cutting swing. The images went on and on, battle after battle, until somewhere along the way Kaz fell asleep.

* * * * *

When the next day came, Kaz said nothing to the kender about the previous night's conversation. For the time being, he allowed Delbin to ride beside him. He still did not want to put Delbin at risk, but silently welcomed the kender's company. Delbin could be so diverting that Kaz might forget for a time the dangers awaiting him in the imperial capital of the minotaur kingdom of Mithas.

For the next two days, they traveled in relative peace,

the only vexation being the kender's relentless questions about the minotaur lands. Some of them Kaz had answered more than once over the years, ever since he first encountered Delbin on a dock in the southern reaches of Ansalon. Now and then the kender asked a question about the minotaur's own life, which Kaz deflected by telling him something fascinating about his homeland.

"One thing I can never understand—why are there two kingdoms?" Delbin asked, for the umpteenth time.

"Because it's more competitive. Each kingdom strives to raise the greatest champions." Although there was only one emperor, the minotaur homeland was divided between the kingdoms of Mithas and Kothas. Mithas, with the imperial capital located within its boundaries, had some advantage, but Kothas was known for its own share of emperors.

"You were in the arena, weren't you?"

"All minotaurs go to the arenas."

"But you were in the arena a lot! You must have been a great champion! Don't champions become emperor if they defeat the old emperor, because that's what I heard, and you said something like that once, so if you were a great champion, then you could have become emperor, which—"

"Take a breath, Delbin!" Kaz suddenly snarled. He tried to be patient with the kender, but couldn't help the occasional angry outburst. The kender overflowed with questions, and endlessly repeated his favorite ones. This time Delbin shut his mouth and remained silent for nearly a mile, something approaching a miracle.

On the fourth night, they made camp near a range of hills. The woods had grown thicker. The forest covered everything. Kaz was vaguely familiar with the lay of the land, but their progress was slowed a bit. All the better— each day's travel brought Kaz nearer a place to which he had no desire to return, a place that in some ways he feared.

After tethering the horses, Kaz decided it was time to tell Delbin that he could go no farther. His life would be in jeopardy. The minotaur was surprised at how guilty he felt about letting his small companion ride this far. But the woodlands would provide good cover for him as he retraced his steps and found other kender to rejoin.

"Delbin—" Kaz started to say, turning . . . but the kender was nowhere to be seen. His mount was tied up and some of his belongings lay near the fire, but Delbin himself had vanished.

The moon Solinari was only a wisp in the heavens, but the stars were visible this night. Trust Delbin to go exploring now. Snorting in annoyance, Kaz searched the ground for some sign of the direction in which the kender had departed. Delbin's race was notoriously light-footed. The minotaur knelt to peer for tracks.

"Kaz! Look what I fou— What're you doing there? Did you lose something? Can I help?" Delbin materialized out of nowhere beside the minotaur and fell to his knees. He earnestly began surveying the ground for whatever he thought Kaz had dropped.

"I was looking for you!" Rising, the beast-man looked down at his small comrade. "That's it!" He overplayed his attitude, pretending to be very annoyed. "Come tomorrow, Delbin, you're heading back to your kind! You can't go running off at night in the middle of nowhere . . . or even during the day, for that matter!"

"I was just curious—"

Kaz thrust a finger at the kender. "In Nethosak, or any other place in the homelands, being curious like that will get you killed, Delbin . . . and me along with you, by the way! I want you to promise to return to your people at first light!"

Delbin Knotwillow looked down. He seemed tiny and vulnerable at the moment, so chastened that Kaz found himself feeling guilty again.

"I . . . I don't want to. They all think I'm so serious! All my friends stay away from me!"

"What? Why?"

"Because I get bored with them! They're not as much fun as you and Helati are, Kaz! Not in the same way! You always come up with interesting things to do, interesting places to see! I told them all about everything we've done, and they were interested at first, but then they got tired of hearing about minotaurs and wanted to hear about anything else, and Noppel even made fun of you, and I didn't like that, so—"

"Take a breath, Delbin." The minotaur blinked. "So this . . . Noppel . . . made fun of me, and you got angry because of that?"

A wide smile spread across the kender's childlike features. "You're my friend, Kaz!"

And obviously a worse influence on you than I could have imagined, the minotaur thought. He felt a slight twinge of shame for making his companion a veritable outcast among his own people. He could not send the kender away . . . not after learning that Delbin had stuck up for him . . . well, at least not right away.

"What did you find?" Kaz asked.

Smiling, Delbin reached into his pouch. "You should see it! I think I know what it is, but . . . Hey, here's my book! Just what I was looking for!"

It was one of the few times that Kaz could recall having ever seen the fabled book. It was battered and filled with loose sheets of paper that he suspected had been "borrowed" from everywhere the kender had visited. Somehow the sheets stayed more or less within the battered leather cover. Before Kaz could make out the lettering, though, Delbin put the tiny book back into the pouch and removed something else.

"Here it is!"

The kender's latest acquisition was almost as unnerving as the medallion. Every muscle in the minotaur's body tensed. Suddenly the forest seemed even darker, more filled with danger, than before.

"Isn't this a neat knife? You know, I think this handle is bone, which makes a pretty sturdy handle, I guess, because bones hold our bodies up pretty good, don't they—?"

"Be quiet, Delbin!" the warrior whispered. He seized the knife, turning it over. The handle was made of bone, just as his companion had said. But what Delbin did not know was that the bone had probably come from a thinking creature, possibly a human or even a minotaur.

Ogres did, after all, have preferences.

The knife was in very good condition and hardly rusted at all. "Did you clean this up?"

"No, I found it just like this—"

Kaz waved him silent and glanced out at the shadowy forest. The knife could have been lost some time ago, depending on the weather, but the very thought that ogres had ventured this far south almost made Kaz want to head back and warn the others. It occurred to him, however, that with the number of minotaurs now living in the settlement, it would take a fairly large force of ogres to attack them. Such a large force could certainly not have remained hidden in this region. Ogres were too clumsy not to leave signs of their passing.

"Show me where you found this."

The kender did. The place was surprisingly close to the campsite. Delbin had found the knife lying next to a tree. It was proof of just how superior the short creature's night vision was that he could have spotted it. Kaz found no other trace of ogres, but he knew the darkness might be masking some proof. When he rose at first light, he would do a thorough search of the vicinity.

The two of them returned to the fire, Kaz still clutching the blade. First the medallion . . . his medallion . . . and now this ogre weapon. There could not possibly be any connection between the two other than Delbin finding both, yet, the weary minotaur could not help but wonder.

Delbin sat, with a hopeful expression, next to the fire. Kaz realized that the kender wanted the knife back. It was a treasure to Delbin. The minotaur started to hand the blade over, then hesitated. He grunted. "I'll give this back to you on one condition, Delbin."

"What's that?"

"Don't find anything else for a while, okay?"

The smile widened. "I'll try real hard, Kaz."

Snorting, Kaz handed back the knife. He turned his

attention to food, his stomach reminding him that it had been a long time since either of them had eaten. The minotaur looked forward to his simple meal. Food had a way of temporarily erasing worries.

Often in the past he had grumbled to himself and others that the gods must surely be out to test him. How else to explain the rocky path Kaz had journeyed over the past several years? In his mind, he had suffered more than his share of trial and tribulation. The short time he had spent in the home he and Helati had built had been the only peaceful period in his life that he could recall. That respite was over now, though. Once more, it seemed as if he had become a pawn of the gods.

Maybe I'm just tired, he thought as he passed a bit of bread to Delbin. Maybe it's just my imagination that the gods are steering me toward some dire adventure.

His arm came to rest against the pouch into which he had placed the medallion Delbin had supposedly been given by the gray man. He yanked the arm away and, ignoring the kender's curious glance, chewed his food as if doing battle with it.

* * * * *

Tap-tap went the staff of the man sitting on the high rock.

"On the path again . . . but do you know the way?"

Kaz stood in the middle of a mountain path. High peaks rose on each side of him. Ahead, the path seemed narrow, barely wide enough for him to pass. Behind him, it was wide and flat. In that direction, the minotaur could make out a beautiful forest and in that forest a dwelling he recognized as his own.

From the mountains in the other direction he heard what sounded like a child crying.

"He who hesitates is lost, they say. Are you lost?" The questioner tapped his staff against the rock again. He was a tall, elderly human . . . elderly but certainly not frail. He wore a hooded cloak that covered most of his form, and on his hands he wore long gloves that went up his wrists, eventually disappearing into his sleeves. On his feet the human wore boots that rose

up almost knee high.

A long gray beard obscured what was a plain yet somehow intelligent face. The gray beard blended into a gray face, which in turn blended into the gray coloring of the cloak.

Kaz's eyes narrowed. Everything about the man was gray, even his teeth, tongue, and eyes.

The crying continued.

"Will that crying never cease?" Kaz rumbled.

"He is out of balance." The explanation seemed to suit the gray man despite its vagueness. "Hail to you, Supreme Champion."

"NO!" roared Kaz, waving his hand in denial. "I've not worn that title or—" He suddenly realized that the medallion hung around his neck. With one massive hand, he tore the medallion from its chain and threw it as far as he could. The gray man watched him do it, his expression perfectly bland. "Not worn that title or that medallion since I left Nethosak! I reject what it stands for!"

"But what swings one way must always swing the other. What one rejects, one must later accept—if one is to remain in balance."

The crying grew more shrill, as if demanding to be heard.

Kaz tried to ignore the sound. "I'm not putting up with such nonsense! I'm going home!"

He turned toward the path leading to the woods, only to discover that instead of the forest, he faced the Great Circus of Nethosak. Cheering rose from inside, and a line of minotaurs stood at attention, awaiting him.

Kaz stepped back, but as his foot came down, the mountain path transformed into the flat, sandy floor of the arena. Instead of the gray man and the rock, a high wooden platform stood before him. The platform was several yards across and towered above him. A dozen of Kaz's kinsmen struggled at levers, their efforts causing the structure to slowly rotate.

Frozen, Kaz watched as a figure hove into view. The figure slowly came nearer as the rotating platform brought him around.

Still the child cried, but now he sounded older . . . not adult . . . but definitely older.

The face of the figure on the platform came into view.

It was his own face.

"About time you got here," the other Kaz called.

Kaz tried to speak, but as he opened his mouth, a great shadow darkened the sky. The other Kaz looked up . . . and was swallowed by that darkness. The arena was gone.

"Definitely out of balance," remarked the gray man, now standing next to Kaz. "The past should be past by this time."

Eyes widening, the minotaur glared at his peculiar gray companion. "I know you, don't I? I've forgotten you, somehow. I remember about Huma and—" His words were cut off as the shrill voice cried still louder. It was too much for him to stand. "By Paladine and Kiri-Jolith! Can nothing be done about that?"

"I can do nothing." The gray man held up his hands, which were bound by what seemed a twisted version of his own staff. He seemed indifferent. "You must complete what you have left undone."

Kaz did not care to ask what the gray man meant, his gaze already turning back to the mountainous trail. The cry for help was stronger, closer. He wished he had his axe, then realized it was in his hands. That was the one thing that so far did not disturb him; Honor's Face always returned to his hands when he most needed it. One of its magical qualities.

"Paladine preserve me!" Kaz grunted, starting up the trail.

"Perhaps he will," replied the gray man from behind him. "He understands the need for balance."

This made the minotaur turn, but when he looked, the man in gray was gone. Snorting his annoyance, Kaz listened again to the cry. It was stronger, closer, but now he thought he heard the sound of running feet and the heavy breathing of determined pursuers. Someone was after the voice.

"Did you hear that, Kaz?" asked Delbin, but the kender was nowhere to be seen.

Keeping the axe ready, the minotaur picked up his pace. If there were others, he had to hurry. They might catch up with their prey at any moment.

Despite his hurried pace, though, it seemed as if he walked through a miasma. Ever so slowly, Kaz made progress along the path, but with each renewed cry, he knew he would be too late.

Then the cry came again, so close that he knew its source

must be just out of sight. All he had to do was reach the point where the path before him twisted to the right. There was still time.

Suddenly Kaz was at the turn. He raised Honor's Face in preparation for a swing and followed the twist in the path.

A shadow loomed over him.

It was a dragon.

* * * * *

Kaz woke with a start, realizing that everything had been but a dream. The minotaur cursed. It was still dark outside. Kaz estimated that he had been asleep for perhaps an hour, possibly two, but no more. He peered around the camp, muttered in annoyance, and tried to settle back down to sleep.

He did not hear the single figure that had been observing the camp move off into the night.

* * * * *

"I told you that story earlier."

"I want to hear it again."

"Not now, Delbin."

"Please? It'll help pass the time, and I always like to hear about it, especially the part—"

"All right." It would be easier simply to relate the tale . . . again.

"Thanks, Kaz!" piped in Delbin. He reached for his pouch. "I should write it down this time! I always forget. It would—say, I wonder where this came from?"

Kaz eyed the newfound object with some trepidation, but it turned out to be only one of his own fire flints. Giving the kender a look, he reached out and retrieved his property. "Just forget the book for now, Delbin, or I won't tell the story."

That gave the kender pause. Kaz sighed, then began, "In the beginning, there were the ogres. They were not the animals we know today, but beautiful creatures, the envy of all other races, including the elves. They built glorious cities and created great works in all fields. All respected their accomplishments and abilities."

"What happened to them?" asked Delbin. He asked the same questions at the same points in the story every time Kaz related it.

"They were decadent, vain. They wasted their achievements, instead playing with power that should've been cultivated in order to cement their greatness. Some of them, however, saw that they were destined for savagery if they continued like that and tried to speak sense to their brothers. The others wouldn't listen, and the race sank further and further into degeneracy. They fell from the grace of the Great Horned One, Sargas, so the story goes, and he finally cast out the ogres, condemning them to be the animals they truly were. Those are the ogres of today, degenerate monsters who can't even recall the wonders of their own ancestors."

"But the minotaurs . . ."

"It's said that Sargas took pity on those who tried to remain on the path of glory." Kaz disliked mentioning Sargas; he no longer followed that god, who many believed was also known as Sargannon, consort to the Dark Queen. Still, this was the story as it had always been told, and Kaz was a believer in the traditions. "Reaching down, he took those most worthy and placed them far from the other ogres. In order to mark them as his true children, he reshaped their forms, making them look like himself."

Kaz leaned forward so that the kender could get a good close-up of his features. It was a theatrical habit he had picked up from his father, who had told the story to him many times when Kaz was a child. The kender shivered, but more in pleasure at hearing the tale than because he was really scared.

"We've taken up the destiny that the ogres tossed aside." Kaz closed his eyes. " 'We have been enslaved but have always thrown off our shackles. We have been driven back, but always returned to the fray stronger than before. We have risen to new heights when all other races have fallen into decay. We are the future of Krynn, the fated masters of the entire world. We are the children of destiny.' That's an old minotaur saying."

"I heard it was the Graygem that changed ogres into minotaurs," Delbin cheerfully interjected. "It just moved through the area, and after it left there were ogres and there were—"

Kaz growled. "Minotaurs weren't created by magical happenstance!" He looked at the kender. "If you want to hear the story again, you'll never repeat such foolishness to me, understand?"

"Yes, Kaz. Sorry."

"Good. Now try to keep quiet for a little while. We have a long day ahead of us."

"What's the minotaur kingdom like?" asked his companion, already ignoring his injunction to be silent.

"Not now, Delbin. Later."

His tone was ominous, and the kender obeyed. The rest of the day passed without incident, as did the night that followed. They were able to get an early start the next morning. The minotaur could scarcely believe their good fortune. Usually, it seemed, his journeys were fraught with daily peril.

"See those mountains in the distance?" Kaz asked, feeling less moody than the day before. "Those are the first signs that we're nearing the minotaur kingdom. We've still got the last part of the journey, though."

"I like mountains," his companion commented, staring at the distant peaks. "Especially ones with caverns."

Kaz shuddered. He did not like caverns. Too many things had happened to him in caverns. "I don't think we need to worry about caverns."

"You found a dragon in a cavern once, didn't you?" Delbin grew more excited. "It was just after the war with the Dark Queen, when dragons were supposed to be gone, but you accidentally found a whole dragon, and she was trapped by this evil sorcerer who—"

"Take a breath, Delbin." Kaz had told the kender the

tale once long ago, but had refused to tell that one ever again. He'd hoped Delbin had forgotten. Thinking of dragons always made him recall the silver dragon who, in human form, had loved Huma of the Lance. Memories of Huma were painful, for the knight had been—would always be—Kaz's truest friend. "I don't want to talk about that now."

"But you flew a dragon once, didn't you? I remember you mentioning that, too."

Despite himself, the minotaur smiled slightly as he recalled that particular dragon. "I flew one during the battle in which Takhisis was defeated. His name was Bolt. Young, eager, and as battle-hungry as I was. He was a bronze dragon, brash but brave." Kaz grunted, the memory turning dark again. "They all vanished after the war was over, both the dragons of light and their darker counterparts."

"But you found the other one *after* that."

Seeing that the kender would not be put off, which was how things generally went, Kaz finally nodded with a sigh. "Only a short time after the war. The dragons had all disappeared. I'd just left Solamnia"—he had left Solamnia after paying his last respects to his friend and comrade— "and was simply traveling. Times were still dangerous, though, and many didn't trust my kind since we'd served as slave-soldiers to the Dark Queen. I was often forced to run rather than hurt innocent fools."

"Don't forget the monster!" piped up Delbin.

"It wasn't a monster, Delbin—"

"You said it was a dragon-man! That sounds like a neat monster. I wish I'd seen it. You said it was taller than you and all scaly! It was made by the mage who captured the dragon and her eggs—" The kender shut his mouth when he realized that Kaz was glaring at him again. "Sorry . . ."

"Why do you even ask me to tell the stories? You seem to know them by heart."

"Please tell it again! I like to hear you tell them, Kaz. You *lived* them!"

Yes, he *had* lived them. Images of the past racing

through his mind, Kaz related the short battle between himself and the creature, who had fled into the night, and then his own capture not long after by a sinister mage. The mage, a human named Brenn, had indeed captured a dragon, a great silver female. He had captured her by stealing her eggs and luring the frantic mother into a trap, using the eggs as bait.

"He was turning her eggs into monsters, wasn't he, Kaz? Making more dragon-men!" Again, it took a severe look from the minotaur to quiet the overeager kender, who still managed to ask one more question. "Why didn't the dragon stop him?"

Kaz recalled all too well. "An illusion. He threatened her eggs, placing an illusion of them just out of her grasp. In return for their safety, he demanded her magic to aid his own in an experiment. She couldn't know that he was using her magic on the real eggs, changing the young into beast-men."

"What happened?"

"With her help, I killed Brenn and his monster, but she died." Her dedication reminded him of Huma's silver companion. "I took what eggs I could find and brought them to a place where I thought her mate, who had also remained behind, would likely come." He exhaled. The story dredged up other memories. "I waited nearly three weeks before he came, and when he did, I thought he would die as well." Kaz eyed the kender as if daring him to interrupt.

Delbin was wisely silent.

"He and his mate had not been the only dragons left, after all. How it also could have been there, I don't know, but there was a great black, one of the most evil of dragons. The silver fought the black, killed it . . . with a little help from me . . . but was so badly wounded that he could barely carry the eggs. You see, once free of the mage's spell, they grew at their normal pace. By the time he came, they were close to hatching."

The kender's mouth formed an **O** of wonder. "Did he live?" he blurted.

"The last I saw of him, he was flying off . . . I think it was to the north . . . with the eggs in a sling that I'd made for him. He couldn't even transform. His magic barely worked." Kaz scratched his chin. "I never knew the female's name, but his was Tiberion, I think."

"That's a good story!" Delbin reached for his pouch. "Oops! I should write it down so I don't forget it!"

Kaz, who had no inclination to discover just what Delbin would pull from his pouch this time, quickly said, "Forget that for now. We've got to pick up the pace. I want to make those lower hills by tonight. Besides, you know the story almost as well as I do. You can always write it down later."

Delbin pouted but obeyed.

They did make the hills by nightfall, albeit barely. Kaz was grateful for yet another uneventful day of travel and hoped it was a good sign. Once they entered the minotaur lands, he would have to be even more on his guard, but until then, the minotaur wanted to be able to relax and build up his strength.

They located a likely spot for camp and dismounted. Kaz took charge of both animals while Delbin cleared the grounds.

"Delbin, see if you can find some food. I'll work on the fire." Regardless of his other traits, the kender was an expert gatherer and trapper when he put his wandering mind to it. Seven times out of ten he was likely to bring both meat and fruit back with him, along with a few items that Kaz had to be convinced to try eating.

The kender scurried off. He would be back within the hour. When he and Kaz had traveled together, they often set traps in the hopes of catching game that they could use for the next day's meals. Kaz would set a few of his own before the evening was over, but he had spent so many years living off the land that this work seldom took long. So far, they had been fortunate, catching a good supply of rabbits and an occasional bird. Nuts and berries added to their repasts.

Kaz had just finished his own tasks when the kender

reappeared. The fire was burning merrily, the camp in good order.

"Kaz! Look what I caught! They practically jumped into my hands!"

The minotaur snorted. Typical kender luck. The kender had two rabbits on a string—rabbits mostly for Kaz's benefit—plus a full bag that likely contained fruits and whatever other plant life Delbin thought edible.

They settled down to sleep not long after eating. Kaz was so relaxed, he immediately drifted off.

He was awakened soon after by a sound he could not identify, save that it somehow seemed out of place with his surroundings. A sense of foreboding coursed through him.

"Did you hear that, Kaz?" asked Delbin, rising from the other side of the fire.

"Quiet!" the minotaur whispered, rising at the same time. He seized the great battle-axe by the handle. "Stay here, Delbin."

"But, Kaz—" The kender clamped his mouth shut at the sight of his companion's ferocious visage.

Staring into the dark forest, Kaz estimated where the noise, whatever it had been, had originated. He took off on foot. His present circumstances reminded him of his dream. True, he was in the forest rather than the mountains, but other than that he felt as if the two were somehow connected.

That was what he was thinking about when a figure as tall as the minotaur nearly crashed into him.

The ogre was as surprised as Kaz, possibly more so. Armed with a studded club, it gaped at the horned warrior, then grunted and attacked.

Kaz met the blow with his axe. Honor's Face cut through the club unhindered, sending a good third of the ogre's weapon flying. The ogre was stubborn, however, and pulled the weapon back for yet another try. Even in the dim light of the moon, Kaz could see the murderous intent in his adversary's flat, brutish face. The ogre snarled, revealing long, vicious teeth accustomed to tearing raw flesh from either a fresh kill or an enemy warrior . . . which was often the same thing to one of its kind.

Kaz did not wait. Even before the ogre could complete its second swing, Honor's Face sliced under the monster's guard, digging in deep at the midsection.

With a cry, Kaz's foe fell back, the ruined club dropping from a lifeless hand. The ogre ceased breathing even before its body struck the ground.

There was more thrashing in the woods as other figures moved in his direction. Kaz made a quick estimate based on the patterns of noise and counted at least four other ogres, all heading his way. One was bad enough, two worse, but if he had to face three, possibly four, at the same time, then he was dead.

Kaz abandoned his position for one farther to his left. He could hear the movements of but one figure over there . . . so he hoped, anyway . . . and against one ogre he would prevail.

The newcomer continued to trample through the forest. Ogres were less concerned with stealth than minotaurs. Brute strength was all that mattered to most of them, though it was never wise to underestimate them. Kaz had been forced to serve under ogres when he had been a slave-soldier in the armies of the Queen of Darkness, and he was fully aware just how cunning and treacherous they could be.

A dim shape materialized, a shape that coalesced into an ogre, with an axe almost as long as Kaz's. The ogre was breathing heavily. It paused and sniffed the air.

Kaz gave no warning. The minotaur warrior emerged from his hiding place with the axe already in flight. To its credit, however, the ogre succeeded in dodging the blow.

"Minotaur," growled the toothy monster. "What do you think you are doing?"

"I would've thought that obvious." Kaz did not want to waste time talking, but the ogre's attitude confused him.

"We've not failed," insisted the ogre. "Camp is near."

They were interrupted by the sudden arrival of a second ogre, this one wild-eyed. "Minotaur . . ."

Two now. Kaz shifted to compensate for the change in numbers. The second ogre carried both a sword and net, the latter one of the throwing kind used by some races when hunting prey.

This ogre eyed Kaz's axe. "Squallin dead . . . by axe."

"You not be from Nethosak," blurted the first at the minotaur. Its axe rose.

Its words were punctuated by a pained growl as Honor's Face caught its weapon arm, leaving a great gash. The axe dropped from the ogre's hand. As the creature grabbed its wounded limb, Kaz whirled on the second one, who was already advancing.

A web enveloped him. Quicker than its partner, the second ogre had tossed the net with accuracy. It covered the minotaur well. The angle made it difficult to properly wield his axe, leaving Kaz nearly defenseless. The ogre's mouth widened in triumph. It raised its sword for a killing stroke.

Bending forward, Kaz charged.

The attack was not what the ogre expected. Kaz's horns plunged into the wide torso of the minotaur's foe, the force behind them more than enough to pierce the ogre's thick hide. The monster's gasp was as much from surprise as pain. As Kaz pulled away, the ogre gasped again and tried to stanch the flow of blood.

The first ogre had retrieved its axe, but its attempt to swat the tangled minotaur with it was spoiled by its awkward swing. Kaz dodged the axe and backed away, at the same time using one hand to pull himself free of the net. The ogre he had gored collapsed.

He had the net half off when the other ogre attacked again. Although he was able to raise his own weapon to defend himself, the angle was such that his opponent's axe clattered and slid down along the handle. Kaz grunted in pain as the edge scraped his arm, nearly making him lose his grip.

Once more the ogre brought the axe up, but obviously being more used to using its other hand, it moved slowly and without precision. It gave the minotaur time to free himself completely and still raise Honor's Face in time to deflect the next attack.

Far to his right Kaz heard a gruff shout. Taking advantage of the distraction, the minotaur charged, battle-axe swinging low and fast. The ogre brought its own axe down in an attempt to pin Kaz's to the ground, but overcompensated. The ogre weapon sank into the earth and before its master could pull it up, Honor's Face cut across both legs.

Its legs collapsing beneath it, the ogre fell forward. Kaz pulled away. Unable to stop, the ogre impaled itself on the head of its own double-edged axe.

Kaz turned to face any newcomers. To his surprise, not only were there no new attackers, but it sounded as if the others were retreating.

They were heading in the direction of the camp.

Delbin was alone.

Snarling epithets at random gods, Kaz ran as fast as he could, fearing he was already too late.

Chapter 4
Ogre Attack

It was only a few minutes before the first of the hunters came within sight. He was only a black outline, but Kaz had no trouble identifying him as another ogre. The hunter carried a net and club.

Just a moment later, a second shadow moved toward the camp, what looked like an axe in one hand and possibly a net in the other. They were surprisingly deft for their kind, but to Kaz they were noisy enough to wake the dead. Leaning Honor's Face against a tree, he removed a knife from the belt of his kilt and moved silently toward the nearest ogre.

The ogre never noticed him, so intent was it on the lone figure by the campfire. Kaz came up behind the stalker, then, when the ogre paused to scout the area, the minotaur struck. With one hand he covered the ogre's mouth. Then, before the creature could comprehend what was happening, Kaz drove the blade into his adversary's throat. The minotaur had no qualms about doing so; the ogre would have done the same—or worse.

With a muffled gasp, the ogre slumped. Kaz held on, cushioning the body to prevent it from falling to the ground too heavily. He gently lowered his victim, then, wiping the blade, looked around.

The other ogre was no longer in sight, but Kaz had a fairly good idea of where it had gone. Crouching as low as he could, yet still move swiftly, the minotaur darted among the trees. Suddenly, he spotted the second ogre waiting impatiently for some signal. Kaz moved at an incautious pace. He was almost on top of the ogre. Only a few steps more . . .

Then something, some slight movement on the minotaur's part, made the hunter turn. The ogre spotted Kaz and hesitated. It would be only a moment before his opponent realized that Kaz was not an ally, so the minotaur did the only thing he could. He threw his blade, burying the knife deep in the ogre's chest. The creature dropped its weapons and tried to reach for the blade, but its life was already draining from it. It fell before its hands were even halfway to the hilt.

Kaz rushed to the body, hoping no one had heard it fall, and reached to retrieve his knife.

A bird called out. The minotaur froze, knowing that such birds were not usually in the habit of chattering at night.

From the other side of the campsite there came the rustling of vegetation and the heavy grunting of moving figures. Kaz heard a gasp that had to have come from Delbin. A deep voice snarled an unintelligible order.

The minotaur cursed. Seizing his blade, he thrust it into his belt and ran for the camp. Even before he reached it, he was able to make out what was happening. His heart sank.

There were five of them, two minotaurs and three ogres. One ogre was trying to hold a squirming Delbin while the others looked around for obstacles to their fun. All of them looked very disappointed.

He did not hesitate. Roaring at the top of his voice, Kaz leapt into camp just behind one of the ogres. The hunters looked up in time to see him raise his arm and open his empty hand. The look of surprise in their eyes when Honor's Face materialized in his grip amused Kaz even though he had already witnessed that shocked look countless times in the past. The magical axe always had returned to him when he most needed it, and certainly now figured to be a time of need.

He cut down the first ogre while the creature was still gaping. The one holding Delbin tossed the kender aside and readied its weapon. One of the minotaurs started forward while the second backed quickly away, retreating into the woods.

Kaz met the ogre axe against axe. The ogre was a veteran warrior, so the two traded blows at first. The other minotaur moved in after that to give the ogre a hand, forcing Kaz back. Behind them he could see the remaining ogre turn on Delbin menacingly.

Hard-pressed as he was to concentrate on anything but his two opponents, Kaz did not at first know why the ogre in the rear abruptly slipped and fell. Only when Delbin's small figure darted past his field of vision did he guess what might have happened.

"Stand still!" cursed the second ogre, rising. It had a sword nearly as long as Kaz's axe and was trying to cleave the moving kender in two. Kaz would have laughed, if not for the fact that his own enemies were separating in order to further divide his attention.

"Surrender and we'll see that your death is swift," the minotaur in the woods demanded.

"I don't surrender to those without honor."

His words angered the other minotaur, who swung

carelessly with his blade. Kaz used that anger to his advantage, catching his foe's weapon by the hilt with the edge of his axe and tearing the sword free. The blade flew at the ogre, who, though it was in no danger of being hurt by it, stepped back in astonishment.

His minotaur antagonist tried to stop the flow of blood from his wounded hand. Kaz immediately turned to the ogre. Its advantage lost and its footing awkward from backing away, the ogre swung its axe far too high. Kaz ducked enough to allow the weapon to pass harmlessly over his head, then brought his own battle-axe down on the ogre's forearm.

Honor's Face cut through the arm with as much ease as it did most everything else. The ogre screamed and pulled away, leaving behind its hand and part of its forearm. The wounded minotaur had retreated.

"Sargas take all of you!" cursed the second minotaur from the darkness, his words for his companions, not Kaz and Delbin. Seeing Kaz about to battle against it, the remaining ogre decided that escape was the best course of action.

Not willing to let any more of his foes escape, Kaz charged after the fleeing ogre. However, he had only reached the edge of the campsite when he suddenly became entangled in a number of tree limbs that materialized before him. Kaz tried to shove them aside, only to discover that they clung to him with the tenacity of serpents.

One of the nearest trees started to move, its branches reaching out in what looked to be an attempt to seize his axe.

"Paladine!" He tugged Honor's Face back before the tree could succeed, then swung it around, slicing through the harassing branches. As they clattered to the ground, more sought to seize him, but he cut through those as well. No normal axe could have severed so many limbs so quickly. If Kaz had used any other weapon, he was fairly certain he quickly would have become trapped . . . or worse.

The animated tree suddenly loomed above him, black shadow in the black night. Kaz hefted his weapon, but as he prepared to strike, another tree moved toward him. It now appeared that the trees intended to crush him on all sides.

Unwilling to accept such a fate, the minotaur gripped his weapon and leapt into the nearest tree, which tried unsuccessfully to seize him. Kaz continued climbing into the upper reaches, avoiding branches from below that tried to drag him down.

Peering down, Kaz caught sight of an unnatural red gleam. He faintly glimpsed a minotaur holding something aloft in his left hand, an item that was the source of the gleam . . . and likely the reason the trees had become so lively. Hooking the axe into his harness, Kaz crawled swiftly along a strong limb that led toward the mysterious minotaur.

Movement to his left and right informed him that the other trees were squeezing in closer. Kaz took one look each way, estimated the distance to the other minotaur, and jumped.

He landed just short, but his abrupt appearance so startled the second minotaur that the latter dropped the gleaming red artifact, a crystal. Kaz, charging forward, did not waste time. The other minotaur tried to retrieve the magic talisman, placing a hand on it just as Kaz reached him. The pair collided, and the gem flew away.

Neither had time for words. The darkness made the battle more confusing. Kaz sought to get a grip on the other minotaur's arm in the hope of twisting it, when he backed into a tree that he did not think should have been there. His amazement might have given the advantage to his foe, but for the fact that the tree *pushed* Kaz forward, sending both minotaurs scrambling.

What in Kiri-Jolith's name? wondered Kaz. Then he realized the truth. The gem gave the minotaur crude command over the trees he had animated. The trees were ordered to capture or possibly kill Kaz, and if the other minotaur got in the way, they would not notice the difference.

His foe crawled out from underneath him, but instead of trying to continue the fight, he took one look at the oncoming monsters and rushed off after his comrades. Kaz did not have much respect for his fellow's sense of duty and honor, though he did have some regard for his common sense. There was no use dying needlessly.

Tree limbs sought him again, but he managed to roll away. Kaz landed against another trunk, this one belonging to a stationary tree. The minotaur took momentary cover.

Attacking with Honor's Face occurred to him, but Kaz did not like the idea of wading into the huge monsters no matter how formidable his battle-axe. There had to be another way. He could outrun ogres, but then he was afraid some other person might run afoul of the animated creatures. Kaz had no idea how long the enchantment would last. The only one who could have answered that question was the minotaur who had been controlling the gem—

The gem! I've been a fool! He quickly scanned the darkness for it, seeking the red gleam. A faint crimson glowed in the foliage to his far left. It could be only the talisman.

One of the trees had shifted closer to try to seize him, but he managed to evade it. Behind him Kaz could hear the animated trees pursuing. Kaz gritted his teeth. He was not far away now. Just a few more yards.

His legs became entangled in some branches. Kaz lost his balance and fell face forward. Almost before he had even hit the ground the hapless warrior found himself being dragged backward. He tried to reach for his axe, but it was difficult. The trees had him in their clutches.

A small figure suddenly materialized near him. "Kaz?"

"Delbin! Find the red gem! It glows in the dark!"

Even under these dire circumstances, the kender's tone was merry. "It does? Gee, that'd be neat to see! I—"

Another set of tree limbs caught hold of his legs. Kaz managed to seize hold of the axe, but doubted he could wield it successfully from his present position on his stomach. "Be quiet, Delbin! Find the gem! Quickly! It's over to your side."

Delbin looked around. "I don't see it!"

Under other circumstances, the kender could have found the tiniest trinket, even if it had been lost and buried for years. Kaz wondered whether he should just surrender to his fate now.

His companion turned his head. "Oh! There it is!" He hurried over to the gem and picked it up. "I've got it, Kaz!"

About time, the harried minotaur thought. "Hold it in your hand and command the trees to stop!"

"It'll make them do that? I never saw—"

"Delbin!"

The kender immediately raised the gem high, shouting at the same time, "Stop, trees!"

Nothing happened. The trees continued their work. One of them was trying to lift Kaz by his legs. The minotaur had the axe out, but trying to strike effectively from upside down was not easy, even with his cherished weapon.

"I said that you should stop, you trees! Stop that!" Delbin paused. "I don't think it's working, Kaz!"

"Break the damned thing!" It was the only other idea he could think of at the moment.

"I don't have anything to break it with. It's pretty hard, Kaz!"

The warrior could think of only one article that either of them owned that might be able to shatter the magical gem. Loathe as he was to give up his only defense, Kaz focused on the kender, cocked his arm, and tossed Honor's Face toward the small figure. "Use the axe! Hurry!"

The other trees clustered around him. His view of Delbin was blocked off. He did hear the kender moving around, but that was all.

"The axe is heavy, Kaz!"

"You don't need to raise it very high!"

His inhuman foes closed on him. Kaz's position became untenable. In minutes the trees would crush him between their trunks.

A brilliant flash of crimson light illuminated the immediate area.

The trees ceased moving. Kaz held his breath, waiting for them to resume, but they did not. He exhaled and laughed.

"Kaz? Are you okay?" Delbin's upside-down head appeared between two of the trees.

"Good enough." He had the arm wound and a splitting headache now, but that was negligible in comparison to what could have happened. "I think I'm going to need your help in freeing myself, though."

"Okay."

With his companion's aid, Kaz was soon able to free himself from the tight little copse. There was no sign of the other attackers. Kaz guessed that he had seen the end of them. Not a very competent group, he thought, not even the minotaurs. He thought about pursuing them, but decided that it was not wise to chase around in the dark. Turning to Delbin again, he asked, "How about you? Are you all right?"

The kender nodded. If anything, he looked thrilled by the night's festivities. It was yet another trait of the race that Kaz would never understand.

Feeling guilty for having left his companion alone, the minotaur added, "Sorry I had to do things that way. I thought we'd have a better chance if I could catch some of them unaware. I'd hoped to do more damage." He was slipping a little, though. He and his companion very well could have been killed. Had his time trying to raise a family dulled his wits some? "I'm sorry."

Delbin appeared unconcerned. The kender looked at the dead ogre and surveyed the remnants of the attack. "It's okay, Kaz. I knew you'd save us."

The statement was said so confidently that Kaz could not dispute it. Delbin resolutely believed in him. Kaz felt embarrassed.

"I knew you'd save us," the kender repeated, looking up and smiling. "The man in the dream said so just before

I woke up."

"The what?" Now that had an unsettlingly familiar ring to it. Kaz's eyes narrowed. "The man in gray?"

"Yes, Kaz! He said not to worry, because the time hadn't come yet to test the balance. He said you'd see us through to that point. We have to be somewhere else for the balancing test."

"By Paladine! That does it!" The minotaur turned his gaze skyward. "I don't know which one of you it is, but I'll not be your puppet again! I'm going to rescue Hecar and then I'm going straight home to my mate and children! Get another to play your infernal game, whatever it is!"

Kaz doubted that the Great Dragon, as the Lord of Good was called by some, was behind this. Paladine was just and fair, but there were other gods, either of Good, Neutrality, or Evil, that, in his eyes, toyed with creatures when they themselves could not act outwardly.

The night sky, of course, did not respond. Kaz snorted in anger and looked at his companion. The kender seemed interested in his words, but made no comment, for which Kaz was grateful. At that moment he came to a decision that he felt was right under the circumstances. It was what he should have done in the first place.

"Tomorrow you'll head south to the settlement and Helati, Delbin. You'll go there and you'll *stay* there."

The kender started to protest, but Kaz turned his back on him, beginning the grisly task of disposing of the ogre remains. He did not look at or talk to his companion again for the rest of the night.

* * * * *

When the next morning came, Delbin raised a protest. "I want to go with you!"

"There were minotaurs with that band that tried to capture us, maybe even kill us. I don't know how they knew we were there or why they wanted us in the first place, but some of them escaped." Kaz did have certain suspicions, but none he wanted to voice just yet. The only ones who had known he was coming to the homeland were the minotaurs of the settlement. "That means we might come across them again, maybe even in Nethosak. They make mincemeat out of kender. I've enough to worry about without worrying about you as well. Go visit Helati again, Delbin. She'll treat you kindly. Wait for me there."

"But, Kaz," interrupted the kender, who was bringing the horses. "I told you! The gray man said I have to go with you to help you."

"Maybe you misunderstood him, Delbin. Maybe he wanted you to be around to help me last night. You've done that, so now you can go back."

The kender thought this over. "Do you think so?"

"I'm sure of that."

"But I don't want to leave! You're my friend!"

The minotaur sighed. Kaz was indeed fond of the kender, which was why Delbin had to leave. He did not want to see him hurt; nor was he very comfortable baring his emotions in this way.

"Listen to me. The minotaur lands are near. They're dangerous. Nethosak is the worst of all. I was a fool to bring you this far, and last night's attack only verified that. I don't know why they wanted us . . . But I think that bringing you to my homeland will only endanger you further. You have to understand that I'm sending you south because I don't want any harm to come to you."

The short figure stared at the ground. "I don't want to go . . ."

"Delbin." The kender looked up. "I hope you understand how serious this is. I wouldn't want anything to happen to you."

"I know, Kaz."

"You'll go south, like I asked?"

"Yes, Kaz, but—"

"No." The minotaur folded his arms, looking as impressive and stern as he could. "Helati needs your help, since I am gone. She has children to take care of." Inside, Kaz winced. Helati would not soon forgive him for making a kender even a short-term member of her household. She cared for Delbin in much the same way as Kaz, but kender had a habit of "accidentally" removing any item left sitting around for more than a minute. Still, Delbin did have a way with children, even minotaur infants, which might prove valuable. That might assuage Helati some.

"I understand," Delbin replied, trying to look big and solemn. Breaking into a smile, he said, "I do like Helati, too! She cooks well for a minotaur and can hunt and knows neat tricks with a dagger, which she showed me once when she hit a target real far away . . ."

The kender babbled on and, although the constant flow of words drove Kaz to distraction, he allowed Delbin to talk freely. And when the kender at last departed, less than an hour later, Kaz felt strangely hollow.

Pull yourself together, he reprimanded himself, once Delbin was out of sight. You're a minotaur, a warrior. That's the way you have to act when you enter the empire. Hecar needs you to be strong.

Thinking of Helati's brother helped strengthen his resolve. Prior to departing, Kaz searched for signs of the hunters' retreat. He counted only five mounts. It was possible there were reinforcements elsewhere. He was positive that his decision to send the kender back had been the correct one. Ogres and minotaurs did not willingly work together unless there was a good reason.

He would find Hecar. There was no question about that.

The day passed slowly. Kaz found that he missed the kender's company more than he could have imagined. Delbin had been as loyal a comrade to him as any he had known . . . more loyal than most.

The woods grew thinner and thinner, becoming simply grassy hills dotted with the occasional copse of trees. The southern end of the mountain range that marked the border of the minotaur kingdoms was only a few days away. As he rode north, Kaz also experienced some bad weather. The wind picked up, with cloud cover coming not long after. It started to rain just before the sun set, and the rain intensified soon after that, becoming a full-fledged storm. Ragged bolts of lightning striking in the hills ahead made him finally decide to make camp.

Kaz found an overhang large enough to conceal both him and his horse. It was no surprise to find it there; he recalled it from another journey long ago. There was no way he could start a fire, so the minotaur satisfied himself with eating cold, cooked meat and fruit left from his portion of the supplies. The rest he had given to Delbin. The kender had been more than fortunate in his scavenging, so he and Kaz both had plenty of food.

The storm grew worse. Unable to sleep, Kaz stared out at the countryside, identifying landmarks. In his thoughts, he considered what he would do when he arrived in Nethosak. Possibly his best bet for aid would be from the House of Orilg. While his relationship with his clan was not as good as it once was, the house had no reason to turn him away. Kaz had cleared himself of any accusations of dishonor, and his reputation outside of the homelands had even given him a unique prestige among his own kind. It was known that the Knights of Solamnia, one of the few human organizations the minotaurs respected, honored him as a warrior.

Of course, Orilg aside, Kaz had one or two other contacts, providing they were still alive. He touched the pouch that contained the medallion Delbin claimed had been given to him in a dream. As much as he hated to lay claim to his past status in the circus, there were those who would aid him simply because he had once owned the rank of supreme champion.

A particularly brilliant flash of lightning lit up the landscape. Kaz leapt to his feet, momentarily disturbing his mount. He could have sworn that he had seen a figure standing untouched in the storm, a bearded figure clad in a long, flowing robe and bearing a staff. It was a figure that, even from a distance, looked much like the gray man from his dream.

"Well, I'm awake now!" he snarled. Suddenly oblivious to the elements, he charged out into the storm, heading for the spot where he had glimpsed the gray man.

Lightning crackled across the sky, but nothing illuminated the figure. Kaz moved swiftly, fearing not only that he might lose his quarry in the dark, but also that he might have imagined everything in the first place. His axe remained behind, but the minotaur did not worry; Honor's Face would be in his grip when he needed it.

Thunder rolled. The rain worsened, slowing Kaz. He peered through the storm. Kaz wondered if the gray man, despite not wearing either the red, black, or white robes of the calling, was indeed a mage; he certainly had the look of one. Something about him was familiar, too, and not just from the dream. It had to do with Huma of the Lance, of that he felt certain, though in all honesty he could not have said why.

Another brilliant bolt lit up the area, revealing to Kaz a form huddled near where he had last seen the gray man. Despite being drenched, the minotaur allowed himself a toothy grin. He had the elusive figure at last.

"Get up!" he roared as he neared the dark, huddled mass. "Get up! You've got some things to answer to!"

Lightning flashed again and, for the first time, Kaz saw that the figure before him was not the man in gray.

It was Delbin . . . and he was bleeding.

Chapter 5
The Minotaur Kingdoms

Water splashed in Hecar's face. He flinched and coughed but could do nothing; his hands were manacled. After a few moments, though, he was able to blink his eyes clear enough to see . . . not that there was anything he needed to see. It was the same grimy cell and the same, squat, scarred minotaur, many years Hecar's elder, who grinned down at the prisoner with a mouth only half filled with teeth.

Molus, so old he was completely gray-furred, was an enthusiastic jailer, ever delighting in ways to further strip his charges of their dignity. "Time to fight again, criminal. Got a good match for you today."

Behind Molus waited four well-armed members of the State Guard. Scurn was not among them. Hecar had not seen Scurn since his arrest, though he was fairly certain the disfigured minotaur had graced the stands at least once.

Every muscle in his body ached, reminding him that at least he was still alive. By rights, he should be dead. Combats involving criminals of the state were usually balanced so that the outcome went against the convicted.

Hecar had fought two combats so far, one against two skilled warriors and the other involving a very hungry bear obviously taunted into savagery by its trainers. He had won both combats, in great part due to tricks he had learned from Kaz, but for some reason his captors were holding back the worst. He knew that many prisoners faced even greater odds. His combats were winnable, as he had proven. Hecar was no champion of the level that Kaz had once been; he was good, even better than average for his kind, but not great.

It seemed as if they were giving him a chance to live longer, and that worried him. It meant they wanted something they thought he could give them.

"Unlock those manacles," Molus commanded. As one of the guards obeyed, he added to Hecar, "Today you fight an ogre . . . then, if you survive, Captain Scurn wants a word with you."

Another fixed combat, this one more winnable than the others. What did they want?

I should have listened to you, Kaz. I should have listened to you—

Kaz? As the soldiers dragged him to his feet, Hecar wondered if he had stumbled on the answer. Was he somehow being given the chance to survive because of his relationship with Kaz?

Scurn might hold the answer to that, providing Hecar survived this latest combat. Perhaps today was when everything would begin to make sense. Hecar snorted, knowing that he had to triumph if only to assuage his own growing curiosity.

He almost pitied the ogre.

* * * * *

Kaz allowed Delbin to continue to slumber while he readied things for the journey. It was clear that he was stuck with Delbin. The wound, which had turned out to be little more than a scratch on the kender's right leg, was the result of an encounter with a far-ranging minotaur scout who had chased the kender for several miles. Of course, Delbin admitted that he had been trailing Kaz, hoping to rejoin him at some later point. Kaz surrendered himself to the fact that he would have to allow Delbin to travel with him or forever look over his shoulder for the irrepressible kender.

The storm had cleared just before sunrise, but the sky was still greatly obscured by clouds. Kaz had the horse saddled and ready by the time Delbin managed to wake. The kender rubbed his eyes, looked around in temporary confusion, then smiled at Kaz. "It's stopped raining."

"That it has. How do you feel?"

"Better."

Most kender, of course, possessed strong constitutions. Delbin seemed almost completely recovered. Kaz, who still felt some of his own aches and pains, marveled at Delbin's recuperative powers.

"Do you remember now how you found me?"

"I just knew." The kender's face was all innocence.

Kaz dropped the question. "You were supposed to go to Helati and the other minotaurs. Paladine's shield! You're likely walking into danger if you stay with me!"

Crossing his arms, Delbin, trying to look firm, replied, "I'm not going back. I want to go with you."

"Oh, you're going to come with me, all right. I don't really have a choice now. Any time wasted means Hecar might die . . . if he isn't dead already. You should've kept going south, but now that you're with me, understand this. Don't stray. Obey every command I give you, even if it seems demeaning or confusing. You're going to act as my slave as long as we're in the kingdoms. I'll have to treat you like one. It's your only chance of coming out of this in one living piece. You understand that, Delbin?"

The kender was undaunted. "I understand . . . and I'm not afraid. Not with you by me, Kaz."

Kaz released an audible sigh. "You've got too much faith in me . . . or did your man in gray tell you something else?"

"No, he didn't say anything else in the dream."

"Did you dream about him while you were riding south? Is that why you came back after me?"

"I only dreamt about him once." Delbin seemed sincerely perplexed.

"You didn't see him during the storm?"

"No, Kaz."

The minotaur gave up. "All right. Mount up. I'll lead the horse a little while until the trail gets better, then we'll ride together for a time. Remember what I said. We may start running across my people, especially an outland patrol or something."

"I'll do good, Kaz. You'll see."

"You'll have to."

The sky never completely cleared, but no additional rain fell. The good weather stayed with them the entire day and the next two as well, by which time they had reached the empire's southernmost border. They were fortunate, at least as far as Kaz was concerned, not to meet anyone else, but that changed as soon as the pair, both mounted, entered the first border pass. A party approached in the opposite direction. Kaz quickly made Delbin dismount. He then looped a noose he had made earlier over the kender's head, tightening it just enough for appearances.

"Looks like a patrol, Delbin. You know what we discussed. Stay quiet and act frightened and obedient. Pretend you've been walking for a while."

"Okay, Kaz." Neither the kender's giggle nor his smile bolstered Kaz's confidence.

They were spotted moments later. The other party immediately turned toward them, cutting them off. The newcomers were indeed members of a patrol, one that had been out in the wilds for some time. The leader, an elder female with two fingers missing from her right hand, called for the two to halt.

"Who're you and what are you doing coming up through this passage?"

"My name's Edder of the clan Mascun." Mascun was an obscure clan that Kaz knew about only because one of his close comrades, during the years he had fought as a slave-soldier, belonged to it. Edder had been a competent warrior whose lack of originality had finally gotten him run through by a Solamnic lancer. No one, not even a minotaur, ought to stand fast when a trained knight on a war-horse came barreling toward him with a long, sturdy lance aimed for his chest. In his excitement, Edder had forgotten that critical bit of common sense.

The female seemed satisfied with his answer, but frowned at Kaz's companion. With her mutilated hand she pointed at Delbin. "And what in the name of Sargas is that *thing* doing with you?"

"I caught him trying to steal food from my camp. He seemed fit enough, so I made him a deal. He serves me or he dies. He's found out it's safer to serve me. It is only proper. After all, we are destined to be the masters of all soon enough, aren't we?" Kaz looked meaningfully at the others. All of them had served as slave-soldiers. Becoming masters of slaves would certainly be to their liking if they were typical of the minotaurs he recalled from his own experience.

The other minotaurs nodded or muttered agreement. The female smiled. "Before long, maybe we'll all have one of those."

"A kender? Why bother?" snorted another. "Let's just wipe 'em all out. Let's wipe out all the lesser races! All of Krynn will belong to us then! We should start with this one here. The only good kender is a dead one, eh?"

More than one member of the patrol seemed to find this an agreeable thought. Kaz decided to cut off the notion before it could gain further support. "And do you feel like cleaning the streets or dumping the refuse? Scrubbing the docks clean? Why should we do that when there are lessers to do it for us! We're meant for battle and adventure, not demeaning tasks like that! If we are to be the masters of Krynn, then we must have menials to command."

"I like the thought of a few slaves of my own," agreed the patrol leader. "I spent all my life obeying humans and ogres who I could've squeezed to death with just this hand!" She held up the three-fingered hand for him to see, grinning. "I like that thought a lot."

"And it'll be soon, won't it, Telia?" called one of her comrades.

She nodded, her attention still fixed on Kaz. "But not soon enough for me, y'know?"

Kaz grinned back. "I'd sell you this one, but I think I've got him trained real nice. Maybe on my way back out . . . if I'm tired of him by then." Kaz urged the horse along. "May your ancestors guide you."

To his hidden relief, Telia replied, "And yours." She shook her head. "Watch that kender, though. Give me a human slave over one of those. I wouldn't trust a mischievous kender."

"He learned what happens when he disobeys." Kaz showed them the wound on the leg. "Come along!" he snarled at Delbin. "We've got a long way to go yet." The kender, mouth clamped, hurried to keep up.

"Mind you watch yourself, Edder," the patrol leader called. "The clerics have been touchy the past few weeks. They've had the guard clamp more than a few in irons for not cooperating. Do what they say and do it fast, and maybe you'll be all right."

"My thanks." He waved, then turned so that none of them could see his face. Whispering, Kaz said to Delbin, "You'll have to hold out until we're far enough so that they won't see us. Then I'll let you ride for a while. A couple more days, though, and we'll both have to walk most of the time. The trail winds."

The kender said nothing, but nodded ever so slightly. Kaz was impressed. Delbin was clever enough to know to keep his mouth shut, and trotted alongside the horse as if he could have done so all day.

They were troubled no more that day, though at one point they did see a trio of riders heading south. Kaz studied them from hiding. While he had nurtured the wild hope that one of them might be Hecar, none of them was. The riders stayed to another trail and soon were lost from sight. Kaz let Delbin ride a little, knowing he would soon have to make the kender walk almost all the time.

On the third day in the mountains, during their midday meal, Delbin looked around at the high peaks and said, with typical kender awe, "I've never seen mountains so high, Kaz!"

"They're among the highest."

"Were there ever dragons here?"

Kaz snorted. "Oh, there were dragons here, all right! Mostly blacks, reds, and blues. This was a favored ground of theirs during the war. More to the north, though. That's where the warlord Crynus kept the bulk of his army. Now there was a true monster, worse than any dragon. Remember what I told you about him?"

As Delbin nodded, Kaz recalled the story he had related to the kender. Until his death, Crynus, a human, had been the Dark Queen's favorite commander. Under his command, her forces had brought desolation to much of the northern and eastern parts of Ansalon. If not for Huma, Gwyneth the silver dragon, and Kaz himself, Crynus likely would have crushed the knighthood and brought Ansalon under his lady's sway. Huma, though, had cleaved the warlord's head from his body in an epic combat . . . then had been forced to find another way to kill him when that had not proven sufficient detriment.

Kaz shuddered at the memory. It had taken a dragon's fire to finally rid Ansalon of the undying Crynus.

"Do the mountains surround the kingdoms?" asked his companion, breaking the spell of Kaz's memories.

"No, they mostly run across the western side and through much of the southern. There are breaks north of here, and to the east there are flatlands, but the journey takes much too long if we circle around to the east." He recalled something from his childhood. "They say that it was Sargas who raised the mountains right after he took the worthy ogres and turned them into minotaurs. The mountains were to protect his children while they recouped their strength and worked to assume their proper place as lords of all Krynn." Kaz thought of his years as a slave-soldier and how often in the past minotaurs had been the slaves, not the masters, of others. The mountains had not done their job very well. "Didn't protect us very well, considering he is a god, did he?"

Weather slowed them by about a day's journey, but two days later they left the mountains and entered the lands of the minotaur kingdoms. At first glance, the landscape seemed no different from where Kaz and Helati made their home. The only change was a definite hint of the sea in the air and a steady wind that seemed to blow from the east. The temperature was also slightly lower, and while this did not bother the fur-covered minotaur much, Delbin required more covering at night.

A day later, they sighted a vast city far to the east.

"What is that place?" asked the kender. He had taken to staring wide-eyed at everything, even though Kaz himself could see nothing remarkable about the area. Of course, a kender tended to find almost anything he saw new and noteworthy, even if he had seen it only a couple dozen times before.

"That's Morthosak, the seat of power in the kingdom of Kothas. Other than Nethosak, it's the greatest place in the twin kingdoms. It spreads all the way to the sea. The port is actually larger than Nethosak, but because the imperial government rules from Mithas, there's more activity up there."

"Are we going there?"

Kaz shook his head. "No, and be glad. Nethosak has its dangers, but Morthosak has a few unique to itself. We'll have enough to worry about in the capital."

Delbin could not completely hide his disappointment at not seeing the port city, but Kaz would not be swayed. He still held hope, fading, to be sure, that Hecar was alive and in one piece in Nethosak. It was still a few days there, and the journey would be further slowed by his having to pretend that his companion was a slave.

Soon the areas they traveled through grew more populated. Larger villages and towns sat nearly side by side as the pair proceeded north. Despite the numbers lost in the war, the minotaur population was by no means depleted. A race used to the rigors of constant battle generally worked to see that its losses were made up for as quickly as possible. Within two generations, the population would be almost at what it was midway through the war, when Crynus had begun recklessly pouring slave-soldiers into the forefront, not caring how he wasted them if it preserved his loyal personal cadre.

Yet, if what Kaz had heard was true, the emperor was not going to wait until his people had fully recovered.

Not all minotaurs lived to fight. It was necessary that there be food to feed the race, so Kaz was prepared for the farms that they began to cross. Minotaur farms were not like those of other races, however, for the state controlled their use. They were lined up next to one another in uniform fashion. A director oversaw the management of each segment of the farm community. Each farm competed with another to raise the best crop, be it vegetable, fruit, or livestock. Honors and promotions were given out to those who achieved the greatest results. There were many rules of order governing how farms were to be run and what allotment of resources each was to receive. All very organized and efficient.

All very much a part of the minotaur way of life.

Delbin stared bright-eyed at everything, but few workers paid attention to him or Kaz, intent as they were on seeing to it that their farm ranked tops in their district. Corn already grew higher and larger than most Kaz had seen during his years of travel. Sheep in one sector were so large that one might have mistaken them for cattle from a distance, save for their woolen coats.

"Everything's so big, Kaz! Did you see that cow over

there?"

"Quiet, Delbin!" Kaz nodded, proud despite his feelings toward those who ruled the empire. "The race is constantly in need of fuel. A healthy child becomes a mighty warrior."

The kender watched the minotaurs working in the fields. "I thought all minotaurs were fighters."

"They are. Even these, who some consider the weakest despite the fact that they keep our stomachs full while we do battle on the field. A minotaur fighter is more than equal to any human or elven fighter." If his people ever did conquer the other races, Kaz suspected that the fittest of the new slaves would be brought to the farms to work, freeing up many minotaurs. There would have to be overseers, of course, but few minotaurs would choose a life of farming over expansion of the empire.

Most of the farms were busy with fieldwork, but now and then they passed areas where the land was barren and had been abandoned. Kaz grunted when he noticed the first of these small wastelands. "The price of too much competition. They've ruined the soil." He noted other farms, lush and active. "The others had better learn from that if they hope to survive. Can't conquer a world if you can't feed your armies."

Kaz avoided the towns and villages at nights, opting for wooded lands that hid them from view of the roads. He kept their fires low, enabling them to pass unnoticed. In order to keep his companion entertained, since a bored kender was an especially worrisome creature, Kaz again told him stories and history whenever possible. More than a few of the tales he told so mixed legend with fact that not even he was certain what was true and what had been inflated by earlier storytellers.

He told Delbin about the minotaurs' supposed enslavement by the dwarves of Kal-Thax. The dwarves had kept Kaz's race slaves for years, according to legend, until the minotaurs finally overthrew and destroyed them. Other races often discounted this version of events. Among the legends of that time was one about a minotaur, Belim, who killed a dozen dwarves and freed enough of his fellows to begin the final revolt before he himself went down under the axes of half a dozen more dwarven warriors. Such acts of heroism were grist for the favorite stories of Kaz's people.

However, the kender's favorites, perhaps because of the emotion with which Kaz recounted them, involved Ganth, captain of *Gladiator*. On Kaz's first voyage, he had sailed with Ganth and Kyri and visited an island that seemed all golden. It was not real gold, which had proved a disappointment, but the voyage itself made everything worthwhile. What Delbin found especially exciting was an earlier adventure of Ganth, when he and his vessel, on one of its first journeys, had approached a mysterious island of giant snakes and great birds. Here Ganth and Kyri had supposedly met Sargas and his daughter, the tempestuous sea goddess Zeboim. Sargas had not wanted to let any of the minotaurs leave the mysterious island, but Kiri-Jolith had intervened and Ganth had killed a giant bird while battling to escape. He and Kyri had married shortly after. Ganth had claimed the episode as the main reason why he had rejected the Great Horned One and become a follower of Kiri-Jolith.

"They had children soon after that adventure. I was their firstborn," Kaz concluded proudly.

"What were they like?"

"Ganth was a bit of a renegade, someone who always argued against the established way things were done." Kaz chuckled. "Which is where I get my rebellious nature from, I guess. Kyri was more typical, a good partner in battle. Of course, she chose to make Ganth her comrade for life, so I guess she was a bit of a renegade, too. They raised us well, kept us fit, cherished us." The minotaur stared off into the distance. "When *Gladiator* sank, I mourned them well."

"Oh." Delbin looked down, momentarily dejected. Then he looked up again, brightening. "But you said 'us.' Did they have more than you? You never told me you had brothers and sisters!"

"There were six of us. Four males and two females." Kaz hesitated, not having thought about his siblings in years. Since he had broken away from his people, he had not contacted anyone from his past, neither friend nor relative.

"Will we meet up with any of them?"

Kaz drifted off. "I don't know . . . not Raud . . . he's . . ." He lowered his hand, touching the pouch that still held the medallion. "Not Raud."

"Who's—"

"It's late." Suddenly rising, Kaz began to gather things together. "We've got more traveling to do. We'll both walk. You'll have to wear the rope again, Delbin. I'm sorry."

The small figure silently obeyed, sensing that Kaz did not wish to speak more about his family. There were some memories too painful to recollect even after years.

I was afraid you'd pop up in my mind if I came back, Raud, Kaz admitted silently to himself. I was afraid you would haunt me again.

It would have happened regardless of whether or not Delbin had asked him about his family. Nethosak was where he and Raud had last met. Nethosak was where one critical decision had forever changed Kaz's life.

It was where Raud had died.

* * * * *

Far off in the heart of Nethosak, death was also on the minds of two weary minotaurs now awaiting an audience with the high priest. They had ridden like the wind after the final debacle, leaving behind the last of the ogres, who was likely dead by now from the loss of its limb. The other ogre had deserted one night and fled back to its own kind, not wishing to face the high priest's wrath. In their hearts, the minotaurs knew they faced punishment for their absolute failure, but pride, so ingrained in most of their kind, had prevented them from simply never returning to the imperial capital. Now they were both regretting the tug of that pride.

The antechamber in which they waited did little to ease

their minds. Tapestries depicting the glory of Sargas, especially his punishment of those who had strayed from the path, lined the walls between high marble columns. Carved on each of the columns was the face of Sargas in his manifestation as the Great Horned One. The faces were all set so that they peered down in judgment at those standing before the entrance to the high priest's sanctum.

The huge iron doors swung open, and a solemn acolyte clad in the red-and-black robes of his calling stepped out to face the pair. "His Holiness will see you now. You will speak only when spoken to and answer all questions completely. Is that absolutely understood?"

Knowing that there was no room for argument, the two minotaurs nodded. The acolyte turned to face the open doorway. "Follow me."

With growing trepidation, they did, one of them pausing only long enough to stare at the huge relief above the doorway. The carving, a great dragon, seemed to stare hungrily down at anyone who walked beneath it. The minotaur shivered, then hurried to keep pace.

The room they entered was the size of a small arena and surprisingly lacking in decor. There were no windows, and the only illumination came from two torches a few yards ahead of them, one on each side of the vast chamber. The ceiling, what they could see of it, loomed high above, adding to the newcomers' sense of inadequacy. Here they were nothing but cogs in the grand scheme of Sargas, small parts that could, if necessary, be easily replaced.

"Come forward."

The voice was strong, commanding, and echoed throughout the chamber. The acolyte stepped aside, indicating that the two should proceed alone.

They had taken no more than three or four steps when high flames rushed from each side, abruptly illuminating the chamber. A row of bright, suddenly flaring torches led to a wide dais more than twice the height of either minotaur. At the top of the dais sat a great stone desk, the front of which also bore the face of Sargas on it.

Behind the desk, quill in one hand, rested the High Priest of the State. His hood and robe were much like the acolyte's, but decorated with a trim of gold along the hood and cuffs and down the front. Beneath the hood was a thin, studious face, one more appropriate for clerical work than the rigors of battle.

Neither of the pair felt any comfort about that. Everyone knew the high priest's brutal power.

"We are not to be disturbed," the high priest commanded the acolyte.

"Yes, Your Holiness." The acolyte bowed, withdrawing. A moment later, the doors closed, leaving the two newcomers alone with the high priest.

"You were given a task."

It took them a moment to realize that one of them was supposed to respond. The taller of the two nodded, then quickly added, "Yes, Your Holiness!"

"Your name?"

"Tosher, Your Holiness. This is Cinmac." At mention of his name, the other minotaur raised a heavily bandaged hand in solemn greeting. Blood had turned most of the bandage red.

The quill did not move. "Where are the others?"

Tosher swallowed, unable to answer. Cinmac finally grunted, "Dead, Your Holiness."

"All of them."

"Yes, Your Holiness . . . except an ogre that ran off."

At last finding his voice again, Tosher blurted, "They came from all around us, Your Holiness! We were outnumbered, and those damned ogres panicked! We would've been slaughtered. We—"

"Silence." The high priest stared at both minotaurs. "It was not that way, was it, Cinmac?"

"No, Your Holiness." Cinmac clutched his wounded hand. "I can't explain it. He was everywhere. It was as if he knew we were coming. I never saw one warrior so effective."

"And what of the item I supplied you with? Why did you not take him with that? Who decided to avoid its use?

Tell me."

The injured minotaur glanced at his partner before replying. "It didn't seem right. Not magic. We're warriors! We know swords and axes, not magical talismans!" Cinmac silently cursed himself for volunteering for the mission, but then, he had thought the favor of the high priest would be invaluable. What he and the others had forgotten was that the disfavor of the high priest was worse to fear. "The blasted ogres surrounded him with the nets, and then we closed in. Don't know what happened next. Some of the ogres just never followed through."

"The magic talisman . . ."

Tosher snorted. "I used it in the end, but he was still too tricky! I made the trees grab him, but he climbed over them and jumped me. He knocked the piece out of my hand. The trees didn't seem to care who was in their way. They nearly got me by mistake. They probably got him."

The quill came down hard on the desk. Tosher and Cinmac both stared as it snapped and the tip went flying. The high priest glared at Tosher. "That had better not be the case. I want him alive . . . at this point. You two have bungled things far more than I could have imagined possible."

With Tosher silent again, Cinmac tried to explain their failure. "He's a champion of the arenas, Your Holiness. You said so yourself. I've never fought a warrior like that. Give us more soldiers, though, minotaurs—not those untrustworthy ogres—and we'll capture him this time. He's got only a"—the warrior shook his head in disbelief—"a kender to help him."

Tosher snorted. "What sort of minotaur is that who'd have one of those little buggers around?"

"An interesting minotaur," the high priest unexpectedly replied. "An interesting one."

"We'll sneak up on them in the night," Cinmac added, "but quieter this time. You still want him alive so—"

"Most definitely." An edge of menace tinged the cleric's words.

"Well, so this time it'll be different, especially now that

we know what to expect. You take that axe, for example! It had to be magic, too! I'll swear by Sargas himself that he didn't have an axe when he appeared, but did just before he cut down one of the ogres!"

"Aye!" dared Tosher again, caught up in the story. "Out of thin air it came, Holiness! An axe that gleamed even in the night!"

"Did it now? Most interesting." The high priest scratched the underside of his muzzle. "Enough talk from both of you. Even with this axe, I still find it astonishing that one warrior sent both of you fleeing. Is this the way of the warrior as you were taught? I think not. You fled from battle when you should have been willing to die on your feet."

Neither of the figures before the high priest dared to utter another word. They knew that what he said was truth. Even Cinmac's terrible wound was not excuse enough.

"I sent you to find one minotaur, one whose presence I require, but whom I do not want others in the kingdom to see again. You cannot track him even though I tell you where he lives, and then you let this one warrior . . . *one warrior!* . . . lay waste to your ranks as though you were children just beginning to learn to walk." The high priest rose. He was taller than either of his minions, albeit slighter in build. His eyes burned down at the pair. "You have failed me. That is the sum of all your excuses. Even with magic of your own, which I reluctantly decided you needed, you failed miserably."

"It was that axe! He had better magic!" insisted Tosher. "We would've had him if he hadn't had the axe! We didn't know we'd be facing that!"

"I grant that, at least. My sources were remiss. You did not know about the magic axe." Reaching up, the narrow figure pulled back his hood. "That does not excuse your failure. As things stand, Kaziganthi de-Orilg will no doubt make his way into the empire and thereafter make known his presence to others." He shook his head. "This makes my work far more complicated than it should have been. There is no room in my empire for such ineptitude as you two have exhibited." The high priest's eyes flared. "No room at all . . ."

* * * * *

A bell summoned the acolyte to the high priest's chambers only moments later. He entered the sanctum of his master, but paused just inside the door. The high priest sat at his desk, hand on chin in contemplation. Of the two hunters who had been waiting, there was no immediate sign.

"Come forward."

The acolyte obeyed, but as he stepped toward the dais, his foot kicked something. He glanced down and saw that it was a hand, half-wrapped in bloody bandages. Nearby was what looked like a foot and the hilt of a sword. The rest of the body was missing.

Trying to ignore the grisly sight, the acolyte stepped past it, then knelt before his master and awaited his command.

"There is a Captain Scurn of the State Guard. Send for him. I have questions I would ask that I believe he might be able to answer."

"Yes, Holiness."

"And remove that refuse on your way out."

The acolyte rose and obeyed. The high priest watched, then, when the acolyte had departed, went back to his contemplations.

"I have waited too long," he muttered. "I have waited too long to be delayed by one fool of a minotaur. When you return to my empire, Kaziganthi, you will have a choice. Join my grand plan . . . or be buried by it."

Chapter 6
A Surprise Reunion

Nethosak.

Kaz found himself at its great walls so soon after passing its counterpart to the south that he almost wondered if the twin kingdoms had moved closer in his absence. He knew that the populations of Mithas and Kothas had multiplied and that Nethosak, as the seat of power, had grown even faster, though it was hard to believe that so much growth had occurred in the short time since the war. Even for a people as driven as his own, the changes were astounding.

Delbin was utterly fascinated by the city, so much so that he tended to forget that he was supposed to be a slave. Delbin's supposed status as slave made it impossible for the kender to ask all of the questions flitting through his head, so Kaz tried to anticipate some of them to prevent Delbin from blurting everything out.

"See that building far over there . . . toward the center, slave?" Kaz asked, pointing at a tall structure with an arched roof. "That's the emperor's palace. Looks a lot like these buildings flanking us only much larger. These are houses of the lesser clans. The great clans are more to the north end of the city, though they've got a lot of influence down here, too." Kaz then pointed out the temple of the state priesthood and the plain, boxlike building that was the quarters of the Supreme Circle. Kaz explained what each of the two groups was, then concluded, "Know them well, slave, for they decide life and death for all and are to be respected, especially by your inferior kind. It'll be they, under the emperor, who decide the fates of all others when we come to rule this world."

The rhetoric sounded hollow to Kaz, but he knew how much most of the minotaurs eavesdropping on them believed in it. Such notions were implanted in minotaur minds at an early age, and while those notions did not always sit well with a few, most of his people were well-indoctrinated through the efforts of the priesthood and the circle.

They passed through an area consisting of a number of the functional but hardly appealing domiciles in which the lowest-ranking minotaurs lived. The air was ripe here, and the structures, while not as decrepit as such neighborhoods in a human city, were dirty and needed repair. Only the streets, whose conditions were monitored by the government, were typical of the order and tidiness for which his race was famed.

As he rode slowly through the well-kept streets into more respectable and pristine sectors, Kaz experienced an involuntary shiver. He was not frightened, but being here unsettled him. Memories of his family, his years in the arena, his combat training, and battles as a slave-soldier serving the likes of ogres and dishonorable humans, all washed over him at once. Now and then, Kaz felt certain that he saw a face he recognized, but he never once stopped to talk to anyone. Someone was bound to notice him before long, but until that happened, he preferred to keep his anonymity.

He debated whether or not to go straight to the great clan house of Orilg and present himself, but in the end decided to delay. Having more or less severed his ties with the clan meant he should make his base at an inn, one that would tolerate his kender "slave."

A small figure darted past his horse, and Kaz's first thought was that Delbin was running amok in the city. Then he saw that the small figure was squat and dirty, a gully dwarf with a collar, a true slave.

It was all he could do to refrain from showing his disgust. If the minotaurs were using gully dwarves to pick up trash, then a kender trained to care for his horse and belongings would almost seem a logical progression—or illogical, Kaz thought wryly.

The buildings grew neater and more stylish as he rode, a sign that they were owned by high-ranking minotaurs. The nearer to the circus and the emperor's palace, the better the quality of life in Nethosak. North of the circus were the major land holdings of the great houses and the clans considered among the most powerful in the kingdom . . . as well as the entire empire. Everyone worked to achieve movement in a northerly direction. Even the lesser clans, whose houses lay in the southern sector, coveted those in the northern neighborhoods. Orilg was one of the first, oldest, and largest clans to have built its domain north of the circus.

The eastern part of the city was near the harbor. After riding through crowded streets for nearly half an hour, then turning and riding east for an equal time, Kaz came across an area of Nethosak that he expected would suit his needs. An inn with the colorful title "The Bloody Axe" seemed the best choice. It was out of the way and looked like the type of place that would respect his privacy . . . for a price.

As Kaz dismounted, Delbin, who had been a true stalwart for hours, quietly asked, "Kaz, what's that?"

The minotaur glanced in the direction the kender was pointing and snorted bitterly. The huge arena that caught Delbin's attention was unmistakable even from a distance. "The Great Circus, the arena where important matters of justice"—he said the last word with distaste, knowing how its definition had changed—"and honor are settled. All grievances and crimes are settled by combat, and the greatest of these takes place each day in the circus." He looked around apprehensively, but no one was paying attention to him and his companion. "Now please be quiet, Delbin. You're supposed to be a slave. Your life very much depends on it."

As Kaz approached the front door of The Bloody Axe, a stout minotaur, one of the few of his type that Kaz could ever recall meeting, came out. His face was as round as his body.

"Welcome in the name of Sargas, warrior. You'll be wanting a room?"

"Yes, for myself and my servant."

The innkeeper cocked an eye at Delbin. "A kender servant? First gully dwarves and now . . . kender? Can our day of mastery be far behind if we've already reached this stage?" His remarks bore more than a touch of sarcasm. Turning his gaze back to Kaz, he asked, "Where do you hail from?"

"Southern edge of Kothas." Kaz gave him the same story he had given the patrol. The innkeeper accepted it without question, then informed Kaz that he did indeed have a room the two could use. As an afterthought, the stout minotaur asked, "Do kender make good slaves? I can't imagine a thieving little rat like that being good for anything."

"He's adequate. But when I return home, he is going to have to start learning more duties in the stable."

It was clear that the notion of a kender slave appealed to the innkeeper. "If you have trained him to be useful, I might be interested in taking the kender off your hands. . . ."

"I doubt I'll sell him just yet, but I'll keep that in mind."

And if you even touch him while I'm here, Kaz thought, I'll see that you won't have a hand left to beat any slave.

The innkeeper introduced himself as Kraggor. Kraggor, no warrior, obviously, commanded little respect in the eyes of other minotaurs. He served a function and was tolerated, but was low in rank. It was a wonder he had survived the war. A slave, however, would have to treat him as if he were the emperor. Kaz did not doubt that if he left Delbin alone at the inn, Kraggor would try to get the kender for himself. In the stables, Kaz informed Delbin that he had better come with him on his mission. Delbin, of course, was happy to be allowed to tag along, but Kaz wished there were some less dangerous option.

The pair drew stares as they walked the city streets, with most minotaurs reacting either curiously or indifferently to the sight of a kender slave. A few looked at the duo with mild disgust, but nobody interfered with them or treated them rudely.

Nightfall was almost upon them. Kaz wanted to reacquaint himself with some of the nearby areas. It might prove necessary to make a quick, unplanned escape at some point.

"Stick close to me, Delbin," he muttered. "And remember to keep quiet." Sooner or later he was certain Delbin would revert to his old kender mischief.

Memories continued to rise from the depths, memories concerning every aspect of his life. Some small children were playing sticks, a game in which one tried to trick one's opponent into losing his or her staff. It was a precursor to the real training that would begin soon for these future warriors. Sticks had determined moves and certain areas of the staff could not be touched without a point going against the attacker. Children were encouraged to play this and other competitive games from the moment they could walk. Kaz noted the hierarchy already developing among the stick players. He saw one with great potential and two who might also become champions of esteem.

Kaz and Delbin entered a market still busy with bartering. If there was one constant in the world, it was the marketplace. Watching his people argue over the price of a new sword or fresh game, Kaz had no trouble envisioning humans in the same milieu doing the same thing with the same sort of gestures and words. He was probably one of the few of his kind who had come to realize just how similar the varied races were. In an ideal world, minotaurs, humans, elves, and the others would live on an equal basis, respecting one another's place in the scheme of things.

He snorted, knowing full well that such a world would be long in coming . . . if it ever came. The minotaur race was proof enough of that, although they were certainly not the only ones to be faulted.

"Master?" Delbin called, smothering a giggle.

"What is it?"

"That minotaur over there's watching you." To his credit, the kender was subtle about pointing.

"Hmm?" He looked around and let his gaze cross over to where his companion had indicated. He saw no one who looked either familiar or suspicious.

"He's gone," Delbin said, keeping his voice low. "But he was watching you, K—Master."

"You did well. Let me know if you see him again."

They continued through the market, then entered an area where woodworkers and smiths worked. The smiths were especially busy. By now their counterparts in most human or dwarven cities would be slowing down and preparing to close up for the evening. Here, however, the activity was so great that it was clear there was no intention of quitting until much later in the night. Kaz eyed the activity with some interest. In the days of the war, the smiths had been very productive, as had the shipwrights and others with similar or related occupations. Now, almost a decade after the end of the great conflict, they were working as if war still prevailed.

Now that is interesting, he mused. Working under war conditions when there is no war.

Some of the minotaurs glanced up from their work as he and Delbin passed, but Kaz paid them little mind, caught up as he was in the question of just what his people were doing. Like all minotaurs, he knew that the emperor—all the emperors—preached for the day of dominion. The smiths, the shipbuilders, were always busy, but now they worked as if the war of destiny had been launched at last and someone had forgotten to tell Kaz.

Kaz stumbled, disbelieving. Despite the rumors he had heard from those joining his settlement, he could scarcely believe that the emperor, the circle, and the high priest could be that foolish. A war so soon after the other had just ended? Even with all it had accomplished since the end of the last war, his race had barely recovered. The effects of the Dark Queen's drive for power would be with it—with all the races—for more than a generation.

His thoughts ever more fixed on the subject, Kaz did not notice the three minotaurs who looked him over, whispered to one another, then continued to stare long after most of the others had returned to their tasks. He became aware of them only a few streets and several minutes later, when the leader of the trio took hold of Kaz by the shoulder and spun him around.

The leader had a short, blunt muzzle, mud-colored fur that was thinning in some places, and red eyes that grew redder as he stared at Kaz. "It is you! I had to follow you to make sure! I couldn't let you slip away again!"

"Who—?" began Kaz, but then he, in turn, recognized the minotaur's face. The name escaped him, but he remembered the face from the circus. He also recalled a vicious temper combined with poor fighting skills that chiefly relied on brute strength.

"It's Angrus, Sargas take you! Angrus!" The bull snorted in rage. His two companions grinned.

Angrus. That was the name. Memories stirred. Twice in Kaz's early days in the arena, Angrus had faced him; twice Kaz had humiliated him with easy victories. Kaz had thought little about it, but Angrus, who appeared to have risen not much further in all these years, had evidently spent his whole life nursing a grudge against the minotaur he believed had humiliated him. Rising to Supreme Champion had left Kaz with more than one venomous rival, such as the more skilled Scurn. What little Kaz recalled of the minotaur before him included the fact that Angrus was a stupid brute who could never accept blame for his shortcomings, admittedly a trait common to his people. There were always those in the arenas who saw their defeats as the fault of others who had triumphed simply because they used—

"Tricks! You used tricks against me instead of fighting honorably! Thanks to you, I lost face."

"Which, by this time, you should've found again," Kaz returned. "I can't be responsible for what has happened to you in the meantime." He made to go, but Angrus spun him around again.

"I should've been supreme champion, not you! I wouldn't have run away like you did!"

"Let me go, Angrus. I've no quarrel with you."

"But I have a quarrel with you!"

"Then I'll settle it with you in an arena after I'm through with the business that brought me here." It was a lie, but Kaz hoped that Angrus would be stupid enough to accept it.

"I can't go back to an arena!" the red-eyed minotaur snarled. "You did that! They won't let me compete in the circus or any other arena!"

Kaz had no idea what his old adversary was talking about, but some vague memory of cheating and dishonorable conduct in the arena did come to mind. He did not recall the details. He wasn't even fighting that day, as he recalled. But somehow Angrus had decided that the second incident was also Kaz's fault. Minotaurs could be very single-minded. "Angrus—"

A fist struck Kaz in the stomach. He bent over, grunting. A knee caught him in the chin and sent him stumbling back.

"Stop that!" called a voice that he recognized as Delbin's. "You leave him alone! He's my friend!"

Don't get involved, Delbin! he wanted to shout, but he couldn't do more than grunt when Angrus took the kender roughly by the arm.

"What's this? A kender slave?" Angrus laughed, a

sinister, hacking noise.

A still groggy Kaz leaned forward and bowled into Angrus, who lost his grip on Delbin. Unfortunately, Kaz's charge was not as overpowering as he had hoped. Angrus, his hands freed, grabbed hold of him and held him tight, keeping Kaz's horns away. At the same time, the other two minotaurs seized Kaz by the arms.

"No tricks this time!" growled Angrus. "Just strength . . . my strength!"

He punched Kaz again. Kaz tried to roll with the blow, but it was not possible. The blow left him almost bereft of his senses.

"You shouldn't have done that, lads!" announced a new voice, one that was strangely familiar to Kaz even in his present state.

The minotaur holding his left arm suddenly released his grip. Kaz pulled himself together and took full advantage of his partial freedom, spinning and punching Angrus's companion under the jaw. The minotaur went flying backward, landing hard on his back.

The newcomer was battling the third minotaur behind him, but Kaz had no time to even glance at his rescuer. He faced Angrus, who seemed just slightly less confident now. "A minotaur fights with honor and skill, Angrus. You've got neither. You've got brute strength and no honor at all. I wasn't responsible for your cheating. You're no warrior, Angrus. You're a disgrace to our people."

Angrus threw himself on Kaz. The power behind his attack gave him a momentary advantage. Kaz, however, used a maneuver that Huma had once shown him, slipping free of his adversary's grip. He then caught Angrus under the chin with his knuckles. Angrus grunted and stumbled back a step or two.

Kaz did not let up. He struck again, this time in the stomach, then swung again at Angrus's chin.

Angrus crumpled as easily as he had those many years before.

Behind Kaz, another body hit the street. He turned and saw the last of the trio lying on his side, groaning. The other minotaur towered over his fallen foe, but his back was turned, making it impossible for Kaz to identify his savior.

"You did it, Kaz!" The kender gave him a quick hug of congratulations. "I thought they had you until *he* came along, but all you needed was a little help. And I was the first to pitch in."

"Thank you for trying to defend me, Delbin," Kaz said, interrupting before the kender could begin a much too lengthy rendition of the struggle. "You should've run off, though. They would've killed you. You understand that?"

The kender quieted. "Yes, Kaz."

"Now that's something I'd never thought I'd have heard from you, Lad. Not as wild and proud as you once were."

Again the voice was familiar, but Kaz could not place it. He looked up and studied the face of the minotaur who had rescued him. It was older than his by many years. He could see that years at sea had weather-worn his features, though his eyes were still lively. In his prime the older minotaur would have had the form of a champion, and Kaz could only hope he would look as strong should he be fortunate enough to live to such an age.

"I thought it was you, Lad, but I could scarcely believe my luck. Have I changed so much you don't recognize me? I suppose a few years lost at sea did make some changes."

Lost at sea? Now that he looked closer at his rescuer, the features looked *really* familiar. If he removed several of the lines on the face, darkened the fur, which was partially gray by now, and managed to straighten the back a little . . .

"Paladine's sword!"

"Not a name I'd go shouting, Lad," warned the other. "The sons of Sargas don't take kindly to competition. They don't even like putting up with Kiri-Jolith . . . something they still seem to blame on me."

It was impossible for Kaz to believe that the figure before him was still alive. Few ever escaped the raging sea, but if anyone could have . . . "Father?"

"That's exactly what your brothers and sisters said, in the same tone yet." The older minotaur cracked a smile. "Aye, Ganth's back. The sea goddess hasn't got me just yet." The smile faded as he added, "But she took your mother willingly enough."

"Father?" Kaz repeated, unable to think of any other word to say.

"And I'll still be your father if you say it a third time, Lad. Now snap to and come with me. You and I have a few things to talk about, including a mutual friend who's in a lot of trouble for reasons I don't like to bandy about."

Delbin peered around Kaz, for the first time drawing the older minotaur's attention. "He's the one who was watching you before, Kaz!"

The graying mariner shook his head. "And we'll have to do something about this little one. By the beard of Kiri-Jolith, Son, you always found the most troublesome companions, you did." He took Kaz by the arm. "Come with me. I know as good a hiding place as any."

Still quite numb at the sudden reunion with his father, who wasn't dead after all, Kaz allowed the elder minotaur to guide him away. Ganth led them from the area, winding through the streets of Nethosak with a determination that finally stirred Kaz from his stupor. This was indeed his father, the famed mariner and explorer. Older, yes, and with a slight limp, but not much off his prime. Somehow he had survived *Gladiator*'s destruction.

Except . . . only Ganth had returned, not Kyri as well.

"Here we are." Kaz's father brought them before a small dwelling. It was one of Clan Orilg's holdings, if the markings were to be credited. Orilg, being one of the major houses, had influence in all parts of the empire, but especially in the major cities of Nethosak and Morthosak. The major houses had holdings in various city sectors, places where business was transacted and members of the clan could retire when matters demanded.

We're more like humans than we think, Kaz mused, thanks to the years under the warlords' rule. The humans had impressed their values and interests on their slave-soldiers. Now, the drive for influence and profit was almost as great as the drive for war.

Two minotaurs flanked the entrance. Kaz recognized

neither, but as young as the two warriors appeared, it was possible he had known them as children.

Neither said a word as Ganth and the others entered, though one warrior glanced skeptically at Delbin. Kaz and the kender were led through a short corridor to an antechamber.

"You're in need of some food, aren't you, lads?" When Kaz nodded, Ganth smiled and led them in a different direction. "Then it's the kitchen for us."

Kaz found himself smiling also. At times Ganth had been even less inclined to the ways of their people than he was. During the long years of enslavement to Crynus and the ogres, he had dared to protest the way his children were more or less taken from their parents so that they could be "properly" trained by approved minotaurs. For two years after, *Gladiator* had been sent on a deadly voyage. Another time, Ganth and his crew had actually been stripped of their vessel and put into ranks marching westward during the second great campaign toward Solamnia. Somehow, Ganth had persevered and recovered *Gladiator* again, only to be sent on another mission of great danger.

Now *Gladiator* was lost, along with Kyri, his mate.

"Dastrun gave me this 'prestigious' post when they brought me and three other survivors back two years ago." Ganth snorted as he led the pair to a simple bench and table. "Should be something left to eat here." He banged his fist on the table. Moments later a young female, lithe and tawny, stepped out. Ganth did not wait for her to speak. "Give me whatever you can rustle up, lass, then you can go back to listening behind the door."

She gave him a disdainful look, but obeyed his commands. Her eyes lingered on the kender as she worked, and it was not until she vanished through the doorway again that Kaz felt comfortable.

"Dastrun's patriarch of the clan now," Ganth commented as he tore apart a piece of dry bread. "Master Hestrith died a year ago, but Dastrun was running things before that, I've heard. When Hestrith passed away, the emperor stepped in and said that, due to the course our people were taking, it was necessary for him to appoint a patriarch with the vitality and dedication needed to help see that course to the end. The high priest and the circle sanctioned the appointment, and that was that."

"The emperor chose Dastrun? As our new patriarch?" As with the emperor, the patriarch of the clan—who could also be a matriarch should a female achieve the position— was chosen by rite of combat. A council of elders in the clan usually approved any such match. Emperors had never dared interfere with such important clan matters.

"The high priest and the circle sanctioned it. That was that. No one protested. They were too shocked, I think."

Dastrun was a cousin of Ganth's. Dastrun and his ilk were more supportive of the emperor and the Supreme Circle than Ganth and his family had ever been. Many years ago, Hestrith had hinted that he would have preferred giving up his position to one of Ganth's line, but after Kaz and his father had disappeared, it was inevitable that Dastrun would succeed the patriarch. Dastrun was a clan champion whose ranking was exceeded only by that achieved by Kaz. His claim to the leadership of the clan was legitimate, but there should have been more debate and the ritual of combat. That was how it was done.

Kaz had a twinge of guilt that he was partly responsible. His staying away had helped put Clan Orilg in his distant cousin's grip. The deadly politics that had developed in the empire since the influence of the Dark Queen's minions was one of the reasons why he had stayed away. Instead of achieving their status through honor and strength, too many like Dastrun had reached it through guile and deceit.

"You're staring off into the sea, Lad. You've changed. You were always more willing to jump into the fray. What happened?"

It should have been Kaz asking questions. He wanted to know what Ganth had been doing all these years and how he had survived at all. Yet, instead he related his own story, beginning with his battle with his ogre captain, his meeting with Huma, and the change in his life caused by the legendary knight. Delbin had heard most of it many times before, but he still listened, enraptured. Ganth was silent, save for the occasional grunt.

When Kaz was done, his father finally unleashed a startling roar of laughter so loud it might have been heard all the way to Morthosak. "You've led a quiet life, haven't you? By the Just One's Horns, Kaz! You make me proud of you! I wish I could have seen all of that, or at least met this knight! He sounds like a warrior true, not like these puppets who now command our people."

"Huma was the greatest warrior, man or minotaur, that I have ever known."

Ganth ceased laughing. His eyes narrowed, and, in a more serious tone, he added, "I see. Then I truly wish I had met him. There are few such warriors these days, if I'm any judge."

"Father, about you—"

"Forget me for now, Kaz. I spent several years on an island with half a dozen others, the remainder of a good crew. Some of them perished there, but I and a couple of others survived . . . not that it seemed to matter much with your mother gone. I kept thinking about the bunch of you, though, and that kept me going. That's all you need to know, Kaz. You and the rest of our young kept me going . . . and now I'm glad I survived, because I can see that I was never meant to fight the final battle at sea. There's too great a battle going on right here in Nethosak."

"What do you mean?"

"Didn't you wonder, Lad, how I happen to be around just when you arrived?"

"I assumed it was by chance . . . but from the way you're talking, I gather it was not."

Ganth smiled grimly, revealing a good set of strong teeth. "I learned long ago that there's little chance in the world. Sometimes I think some god, probably old Sargas himself, is still out to plague me."

Kaz nodded, interested to find out that he and his sire thought similarly.

"No, I wasn't there by chance. I've been watching for you for more than two weeks, ever since he was taken."

Ganth shook his head. His horns were even longer than Kaz's, but years at sea had weathered the tips, making them rounder. "I thought I'd never see you again, and then I found out that Dastrun's bunch has known where you were for the past couple years."

While not completely surprised to hear that the clan had been keeping track of him, Kaz felt a growing unease. If Dastrun had been monitoring his movements, it was possibly because the new patriarch was keeping a wary eye on a potential rival. He supposed that as long as he had remained at the settlement Dastrun had not cared, but if the patriarch discovered that he was now in Nethosak, things might be more precarious.

"Should I be worried about that?"

"Probably not. Dastrun's not going to undermine his already shaky position by acting against a clan member of your reputation, Lad. Not directly, anyway. You've made the clan proud of you even if it doesn't always admit it. In fact, you've become something of a legend to more than just Orilg."

"I could live without that."

"Aye, I know that feeling well." Ganth drank some wine, then tore off a piece of meat. Neither Kaz nor Delbin could keep pace with him. "I knew you'd come. One thing that hasn't changed is that you're loyal to your friends . . . deathly loyal sometimes. When they took him, I knew you'd be by before long. Of course, I'd have done the same thing."

"Hecar?" Kaz forgot the food and drink. He rose and leaned forward, hopeful and anxious at the same time. "You're talking about Hecar, aren't you, Father?"

"The same Hecar whom we both knew. Aye, Kaz. Your friend and mine. A clan member, too, though Dastrun won't help him, especially as there's no real blood relation. He's got to know about what's happened, but against the high priest and the emperor he won't do a blessed thing."

"Where is he? Where is Hecar?"

"Sit yourself down, Lad. You're squirming around like a dragon shark about to dine after a bloody sea battle. Not as patient as I thought, though I can't blame you, really. Just give me a chance. You won't be going anywhere tonight, anyway. Not there, at least."

Kaz forced himself to calm down. "Where is he, Father?"

"They've got him in the circus, Lad, tried and convicted as a criminal."

"The circus?" Kaz knew what that meant. As a criminal, Hecar would be given an opportunity to redeem his lost honor by facing impossible odds. He would fight to the death . . . his death. The odds against him would always be too great, but that was how it worked. If he died bravely, he redeemed not only himself, but the clan he had shamed. "I've got to get him out of there before it's too late."

"Before you do that, let me say something. He's fought three combats already, Kaz. Think about it. Three."

"Three—? That's impossible!" Hecar was good, but not that good. Not under such conditions as the circus would have imposed.

"Three fights that a good warrior like Hecar could win, as difficult as the odds were." Ganth scratched his chin as he eyed his son. "If I was a suspicious sort, Lad, I'd think they were giving him a fair chance of surviving. Put him in danger, but danger he can handle. That's not how it works. They're supposed to give him impossible odds so he can die heroically. Makes me think they really want him to live for some reason."

"What purpose would that serve?"

"Just a thought," Ganth replied, shrugging.

"We have to get him out of there, Father." Kaz paused, "I have to get him out of there."

"Hecar's my friend, too, Kaz, not to mention a former crew member of mine. I don't take kindly to my lads being mistreated, not by the enemy or the emperor, which is almost the same thing these days. We'll get him out." Ganth yawned. "But a good battle plan was never forged by slumbering fools. We should get some rest. Hecar's not scheduled to fight again just yet. I've got some friends who know about these things, in case you're wondering. We can figure out what to do tomorrow."

Kaz agreed, despite the urge within him to go charging into the circus and kill everyone who stood in the way of rescuing Helati's sibling. "Tomorrow, then."

"You'll stay here. I can find room for you and the . . . Delbin here. It'll be safer than anywhere else, and it will save us time."

"My things are at an inn."

"Yes. Can't you leave 'em, Lad?"

"Most, but not my horse. It won't take long. I'll be back soon." Kaz made to rise.

"I'll send someone."

"The horse won't like that." Only those whom Kaz introduced properly to the horse could get near the fierce steed without risk. Delbin was one of the few he could recall who had not had difficulty becoming acquainted with the massive Solamnic war-horse. "I'll have to do it."

"I'm going, too!" announced the kender, who had, up to this point, maintained yet another remarkable interlude of silence.

"No, you're staying here. Your kind isn't cared for much. I'll stay with you."

"I'm going with Kaz!" The kender folded his arms, eyeing his companion.

Kaz looked into those eyes and knew that, if he left the kender here, Delbin would somehow follow him just as he had in the mountains. "I'll take him with me, Father. If I don't, I can promise you he'll find a way to slip away. Better I keep him under my wing for now."

His companion smiled. Ganth grunted, but held his protest. After a moment's consideration, he finally said, "Then I might as well go with you and help. Besides, we've still got a few things to talk about. You know, they'll be watching Hecar more than the other prisoners, if only for what he did."

"What was that? What do they claim he did?"

The elder minotaur looked startled. "Didn't I tell you? Hecar's supposed to have killed a cleric . . . one of the high priest's staff, yet!"

Chapter 7
The High Priest

Ganth's words echoed through Kaz's head as they made their way back to The Bloody Axe. Hecar had killed a ranking priest? That hardly sounded like Helati's brother. Hecar was no murderous fool, forsaking all sense of honor to strike down one of the state clerics. True, Hecar had little love for them, but even he would not have attacked one without strong cause.

Ganth insisted there was evidence of the incident. Kaz assumed his mate's brother had acted in self-defense. For some reason, they must have set on Hecar and tried to take him into custody. He had been warned about such happenings. Hecar might have resisted, knowing that his arrest was false, and in the struggle with the guard accidentally killed the cleric.

That made some sense, but did nothing to ease Kaz's anxiety. A prisoner who was accused of such a monstrous crime would be heavily guarded. The high priest would want to make a prime example of Hecar . . . which made the fact that Hecar was still alive all the more puzzling.

Not for the first time did Kaz feel like an absolute stranger in the land that had given birth to him. Nothing made sense anymore.

Things had at least partially quieted in the neighborhood near The Bloody Axe. That suited Kaz; the less who noted his presence, the better. He was hoping he could get away before the nosy innkeeper spotted him.

"Do you have things up in your room?" asked Ganth.

"Yes, and it'll make for less curiosity if I take everything. If I leave some things, they'll wonder what I'm up to. Someone might start asking questions."

"Then let me clear out your room while you take care of your mount. Just tell me where to find the stuff. I'll leave a few coins for the proprietor so he doesn't bark about your sudden departure."

Kaz gave Ganth directions, then he and Delbin headed to the stable. It would take his father only a few minutes to return with his things, so Kaz needed to hurry. He hoped there would be no one in the stable. The less talk, though, the better.

It was hard to see in the darkened stable, causing Kaz to momentarily flounder around. Delbin immediately pointed out the animal. Once again the minotaur was impressed with the kender's keen eyesight.

"Help me with the saddle, Delbin. It'll be quicker if both of us pitch in."

"Okay, Kaz."

They completed their work in short order despite the dim light. Ganth had not yet returned, so Kaz decided to take the horse outside. He had just maneuvered the horse around when a voice near the entrance called out, "Hold right there!"

"It's all right. This is my mount. I can easily prove that."

Only after he had spoken did he notice there was more than one shadowy form blocking his path. The owner of the voice was now flanked by two others, and at least one of them carried a glittering blade.

"Kaziganthi de-Orilg, you will surrender yourself and your companion to us in the name of the emperor, the circle, and the Holy Orders of the Stars."

The State Guard. Kaz snorted, wondering how the guardsmen had tracked him so swiftly and, more important, why they wanted him in the first place. He had done nothing wrong . . . but then, he doubted Hecar had, either.

"There must be some mistake. Why would you want me to surrender? I've done nothing to merit your attention."

"You will surrender now," insisted the leader. "Throw the magic axe to the ground and step away from it. Do it now."

They were determined to arrest him. No amount of protest would deter them. Interesting that they knew about the axe and its abilities. Few minotaurs in the homeland knew. It could be no coincidence; the same power that had sent the hunters in the woods had also dispatched these guards . . . but who was it? The circle? The priesthood? The emperor himself?

Hecar had killed a high-ranking cleric. That couldn't be a coincidence either. The priesthood must lie at the heart of the conspiracy.

The warriors began to stalk toward him, swords raised. Kaz took hold of his axe and confronted his dark adversaries.

"Put down your weapon," commanded the leader, a little uncertain.

"I've done nothing wrong. I'm certainly no danger to our people. Why do you want me?"

The guard leader did not answer. Behind the trio Kaz saw two more figures. Here in the crowded stable, Honor's Face would be limited. The stalls, the posts, and the horses would confine his abilities. Kaz didn't mind risking his own life, but there was also Delbin's to consider.

"The kender is of no consequence to you. Leave him be," Kaz demanded.

They ignored him. A sixth figure appeared some distance behind. The odds mounted against him.

Raising his free hand, the guard leader signaled the others. The figure in back suddenly let out a loud cry and charged into the others from behind.

Taken by surprise, most of the guards were pushed aside. Weapons went flying. One warrior managed to charge Kaz, who met him axe to blade. The close quarters prevented Kaz from making full use of his weapon, but Honor's Face still presented a respectable threat.

"Away with you!" roared Ganth, his tall figure looming over the pack of warriors trying to regroup. Ganth pulled one up and struck him in the jaw, sending the minotaur falling to the earthen floor.

Two minotaurs faced Kaz's father. Another warrior joined the one already dueling Kaz. Against both of them he was hard pressed, unable as he was to fully employ his axe.

Beyond his attackers he could hear swordplay. Ganth laughed and said something, but to Kaz the words were unintelligible.

One of his adversaries suddenly shouted in pain and hopped away. Something brushed Kaz's leg. Delbin, he realized. The kender had something long and sharp in his hands. Kaz identified the shape as a pitchfork the stable hands must have left behind. A brave, loyal companion as always, Kaz thought. It inspired him to fight that much harder.

Thanks to Delbin's diverting action, he was able to press forward. Ganth, too, looked to be pushing his pair back.

A shout came from outside. The entrance to the stable was filled with more armed figures, one of which barked out commands. Reinforcements had arrived to help the beleaguered soldiers.

There was no hope of Kaz and his father escaping now,

but there was a slim chance at least one could be saved. "Delbin! Get out of here! Run and hide! The southern gate's only a short distance from here!"

"But, Kaz—!"

"Do it! I'll keep them occupied! Do it for me!"

The kender had more of a chance on his own. The small figure was clever and agile. "Go!" Kaz shouted again.

Delbin dropped the pitchfork and obeyed, not even looking back. The minotaur fighting Kaz turned and tried to seize him, but Kaz thrust and caught him in the side with the upper edge of the axe blade. Grunting, his adversary slumped to his knees, hands covering his wounds.

Angry shouts informed him that Ganth was now under assault. Suddenly Kaz himself had three more warriors pressing him. He was backed into the stall. As he was pushed back near his horse, the animal reared up and, whinnying, struck out at the nearest member of the guard. The unsuspecting warrior was flung backward by the blow, but almost immediately two others moved to take his place.

Again the horse kicked out. Although he missed this time, the stallion prevented anyone from reaching his master. The reprieve was a temporary one at best, but Kaz was grateful to the loyal animal.

"Get back!" commanded a new voice.

Kaz's opponents retreated. Someone brought a torch into the structure. Kaz found himself facing a minotaur with a scarred visage. It was another familiar face, not Angrus, but a more intelligent opponent.

"Surrender now, criminal."

He was all too familiar, but Kaz was more immediately concerned with the bound figure four members of the guard were dragging forward. It was Ganth, still struggling. He was bleeding from minor wounds on one arm and his chest. There was also a patch of blood on his face, but it did not appear to be his own.

"Surrender, Kaz, or I may be forced to execute this old one here and now."

Something in the voice made him remember. "Scurn!"

"Captain Scurn of the State Guard, Kaziganthi de-Orilg." The way Scurn pronounced the clan name made it seem a vile curse. "And you'll surrender now. Understand?"

To emphasize the point, one of Scurn's men brought the tip of his sword up against Ganth's throat. Kaz's father snorted in contempt. "No honor in the guard anymore, Lad?"

Scurn pretended not to hear him. "What's it to be, Kaz?"

Lowering his axe, Kaz stepped forward. "All right. I yield to you."

"Bind him."

As two of his warriors seized Kaz, Scurn looked around. "Who has the blasted kender?" When he received no response, he grew angry. Scurn's eyes took on a reddish glow. In the flickering light of the torch, his eyes looked wild. "Fools! You let a kender sneak away into the city? Search the area at once!"

Nearly half the patrol immediately departed the stables in search of Delbin. Two others began prodding the corners and the piles of hay in the possibility that the wily little fellow was hiding.

"Lose something?" Ganth asked with a touch of mockery.

"Not as much as you'll lose, Old One, after His Holiness is finished dealing with you." He indicated Kaz. "Harboring a fugitive is a criminal offense."

"Now what would the high priest fear from my little boy? What danger could he be?"

"That's not for you to know." As Scurn replied, however, Kaz noted his brief look of annoyance. Evidently, Scurn, too, would have liked an answer to that question. He obviously was not important enough to have earned the right, though, and for someone like Scurn, that fact had to be bothering him.

"Not in here, Captain," announced one of the pair searching the stables.

"Then get outside and help the others. I don't want you back until you have that little vermin . . . and don't kill him! The high priest might want him since he rides as companion to this one. Anyone who fouls up will be speaking to His Holiness personally."

That was warning enough for any minotaur. The pair ran outside, leaving only Scurn, the torch-bearer, and the soldiers holding the two prisoners. Kaz's old enemy walked past him, eyeing the axe, which now lay on the ground, and then the war-horse. "Don't worry about these, Kaz. I'll keep them for you until you need them back." He laughed, then picked up Honor's Face. In the light of the torch, the axe gleamed. Scurn held it high, admiring the workmanship, especially the mirrorlike finish of the head. "I'll keep them both safe, all right." A grunt of surprise escaped the captain's lips. He glanced at Kaz. "It reflects the torchlight, but there is only a vague image of me in this blade! What sort of trickery is that?"

"A minor one," Kaz returned. And not surprising, either, he thought, to find that you've so little honor left in you, Scurn. He was tempted to tell Scurn the truth, that only those with honor were reflected in the axe face, but decided better of it.

"I'll examine this oddity later." He noticed the pouches hanging on the belt of Kaz's kilt. "What have we here?"

Kaz squirmed, but could not keep Scurn from taking not only the pouches, but also Kaz's knife. The captain put the blade in his own belt, then inspected the contents of the pouches. One bag he tossed away with disgust, no doubt having located nothing of value. From the other he removed several coins and, lastly, the medallion that Delbin had brought to Kaz from his dream.

"So, a souvenir of greatness." Scurn snorted in disdain. "Don't know why you kept this. You never cared about it much."

If Scurn expected a response from Kaz, the prisoner was more than willing to disappoint him. Kaz watched his captor pocket the medallion. Then Scurn commanded, "Bring these two. The high priest wants to see them."

"What would the high priest be wanting with simple folks like us?" asked Ganth, still maneuvering for some information."

"You . . . nothing. Him . . ." Scurn used Honor's Face as a pointer, thrusting it at Kaz. "He's been in the high priest's eye for some time now." The disfigured minotaur snorted with laughter. "When I was told that Hecar was coming here and that I should arrest him, I was glad to do so, even if I didn't know why. Now I know why . . . You were baited, Kaz, baited like a fool of a fish."

One of the searchers came up to them as they departed the stables. He saluted Scurn. "No sign of the kender yet, Captain. It's as if he vanished. No one's seen him. We're questioning everyone nearby."

Kaz brightened at this news. Grinning, he said, "Looks like the high priest might be a little annoyed with you, Scurn. You let a kender slip out of your grasp and escape into the city. Nethosak will never be the same."

Scurn spun and struck Kaz with his hand, sending the prisoner staggering back. "It might be that he'll be annoyed about that, but we'll find the little pack rat. He can't escape Nethosak." To the warrior who had reported, Scurn commanded, "Return to the guard. Get another squadron out. I want the entire southern part of the city searched from top to bottom. He'll try for the gates at some point, probably before daylight. I want him."

"Aye, Captain."

When the warrior had departed again, Scurn studied both of his captives, giving special attention to Ganth. "Now I remember you, Old One. I thought you were dead."

"I have a way of coming back."

"Not this time. Not you or your son." Scurn grinned at Kaz. "Now you'll answer for everything you've done."

"The past is over. It was settled long ago. I don't understand you, Scurn. I don't understand you at all. You still think about the past, even now?"

"You betrayed the dream, Kaz. You turned your back on our destiny. That's the greatest of your crimes in my eyes. No one can turn their back on our destiny. You're a coward. You have no honor."

"Funny," interjected Ganth, "but I was just thinking the

same about you."

Scurn looked ready to lash out, but chose not to. Instead, he turned on his men. "Well? What're you waiting for? The high priest wants to see them both right away. Move!"

As they were dragged off, Kaz quickly looked around, searching for some sign of the kender. He saw none. Paladine, hear me, Kaz thought. Let him be careful if he flees to Helati.

There had to be a spy among those in the settlement. That was the only way they could know so much about him. One, possibly more, of the refugees was an agent of the guard. If Delbin went there, the high priest would hear of it. Kaz knew they would stop at nothing to satisfy the high priest . . . even if it meant destroying the settlement itself and everyone who was a part of it.

"Helati . . ." he whispered. No one would have any notion of the danger they were in, and Kaz could do nothing to warn them.

* * * * *

Delbin ran out of the stables, darting past a minotaur occupied with trying to subdue Kaz's father. He felt terrible about leaving both of them, but Kaz had said he had to leave, and he always did what Kaz asked . . . even if he usually changed his mind later and did the opposite. Delbin was determined to rescue his friend, but first he had to make certain he lost any of the bad minotaurs who were dogging his heels.

I'll rescue you, Kaz. You'll see! Kaz was a true friend, the nearest thing to a family Delbin really had. Kaz always got uncomfortable when Delbin mentioned what a good friend he was. Yet the minotaur understood him better than other kender did.

Behind him he heard a minotaur shout. The shout was far away and probably didn't even concern him. Delbin started thinking about where he should go next. The minotaur city was so fascinating that he kept wanting to stop and look at things, but he knew that Kaz was in trouble, so he had to hurry.

I have to do something to help him and Ganth! He liked Ganth, too, in great part because the elder minotaur treated him almost like a grandson. But what could a kender do?

"This way!" roared a deep voice, this time definitely a lot nearer.

Delbin looked behind him and saw an enormous shape closing in. They were very near, all right. He had the advantage of being small, which made it hard to see him in the dark, but he was unfamiliar with the area. It would have been nice to set a few traps for his pursuers, but he was in a hurry. Maybe he'd even have to kill a few of them, albeit in self-defense. Kaz would be proud of him if he did.

"Cover that street!" shouted the voice.

They were even closer now. Delbin spotted a darkened alley ahead of him and giggled. Like all kender, he was good at playing hide-from-the-bad-guys, a game all youngsters of his race learned in their childhood, just in case. The alley looked as if it led to another good hiding place. There were all sorts of good buildings in which to hide.

Delbin giggled again, then shook his head and whispered to himself, "You should be quiet, Delbin, because if you don't, those soldiers might hear you, and then they'll catch you before you can kill a few . . ."

He squeezed down the alley, then slipped through an even more narrow opening between two buildings. The minotaurs could certainly not follow him here. Delbin cracked a smile as he darted around another corner. This was actually fun. He just wished Kaz could be here to enjoy the game.

"Don't worry about that!" Delbin whispered, reminding himself. "Find a good place to hide, then come up with a plan to rescue Kaz!"

He was certain he would think of something. He had always been a clever fellow. Had not Kaz said so? Delbin had helped him against the dark elf Argaen Ravenshadow and those nasty ghosts down in the cold south. He could certainly help his friend against a few stupid minotaurs.

"I'll come up with a real good plan, Kaz. You'll see! I'll save you and Ganth and Hecar, and then we'll all ride home together. I'll make it a really good plan that you'll be proud of and all the other minotaurs will be surprised about!"

Delbin, of course, was blissfully unaware of how Kaz, not to mention the others, would have cringed at hearing any plan of his. A kender plan was more likely to backfire on those involved than it was destined to succeed. Of course, to kender, that was part of the fun.

They just could not understand why others never seemed to see it that way.

* * * * *

Their captors dragged Kaz and Ganth to the temple, where the high priest awaited them. Inside, the acolytes were very attentive. One of them guided the party through the temple. He led Scurn and the others to two great doors. There, two more acolytes opened the doors, then stepped away. Scurn paused at the entrance, giving Kaz a moment to study the place in detail. The artwork did not concern him at all. What he wanted was some way out should the opportunity arise.

His eyes drifted to the carvings. Most, especially the faces of Sargas, were familiar to him, since copies appeared on structures throughout the empire, but the dragon was something uncommon. It was startlingly real. It unnerved him almost as much as the thought of facing the high priest.

"Your party may enter, Captain Scurn."

The voice echoed throughout the nearly black chamber and caused the hair on the back of Kaz's head to stiffen. Like all minotaurs, he had been raised with a healthy respect for the high priest. But, just standing there, he felt an unreasoning terror. This is nonsense, he told himself.

The cleric's as mortal as anyone else here. An axe in the hand will cleave him in two just as easily as it would Scurn.

Nonetheless, it was all he could do to keep from quavering when they pulled him forward.

Torches suddenly blazed, revealing not only the immense chamber, but the dais ahead of the party. Seated at the desk atop the dais was the high priest, who stared down at them.

Studious features were half-shadowed by the cleric's hood. Kaz had met this particular minotaur before, but he could not recall when. Was his past out to destroy him? It seemed that everyone he had ever met was turning up in his life again, wanting to dispose of him.

Scurn led the prisoners up to the dais. Kaz was pleased to note that his captors seemed nervous, too. Everyone was afraid of this high priest.

The high priest leaned forward, studying the two prisoners. His eyes raked Kaz, then Ganth, almost as if he intended to dine on their corpses. The hooded figure studied them for a moment or two longer, then turned his burning gaze on Scurn.

"There was a kender, too, was there not? Where is he?"

Steadying himself, Scurn replied, "The guard is still out hunting him, Holiness. He escaped in the confusion when these two resisted."

"A kender, a lowly kender, escaped a squadron of the guard? Are you becoming that incompetent? The kender should have been the least difficult of the three."

"We weren't expecting this one," protested Scurn as he pointed at Ganth. "We were told to watch for Kaz, not the old one."

"And who is he?"

"I am Ganthirogani de-Orilg," announced Kaz's father, standing proudly. "I'm a loyal son of the empire, which is more than I can say for these bits of flotsam. You should know me—"

"You will not speak again unless spoken to," intoned the high priest, cutting off Ganth. He leaned back and studied Kaz again. "Kaziganthi of the clan Orilg, we have watched your activities for some time. Your reputation is both a credit and a shame to the minotaur race. You have fought bravely against great foes, but you reject the destiny of your people. You act as an independent when you must play your part in the great plan. Your place is here, working for the future that is to be ours, but you rebel, fomenting discord among your own kind. Because of your past, you could be forgiven, but now you return to the empire, attempting to increase your power at a time when all minotaurs are needed for the grand conquest."

"That's ridiculous!" snapped Kaz, surprising himself.

The high priest ignored his effrontery. "What you have achieved is admittedly admirable in many ways, but it cannot be allowed to go on, I'm afraid. For the sake of the future, a settlement such as yours cannot be tolerated. The minotaur race cannot be divided so. We must be one strong axe arm ready to cleave all foes in our path. No minotaur can be allowed to act alone."

"I always thought we prided ourselves on our fairness," Kaz returned, more defiant than fearful now that he had heard the high priest's exalted words. "We are the race where anyone may become emperor, where males and females are equal, and where honor is individual."

The high priest visibly checked his anger. Putting on a smile as false as his words, the hooded figure shook his head. "This is a time of sacrifice, my son. In the name of the Great Horned One, we must put aside some of our freedoms so that we can sooner claim the world for him. The time is ripe. The unity of the race is now paramount, greater than the personal desires of one rebellious minotaur. You should understand that."

"I understand much."

"Do you?" The high priest shifted. "I make you an offer, Kaziganthi. Talent such as yours should not be wasted. There is room for you in the empire, but only in service to the empire. What you have achieved in the wilderness could be put to good use here. Commanders who compel such respect and loyalty from warriors are always invaluable to the cause. You could be the greatest commander since Mesonus, who led the attack against the elves even though he and his warriors were outnumbered three to one!"

"Mesonus lost that battle, however glorious it's been proclaimed since," Ganth returned, snorting.

"You will be still, Ganthirogani. Think of it, Kaziganthi. Legions at your command. You are respected by humans. You can be feared by them in the same way. You understand their tactics better than any of our present officers. Your service to your people could lead to the throne itself before long, you know."

"I've no desire to sit on that piece of abused marble."

"Consider carefully. This offer is not made lightly."

Kaz snorted. "That's no offer. That's a threat. I want nothing to do with your coming debacle."

At a slight nod from the cleric, Scurn abruptly turned on Kaz and slapped him with the back of his hand, causing his head to rock to the side.

The high priest eyed him quietly for some time, then glanced at Scurn. "Captain, the criminal Kaziganthi is guilty of endangering the integrity of the state. He has become the focus of dissension and has undermined the authority of the emperor himself. The patriarch of Clan Orilg has already agreed that there is a debt of honor here so great that it can only be judged in the circus."

"What's that?" Ganth snarled. "Even he wouldn't agree to such nonsense! You can't mean that! What could have gotten into you, Jo—"

A member of the guard struck Kaz's father. Ganth clamped his bleeding mouth shut, but continued to glare at the high priest.

Despite what had happened to his sire, Kaz remained silent. He listened carefully to what the cleric said.

"They will be brought to the circus, there to face a chosen adversary against whom they will be allowed to regain some portion of the honor they have squandered."

"Yes, Holiness." Scurn looked at his former opponent with some satisfaction. "You heard. Come with us willingly or be dragged, Kaz."

Kaz smiled slowly, allowing both the high priest and Scurn to digest the smile. "Let's go, then."

His attitude disconcerted not only Scurn, but, much to his satisfaction, even the high priest. The cleric was quick to recover, however, "Remember, my sons, you will be fighting to recover your lost honor. Dwell on that thought."

And at the same time, remember we're not supposed to survive, honor or not, Kaz thought. He snorted at the hypocrisy.

"Come on," growled the captain.

"One more thing, Kaziganthi," called the hooded figure. "It is always possible for you to avoid this sentence if you see the error of your ways. Not simply you, but also those close to you."

"I'll try to remember that."

The high priest turned away from them.

As they were taken from the audience chamber, Ganth muttered, "I can't believe what's become of that lad! He's turned into a foul creature, he has!"

"What're you talking about?" asked Kaz, only partly paying attention. He had been thinking that despite their predicament, this was still an opportunity. Hecar would be in the circus also. This would be a chance to speak to him. Kaz knew the circus well, including the underground passages and gates. Once they located Hecar, he could see a possibility of the three of them escaping. Honor's Face would prove invaluable there. Scurn might have it for now, but it would turn up when Kaz needed it. It always did.

"It's him! Jopfer!" Ganth hissed. "He sailed on *Gladiator* when Hecar did, then went to work for a member of the circle. He was a studious boy who should've been seated in the circle by now. How, by old Sargas, did he come to be the high priest . . . and why does he act as if he doesn't know us?"

"Jopfer?" Slowly the name brought recognition. That was why the high priest seemed familiar. Kaz had a memory for faces, even ones he had seen only once, but that had been years ago and Jopfer was much older now.

"He was one of Hecar's best friends, once."

Hands shoved both of them forward. "Pick up the pace and stop talking!"

Kaz grunted, wishing his hands were untied. To Ganth, he finally muttered, "Well he's not one now."

* * * * *

With some concern, the high priest watched the two prisoners depart. Kaziganthi was a minotaur of impressive personality, the type that could be a great asset to his plans if only it were possible to make the prisoner see that his best hopes lay in cooperation, not defiance. A minotaur like this one, however, would be hard to break, much less bend. The techniques that could have been employed would leave him a shell. Someone like Kaziganthi would grow only more stubborn under torture. The high priest knew that. He had spent lifetimes studying the race.

No, Kaziganthi and his equally recalcitrant sire were best left to the circus for the time being. If, in the end, the former could not be convinced to join, not even for the sake of his companions, then the master cleric would see to it that their deaths would make them sterling examples of what happened to those who defied the destiny he had worked so long to impress upon the minds of his children. Their deaths would spell the end of Kaziganthi's settlement. There would be no more desertions. The plan he had worked on for so long, first for her, and now, astonishingly enough, for himself, had to proceed. There would be a master of Krynn, and it would be he.

I will let neither a rebellious minotaur . . . nor a potentially volatile infant . . . destroy what I have worked centuries to build, he thought. The minotaur will die in the arena if necessary, and the female . . . my female . . . will remain my permanent guest. So it will be.

Thinking of the other, the one who was most important to his continued existence, the high priest decided it was time to visit again his secret guest. If the fools who followed his commands only knew what she was, they would have fled from the citadel in outright fear. Fortunately, even she did not truly understand the truth.

By the time she did, she would be his puppet. By then, Kaziganthi de-Orilg would also be his to control . . . or dead and burned, a memory of ashes soon to fade from the minds of his children.

However, there was one matter with which the hooded cleric still had to deal. He reached to his side and pulled an almost invisible cord. A few moments later, one of his chief acolytes appeared.

"Yes, Holiness?"

"Tell the emperor I wish to see him . . . now."

"Yes, Holiness."

The high priest ignored the acolyte's departure; his thoughts returned to the future. His future.

I will not let this opportunity escape me. The world is ripe for my picking . . . and the minotaur, if he will not obey, is expendable in the end.

Chapter 8
Escape Plan

Helati carried the infants outside and stared in the direction in which Kaz had ridden off so many days ago. She knew he would not suddenly come riding up to her, but the desire to see him was so strong that she could not help but continue to wait and hope. The twins were unusually quiet, as if they, too, watched for their father's return.

"Not back yet, is he?"

She had been so preoccupied that she had not even heard the newcomer. Turning, Helati shook her head and replied, "No, Brogan, but it's much too early. You know how long it takes to reach the empire, much less Nethosak.

He will have just entered the city by this time."

"Which doesn't make us any less concerned about him." Brogan walked up next to her and leaned forward. His voice was steady. "Just say the word, Helati, and I'll gather the others. We'll ride to Nethosak and help him."

"I can't do that, because he wouldn't want me to do that. Kaz works best with little assistance from others."

"Then what about that kender? I still can't believe you'd tell that little thief where he is but not let us follow! What aid can one of those creatures give a minotaur?"

The twins began acting up. Helati hushed them. "You don't really know Delbin or you wouldn't ask that. He's a kender, true, but he's come to Kaz's rescue more than once."

Brogan snorted. "I find that hard to believe."

The conversation died abruptly as the sound of hoof-beats made both look up. Helati's heart pounded, but her wild hope that it was Kaz and her brother faded as she saw that the riders were unfamiliar. There were two, yes, but one was a male and the other a female. New additions to their community, they had a look to them she had come to recognize.

"May your ancestors watch over you," Helati said, approaching.

"And yours, you," replied the male. He glanced briefly at Brogan, then returned his gaze to Helati. "I am Zurgas, and this is my mate, Keeli. Is this the clan Kaziganthi? We were told we could find others like us here. Others . . . who have tired of the old ways."

Clan Kaziganthi. Helati glanced at Brogan, who, despite their conversation, could not repress a smile. Kaz's fame had grown more than either of them had realized if the settlement was already being called by such a title among the people.

"This is the place, friends," Brogan replied, "and you're welcome here."

The two riders looked relieved, but Helati, despite her forced smile, was not. If these minotaurs had come to call the settlement the clan of Kaziganthi, then so did others.

Soon, if not already, the emperor's people would hear of this new clan, one that did not acknowledge the power of the emperor, the circle, or the high priest.

What would happen if they heard of this while Kaz was still in Nethosak?

* * * * *

It was not until the next day that Kaz was reunited with Hecar.

An older minotaur with half his teeth missing chuckled as they were led into the prison section of the circus. He eyed Kaz with great joy.

"I heard they had you in their clutches! By Sargas! It'll be good to see you in the circus again, even if it's for a short time!"

"What's that, Molus?" asked one of the guards, curious at the jailer's remark. "Who's this supposed to be?"

"You're young. You would've been a child. This is Kaziganthi, of the clan Orilg!"

"I know who he is."

Molus shook his head. "You know a name. This is Kaz the Undefeatable! He fought his way to the rank of Supreme Champion! He was the greatest gladiator in all the empire! There's been none like him since!"

Kaz pretended indifference but, beside him, Ganth smiled.

The guards were all impressed, but the same one who had asked Molus the question persisted. "If he was supreme champion, why isn't he emperor or dead?" Those were the only two routes generally left to the supreme champion. He had to challenge the emperor and defeat him or die in the attempt. "What happened?"

Molus eyed Kaz with curiosity. "I don't know why, but he quit. He abandoned the circus, abandoned everything he'd fought for. He turned down commissions, rank benefits, and every sort of glory that should've been heaped on him. He went into the war just a simple warrior!"

The others, save for Ganth, looked at Kaz as if he had

suddenly turned into something distasteful. The guards muttered among themselves, trying to understand so uncharacteristic an action. Any warrior who had made it to the most exalted rank of Supreme Champion was expected to seek the throne. It was insane to work so hard and rise so high otherwise.

"Just why did you quit?" Molus asked Kaz.

"I saw no good reason to continue."

"Maybe he turned coward," suggested a guard.

"Him?" The jailer laughed. "Not likely. But it doesn't matter. He'll be fighting in a day anyway. You boys should watch. It'll be a good battle, even if it's a little one-sided." He turned away. "Bring them this way. They can share the cell with their friend."

Kaz and Ganth were dragged to the door of a dingy cell that contrasted greatly with the clean environment of Nethosak. Molus unlocked it, signaling the guards to put the prisoners inside.

The cell was dark, which was why they did not see Hecar at first. When the flames of one of the guards' torches finally revealed the other minotaur, Kaz and Ganth dropped their jaws at the pitiful sight.

"He was . . . more skilled . . . than he looked," Hecar muttered, forcing a smile onto his battered face. "I heard them . . . talking about you coming here. I'd like to say it's good to see you, Kaz, but—" Hecar glanced at the other minotaur and frowned. "Ganth?"

Hecar had lost a great deal of weight, and scars covered his chest, arms, and legs. Bandages were wrapped around both his left arm and his right leg. He was covered with the grit and grime of the arena, not to mention a layer of dried blood.

"This is no way to treat a minotaur," Kaz snarled at his captors, losing his temper for the first time since being led from the sanctum of the high priest. "By right of victory, even as a criminal, his wounds should be cared for and his body cleaned."

"By right of victory, he should be a free warrior now," Ganth pointed out, eyeing Molus. To his credit, Molus lost some of his good humor and briefly looked even a little guilty. "He should once more be an honored member of the race."

"The orders come from the emperor and the high priest," the jailer mumbled. To the guards he commanded, "Chain these two up next to Hecar. He can entertain them with stories of what to expect."

"Where's your honor, Old One?" snarled Kaz, struggling against his captors. "What has happened to the honor of the circus?"

As they forced the two new prisoners to the wall and chained them, Molus whispered, "You idealistic fools wouldn't understand."

Moments later, Molus and his guards departed, leaving the trio to themselves. Kaz's eyes grew accustomed to the cell's dimness. He looked at Ganth, then at Hecar. "What happened to you, Hecar? How did you end up here?"

"I don't really know." Hecar sounded better now that their captors had departed. There was a glint in his eye. He was obviously worn out, but evidently hardier than he wanted the jailer to know. "I've broken no laws that I can recall. I looked around, asked a few questions, and suddenly found others asking me questions. I stopped to see an old friend, but I couldn't find him. That's when they came for me." He took a breath. "Kaz, you remember Scurn?"

"We met him," interjected Ganth. "He brought us in."

Hecar looked at the older minotaur for some time. "You! You're supposed to be dead."

"You should be, too. Give me time."

"But *Gladiator*—"

"He'll explain later, Hecar. Go on with your story." Kaz needed to hear everything.

"They seemed interested that I knew Jopfer, but—"

"I told you he did, Kaz, remember?" Ganth said, interrupting again. To Hecar he asked, "And did you ever get to see Jopfer?"

"No, I didn't."

"You would've, if you'd been brought before the high

priest himself."

Hecar snorted. "What does that mean?"

"What he's saying in a roundabout way is that your old friend Jopfer is the high priest now."

"Jopfer?" The other minotaur sounded incredulous. "Jopfer as high priest? This is a jest, isn't it? A sorry jest."

"It was him all right, even if he pretended not to know me. Imagine that. Me!"

"Jopfer?" Hecar still sounded incredulous. "Jopfer never cared much for the calling. He followed Kiri-Jolith if he followed anything."

"Well, he's the high priest now, and a mighty strange one," Ganth concluded.

"Jopfer . . ." Hecar shook his head. "If he is high priest, then what's he up to? And why would he throw me into the circus just for asking a few innocent questions?"

"They're worried about the settlement, Hecar," Kaz said. He told the other minotaur about what the chief cleric had said and how there had to be at least one spy among the settlers. "This is a nation at war. Everything seems tensed toward some lightning strike. They expect to use a fleet, but whether they intend to travel north or south, I don't know."

"I think it might be south, Lad. Good land down there. Makes sense to spread the empire where the resources are best. Doubt if anyone there will be expecting an armada of minotaurs."

"Maybe, but I'd opt for north, Father. That place, Istar, is growing too, despite the effects of the war. It'll probably be the next big empire. I'd go there. It would satisfy their taste for revenge, since we've been beaten back before, plus it would quickly remove the biggest threat to our western border."

The old mariner considered that. "You could be right."

"Which still doesn't help us any," Kaz added. He tried the chains, but they were of good minotaur workmanship and easily held despite his most strenuous efforts.

"I've tried that over and over with my own chains," Helati's brother informed him. "I've pretended to be weaker than I really am just so they don't tax me in the combats. Now that you're here, though, I guess they won't worry about keeping me alive." He grunted. "All I am is bait."

"The emperor wants to tidy up loose ends before beginning his campaign. Kaz here was a big loose end. He was giving the people an option other than blind obedience to the cause. He told my boy to either join up or meet his end in the circus." Ganth broke into a smile. "Strange as it might sound, I'm happy to say that he turned the bugger down."

"I don't think it's the emperor as much as the high priest, Father," Kaz remarked. "I think *he* runs the empire, not whatever fool happens to sit on the throne."

"It's still Polik, Son."

"Is it?" Kaz grew silent.

Beside him, Ganth snorted in anger. "Polik, yes. They left that scraping cur in power even after he more or less played a puppet on a string for the warlords!"

"He keeps winning all of his blasted challenges," interjected Hecar. "That's enough to keep him in power, Master Ganth. He wins about ten to twelve challenges a year, all of them issued by him."

"And he wins—"

"He killed Raud, Father," interrupted Kaz, unable to keep the fury within him a secret. "He challenged Raud to combat even though Raud hadn't achieved the Grand Champion level yet."

"Raud . . ." Ganth stared at his son. "By the horns of the Just One!"

"Now that I think about it," Kaz continued, "the combat had to be sanctioned by the circle . . . and it was, after support for the emperor's challenge by the high priest himself. Not Jopfer, but his predecessor, I think."

"Comes back to the sons of Sargas again," Ganth muttered. There was still a trembling in his voice. "You had just become supreme champion, then . . ."

"He should've beaten the emperor, Father. Raud was good enough that he could've beaten me, eventually . . .

not that he wanted to face me. Raud said he wanted to become a grand champion, then use the title to get the ship he wanted."

"How'd he lose? How'd Polik beat him?"

How indeed? Kaz recalled the day of the fight. For some reason, he had been kept from visiting his brother, who was preparing for single combat. An emperor could issue his own challenges, in this way eliminating rivals before they were ready to face him, but never could anyone recall someone below the rank of Grand Champion being challenged. Grand Champions were the top gladiators of a minor circus, of which there were eight in each of the two capital cities, Nethosak and Morthosak. Only after achieving this rank could a warrior move on to the next level, the Great Circus.

Although Raud had not been a grand champion, he had risen to fourth on the list at his particular arena and would have achieved his goal in less than a year. Kaz now knew the true reason for the challenge. His other siblings, save for a sister who had just given birth to her firstborn and another sister, Fliara, who was too young herself, had all been active in the arenas; but none had risen as high in ranking as Kaz or Raud, the sons of Ganth and Kyri. They were often touted as the champions of Orilg with the best hope of becoming emperor.

Polik was a tool of his masters. He had been chosen more for his ability to keep the race under control than anything else. It was essential that someone like him and not someone like Kaz be ruler. The human Crynus had desired that. Yet, even the Dark Lady's most devious warlord had known that to outright assassinate a supreme champion would turn the minotaurs on their masters. Even Polik would be unable to keep the revolt from spreading.

Raud had been challenged. Kaz had been shocked. Something was amiss, and he had tried to convince his younger brother of that, but Raud was too honorable and competitive to reject so important a challenge. He did not want to become emperor, but neither did he care to lose face.

They would not let Kaz see his brother, and so he had sat in the stands with the rest. His brother had come out onto the field, but only Kaz had noticed that he moved a little slower than usual and seemed hesitant. Nonetheless, Raud had made it to the huge, rotating platform where a combat against the emperor always took place. He mounted the platform and faced the emperor with determination. To all, save those who knew him as Kaz did, Raud seemed ready and able.

He died within a minute of the fight's beginning. His reactions were too slow, his moves foolish, unthinking. There were only two ways to leave an imperial combat: victory, or death. Kaz could do nothing as Polik brought his axe down and ended Raud's life. He could do nothing, not even voice the truth. Something had been done to his brother to prevent him from making full use of his mind and skills. It was almost as if he had been drugged or bespelled. The outcome had been decided before the start.

Furious, Kaz had almost leapt to the floor of the circus, but then Polik had glanced his way. The look in the emperor's eyes said many things to him. He understood that if he challenged Polik, he would enter the arena in no greater condition than his brother had. More important, his other siblings would also be marked, not because they would ever be any great threats, but because of Kaz.

Shortly after, he had simply quit the circus, given up his special status, and been added to the ranks of the slave-soldiers. As it worked out, he was suddenly thrust into the war as part of the latest advance. It must have galled Polik that he had survived the war. Paladine knew that it galled Kaz to think Polik still ruled.

"The only way Polik could ever win," he finally responded to his father's question.

His statement was enough for Ganth. "Then we can't expect much when they take us out there. There'll be none of this foolish stuff they have been doing with Hecar while they preserved him as bait. Whatever we face will be ready and able to kill us." Ganth tugged at his chain again. "Well, I'll make them remember how I went down. They'll be talking about it for years!"

"We have some hope." Kaz leaned closer to the others. "We have to wait for night before we can do anything, though."

"What've you got in mind, Lad?"

"Given the proper weapon, we could break out of here. That's why they never give out weapons until we're sent out onto the field. They can't know that I have access to a weapon."

A slight gasp escaped Hecar. "You mean Honor's Face!"

"Honor's Face? What's that?"

Kaz told his father the tale of how the good elf Sardal Crystalthorn had given him the battle-axe, and the powers Kaz had eventually discovered the weapon contained, including its ability to materialize for Kaz whenever the minotaur needed it.

"That was the weapon you carried, and you didn't mention all that sooner, Boy? I'd have liked to have hefted it once!"

"You'll get your chance after we're out of here."

"Now I understand why you weren't so disappointed when Jopfer had us sent here."

"Where is the axe now?" Hecar asked.

"Scurn has it. For some reason, he couldn't see his face reflected very well in it."

Helati's sibling grunted. "I'm not surprised . . . but I guess he'll be a little taken aback when the axe disappears."

"What about your little friend, Lad?" Ganth suddenly asked his son. "Think he'll be okay? I feel sorry for the little one. I've met some kender, and they're not too bad . . . from a distance. He's a good one, though, a real surprise. I hope he makes it to safety."

"They haven't told us anything, which makes me think he's managed to avoid them. I can only hope Delbin gets out of Nethosak and heads west or south. If west, he can join up with his own kind again and disappear. I'm wondering, though, if maybe he might go to the human areas in Solamnia. He always liked the knights. He might very well ask them for help." Kaz shuddered, thinking what might happen if Lord Oswal or Sir Bennett took Delbin seriously. Would they try to send aid? He hoped not. That would only tangle the situation further.

"He'd go there all by himself?" Hecar asked, astonished the kender was capable of such a trek.

"You'd be unwise to underestimate him, Hecar. Scurn and his bunch have made that mistake. So have a lot of others since I've known Delbin. I cannot guarantee that he will make it, but he has a better chance than most."

"A kender. He's that dedicated to you?"

"He is. Never underestimate their kind. I know."

"Well, his chances are better than ours right now, Lads, so what do you say we think on it while we wait for our meal . . . We do get one, don't we, Hecar?"

The other minotaur grunted. "Some might call it a meal, Master Ganth. Some might even dare call it food. You'll see what I mean, but I'll warn you now not to smell it, or concentrate your hopes on the taste."

Ganth and Kaz looked at one another. The former finally spoke. "We'd better see about trying to escape soon, then. Dying in combat in the circus is one thing, but dying from bad food would be an embarrassment to our ancestors."

* * * * *

Delbin sat in the dark, in the small room he had discovered the night before, chewing on a piece of meat that had somehow found its way into his hands. Delbin Knotwillow had an amazing tendency to find just what he needed, just when he needed it.

I hope I can get him out.

Delbin was fairly certain that Kaz was somewhere near the circus. Had not Kaz said that matters of justice were decided there? Since he had been taken by the guard, he would probably go to the circus at some point. It sounded good to the kender, who was naive enough to discount a thousand other places the prisoners could have been taken. It also sounded good because Delbin wanted to see the circus anyway.

Delbin had no way to accurately measure time, but he was certain the other minotaurs had long ago ceased searching this area. Still, to go out in the daytime might be too risky, even for him. Kaz would have thought so, and Delbin was trying to think like Kaz as much as possible.

At least he did not have to fear discovery here. Delbin had found a small room in a storage building that was filled with equipment used for sailing . . . or so the kender had decided after a cursory examination of some half-hidden objects. Delbin had no idea what some of the other various items stored in the building were used for, but they had a military look to them.

I have to go outside soon, Delbin decided. Something terrible might happen to Kaz. Yet, still he did not move. He needed a brilliant plan.

He ate a piece of fruit that had accidentally fallen into his pouch, and wondered where all the food had come from. Fortune had smiled on him.

His journey through the city had been a fun time, despite the danger. Delbin had come seen gully dwarves running around picking up trash, and had used their similar heights to fool a couple of his pursuers. In fact, any time he thought someone might have noticed him, he squatted low and put on a befuddled expression. No one had stopped him, so he was pretty sure they thought him a gully dwarf, though Delbin didn't think it was right that the poor creatures were forced to clean the streets in the first place.

He thought about Kaz and his possible whereabouts. Kender liked to talk, and so, with no one else to talk to, he went over matters with himself, the most loyal audience any kender had. "He should be at that big arena they call a circus but which really isn't, because I always thought a circus was a fun place with animals and jesters, but this is supposed to be a really big place where a lot of people just fight one another, and sometimes they must fight animals, because there's supposed to be a menagerie there, too, but I don't think—"

Delbin absently took another piece of fruit from his hoard and bit into it. Swallowing, he continued, "I'll bet they've got some cells really deep down below the big arena. They've probably got Kaz and Ganth prisoner down there. I'll bet if I went there, I could find a way to free them . . ."

The kender thought hard, his expression as intense as possible for one of his kind. Delbin wanted to do his best to find Kaz and rescue him. Kaz would do the same for him, after all.

"I'll have to wait until night, that's what I'll have to do, because then I can go looking in the circus without a bunch of big minotaurs bothering me. I can at least see what's there, so that I can think of a really good plan." The kender frowned. The topknot in his hair bobbed back and forth as he shook his head. "But Kaz would want me to stay away from there, because if I go there now and they see me, then maybe they might catch me—"

Delbin straightened, steeling himself. Even if Kaz got mad at him, he had to try to help the minotaur. Ideas began to form, neat, ingenious ideas . . . at least in the eyes of the kender, that is.

It would be so simple, so masterfully done . . . and even if there was an element of danger to it, the kender saw that only as added excitement flavoring this new, grand adventure.

"Don't you worry, Kaz," he whispered into the dark, eyes shining in anticipation. "I'm coming to save you!"

Chapter 9
A Secret Prisoner

"I am disappointed in you, Captain Scurn."

Scurn shivered as he faced the high priest with the news that the blasted kender was still at large. Scurn was no coward and, despite his exalted position, the high priest was more a scholarly type than a great warrior. In single combat the soldier was certain he could easily defeat the figure looking down on him. Of course, that was an opinion he would never dare voice to others.

The high priest was not alone. Acolytes lined the path to the dais, strong sons of Sargas, who Scurn knew would willingly throw themselves at him unarmed if their master so commanded. They stared straight ahead, but the captain knew very well they watched his every move.

"Holiness, the guard is still looking. It's only a kender, anyway. A mischief-maker, nothing more! My commander—"

"Has nothing to do with this, Captain. You presented yourself to my subordinates as someone striving to rise in rank and who saw, wisely, that such a path must be harmonious with my goals. You have benefitted from my goodwill, but in return you have not given what I required of you." The high priest leaned forward angrily. "I want the kender found. This creature is loyal to Kaziganthi. Not only might he cause unnecessary and politically embarrassing trouble in some kenderish attempt to redeem his comrade, but it has occurred to me that he of all of them might be used against the prisoner. This Kaziganthi sees himself as something of a champion to the small, I think. Therefore, I want him found. He cannot have escaped the city. The gates are too closely guarded. Find him. Do you understand that, or shall I endeavor to find out if any of your men can do better?"

"No, Your Holiness. I'll find the little vermin. I will."

Leaning back, the high priest regained his composure. "You had better." He waved a hand, dismissing the subject. "You will be pleased to know that on the morrow the criminals will face separate challenges that shall give them a chance to recover the honor of their clan . . . and shall put an end to at least one of them if Kaziganthi does not cooperate."

"Tomorrow?" Scurn was unable to hide his surprise. The leader of the temple worked in swift fashion. "Which one?"

"That is undecided, but I believe it will be the one called Hecar. His usefulness is at an end, but as the brother of Kaziganthi's mate, his death will have a profound impact. It may be enough."

"That's good news, Holiness."

"It will not be such good news if you find yourself joining them, Captain. I still desire the kender. If necessary, I will have Kaz's family and friends executed one by one until he sees the error of his judgment." The high priest steepled his fingers and sighed. "The fate of the cause outweighs the regret I feel for being forced to such dire actions. Kaziganthi is a symbol to many, Captain, a symbol that can still be wielded for the greater glory of the minotaur race . . . but only if he can be turned."

Scurn got the hint. "I'll double the number of soldiers involved in the search. By tomorrow, we'll have the kender . . . though why the creature is important to Kaz, I'll never understand."

"You do not need to understand. That is my concern. Simply find this valuable little creature. And do so very soon, lest you share the fate of the criminals in the field."

The captain swallowed. Then, realizing he had just been dismissed, Scurn bowed and quickly retreated from the chamber.

When he was gone, the high priest looked down on his subordinates. As one they turned their gazes to him, respect and fear combined in their eyes.

"What word from our own?"

The acolyte nearest his left side replied, "They find nothing so far, Holiness. No sign has been seen of the kender."

"He has certainly not taken himself from Nethosak through magical means. I think I would have been able to sense that." The high priest allowed himself a slight look of frustration. "Not that I would expect magic of a kender."

An acolyte across from the first spoke. "Holiness, there have been rumors."

"Rumors of what?"

"That a kender has been sighted in the streets. These rumors have not been verified. No trace of any such creature has been discovered—"

"But it is not the type of sighting to arise without substance." He rubbed his jaw in contemplation. "I wonder . . . yes . . . the kender would probably do that. If he's as loyal as reported, general mischief would be less likely. It's more possible he will seek to emulate his brave friend.

This is good. We shall let the kender wander about."

"Master?" asked the second acolyte, not understanding.

"If the guard and our own cannot find the kender, perhaps the kender will reveal his whereabouts to us." The high priest actually smiled. "A determined kender will generally find what it seeks, and this particular one, I think, seeks his minotaur comrade. I will have notices put up, reminding all that the criminals of the state will be sent into the circus on the morrow."

"But how will this help us find the kender, Holiness?" asked the first acolyte.

The high priest grew visibly annoyed. "The kender has proven through his determination that he cares about his companion, the great minotaur warrior. He will, in his own way, seek to free the minotaur. We must see to it that he is encouraged to investigate the circus just in case he does not understand they are being held there. A way must even be left open for him, the better to trap the insipid creature. The guards at the circus must be forewarned. You, Merriq, for being so inquisitive, have volunteered to lead a group of our own people in searching the circus from top to bottom, after which you will coordinate the successful capture of this pack rat."

Merriq bowed and asked no further questions, realizing he had already pushed his luck.

The high priest rose and leaned over his desk. "I think perhaps that some of you have grown lax in your work and, perhaps, your faith. We have been entrusted from time immemorial with the heavy task of keeping the vision strong, of preaching to the masses the dream of destiny set down by Sargas when he took a few worthy ogres and transformed them into the first minotaurs. The Supreme Circle is the arm, making certain the empire functions on a physical level. The emperor is the heart, the symbol of perfection that all strive for in battle. We, however, are the soul, and that is the most important of the three. If the people lose faith in their destiny, we have failed. The arm will grow weak and the heart will cease to beat. That is why you must all be strong, determined in your tasks and belief. There can be no room for the weak."

The acolytes nodded, but remained silent.

Stepping around the desk, the high priest raised his hands high in supplication to the sky. "We stand as warriors in the circus of the soul. We must triumph, or our entire race will fall into the degeneration that befell the ogres. Merriq, you will begin the litany."

The senior acolyte bowed, then, clearing his throat, began, "We have been enslaved, but have always thrown off our shackles . . ."

Around him, the others repeated his words. All closed their eyes and, imitating the high priest, raised their hands skyward.

The figure on the dais lowered his hands and watched those below, satisfied that there would be no hesitation, no matter what commands he gave them. They were dedicated to the dream, though they did not know he had altered that dream. They would do anything in the name of Sargas, but in reality it was he they worshipped. He was their god, even if they did not realize it.

Before long, however, everyone would know . . . and by then it would be too late.

* * * * *

Night crept forth, but in the cells below the circus it was hard to tell the difference between darkness and light. Only the change in guards and the fact that they had been fed at least an hour before gave Kaz and his companions any notion of the late hour.

"I feel as if I've been rotting down here forever," Hecar grumbled. "If you'd not come when you did, it's very likely I'd have lost my next challenge simply to put an end to this infernal monotony."

"That's no way to talk. A warrior must always look to victory."

"This place has a way of sapping any such enthusiasm, Master Ganth. Trust me."

"We still have to wait a few hours more. They'll relax

their guard by then. No one has ever escaped from these cells." Kaz tried to make his voice encouraging. "We will be the first."

Ganth grunted. "Maybe you'll tell me how we'll escape even if you get your wonder weapon, Lad. You won't be able to swing it too well from inside here."

"You don't know the power of Honor's Face, Father. Trust me."

"I promise not to leave your side just so you can prove me wrong." The older minotaur chuckled for a moment, then grew silent.

More time passed. Kaz spent the time twisting his wrists this way and that, trying to find the best angles for what he planned. He could succeed with such a mad plan only because of the magical axe. Any other weapon would be either too dull and blunt or too unmanageable. Only his magical battle-axe had the ability to cut through almost anything as if it were water.

He had a suspicion that Polik would be in the audience in the arena tomorrow. He knew the Polik of old well enough to know that the emperor would want to watch the death of his onetime rival personally. That suited Kaz just fine. He had learned to throw his axe great distances with surprising accuracy. After that, the minotaurs would need a new emperor . . . something that, in his opinion, was long overdue.

Of course, if the high priest was also present, Polik might survive after all. Kaz had a fair notion of who was the true power, and if he had only one chance to throw his axe, Jopfer would be the one.

The hallway outside suddenly resounded with the clatter of arms and the marching of feet. Beside him, Ganth stirred and Hecar, who had been slumbering, woke. They listened in consternation as guards continued through the hall.

"All corridors must be checked! All cells lit! Let no space large enough to hide a rat be left unsearched!"

"What in the name of Kiri-Jolith is going on out there?" Hecar whispered. "Why are they suddenly so active?"

"I don't know," Kaz replied, "but it's some kind of

search. Maybe a prisoner has escaped." He snorted. "Couldn't have happened at a worse time."

"Maybe they'll go away soon and things'll calm down, Lad."

"Maybe." This was no ordinary search, however. It sounded as if they were stationing men as well as searching the cells.

Sure enough, the door to their cell flew open and a pair of the State Guard's men marched inside, swords ready. Each also bore a torch.

"You should've warned us you were coming, lads," called Ganth. "We would've been better prepared. Sorry there's nothing to eat or drink."

"Quiet, you!" snarled one of the newcomers. Two of them prodded at dark corners with their swords, then double-checked with their torches.

"I'd be more careful," Kaz added. "The rats don't take kindly to being disturbed."

One of the guards gave him a dark look. "The only rat we're looking for has got two legs, and we'll find him yet."

The guards retreated from the cell. The door was once more bolted shut. However, activity still continued outside.

"What in the name of infernal Sargas is going on out there, Kaz?" Hecar strained to see. The occasional head or axe went by in a blur.

"I don't know, but pray they quiet down and go away soon or we may not be able to try to escape. Even Honor's Face won't be enough to deal with all those soldiers."

An hour later, however, it was clear that the searchers were not going to leave for quite some time. Kaz fidgeted. He knew how much more difficult it would be to try to enable any of them to escape if they had to do so from the arena itself. But there seemed no choice.

So be it, then. I'll do what I can for them and die myself if need be. Kaz grimaced. And to think I swore I'd never let myself die in the circus, not for the pleasure of the emperor!

Kaz swore a new oath then, one in which he vowed to make certain that neither Polik nor Jopfer would find pleasure in his death.

The night continued to dwindle. Dawn had to be only two or three hours away. Kaz and the others had just about given up hope that the search would end when the halls suddenly grew quiet and the torchlight dimmed. Hecar nudged Ganth, who had dozed off. Kaz twisted in an attempt to see a little more of the hallway, but the bit of blank wall he could make out told him nothing. There might be a legion of sentries out there, and then again there might not be.

"Are you going to try it, Lad?" whispered his father. "Time is getting short."

"Maybe in just a minute—" He cut himself off as a clicking noise warned all three that the door to the cell was being opened. Kaz stared, wondering who or why . . .

The door moved slowly, then stopped before there was barely enough room for a jackrabbit to slither through. A wary breath later, a small figure peered through the crack and smiled at the trio.

"Delbin!" Kaz barely managed to keep it a whisper.

"Hi, Kaz!" Of course, to Delbin the entire situation was probably like a bizarre game of hide-and-seek. "I found you! I knew it must be you in here when people said they brought in some warrior who didn't have the sense to surrender against a full squad of the guard—"

"Delbin, what are—?"

The wiry figure put a finger to his lips. "Shh! I can't save you now, Kaz, because the guards are coming right back and you can't sneak into the places I can, which they did check, but they don't look very hard or very well, and you wouldn't want to hide in some of those places anyway . . ." He clamped his mouth shut, then, much more slowly, added, "I just wanted to tell you I think I found a good way to rescue you—"

"Delbin! Get out of here. I want you to get out of Nethosak as I told you to do the first time!" Only Paladine knew how the kender had been able to get in here, but Delbin was only endangering himself. He could not possibly help Kaz. "Go now!"

"But I wanted to tell you how I'll rescue you from—"

"Get going," added Ganth, ears straight as he listened for the return of the State Guard. "Or come morning you might end up helping us entertain the crowds in the arena!"

"You're going to be in the arena?" The kender's tone was so cheerful it grated on the minotaurs. "That'll make it so much easier for me! Just wait!"

To their surprise, the kender stepped back and began closing the door.

"Delbin!" called Kaz as loud as he dared. "Leave the city!"

The door closed, but a moment later, the minotaur's tiny friend pulled himself up so he could see through the bars. Still smiling, Delbin replied, "Oh, don't worry, Kaz! I'm not going to leave without all of you! I'll rescue you tomorrow, real dramatically, when you're in the arena!"

Before Kaz could say anything else, Delbin abruptly dropped out of sight. Several moments later, a sentry thrust his ugly muzzle against the bars.

"No more noise! Sargas take you, you fools! You should get some rest so you can at least put on a half-decent showing before you're all killed." He snorted. "Now quiet down. Soon it'll be first light."

He stepped away from the bars as one of his comrades joined him. The second guard was more agitated.

"A representative of the high priest is here! He's got men of his own, and they're coming down here to search the area and check on the prisoners!"

The first snorted in disbelief. "We just finished searching this place from top to bottom at the orders of the circle! What's a cleric going to find that the guard hasn't?"

"We may find nothing, my son. But then again, we may," replied a third voice. "It is not for us to question the wise actions of His Holiness."

"My—my apologies! I didn't mean—"

Kaz and the others looked at one another. One of Jopfer's acolytes? With a new band to search the cells?

They obviously had not discovered Delbin or someone would have mentioned it already. That was some relief to Kaz.

"I am Brother Merriq. You shall assist us in any way necessary. Those orders come from both your superiors and the office of the high priest."

"Yes, Brother Merriq."

"Search there and there," the prisoners heard the cleric command. "You search over there."

"That's done it, Boys," Ganth commented sourly. "They aren't leaving anytime soon. It's to the arena with us. At least we'll show them how a true warrior fights!"

Kaz shook his head. "I've got a plan for that, too. Riskier, but the only choice we've got, it seems."

"Lad, what could you possibly hope to do in the arena? Is this something to do with that kender?"

He had momentarily forgotten Delbin's plan . . . possibly because he did not want to think about what sort of wild notion had been at the core of it. "No, nothing to do with him. We can't talk about it now, though."

His words were truer than he thought. A new face suddenly thrust itself into the barred window. Calculating eyes studied the three forms. "This is them, then?"

"Yes, Brother Merriq."

The representative sniffed. "Not much to look at . . . and even less to look at come the day. Their combats are scheduled?"

"Aye. Molus has the proper list, but I think the one who's been here longer goes first, then the old one, and then the one called Kaz."

"Change that." Merriq's eyes focused on Kaz, who stared back, determined not to lose this small but crucial test of willpower. "His Holiness would prefer that Kaziganthi of the clan Orilg be the first of the three to face combat. Here are his orders."

The sooner I'm out of the way, the better? Or is it that you still think to scare me into renouncing my life and becoming your symbol to the masses?

Clearly Merriq awaited some reaction from Kaz, but when the prisoner did not satisfy his desires, the robed figure turned from the door. "I trust there will be no trouble seeing to it that the change in schedule is made."

"No, Brother Merriq! I'll alert the Master of Combat even now if you like."

"Simply tell him when he arrives. That should prove sufficient, don't you think? He will not argue with it much, will he?"

"As you say, Brother Merriq."

"Open the cell door."

"Yes, Brother Merriq." The door rattled, then swung wide enough to admit both the high priest's man and one of the sentries."

As he entered, Merriq looked around. "This cell was searched from rafter to floor? All corners?"

"Aye, Brother." .

"Then it should be secure, I suppose." The tall, robed figure strode over to the captives and stared down at Kaz. "You are Kaziganthi de-Orilg."

"Since you were there when I was brought to your master, that should come as no surprise, even to you."

"A flippant tongue, typical of a heretic and traitor. Also typical of a fool. One would think you might start pleading for clemency by this time."

Kaz snorted. "Now what good would that do? Your master would never grant it, and we both know that."

"True, but you could try anyway." Merriq squatted, the better to stare Kaz in the eye. "Things could be made easier for you and your friends if you would change your mind. His Holiness has offered you such as most warriors only dream of achieving. Only a fool or a lunatic would reject such glories."

"I can only give you the same answer I'd give your master again. I'm no one's puppet. It would go against my honor . . . which might be something you'd never understand, Brother Merriq."

The cleric glared, but did not respond to the slight. "It would also be wise to tell us where the kender is. He will only come to worse if he is not placed safely in custody."

"Hopefully, he's far from Nethosak and far from your reach."

"He is still in the city," Merriq returned. "We are certain

of that. You would do him a great favor by telling us where to find him. There are many ways to die."

"I think the man must be deaf, Kaz." Ganth shook his head. "He asks a question, gets an answer, then asks the question again."

Kaz grunted. To his inquisitor he said, "As if your master cares about a kender's safety."

"The high priest cares about all the children of Sargas, even those of the lesser races."

The high priest wanted Delbin alive . . . alive to use as a threat against Kaz. More and more, Kaz wondered what sort of game Jopfer was playing. Even the emperor and the Supreme Circle might not know Jopfer's agenda.

"I can see there is nothing to be gained in trying to talk sense to you," Merriq remarked. "Very well. Then, by the will of Sargas, I pray you fight well tomorrow and, by doing so, redeem your lost honor in the eyes of your fellows. Fight well and your memory may still be honored."

Merriq departed without a second glance. The warrior who had let him in gave Kaz and the others an almost sympathetic glance before quickly following.

"We must search down this hallway again. If the kender shows up, he will have to make use of one of these exits," Merriq said to someone. His voice dwindled as he moved off. However, guards still continued to move through the corridor and Kaz could make out the horns of a sentry on duty across from his cell door. He suspected it was one of the temple soldiers and not one of the State Guard's men.

"That's it, then, Lads. It's the arena for certain now."

"What can we do?" asked Hecar. "Kaz goes first. You heard that robed serpent. They want him first so he's out of the way as swiftly as possible. Why don't they just kill us in here?"

"Now that wouldn't be sporting, Hecar! Must keep up illusions, our high priest. Besides, I think you, Kaz, are supposed to live. Hecar and I, we are more likely to be the object lessons. Still, I could be wrong. I'm certain that more than a few will remember my son and the last time he was out there. Maybe this is also an attempt to prove that no one can defy the emperor and the others." Ganth shook his head. "I don't know what to think."

"The emperor? No real need to defy him." Hecar grunted. "Polik's the high priest's puppet. That's obvious."

"Worse than that," Kaz responded, finally stirring from his thoughts. "Jopfer's got the Supreme Circle in the palm of his hand, too, I'd say. Which doesn't matter for the moment, I suppose. What matters is us getting out." He forced a smile that he hoped looked cunning. "You two be prepared to act tomorrow. Watch me. As soon as I move, you've got to head down a certain tunnel across the field that I'll point out. It's the quickest and easiest way out. They keep the animals they use in the circus in that area. There'll be fewer sentries on duty there. In a situation of great chaos, it won't be that hard for you to slip free."

"What about you, Lad?"

"I'm the great chaos," he said. "And I'll be right behind you," he added, lying.

Hecar's brow was furrowed. "What sort of situation could cause enough chaos to make them ignore us?"

"You'll be better off not knowing. Just trust me. It'll work." He had his doubts, but did not voice them.

"What about Delbin, though, Kaz? He said he had something in mind. What happens if he puts whatever mad idea he has to work just as you're about to put your own plan into play?"

Kaz did not want to consider that particular problem. Hopefully, Delbin would follow his wishes and leave Nethosak. If not . . .

"Pray Paladine and Kiri-Jolith can use some good warriors at their side, because if they don't, old Sargas is going to have the last laugh in the afterlife."

* * * * *

Delbin returned to his hiding place with little more than two hours of darkness left.

"Well, I found them," he said to himself, speaking quietly but firmly in order to keep his thoughts organized the way he thought Kaz would in his position. "They're in a place under the circus, but it's not a very nice-looking place, and it's got rats in some places, which seems strange, since everything aboveground is so clean. They're locked up, and I would've gotten them out except some minotaurs in funny black-and-red robes who I heard worship Sargas, who is a peculiar god to worship since he's not very nice, came in and started looking for me. I had a good talk with Kaz and told him I'd be back because while I was there I got a great idea for a really big diversion that'll keep everyone there busy while they escape." He smiled in the dark, pleased with his personal rundown of events. Kaz would have been proud of him, Delbin was certain, even if the minotaur had declared he ought to leave the kingdom.

The kender set to work on his master plan. Everything was falling into place.

* * * * *

The high priest did not sleep as others slept. Sometimes he thought and plotted; other times he simply paced. Soon he could reveal the glorious truth to his children. Until then, however . . .

This dark morning, dark because there was at least an hour before sunrise, he had to visit his guest. She had grown unsettled of late, something which in turn unsettled the high priest. In the short time since she had become his guest, a decision not of her making, she had been, for the most part, quiet and frightened. The high priest preferred that. He encouraged those emotions, while at the same time being careful that she did not come to harm. Her good health was vital to everything. She had to be kept secured, but otherwise he made certain she did not hunger much or grow unduly ill.

Deep below the main part of the temple, in the special cells in which declared heretics were once placed, she awaited. The cleric walked unescorted past empty cells, turning corner after corner until at last he found the only one presently occupied.

Something scurried away from the door of the cell, a short, dumpy little figure whose presence disgusted him. "What are you doing there? Get away from that door!"

"Sorry, Great One! Sorry! Galump mean nothing!"

"Get away from here! Go back to your garbage! If I see you here again . . ." He let the threat trail off as the gully dwarf scurried away. If the little creature had not been trained to perform certain acts of spying for the priesthood, the high priest would have dealt with him there and then.

A slight clink from within the cell informed him that his guest was awake. Had she been talking to the foul little creature? The only other ones she saw were the guards that watched the corridors. But they were strictly forbidden to speak to her. No one was allowed to speak to her but him.

Moving to the door, he peered into darkness. "You are awake, my little one, so do not pretend otherwise."

From the darkness of the cell there came the sound of chains clanking. A moment later, the prisoner appeared out of the darkness.

In Solamnia, Ergoth, or any of the human lands, she would have seemed perfectly in place. Here in the empire, she was a striking contrast. Humans were not often seen or well-liked here, especially after years of domination by the warlords. Crynus had left a legacy of hatred.

"What do you want of me? Why can't I go home?"

She appeared young, perhaps fifteen, sixteen summers if he was a judge of human looks, but the cleric knew appearances could be very deceiving, and the girl was perhaps the greatest deceiver of all. Her innocent face, draped by long, silver hair that might have seemed more appropriate to an elf, belied what he and he alone knew to be the truth: there was power within her.

"This is your home, female. This will always be your home. Understand that now, and all other things will become much easier for you to accept." He indicated the cell. "You have a comfortable chamber. I have seen to that.

The chains are required since you have yet to acknowledge that I am your master. My will is your will. When you truly accept that, then they may be removed."

"I want to go home!"

"What home is that? What life do you recall other than wandering by yourself, surviving by yourself, in the mountains and forests? Running from others who understand less than you yourself do. Surviving on what you were able to scrounge." Despite himself, the high priest grew angry. "Is that what you think your life was meant to be? Do you realize the danger you face, not having been trained in your abilities? You could be killed, either intentionally or accidentally. Do you know what that would mean?"

Her frightened yet still perplexed expression infuriated him. There was much he wanted to tell her, information he needed her to know in order to better understand. But to tell her this soon was to increase the potential of a deadly threat.

"I don't understand you at all," she insisted. "You keep talking as if I'm so very important to you. Of what importance can I be to you? I don't even *know* you."

"You are very intelligent, female, despite a lack of training. You have always known more, learned easier, than those around you. Look into yourself, then look into my eyes and see how closely we are linked. Look closely . . ."

She raised her hands, palms toward him. "No!"

Her hands glowed white.

The chains shimmered blue.

With a gasp, the young girl slipped to her knees, barely able to keep from falling to the floor. As her hands ceased glowing, the chains did the same.

"That is an object lesson. You must cease attempting to defy me. I do not like having to hurt you, but I will be obeyed. There is too much at stake here. I have worked too long for either you or a recalcitrant minotaur to disrupt things."

The girl did not answer him. The high priest frowned, deciding this was a waste of his precious time. The female had been in moods like this before. It was a sign of her childishness. Under his tutelage, such moods would soon become a thing of the past.

"Sleep now," he finally commanded. "Tomorrow we will talk again. Tomorrow we will begin new lessons."

As he turned and walked away, he heard her begin to cry. The sound encouraged him. She was at last beginning to break. Soon she would be his obedient servant . . . and her power, matched with his, would make his dream unstoppable.

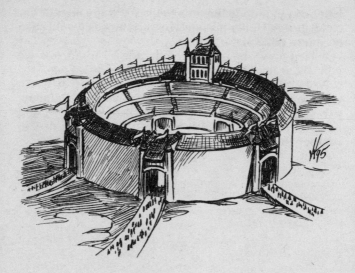

Chapter 10
The Great Circus

Molus was not as enthusiastic as Kaz would have expected him to be. He soon found out why. Word of the cleric's command to make Kaz the first of the three prisoners to face death had reached the jailer, and the older minotaur was clearly put out by the new orders.

"No sense of timing and drama when it comes to the arena! We should lead off with your friend, who's been out there before and whose blood the spectators are ready to see, then schedule your father, who should make for a good warm-up. Then, and only then, should you go in, Kaziganthi! By Sargas! You should really be the last battle of the day! Word's gotten around, and there're plenty who recall or have heard of you. Heard some good bets as to how long you'll last . . . 'course it depends on who or what you face, doesn't it?"

"And would you happen to know?" asked Kaz. He would prefer to know whether he was going to face several gladiators or possibly a savage animal or two. His attack would be timed accordingly.

"I do know, but it's going to be a surprise. The emperor's own orders. Doesn't want you too prepared, I'd guess. He remembers you well."

"I remember him, too."

Molus studied his expression. "I'll just bet you do."

"At least am I going to be allowed a weapon?"

As they talked, guards had been busy preparing all three. Kaz was counting on the trio being taken up to the waiting area together. That had always been the habit in times past, and he was pleased to see that in typical minotaur fashion no one had bothered to fiddle with tradition. Had Hecar and Ganth been left behind, Kaz would have been hard pressed to devise an escape plan.

"Aye, you'll be carrying a short sword."

Short sword. That probably meant he was fighting another warrior. Kaz was glad to hear that. If so, he wouldn't have to worry about the unpredictability of animals. Gladiators, on the other hand, were quite predictable.

Bracelets replaced the wall chains. Kaz and the others were then led out of the cell and down the corridor leading to the vast field of the arena. Vaguely familiar with the path from years ago, Kaz estimated the time the others would need to escape once they made it across the field. Four minutes, maybe five, to traverse the long corridor through the menagerie. That, of course, did not include any resistance they might meet, but the menagerie was generally guarded by only a pair of sentries and one or two handlers.

Overconfidence. No one expected anyone to attempt such a bold escape. Minotaurs fought and died; they did not flee. He only hoped that Ganth and Hecar could get away in time.

Cheers erupted from above them. The entire corridor shook with pounding feet. There must be a good combat going on. The better the combat, the greater the crowd reaction. Pounding feet was one way in which the spectators sounded their approval, and gaining the crowd's favor had turned many a combat.

As they reached the holding area, a barred space from where they could watch the other duels, Kaz noted a familiar figure waiting for the prisoners: Scurn. In one hand he held an object that Kaz did not at first recognize. Only when the two stood almost face-to-face did Scurn reveal what it was he held.

It was the medallion honoring the supreme champion, the same medallion he had taken from Kaz after the latter's capture.

"I would've preferred to take this from you in combat," the scarred minotaur said.

"You've got the medallion now. Just wear it."

A dark expression covered Scurn's mutilated features. "I would not dishonor it so. I never won it, so I can't wear it."

It was odd to think that someone like Scurn could still think in terms of honor. Kaz was about to make a scathing reply when the other minotaur suddenly reached out and offered him the medallion.

"Take it. It's still yours, won in combat in the circus. The high priest and Polik won't like it, but it's still your right to wear it. Even your crimes can't take that away from you, though your death will." He snorted. "I should be the one fighting you. This isn't right, to—"

"Never mind about his combat," the older minotaur quickly snapped. He pointed at the medallion. "Go ahead and take it," Molus added. "It'll make for some added excitement once they see what you're wearing."

Kaz wanted to reject the medallion. He saw no purpose in accepting the honor, not when he did not believe in it. All it meant was that he had wasted a portion of his life fighting and injuring others for the sake of the handful that ruled the minotaur race.

"You *should* take it, you know. It may come in handy."

Stiffening, Kaz glanced around. He recognized the voice. The only time he had ever heard it was in a dream.

It was the voice of the gray man . . . but he was nowhere to be seen.

Without really knowing why he did it, Kaz turned and took the medallion. Even with his wrists banded together, he managed to place it around his neck. A warmth spread through him. Scurn nodded, then stepped back. Anticipation was evident in his eyes, anticipation and perhaps a little envy. Someone else would have the honor of killing Kaz.

There was no sign of Honor's Face. The axe Scurn wore was one of the service axes that the guard issued to its members. Of course, Scurn would never risk an excellent weapon such as Honor's Face for the mundane tasks of the guard. Likely he planned to use it in the circus or in battle. Unlike the medallion, he had no intention of giving it back to its original owner even for one last battle. Scurn's sense of honor went only so far.

Another roar shook the colosseum, followed by more foot stomping and clapping. Whatever match had been going on had now ended and, from the sounds of it, Kaz suspected that one of the combatants had suffered a fatal defeat.

We might conquer the world a little faster if we didn't keep disposing of our warriors in the arena, he thought with disgust. That made him think of Raud, which in turn made him think of Polik, who was probably in the audience already.

"Let's get this going," Kaz snarled, holding out his hands so that the jailer could remove his bracelets.

"That's the spirit!" chuckled Molus. He released Kaz. Ganth and Hecar were also freed from their bonds. None of the three were taken to the barred area, which was as Kaz had hoped. Again, minotaur habits worked to Kaz's advantage. Since his father and Hecar would follow Kaz, Molus and the others saw no sense in wasting time locking them up. With half a dozen guards surrounding them, it seemed unlikely that the pair would be able to try anything while Kaz was fighting in the arena.

Of course, with a distraction such as he planned, the guards would be too stunned to react immediately when their prisoners attempted to escape. Everything counted on the minotaur race's penchant for routine.

Had Kaz been of another race, say a human or elf, he would not have been as fortunate. Rarely were creatures of other races, with the exception of ogres, brought to the Great Circus. The smaller arenas dealt with the other races and usually allowed no chance of escape. The Great Circus was for the minotaurs almost exclusively. The few outsiders who fought in it were watched closely, since it was known that only members of the chosen of Sargas were truly honorable.

"They've cleared the field," Molus announced. "Move on, Kaziganthi. It's your time."

With two guards flanking him, Kaz walked out onto the field. In the stands, a sea of black, brown, and white forms, with a few other colors sprinkled here and there, watched and waited.

At first there was silence. Generally it was so when criminals were brought out, for a minotaur who had dishonored himself was only half a minotaur in the eyes of his fellows. Then, perhaps because of the medallion hanging from his neck or the fact that at least some in the crowd had recognized him despite the many years, a murmuring arose. It grew in intensity and by the time Kaz and the guards reached the bloodstained center of the arena, it had risen almost to a cheer. In fact, there were more than a few who were indeed cheering . . . for him.

From another entrance, more than a dozen warriors armed with a combination of swords, axes, spears, and nets appeared. They marched toward Kaz, each of them sleek gladiators in their prime. They were not champions of high rank, but definitely seasoned warriors. There were at least five females, but Kaz did not discount them. Helati was a prime example of what a female warrior was capable.

So it was to be combat against overwhelming numbers. Kaz estimated sixteen warriors. That meant eight would do battle while the other eight surrounded the circle where Kaz would fight. If one of the first eight died or was unable to continue the combat, another, designated earlier by lottery, would enter the fray. Warriors would continue to join the struggle until the criminal was outlasted—and dead. There were variations on this, but for the Great Circus, this was the accepted system. Hecar had been given a lesser risk only because they had wanted him alive as bait.

As the warriors began to surround Kaz and his escort, one of the guards handed him a much abused short sword. Kaz grunted, but did not otherwise protest. His weapon should have been better, but he knew not to expect otherwise. Polik and the high priest wanted to take no chances.

Thinking of the pair, he quickly scanned the crowds. The emperor was usually seated in a box at the center of the longer side of the arena. His box was higher than most other seats. Beside him would sit Jopfer and members of the Supreme Circle.

Sure enough, the box was occupied. Kaz squinted. Polik was there, a little heavier and wearier than years ago, but otherwise hardly changed. He still bore the physique of a champion, but Kaz could not see how he could have won every challenge he had faced in all these years. The emperor was clad in an elegant robe of brown and red and wore a crested helmet that was obviously used only for ceremonial purposes.

It's true, then, the prisoner thought. The warlords brought Polik in because he could be managed, and the high priest and circle kept him in for the same reason.

Polik was not looking at him, but was arguing with another minotaur, an armored figure that Kaz guessed was a member of the circle. He was tapping his chest again and again. It took Kaz a few moments to realize that Polik was complaining about the medallion. Even from so far away, most would recognize it as a symbol of a high-ranking champion. Those who still recalled Kaz would likely also remember that he could have challenged Polik if he had not abandoned the circus. The emperor did not like to be reminded of that.

The emperor pointed at Kaz, then at the warriors. The minotaur beside him shook his head, but Polik was adamant. His companion signaled a guard. A few quick words were shared, then the guard hurried off.

Horns blared. Kaz glanced to the side and saw a herald walk out. They were about to announce the battle. Not caring what the herald was going to say, he continued looking around. Polik and at least three members of the circle were in the audience, but the only representatives of the priesthood were Merriq and a pair of lesser acolytes. Of Jopfer there was no sign.

His target would be Polik after all.

"Wake up, you fool!" whispered one of the guards. "Or are you planning to just stand there and let them run you through?"

Kaz snapped out of his reverie, realizing that the herald had finished and the warriors were readying themselves. Once they were all in place, eight surrounding Kaz and the other eight forming an outer circle, the guards backed out of the way and returned to where Ganth and Hecar were being held.

Kaz had only a moment. He had to dispose of the weapon, distracting his opponents at the same time, then summon Honor's Face to him. Only Honor's Face, with its magic, could do what Kaz desired. Only the axe could fly as straight as he desired, and end Polik's reign once and for all.

Another horn sounded. The gladiators paused, clearly confused. Kaz was also confused. The new signal commanded the gladiators to retreat, which they undertook in slight disarray.

Yet another horn sounded. This time, no gladiators paraded out. Instead, a gate to the side opened. The minotaur's eyes widened. He knew what the gate meant. Someone had made a change in plans. Kaz no longer faced warriors.

A roar echoed from the corridor behind the half-open gate. Instead of gladiators, Kaz was to fight an animal.

The second roar was greater than the first. The crowd was excited. The audience, too, knew this was to be no ordinary confrontation.

Then, a great head thrust out of the tunnel, massive nostrils sniffing the air in suspicion. Reptilian eyes slowly adjusted to the light. A maw of dagger-type teeth opened, and a thick red tongue darted out and in.

A meredrake, a creature larger than the largest bear and resembling the dragons of lore, lumbered out. While only a reptile and not related to the great leviathans, it was still a vicious beast. This one was nearly full-grown.

Many in the audience clearly saw the unfairness of the match-up, and even though Kaz was supposed to be a criminal, there were grumbles of protest. Polik pointedly ignored them, watching the prisoner with satisfaction. The reptile stalked toward the center of the field. The meredrake's tail swished back and forth, the beast growing more anxious as it smelled so many minotaurs.

Then it saw Kaz.

The meredrake hissed. One minotaur was not a threat to it, but rather a meal. Meredrakes were always eager to eat.

Kaz gripped the short sword in one hand. He did not want to make his move right away. He wanted to study the monster for a minute to determine how to fight it. If the meredrake moved true to form, he had some hunches. If it surprised him, then it was very possible that Kaz would die, ripped to shreds by claws and teeth.

It was not how he had hoped to die. He only wished he could take Polik with him.

The beast raised its head and opened its jaws wide. To anyone else, the sight might have been enough to terrorize the hapless victim. Kaz, though, had faced dragons and other creatures far stranger and more deadly than a meredrake.

Hissing, the meredrake abruptly charged to Kaz's left, moving with a swiftness and dexterity that its lumbering, reptilian form did not suggest. The crowd roared, protest mingling with cheers.

Kaz roared at the charging beast, which stumbled momentarily. The seasoned warrior shifted his grip on his blade so as to be able to throw it, then threw the worn but still serviceable blade at the monster.

The sword flew with the accuracy of a javelin, and the speed with which it moved was so great that its intended target had no time to get out of the way. The blade sank into the meredrake's shoulder. This time, the monster did more than stumble. It roared in pain as it raised one paw to knock the projectile from its wounded body.

Even as he released the blade, Kaz held his other hand high. Honor's Face materialized. The crowd's tone shifted to confusion, but Kaz did not care what they thought. The great reptile had already batted away the sword as if it were a twig, something Kaz had not expected it to be able to do so swiftly, and the minotaur needed something better.

Kaz stumbled back as the monster charged forward. The meredrake got one set of claws on the bottom of the axe head and pushed down. Honor's Face was ripped from the minotaur's grip.

The huge monster charged forward again. Kaz threw himself onto the back of the beast, which hissed and tried to shake him off. The minotaur held tight and willed the axe to come to him.

It did . . . just in time for the warrior to lose his seat. Kaz slid off the reptile's back to the loud reaction of the crowd. He did not know whether the audience was disappointed that he had failed or hoping that now the meredrake would turn around and tear his chest open.

The meredrake turned. Kaz fell on its tail, seizing the appendage with his free hand. The tail dragged him along when the reptile moved, at first baffling the beast. After a few almost hilarious turns, the meredrake finally realized what was happening and whipped its tail to its open maw.

Kaz released the appendage and rolled in the opposite direction. Rising to one knee, Kaz brought Honor's Face around and dug the gleaming blade deep into a half-raised paw. Blood splashed over the minotaur's head. Kaz tried to blink away the blood, which stung his eyes so much he could barely see.

It nearly cost him his life. In agony, the meredrake swung wildly about, throwing Kaz and the axe into the air as easily as a child might toss a pebble. Kaz could do little to control his fall. He struck the ground with enough force to shake Honor's Face from his grasp.

Only the enraged reptile's thundering movements warned the minotaur that he was once again in its path. Kaz rolled quickly to the side. His vision had returned, just in time to catch sight of the meredrake's jaws trying to close on his leg. The warrior snapped his leg back and kicked it forward into the meredrake's snout.

The action stunned the beast, but not as much as Kaz had hoped. It managed to raise itself high on the three limbs it had that still functioned. It clearly intended to fall on its prey and crush him.

Body aching, Kaz willed Honor's Face to him as the meredrake fell on him.

Honor's Face formed in his hands. Kaz did the only thing he could. He tried to shift to the side with the head of the axe edgewise against the ground. That left the other edge in the monster's direct path.

Several hundred pounds of reptile drove the air from the minotaur's chest as the meredrake landed. Kaz was certain he would be crushed to death, until the monster shivered and rolled away, a fresh stream of blood dripping over the minotaur. The magical weapon's astonishingly sharp edge had saved his life.

Yet the meredrake was still not defeated. It breathed in long gasps. Its chest wound was deep, and one limb was nearly useless, but the massive jaws were still a threat to Kaz. Fortunately, Kaz had access to its throat. He rolled onto his stomach, Honor's Face cradled in his arms. The angle was such that a strong swing was impossible, but the axe could be just as deadly a thrusting weapon. The tip was sharp and long enough to kill.

He rose to his knees immediately after rolling onto his stomach, but as he positioned himself to dart under the massive jaws of the beast, the meredrake shifted. It was clumsy and stiff, yet the combatants were in close proximity. Honor's Face was the only way Kaz could prevent the meredrake's jaws from getting at him. Kaz thrust the magical axe up into the creature's maw as hard as he was able. And there it stuck, in the meredrake's mouth, with Kaz holding on for dear life.

He gritted his teeth.

Paladine . . . Kiri-Jolith . . . guide me now, the warrior prayed. Releasing his hold on the axe, Kaz threw himself forward. Hissing, the reptile swung its head to the side, knocking the weapon to the ground.

Kaz gored the meredrake in the throat and neck so hard that both his horns sank deep.

Hundreds of pounds of monster threatened to fall on the minotaur, but he remained where he was, pushing upward as hard as possible. Cold blood poured down on his head. The meredrake tried to swipe at him with its injured paw. Kaz felt the beast shiver.

With effort, the minotaur pulled free. The meredrake barely noticed. It rocked its head back and forth, its life fluids draining onto the circus grounds, then stumbled a few steps. Kaz scrambled away as best he could, exhaustion preventing him from going too far.

The meredrake shivered, gave a gurgling sound . . . and collapsed on the field.

The crowd roared. In all his time as a champion of the arenas, Kaz could not recall a cheer as great as the one that now echoed through the circus.

Forcing himself to stand, Kaz retrieved his axe. It was still not too late to kill Polik. Honor's Face would fly straight and true.

All of a sudden, from the entrance emerged a squad of gladiators. They swarmed toward him, ready to do battle. The cheers of the crowd turned sour. Clearly most did not think that even a criminal deserved such a short reprieve. Kaz had likely vindicated himself in the eyes of many.

Polik did not care for that. The emperor had risen and was demanding that the gladiators charge the prisoner. All he cared about was that Kaz died and died quickly before sentiment for the renegade increased.

The gladiators did not move toward Kaz with much enthusiasm. Any warrior who could single-handedly kill a meredrake was one to be reckoned with, even one as exhausted as Kaz. He was grateful for their hesitation. Each second meant he would be able to give them a better struggle.

"All right," he growled. "Who'll be first?" His brave words were intended to make them even more hesitant.

A roar from the other end of the arena made even Kaz lose concentration. Both he and the gladiators turned in the direction of the roar, duty giving way to surprise.

A lion charged out onto the field. It was a full-grown male. Even before the shock of its appearance could subside, it was joined by two, then three females, all roaring fiercely.

The animals' escape had only begun to register on those on the field when a second meredrake the size of a large wolf lumbered out. It snapped at the lions, who, despite their numbers, decided it was risky business. They spread out, coincidentally creeping closer to the guards and Kaz.

Smoke began pouring out of the entrance to the menagerie.

"Fire in the menagerie!" someone with a high voice called. "The animals have all escaped!"

There was something faintly dubious about that voice, but those able to hear it registered only the alarm. Weapons were forbidden in the audience, due to the minotaur tendency to end all disputes, especially wagers, with combat. Only the State Guard, clerics, members of the Supreme Circle, and the emperor were permitted weapons here. Minotaurs were not fool enough to go up against a lion or a meredrake with their bare hands, not even after watching the great feat of Kaz. The fire was also worrisome. Many of the spectators near the menagerie began to abandon their seats.

Other animals began emerging from the smoky entrance, horses, bears, and more. Kaz could not even identify some of the beasts, but anything that had teeth as long as his fingers or claws as big as his hand was to be avoided. There were bulls and sheep, the latter used mainly for feeding the predators. Some of the animals fell upon other animals, but other predators seemed more inclined toward two-legged meals, perhaps because they had been trained to attack when in the arena.

Kaz was forgotten as the gladiators moved to defend themselves from the more immediate threat. There was no sign of the handlers, but Kaz guessed they were either dealing with other animals that had not made it outside or were already dead.

"Delbin!" he muttered. The kender had promised to create a diversion, and had. It was up to him to see that Delbin's efforts were not in vain.

He backed away from the animals and the gladiators, Honor's Face at the ready. One of the other warriors glanced at him, then evidently decided that Kaz was the lesser of two evils.

Two more warriors passed Kaz, holding nets and tritons. Deciding he was momentarily safe, Kaz turned to see what had happened to Ganth and Hecar.

They had taken advantage of the confusion caused by the escaping animals and sought to escape as planned. The pair had made it out in the open. Ganth had grabbed a short sword, but now they were being harried by one of their guards and the stubborn old jailer. For an old minotaur, Molus was quick with a weapon.

Ganth and Hecar were still bound, which made it difficult for the former to wield his blade. Somehow Kaz's father was managing to fend the pair off.

Roaring, Kaz charged in their direction. Molus turned first and actually smiled when he saw who it was who was coming. He turned away from Ganth and started toward Kaz, but suddenly another figure darted between them. The figure held an axe almost as large as Kaz's own.

"Take care of your prisoners," snarled Scurn. "I'll deal with Kaz." The look he gave the jailer allowed no room for argument. Molus backed away and went to help the other guard.

"I beat you in the arena, and I beat you when you came for me, Scurn. Don't try again."

"You should've killed me the last time, Kaz. I asked you to. I couldn't face the clan after such a humiliating defeat!"

With that, Scurn attacked. His swing was more precise and swift than when he had faced Kaz in the past. Startled by both the vehemence and skill the other minotaur displayed, Kaz backed up.

Smoke almost distracted him. New fires had started up in more of the underground sections of the Great Circus. Kaz wondered exactly what Delbin was trying to do. If he continued like this, it was possible the kender would burn the colosseum to the ground, in the process killing his friends as well as his enemies.

Scurn swung again, his axe nipping the air just in front of Kaz's muzzle. Kaz brought Honor's Face up and caught Scurn's axe head. The two weapons remained locked for several seconds, then the disfigured warrior pulled his weapon back and tried to ram Kaz with the axe's long, pointed head. Kaz managed to fend off the attack, but the head of Scurn's axe sliced the air just an inch or two above Kaz's horns.

Kaz's injured arm began to act up, causing his grip to loosen. Struggling against pain, he knocked aside his opponent's axe and struck Scurn in the jaw with the lower end of the shaft. The other minotaur grunted, stumbling back. Kaz pursued his assault, striking Scurn again.

Disoriented, Scurn brought his axe around again and chopped at Kaz. His swing was off, however, and he was left wide open to his adversary. Kaz wasted no time. Again he struck with the shaft, driving the blunt end into the other's stomach. Scurn fell to his knees, dropping his axe. Unable to bring himself to kill so helpless a foe, Kaz took the only recourse left to him. He raised a fist and punched the gasping figure before him.

Scurn collapsed.

"Consider yourself fortunate," Kaz muttered. He then turned to the guard and Molus, who had forced Ganth back. Ganth was obviously tiring. Raising the axe, Kaz gave a battle cry and charged at the guard. The guard turned, and his eyes went wide at the sight before him, but to his credit, he charged back.

Molus was pushed back by a revitalized Ganth. Worse for the jailer, he had to keep an eye on Hecar, who began to swing around to his left.

The guard was not the warrior Scurn was. He tried to defend himself, but Honor's Face slashed through his guard and, at the same time, severed his sword hand. Kaz thought that would be the end of it, but the guard snatched up his bloody blade with his remaining hand and made a run at Kaz. Grunting, Kaz gave his adversary no quarter. This time he struck to kill.

The axe buried itself deep in the other minotaur's chest. Kaz did not even wait for the guard to fall as he pulled the weapon free. He moved in on Molus, but the jailer saw him and, abandoning his attack on Ganth, fled.

"Let's get going, lads," Kaz's father cried.

"One thing first!" Kaz took one edge of Honor's Face and ran it across the older minotaur's bonds. The severed pieces fell to the ground, joined there a moment later by the remnants of Hecar's bonds. "Grab a weapon and a net if you can, Hecar! We have to hurry now!" His last words were punctuated by the noise of a gong. Kaz looked around and saw smoke coming from yet another area.

Most of the crowd on the menagerie side of the circus had chosen to flee rather than face the fire and the animals, but many others remained, doing what they could to alleviate the problems. Some of them served only to further the confusion, for which Kaz was grateful.

The trio hurried toward the menagerie entrance. There were several dozen creatures scattered throughout the arena floor, and at least two had climbed into the lower seats, where members of the State Guard were trying to control them. The first meredrake to escape had been joined by a second, smaller one. Wolves darted around the nets of gladiators. At least two minotaurs were down, what was left of their bodies not a sight Kaz cared to dwell on. Several of the predators had been captured, but every now and then, one or two other beasts would charge out into the arena from the opening the prisoners needed to reach.

"We'll have to keep a careful eye out when we get to the other side," Ganth called. "Or we might find ourselves running into the jaws of a meredrake!"

A ram burst past Hecar, followed quickly by a pair of wolves that veered after their prey.

A minotaur scream cut through the chaos. It made Kaz look around. Although he did not spot the unfortunate warrior, he did see something else . . . or perhaps "not see" was the better term. There was no sign of Polik or the representatives of the circle. Even Jopfer's man, Merriq, was missing. No doubt he had been among the first to retreat.

"Kaz! Watch it, Lad!" Ganth was suddenly in front of him, sword slashing downward.

He backed away in surprise. His father tore past him. It was not an animal that threatened them, but a gladiator who had noticed them moving around and had elected to try to block their escape.

The other warrior tried to spear him from the side. Fortunately, Ganth shoved the spear aside with his blade. The spear dug into the earth, jarring the would-be attacker. He pulled the long weapon out before Ganth could follow through, then retreated when he saw he would have to deal with all three minotaurs at once.

"He'll be back with some friends very soon, Lads. Mark my words!"

"Then we'd better get out of here," Hecar rejoined.

Ahead of them, an arrow suddenly sprouted from the side of one of the female lions. The lion stumbled, fell, and managed to rise again. Blood dripped from the wound, but she managed to stay on her feet. Archers began appearing on the walls. A second arrow caught the lion. This time she fell.

"We'd better move faster! They're getting organized!"

They reached the entrance to the menagerie almost in time to collide headlong with a huge bull. Kaz wondered if the kender was purposely releasing them a few at a time to keep the melee going.

"Inside!" Kaz called, hoping that Delbin had not released anything else along with the bull.

The smell of many years of animal captivity made the trio recoil. Evidently there was a place that could smell worse than the prisoners' cells. Smoke made it uncomfortable but not impossible to breathe in the underground region. There was no sign of fire yet.

Two minotaurs lay crumpled on the floor of one cage. He scanned the rest of the room. The area was clear of threats. Several animals were shrieking in their cages, but most of the doors were open and the cages bare. The cause of the fire was a pile of baled hay that burned within one of the empty cages.

"There're still probably horses in the circus stables, Kaz," called Hecar. "Do we take them or try on foot?"

"On horseback we'll be more noticeable," called Ganth. "We'd be better off sneaking around on foot. The time to fight is later on."

"We can go this way," Kaz said, indicating a wooden door slightly ajar. He and the other minotaurs started for it.

Kaz wondered where the kender was. The brave little creature had a tendency to forget that he could be captured or killed . . . "I have to find Delbin."

"We've no time, Kaz," Hecar protested. "It's the will of Kiri-Jolith that we've gotten this far. We have to keep going. He'll catch up."

"We've no idea what else the kender had in mind, Lad." Ganth looked grim. "He might've figured that the animals and the fire weren't enough."

Kaz stared off into the distance. "You two go on ahead. I have to find him."

"Lad, from what you've said about Delbin, why not wait until he just shows up again? His kind are clever when it comes to escaping."

"Because I can't take the chance. He's helped me too much in the past. I will not abandon a comrade. You two had better get going."

Before they could stop him, he was already out the doorway.

* * * * *

Delbin hid behind the door as three minotaurs raced past to stop his latest fire. He was proud of himself for what he had accomplished.

He was not normally so adept at lighting fires, but he'd been assisted greatly by a strange bottle of oil he had discovered in his pouch. The bottle bore the mark of the circus, but Delbin could not fathom how it had found its way into his possession. Nevertheless, he had made good use of it. The torches positioned every now and then in the walls helped. Between the oil and the torches, Delbin had created some masterful blazes.

That he might be captured was a thought that occasionally occurred to him, but Delbin did not worry too much. He already knew some neat places to hide and others that could serve as escape routes.

One more. I should do one more. Kaz and the others might still need more time.

Seeing no one in sight nearby, he slipped around and headed down the hall. This one corridor seemed to encompass the entire circus and had so far made it simple for him to move from one place to another. His size helped, of course. Someone as large as Kaz would not have been able to hide in such cramped places. Surely his minotaur friend would be proud of him.

He saw his next potential target moments later. The corridor was still deserted, most of the minotaurs having either fled the threat of fire or fighting to subdue the animals outside. Delbin saw a wooden cart. He had no idea of its uses, save that it might be needed to haul things out of the circus. Remembering what most often had to be hauled out of the arena, Delbin made a face. That was a part of minotaur life he did not like. Then the kender started forward.

"Well! Sargas watches over me this day!"

Heavy hands clamped on to the small figure's shoulders. He was drawn backward, then flipped around to face the source.

It was a tall minotaur clad in a black-and-red robe that Delbin knew was the clothing of the clerics of the minotaur empire. He had seen them and knew something about their organization from Kaz, but this was the first time he had been so close to one.

With the robed one were two warriors who looked similar to the ones who had captured Kaz. They each took hold of an arm and dragged the kender nearer to the cleric.

"I am Merriq, representative of His Holiness, the high priest. You have an appointment with him. Resist and we shall drag you there. You cannot possibly escape."

"You let me go or you'll be sorry!"

The minotaurs laughed. Merriq, still smiling, said, "You are a kender, and a young one at that. You are next to nothing, and if it was not that the high priest himself requested your living presence, I would have you tossed into the arena to distract the beasts while our gladiators find and destroy your friends. They have not escaped, you know."

"You're lying!" Despite saying that, Delbin was slightly shaken. Had Kaz and the others been captured?

"The minotaur Hecar and the old one are the prisoners of the circus again." Merriq steepled his hands as if in prayer. "The criminal Kaziganthi died fleeing in dishonor from a meredrake that eventually bit him in two."

Delbin reacted without thinking, with the same temper that had caused him so much trouble among his own kind. Both Merriq and the guards seemed a little startled by his vehemence. Having no weapon in his hands, Delbin threw the only thing he had, the bottle of oil.

The bottle broke against the cleric's chest, splattering him with oil and fragments. The minotaur growled and stumbled backward, trying to rub his injured eyes.

Delbin squirmed out of the guards' grips, but collided with the cleric, who could not see.

Losing his balance, the blinded Merriq fell against one of the lit torches, which fell free. Flame from the torch grazed his robe, and the screaming cleric burst into flames. The oil helped to create an inferno that quickly spread over most of the minotaur's body.

One of the guards seized Delbin. The other tried to aid Merriq, but it was too late. The cleric collapsed. More guards began to arrive.

A guard behind Delbin struck him on the head with the hilt of a dagger and sent the kender to the floor, his thoughts reeling. Delbin tried to rise, but the world went crazy, refusing to settle down. At last, unable to struggle further, the kender collapsed.

Oddly, he did not black out. Instead, Delbin found himself standing by a mountaintop, with the man in gray beside him. They looked out onto a landscape covered in great part by a city. Nethosak, to be exact.

"The road is harsh. I'm sorry about that," murmured the gray man. "But the balance must be maintained. I swore by Lunitari, Solinari, and Nuitari that I would see to it. I have yet to be released from that oath. I will do what I can for Kaz. I promise you that, young Delbin."

"I don't understand," the small figure said, looking at the robed man.

"Neither did Huma of the Lance, but he fulfilled his destiny. This is all about destiny, Young One. Yours and that of the entire minotaur race, who deserve better and worse than they've received these past centuries, Kaz especially. Destiny demands the balance, though."

Delbin understood even less now. He started to open his mouth, but then a roar echoed through the city below. It was a terrible roar, as if some great leviathan had just awakened in a foul mood.

The gray man shook his head. When the roar died down, he smiled sadly and added, "It is almost time, I'd say. Wouldn't you?"

Chapter 11
A Kender Captured

Kaz caught sight of the soldiers as they were carrying Delbin's limp form out of the corridor and into the streets. The high priest wanted Delbin alive and unharmed, which meant that at the most the minotaur's friend was unconscious. Still, he intended the captors to pay for what they had done.

The corridor smelled of fire, smoke, and some other odor that made the minotaur's nostrils twitch. He started after the guards. He had to stop them before they left the shadow of the arena. Anywhere else, and an attack would be too conspicuous. The other minotaurs, busy with their charge, did not notice as he slipped out the entrance after them. Kaz counted only two. A good number. Two he could take with ease.

He was suddenly seized by strong arms that tore the axe from his grip, secured him, and covered his muzzle before he could speak. The minotaurs with the kender did not even notice the swift and silent scuffle behind them. There was no one now who could save Delbin from becoming the high priest's prisoner.

A hard female voice whispered in his ear, "Kaziganthi, you are summoned before your patriarch."

Patriarch?

He had been captured by his own clan? Kaz felt like a fool. Of course they would have been in the audience. Possibly even the patriarch himself.

"Give your word of honor and we shall let you walk. Refuse and we shall be forced to bind you hand and foot and drag you. We haven't much time, so you'd better make up your mind fast."

She meant what she said, especially about dragging Kaz. The clan of Orilg did not make empty threats. Kaz quickly nodded.

The minotaurs relaxed their grips, though at least one blade grazed his back. Kaz glanced around him. The others were all young, strong, and lean. He could have taken two, possibly three captors, but the clan had surrounded him with six, which was something of an honor, he supposed.

Able to speak again, Kaz said, "Listen to me! There is a kender with those two! It's important that we rescue him! The high priest must not get his hands on that—"

"We've orders concerning only you, Kaziganthi. The patriarch saw you flee the arena and desires to speak to you."

"The kender is my—"

"Your word's been given. Resist and we'll have to act accordingly, Kaziganthi."

He had no real choice. Kaz glanced at the receding figures. It was already too late. The State Guard had carried

Delbin off into the crowds. It was fortunate that only his clan had so far caught up with Kaz.

I'll get you out, Delbin, he silently promised. I'll teach Jopfer to regret his scheming.

Another thought occurred to him. Ganth and the others. As far as he knew, they were still inside. He turned back to the female. "The others—"

"We've been ordered only to bring you. Now move on before someone notices who you are. If they recognize you, we can't help you."

He almost laughed. He had escaped, only to be captured just outside the circus. Now not only was Delbin lost to him, but so were the others.

"All right, then," Kaz growled. "Let's go see old Dastrun. Maybe it is time I had a few words with him."

For the first time, he managed to disconcert the female. He could tell by her expression. Looking at the others, she commanded, "Keep an eye on him at all times, but make it look casual." To Kaz she added, "Don't fight us, Kaziganthi. We are clan, remember."

"Does Dastrun remember that?"

There was no reply. The female started off, as did the others. It made for a long and sobering march to the clan house.

* * * * *

"So this is how you spread the glory of Clan Orilg," Dastrun commented.

Kaz had always recalled Dastrun as a wiry sort, and in the years since he had last seen the elder minotaur, Dastrun had grown even more wiry, almost emaciated. His fur was nearly white. Yet there was strength in those limbs and voice, despite the signs of old age. He had to admit that the robed figure seated on the chair was very much the image of a clan patriarch. He even might have respected Dastrun despite their differences if only the patriarch had not been chosen for his position by the emperor, possibly at the high priest's urging.

The patriarch was seated on a high-backed throne placed at the top of a short dais. Seated on each side of the huge chamber to which Kaz had been brought were other elders of the clan. Standing along the walls were guards. Kaz and his captors were the only others in the meeting hall. Dastrun was trying keep Kaz's presence a secret as long as was possible. Whether that strategy would succeed, the prisoner could not say.

"No, this is how I try to live," Kaz finally remarked. "This is how I uphold the honor of Orilg."

Dastrun sighed. "The same old Kaz. You were always one who would not bend when it was best to do so. Your sense of honor, your *personal* sense of honor, was always more important than the good of the clan."

Kaz stared at the minotaurs gathered in the chamber. Most of them he recognized as followers of Dastrun. Some, he was pleased to see, were from parts of the clan that would never, ever, accept the elder as a legitimate patriarch. In their eyes, there were some traditions that should not have been flouted.

"All I ask is to be left alone."

"You were left alone."

"Only when it was convenient, Dastrun. Only when it was convenient."

The patriarch waved the matter away. "I came to the arena to see if you would at least die with your honor intact. You could not even do that. When I saw that you intended to flee, I commanded Fliara to keep watch for you. I knew she would understand your thinking."

"Fliara?" Kaz froze, then slowly turned to study the younger female. "Fliara?"

Her acknowledgment was formal, nothing more. "Brother."

"Fliara." She was his youngest sibling and had been little more than a baby when he had last seen her. Fliara had often tagged along behind him, watching with great interest what her eldest brother did. Now she seemed not to care. "Why didn't you say anything to me?"

"The patriarch had commanded me not to reveal myself

unless you recognized me." If she felt any emotion, it was well concealed by her indifferent expression. "You did not."

She looked away as she finished speaking.

"Our father was back there."

Her eyes darted to Dastrun, then to Kaz. With clipped words, Fliara quietly said, "I know."

"Fliara understands that her duty to the clan outweighs all else. Family is important, as Sargas teaches, but it must not be forgotten that the clan is the greatest of our families. One individual may be lost, but the integrity of the clan must be maintained. Without it, all that has been built since Orilg became patriarch will collapse."

Kaz found himself wondering if Dastrun knew about the clan-in-the-making Kaziganthi. What would the elder say about that?

"I've striven to keep Orilg strong. You've not been here much the past decade." The tone was almost accusatory. "Things have changed, especially in the past couple of years. Attitudes have changed. The way things are done has changed. To survive and prosper, Orilg has had to make some changes, too."

"Yes, I've noticed," Kaz commented, purposely ignoring the look of disapproval on Dastrun's features. One simply did not interrupt the patriarch. It just was not done. "Some traditions change as well, things like how the young are trained, what honor means, and how those who rule are chosen."

"I could have turned you directly over to the State Guard," the patriarch pointed out, still angry at being interrupted. "It is what my duty to the glorious minotaur empire demands."

"Should we leave now, then? Since I'm going to be handed over to them when you're done trying to excuse yourself, we may as well get going."

Dastrun started to rise. "You impudent—" Then his anger suddenly dissipated, leaving an older, world-weary figure who looked away and sighed deeply in frustration. Kaz actually found himself sympathizing, briefly, with this vulnerable Dastrun behind the mask.

"Tell him what's been decided, Dastrun," said a clan elder on one side of the chamber. Kaz peered curiously at the new speaker, vaguely recognizing the squat, wrinkled visage as a former tutor of his, a sword master. He was still formidable, though lacking one arm.

"I will, I will." Regaining some of his composure, the patriarch eyed Kaz. "There's been some . . . discussion, concerning how best to deal with your presence—"

"Send me home."

"That would not be easy. Kaziganthi, you don't realize just what you've become here. You don't realize that you've become a symbol. You don't realize just how many stories of your . . . recklessness . . . have reached Nethosak. Most of the stories are sheer nonsense, of course . . ."

Kaz snorted, then added, "Of course."

"But such tales grow in credence the more they are repeated. You've done more to disrupt the course of destiny here than the years under the rule of the Dark Lady's warlords."

"I've already heard such words from the high priest, Dastrun. Unless you have an original point, you can forego the rest of your speech."

"Same arrogant little Kaz," snarled one of the other elders. "Never did know his proper place."

Kaz gave the elder a look. "I thought that was one of the driving forces behind our people, the fact that we have dared strive to improve ourselves and achieve greater heights. . . . Of course, that was in the old days."

The elder muttered something about insolence, but there were many others who nodded agreement with Kaz. It was then he saw Dastrun's predicament. Kaz's father had mentioned that Dastrun's position was not a secure one; he was the emperor's designate, not the clan favorite. Perhaps things might have been different had he gained his position by the old ways, but now no one would ever completely trust his wisdom. He ruled because Polik said he should rule.

A puppet pulling the strings of a puppet, thought Kaz.

He suspected that all the strings, be they attached to the emperor, various patriarchs, the military, even the circle, led back to Jopfer.

"Very well," the patriarch grumbled. "When you were sent to the circus, there was some question as to the fairness of your sentence, but Orilg is not influential enough to change the commands of either the emperor or the state priesthood. It was hoped you would fight honorably and prove that any crimes you might or might not have committed were of no consequence. You would have been kept on the rolls of honor, forever a symbol of Orilg greatness."

"How flattering."

"Of course, you couldn't bring yourself to do what was best, could you? I was in the crowd when the chaos began. I left immediately, of course, but left word to keep track of you." The elder minotaur's tone indicated that he suspected the chaos was part of a plan to engineer Kaz's escape. "The warriors of the clan did their best to see that you were brought here rather than be recaptured."

"You seem to have forgotten my father and Hecar, who also are clan members."

Dastrun looked at the other elders. A narrow-muzzled female that Kaz thought might be an older cousin of his nodded. The patriarch turned back to Kaz. "There are others watching for them. Fliara and her group were ordered to watch for you. It's you that causes the most concern to the clan."

Kaz glanced sideways at his sister. She stood stiff and emotionless, a fine example of the sort of warrior that was being reared in the homeland these days. Did she even care about her father? Granted, much of her early upbringing was owed to the teaching prescribed by Warlord Crynus and his ilk, but the years since Kaz's departure had not improved Fliara.

"It is fairly certain now that we will request an amnesty for your father. He will even be given a chance to crew his own vessel again despite his past carelessness." A few elders muttered at the choice of words. Dastrun pretended not to notice them. "Hecar may join him as well."

They would be virtually exiled on the high seas. It would not be the first time the unruly were cast out in such a way. More often than not, they did not return, falling overboard during storms or wasting away, through no choice of their own, on some lonely island.

"And me? The high priest has already offered me a chance to rejoin the cause, to help take us further down the path of ruin." Kaz's words ought to have been considered sacrilegious, but instead he received little more than a weary stare from Dastrun and concerned expressions from the others. Even Fliara was looking at him oddly. "My apologies. I meant the emperor, of course. I wouldn't dare suggest that he followed the priesthood's commands and not the other way around."

It took the patriarch a while to collect himself enough to continue. "I've been petitioned by some within the clan to act on your behalf. There is a chance to save you, and it's a path I suggest you accept. It's believed that the emperor will permit it. There is a ship, an explorer under the banner of Orilg, sailing to the continent east of here."

"Another continent?" Now and then, there were rumors of another continent, and, despite his reluctance, Kaz's curiosity was piqued.

Observing Kaz's reaction, Dastrun pressed on. "Yes, another continent. An opportunity to expand even further. We've already made some inroads there, Boy. The few inhabitants discovered there so far have been . . . of no consequence. However, we've explored only a little into the interior. There's room for adventure and opportunity."

Sail to the other land and become one of those who pioneered the way for the rest of the people. It was exciting, an offer Kaz would have accepted gladly under other circumstances. But several concerns held him back. One was that he could never leave Helati and the children behind. Another was that he knew, despite whatever Dastrun and the others believed, that Polik and Jopfer would not agree to the offer . . . or they would send Kaz off, only to have him suffer an 'accident' once he was far from home.

Kaz wondered if Dastrun himself made the offer in

good faith or was aware of what would likely happen.

"A tempting offer," Kaz finally commented, still pondering. Whatever happened to him, Kaz refused to let others assuage their guilt by sending him somewhere far away where his fate could not be tied to them and their tainted sense of honor. "But you might as well turn me back over to the circus if that's the best you can do."

"Don't be a fool, Kaziganthi!" warned Dastrun. He rose from his chair. "We offer you a chance not only to maintain your own honor, but to increase your standing! At the very least, the honor of the clan should mean something to—"

"You're the fool, Dastrun, if you expect us to believe that honor is still of such import that we're willing to sacrifice one of our own like this!"

Kaz and the others looked to the source of the voice. Somehow, Ganth had found his way from the circus and slipped into the audience chamber. There was no sign of Hecar, but at least Kaz's father was safe.

"You are not a part of this meeting, Ganth!" snarled the patriarch. "You'll leave now!"

"Ganthirogani has as much right to speak as any of us!" pointed out an elder. "More than some, even."

The consensus of the majority of the elders was the same. Dastrun might be patriarch, but even he could not argue against certain precedents. One of the foundations of clan life was that each minotaur was allowed to voice his opinion, and those who achieved the age and status of Kaz's father were entitled to speak during matters of council. The race considered itself the most democratic of all the peoples of Ansalon.

"Aye, it's good to see that some haven't forgotten that." Ganth marched forward until he stood next to Kaz. He glanced briefly at his daughter, who looked away in what might have been embarrassment, then at his son. In a low voice, he told Kaz, "I can say only that Hecar waits outside. More'll have to wait until we get you out of this."

To the others, Ganth addressed these words, "I've missed a few years among my kin and clan, I'll be the first to admit, but there are some things that shouldn't have changed completely in that time. We're minotaurs, the greatest race ever to walk Krynn, greater than the ancient ogres from whom we're descended. Only dragons could be considered superior, and they've left this world to us now."

Kaz watched as his father appealed to the vanity of the race. To him, the words were almost a jest, but to the others, who had never lived outside their small world, they were true and monumental.

"What's happened now, though?" the older minotaur asked, giving a theatrical performance that Kaz would not have expected his mariner father capable of delivering, but he had the crowd. "We've become willing to set aside our personal honor, to set aside the clan and our esteemed ancestors, including great Orilg, who once fought a dozen ogres to save his children. Our ancestors watch us now, Dastrun, and what do they see? That's the question you should all ask yourselves. Are we being true to our ancestors? Are we being true to the honor of Orilg?"

He had most of them agreeing with him, except for Dastrun, of course. The patriarch snorted; then, seating himself again, he countered, "Pretty words, Ganth, but they say nothing. Are we to presume you speak for our ancestors, most especially great Orilg? More to the point, have you forgotten that we also belong to a larger family? We're the children of Sargas! Even Orilg would give Sargas his due." He shook his head and looked at Ganth as if Kaz's father was a dim-witted child. "The high priest teaches us that sometimes there must be sacrifice for the greater good. That is what we must all remember, even you and your son."

"I know what the Great Horned One's like, Dastrun, which is why I've chosen Kiri-Jolith to be my lord . . . or is such a choice now also forbidden?"

"Ah, yes." Dastrun nodded. "You met them both, didn't you?" He chuckled. "Quite a yarn that was."

The old mariner drew himself up to his full height. He still had the presence to impress most around him. Kaz was proud of his father. "Aye, I've met them both.

Whether you choose to believe that or simply toss it aside as a sea tale, you'd do well to remember one thing: It's honor we've been brought up to believe in more than anything else, even more than our so-called destiny. It's honor that's at the core of our kind, even more than among the humans of the Solamnic knighthood. 'Honor is our blood and our blood is honor.' Recall that? Orilg liked to quote it. It's carved on the outside and inside of the circus and every minor arena throughout the land. It's carved high in the walls of the palace and the headquarters of the Supreme Circle." Ganth crossed his arms and looked up. "Why, it's even carved up there."

Many others looked up, nodding. Even Dastrun could not help glancing in the direction that his rival had indicated.

"Of course," added Ganth, looking at the other minotaurs, "I know it can even be found in the temple itself, of all places. The home of Sargas, they say." He stared at the patriarch. "And you know why it's especially interesting that it's there, Dastrun? Because it's supposed to be a direct quote from your Great Horned One himself. He's supposed to have spoken the words to Istvanius, the first high priest, who we all know was a paragon of virtue and truth. Therefore, the words must be true."

"Your point?" Dastrun demanded. The patriarch seemed to have shrunken in size by a third.

"That even Sargas points out the importance of honor to our kind. So I ask, has the clan of Orilg forsaken honor? Have we forsaken the most important of the teachings? If Orilg cannot survive without compromising its honor, should the clan even continue to exist? Are we worthy of those who came before us, not just Orilg, but Bestet the One-armed, who fought the elves even after one limb had been sliced clean off by a magical sword? Or Tariki? She sailed her burning vessel into the enemy after commanding the remnants of her crew to abandon it! Two enemy ships caught fire and more scattered before they could finish sinking her. Just two examples of what Orilg has produced." Ganth looked at his own son. "And whatever you might think of Kaz, this one has led a few momentous victories that our ancestors would have been proud of."

Dastrun might be patriarch of the clan, but he was isolated in his opinions. Ganth's words touched the very fiber of every minotaur gathered there. Even Fliara nodded.

"Ganth speaks truth!"

"It's a matter of our honor! We cannot abandon Kaziganthi!"

"What of the emperor? What of the high priest?"

"What of them? This is for the honor of the clan!"

Words went back and forth as the elders debated. Ganth nodded confidently to his son. Now it seemed that Polik's influence was as weak as his claim to the throne.

Seeing his support crumble, Dastrun abruptly acted. Standing, he called for order. At first no one heeded him, then Dastrun seized a staff and began to pound on the floor. "Give me order! I command it!"

He still carried enough sway that the others lowered their dissenting voices. Dastrun looked around, seeking sympathetic faces. Kaz doubted he found many. He almost felt sorry for the patriarch.

Drawing himself up, the robed figure spoke. "Points have been made by the esteemed Ganthirogani. His words touched us all, I'm sure." There was assent at this, but no one interrupted. Dastrun took a deep breath and tried to sound imperious. "Long have I labored over the very same issues that he's touched on, trying to weigh what is right and what is most honorable." Now there was renewed muttering. The patriarch quickly went on. "Sargas preaches to us about the utmost importance of honor. It is the cornerstone of our lives. Who are we to argue against the will of the Great Horned One? Was it not he who deemed our ancestors worthy? But wasn't it also their dedication and their sense of honor that made them worthy in the first place?"

"The old boy can still talk when it's to save his hide," Kaz's father whispered to him.

"I've considered further," Dastrun continued, "and I must agree. We would shame the memories of our ancestors if we did not act to preserve a son of Orilg. This will not be simple. I must therefore ask that all of you take a hand in this. The guard will no doubt come to the clan house before long." He turned his gaze to the pair standing before him. "The sooner you are ready to leave, the better. It will be difficult but still possible to help you through the southern gates without anyone noticing. A handful of volunteers will take you to the mountains. From there you may journey anywhere you desire, just as long as you do not return."

"That's preposterous!" called an older female. "What sort of solution is that to the problems confronting Kaziganthi, Dastrun?"

"Do you have a better one . . . any of you?"

None of the other elders did. It was one thing to spirit Kaz and his father away and out of sight of the emperor and Jopfer, but it was another to allow them to stay and openly defy Polik, the priesthood, and the Supreme Circle. Once Kaz was away, the clan could claim no knowledge.

Not that it really mattered. Kaz had no intention of leaving without rescuing Delbin, who was imprisoned only because he had been too loyal. "You don't have to worry about me at all, none of you. Let me go and I absolve the clan of all obligations. I've got only one objective now, and if I happen to survive, I'll be leaving here. If I don't survive, you're welcome to condemn me for my dishonorable ways. I could care less at this point."

Ganth stood closer to his son. "The same goes for me."

Fliara gasped, actually raising a hand in feeble protest. Ganth turned and gave her a smile. She closed her mouth and again pretended indifference. Ganth's smile grew broader.

"Exactly what are you saying, Kaz?" asked the female elder. "Are you suggesting we take no action? Simply let you go without knowing what's to befall you?"

"Oh, I could tell you what I've got planned, but you wouldn't want to hear about it, trust me."

She was about to differ with him when Dastrun quickly interjected, "No. We wouldn't. You can spare us such incriminating details. You wish us to do nothing then? No matter what happens, the clan is not required to defend you, or your actions?"

Kaz surveyed the assembled elders. "I never intended to draw Orilg into my activities. I came only to claim a friend, another member of this august clan, who was missing. Now I find I have to go claim another friend, an innocent who doesn't deserve what's happening to him. Clan Orilg may wash its hands clean of me. I swear this by Orilg himself and all my ancestors."

"What do you plan to do?" the female elder asked.

"It doesn't matter," the patriarch said curtly. Then Dastrun cleared his throat. "Very well, Kaziganthi. By your own words shall this be decided. The clan will do nothing to hinder you, but neither will it assist your mad— your activities."

There were voices of protest, but Kaz himself signaled for silence.

The patriarch nodded. "No word shall be given to the guard concerning your whereabouts. That holds true for your father and your friend, too. You'll be taken to a place where you may hide until dark." Dastrun gave the pair a magnanimous expression. "Then you are on your own, just as you've requested. Should you be captured or killed, we will abide by your decision and make no claim for you."

"You are very gracious," Ganth said with more than a little sarcasm.

Ignoring him, Dastrun faced the elders. "Is there anyone here who'll dispute the agreement made between myself as clan leader and this renegade warrior?"

No one could dispute the decision since Kaz himself had made the proposition. No one, that is, except one young warrior. "Patriarch, I must ask that I be included with these two. I make that request through blood rights."

Both Kaz and his father looked with astonishment at Fliara.

"Lass, think what you're saying! This is our doing and ours alone!"

She raised her chin in a manner reminiscent of both her

brother and her father. "I will do no less than my own kin. I am as honor-bound as either of you."

"Talk sense to her, Kaz!"

"Listen to our father, Fliara. If I could, I'd make even him stay, but he's already involved and there's no way to extricate him from this. You don't have to follow us. If we survive . . . and I say 'if' . . . we will never return to this land again."

"I have already considered that." She straightened. "I stand firm on my request."

"And your request is granted," Dastrun announced before anyone could volunteer an opinion. "Your spirit is a credit to the clan."

"The same clan that'll now ignore her if she falls prisoner to the guard!" Ganth quietly growled. "Do something, Kaz! I'm bereft of any ideas. What's got into that girl?"

"Evidently she's one of yours after all, Father."

Fliara moved to join them, keeping her eyes on the patriarch. Dastrun looked around as if to see if anyone else was going to defect. When he saw that was not the case, he peered down at the trio. "By will of the clan, I commend you and send you on your way. Your path diverges from ours now, but your duty to honor remains strong. Oaths have been sworn and must be upheld."

"Don't put him in a terrible bind with the emperor is what he's saying," whispered Ganth. He snorted. "And he talks of honor and duty."

Dastrun raised a hand, pointing at the door. "Go now. May Sargas and the spirit of Orilg guide you. I deem this audience at an end."

That was it. The assembled elders rose and began to depart. Clan Orilg had always been known for its efficiency and order.

"Come with me," Fliara said. Ganth hesitated, still glaring at the patriarch, but Kaz shook his head and steered his father toward the entrance.

Kaz, while not happy, was at least relieved. The clan would leave him alone for now. Its intervention would have been more hindrance than help, especially with Dastrun in command.

"Why'd you do it, lass?" Ganth was asking Fliara. "You needn't have concerned yourself with our folly. It's not been your way, ever."

Kaz's sister looked from father to brother, then shifted her gaze ahead again. "No, it's not. You didn't recognize me at all, did you, Kaz?"

The question caught him by surprise. He looked at his younger sister. Up close, he could see some family resemblance, but, it was true, she was virtually a stranger to him.

"No, I didn't recognize you. It's been years, though."

"But you didn't know me."

"I just said that."

Fliara looked at both of them. "That's my reason."

She would say no more. Kaz looked to his father for clarification, but Ganth merely shrugged. He understood no better than his son.

They came to the chamber where Hecar waited. Helati's brother was pleased to see them. He had been expecting the worst. "They wouldn't let me move from this chamber," Hecar told them. "There were guards at the door."

"Dastrun's thorough, I'll give him that," Ganth noted.

"What happened in there, Kaz? Are we to be returned to the circus for the emperor's amusement?"

"No, Hecar, we're being allowed to go on our way. In return, we won't involve the clan in our doings and it'll pretend it knew nothing of our whereabouts."

"Very kind. Hmmph. Better than I'd have expected of old Dastrun. Who's this? Someone to see us out into the street?"

"I'm coming with you, Hecariverani."

Hecar peered at her. "Hey, I know you."

"It's my daughter, Fliara. You saw her a couple of times when Kyri brought her around."

"That little—" He ceased when he saw her bristle. Fliara was every inch a warrior, sleek and muscled. There was nothing diminutive about her now. "She's turned into a fine fighter, I can see now, a credit to you and your mate, Ganth."

Ganth chuckled. "Well and quickly spoken, Hecar. She's every bit as headstrong as the rest, which is why she's one of us now. The foolish female just abandoned the clan to help us."

"Better to follow you than the clan these days," Hecar returned. "I learned that a long time ago." He thrust out a hand to Fliara. "You're welcome to join, only you might change your mind. Your brother and father have a habit of getting into the worst of situations."

"And whose fault was it this time?" Kaz pointed out.

"What is it with Jopfer?" Ganth asked his daughter, wisely changing the subject. "Why did he choose to go from the service of the circle to the state priesthood . . . and how was he selected to replace the former high priest? I've never heard of someone other than a cleric rising to that position."

"It was abrupt," Fliara answered. "The old cleric was still going strong, but then one day he suddenly announced he was searching for a successor." Her eyes narrowed. Kaz and Hecar were listening intently. "The priesthood had been adamant about supporting the warlords, and their position was weaker after the war because of it. I think the old high priest decided to quit. The circle was different. There were a lot of new members. Jopfer was one of the new generation, one with vitality, and he didn't have any connection to the Dark Queen's minions. That was important to gain people's trust. He grew very popular very quickly."

"I'm beginning to smell a deal between interested parties," Ganth grumbled.

Kaz agreed. "Looks like either the circle offered Jopfer as a replacement or the high priest preferred him as a way of keeping the sons of Sargas from falling further from grace in the eyes of the people." He shook his head. "Nothing sounds quite right. We must be missing something. Even if the clerics had lost their standing, why accept a minion of the circle as their master?"

"Jopfer's no minion of the circle," Kaz's sister offered. "In fact, they seem afraid of him now. He took to the role of high priest as if born to it. He's not only brought the state priesthood to the forefront again, but eclipsed his predecessor."

"Things make even less sense, then."

They were interrupted by the sounds of armed warriors behind them. Some of the group who had accompanied Fliara at the circus waited just beyond the chamber. One of them stepped forward and curtly pointed.

"I think, my children, that we're being asked to leave this place."

The warrior in the lead responded, "The patriarch has found a house where you'll be safe until tonight. He feels you should go there as soon as possible. We've been sent to escort you."

"What then?" asked Hecar.

"I'm going after Delbin. He freed us in the circus. It's because of me he's here in the first place, and I owe it to the kender to get him out."

"Get him out of where? Who's got him? The guard?"

"No, I'd say the high priest." When he saw Fliara start, Kaz reassured her, "You owe no obligation to us. I'd even make Father stay behind if I thought I could convince him to do so."

She gave him a look that was reminiscent of one Kaz himself had been known to give people in certain situations. "And you think I could do any less?"

Ganth sighed. "What sort of children did I raise?"

"The high priest," Hecar mumbled. "We'll be assaulting the temple itself . . ."

"Probably. I can't think of anywhere else they would keep him. There are supposed to be cells below the main building."

"The temple . . ." Helati's brother grunted. "All right, then. How do you expect to gain entrance to that place? We can't just walk in, can we?"

Kaz lowered his voice, making certain that the warriors impatiently waiting by the door could not hear him. "No, but there is someone else who can."

"And who's this? A cleric?"

Kaz turned away from him without answering, and said to the guards, "We expect our weapons back before we go."

Honor's Face and the other weapons were brought forth. The leader said, "We'll give them back to you at the safe house."

"That'll do." Kaz looked at the others. Hecar was still waiting for an answer. Kaz smiled grimly. "You haven't figured out who has the key to the temple? I'll give you a guess. He's not a cleric."

"Lad, you're not talking about—"

Kaz nodded to them. "Yes, Captain Scurn. He is no doubt looking for us even now. I think we should help him find us."

Chapter 12
A Traitor in the Midst

Helati looked the children over one more time before settling
down. She could not sleep, not just yet, so she spent the
time in quiet contemplation of what she and Kaz had
expected to do with their lives over the next few years.
They wished for more children and had intended to
expand their dwelling accordingly. However, the growth
of the settlement was going to force them to rearrange
some of their plans. Like it or not, Kaz was going to have
clan responsibilities.

Helati was not so put out by that. If anyone deserved
such an honor, it was her mate. Had he not fought well in

the war, faced mages and monsters, and earned the praise of other races, the last the hardest thing for any minotaur to attain? Clan Kaziganthi had a good ring to it, though it would no doubt be shortened to Kaz, as her mate expected.

Her reverie was disrupted by a slight sound, a movement outside. It might have been only an animal, but Helati doubted that. Like Kaz, she had come to sense the difference between various intruders. This seemed more the two-footed kind.

Easing the dagger from her belt sheath, Helati pinpointed the location. Even in her home she always wore a blade, a notion Kaz had introduced to her, for which she was glad. Her other weapons were nearby, but the sound was close to where the children slept. The dagger would be better.

The sound was repeated. A footfall, all right. She poised herself, ready to strike.

"Mistress Helati?" whispered a female voice.

Many of the minotaurs had started calling her by a number of titles such as "lady," "matriarch," and "mistress." Like Kaz, she preferred simply being called by her name, but the others would not hear of it.

"Come in slowly," she called, "with both hands visible."

The other obeyed. A moment later, a female called Keeli entered. Helati recalled her as the mate of Zurgas. The pair had been busy since their recent arrival, already having located a place to build their dwelling. "Forgive me for disturbing you at this time, but I wanted not to be noticed."

Helati lowered the dagger, but did not put it away. "And why is that, Keeli?"

The other female looked around, making certain they were alone. "I had something to tell you, but I was afraid others might be around, others who might be the wrong ones."

"Including your mate?"

"Zurgas knows, but since this is my knowledge, he agreed that it was up to me to tell you. He waits back at our campsite."

Helati did not know whether she was supposed to feel more secure knowing that or not. She was not certain she could trust the newcomer. "Perhaps if you explained what knowledge it is you have. . . ."

Keeli cleared her throat. Her gaze fixed on Helati's suspicious eyes. "I am of the clan of Sumarr. It's not a large clan, but it has links to others. Through those links, I gained a position working as a low-level subordinate for a member of the Supreme Circle. At the time, I was proud of the honor. My work involved seeing to it that his dictates were followed by the State Guard. That was how I met my mate. He occupied a similar position for another member of the circle. We had cause to meet often, though we kept our interest in one another quiet for some time."

"Understandable." Members of the circle were terribly rivalrous and, as such, leery of interaction between their subordinates. "What does this have to do with me?"

Keeli looked down. "I am sorry. Let me move on. Months later, Zurgas and I came to the understanding that we could not love one another and still work for our masters. For our own good, we resigned to seek our futures elsewhere, perhaps in sailing. If either of us remained as a servant to a circle member, the other might be suspected of betraying secrets. You understand what I mean?"

"I do. Go on."

"It was but a short time before I was to leave. I was doing what I could to make certain my master would have no reason to fault my work since I hoped he would still give me a recommendation. I worked late hours that day, trying to organize everything. That was when he came."

Helati said nothing, relieved that the other female had at last gotten to the point. The younger minotaur had begun to remind her, with her long-windedness, of a certain kender named Delbin.

"He was a representative of the high priest. He seemed annoyed to find me there, but dismissed me a moment later as not being worth his interest. I recalled seeing him once or twice before, but only glances. He wore a robe that marked him as a cleric of some ranking. Since it was not entirely uncommon for the high priest and the circle to communicate, I thought nothing of it, but now that I've seen him again, I thought you ought to know."

It took several seconds for the statement to register. Kaz's mate chose her words with care. "Let me see if I understand what you're trying to say. You are talking about a high-ranking cleric who visited the sanctum of your master, one of the Supreme Circle, and then you claim to have seen him again. . . . Do you mean here?"

"Yes! His appearance has changed, but I remember him. I've always been good at recalling faces."

A cleric among the settlers? High-ranking clerics especially did not simply give up their positions and walk away. She could think of only one reason why a cleric would be among her people: to spy for the priesthood.

"You say he's changed his appearance?"

"Aye, Mistress Helati. The hair is shorter and his face did not wear such a beaten, gladiator look to it. Both horns were intact, too—"

Helati stopped her there. She could not believe what she was hearing. "One of the horns is damaged?"

"Broken off. I was afraid to say anything at first, for he stood next to you when we arrived."

Brogan.

"The one who greeted you when you first met me?" she asked Keeli, hoping somehow the other would deny it. "Brogan?"

"That was him. I swear by the sword of Kiri-Jolith."

Brogan a spy? How long had he been among them? He was one of their most trusted. Helati could not believe what she was hearing, and yet . . . there had been times when both she and Kaz had wondered if they were being monitored from Nethosak. The powers were suspicious of anything that threatened their supremacy.

She could not condemn him without hearing his side. It could be that Keeli's memory for faces was not so perfect. It could also be that Keeli herself was the spy. Helati tried not to let paranoia guide her emotions.

"Come with me." Sheathing the dagger, Helati returned to the children. With great care, she gathered them up, still slumbering, then turned to Keeli and commanded, "Walk before me. I'll direct you where to go once we're outside."

The younger female did not understand, but obeyed. They abandoned Helati's dwelling, at which point she ordered Keeli to turn right. The dwelling they soon reached belonged to another mated pair raising a child of their own. The mother was a friend of Helati's, named Ayasha. Ayasha could be trusted. She and Helati had been friends once, long ago in the homeland. It had been one of Helati's greatest pleasures to greet Ayasha when she and her family had arrived in the settlement.

She left the twins with Ayasha, her explanation a simple one, then briefly returned to her own dwelling. Moments later, sword dangling at her side, she journeyed to the home of Brogan. Keeli followed her halfway there, but Helati decided it was best if she went the rest of the distance alone. If, for some reason, the accusations were not true . . . or even if they were . . . she did not want Brogan knowing who had informed on him.

Keeli protested. "You should not be alone with him."

Helati touched the hilt of her sword. "Don't worry about me. You return to your mate until I call for you."

Still protesting, the younger female departed. Helati did not mention that she hoped Brogan was innocent. In any case, it would be easier to talk to him alone.

The light from a small, crude fireplace burned in Brogan's modest dwelling. He lived alone, far from most of the others. Helati glanced about, studying the lay of the land. Neither she nor Kaz were overly familiar with the one-horned minotaur's home, for Brogan generally visited them.

Brogan a spy? The distance of his home from the main settlement and his constant interest in what Kaz was doing spoke against him, but could easily be excused for other, more mundane reasons. Helati felt rather foolish about accusing him, but could certainly not ignore Keeli's words.

She remembered that Brogan had tried to form an armed force to accompany Kaz to Nethosak. Had that also been a ploy of some sort?

Enough paranoia! she scolded herself. Time to be a warrior.

It was tempting to peer through a window, but Helati boldly knocked on the dwelling's crude wooden door.

"Who's there? Who is it?"

"It's me, Brogan. Helati."

"Helati?" After some noise, the door swung open. The one-horned minotaur blinked, then smiled. "Some news of Kaz, I hope?"

"Possibly." She had not given any thought to what to say to him. Accuse him outright? "May I come in?"

"Of course! Enter!"

As she walked through the doorway, Helati noticed the mark of Kaz on the dwelling. Her insides twisted. If Brogan was innocent, what she had to say would greatly insult his honor. Yet if he was guilty, the mark of Kaz was of great insult to her and her family, a mockery of the friendship they had extended to Brogan.

There were few furnishings in the minotaur's home: a table, two stools, and a box in which personal effects no doubt were stored. Brogan apparently slept on a bedroll to one side of the single room. The fireplace was very small, almost as if an afterthought. A few items were scattered about, but overall the place seemed orderly. A battle-axe hung on a wall near the bedroll. The table was situated so that if Brogan sat down, he could reach the handle with little effort.

In fact, Brogan led her to the table and offered her a seat. Helati shook her head. "I won't be staying long. Just a few minutes at best."

He frowned. "Is something wrong? Have you heard some bad news?"

"I'm not certain." She did not know how to proceed. Had Kaz been here, Helati suspected he simply would have pushed ahead. She must do the same.

"I'm worried that Kaz might be in danger, that he might

also have been captured and imprisoned along with my brother."

"Well, as you indicated not long ago, Kaz hasn't been gone all that long. He might even be on his way back by now."

"Maybe. What makes me fear that Kaz is a prisoner are some rumors." She hesitated for effect. "I've heard there might be spies among us, Brogan."

"Spies?" He sounded genuinely concerned. "Here? Who?"

"There may be more than one, but I've heard that there's at least one who might be acting as a servant of the high priest himself." She watched him for some sign of guilt. So far, he seemed perfectly at ease.

"The high priest, eh?" He rubbed his muzzle and turned toward the fire, staring into it. The battle-axe was only a step away, but Brogan made no move toward it. "I don't like the sound of it. The high priest, he's a deadly sort. Not a gladiator. More like a serpent. That's what he always reminded me of."

"Then you've seen him . . . often?"

"Now and then." The male squatted by the fire and, seizing a loose stick, prodded the fire into greater life. "From a distance."

"Do you have any idea who might be the spy, Brogan?"

The question startled him more than it should have. Helati saw that. Her hand shifted slowly, almost casually, to the hilt of her sword.

"I used to be one," he replied, still stirring the fire.

The outright admission was so unexpected that Helati froze where she stood, not quite certain how to continue. Her grip tightened on the sword. "You're the spy, then?"

He looked up at her. "No, I said I used to be one. When I first came here, I was a spy for the high priest. I sent messages through various means back to Nethosak. The past four months, though, I've been sending misleading messages."

"Why would you do that? More to the point, why should I believe you?"

Brogan finished tending the fire and rose. "When I came here, I was a fairly high-ranking cleric. That's why they trusted me to send them accurate intelligence about this settlement and its growth. His Holiness does not like this place. Everyone and everything here defies his preaching. I was ordered to assess the situation and report on it. I did so for the first several months."

"What changed your mind?" Helati found herself wanting to believe that Brogan was a friend, not an enemy. But he might simply be an excellent liar.

The one-horned minotaur looked her in the eye. "Kaz. You. The lives I saw around me. There's more life, more satisfaction here than in all the homeland. Oh, everyone works frantically to fulfill our 'destiny,' but we are losing our individuality. We are becoming the servants of the dream, not the masters we were supposed to be." Brogan shook his head. "Honor has become like a sword without a warrior to wield it. We're heading in the same direction as the ancient ogres. Even if we do conquer the world, we will eventually fall. Without honor, without vitality and respect for ourselves, we're lost."

Helati's grip on the hilt loosened. Brogan sounded honest, but could she believe him? "Pretty words. I'd like to believe that being here has somehow converted you, but I've got no proof, Brogan. Can you tell me anything that'll make me more willing to accept your words?"

"No. Nothing. My words are all I've got. I saw in Kaz the embodiment of what we should be. I decided to follow his example. To be a true minotaur warrior, I could do no less."

More words, but still no proof. She had to make a decision. "Brogan, what you've said sounds good, but I can't accept words alone. I think you should come with me. I think some of the others need to hear what you've said."

"I understand that, but could I ask you a question?"

"Ask."

"Who told you about me?"

"I just found out, that's all."

"It was the two newcomers, wasn't it? They're the only

source of recent news. I wondered about them. I thought the female looked familiar—" His eyes brightened. "She worked for the priesthood . . . no . . . the circle!" He grinned. "Of course, that amounts to the same thing these days. At least three members of the circle are under the thumb of Jopfer, especially his old mentor! Hah! To think that old war dog thought he was being handed the state priesthood when they offered to make his aide high priest in return for concessions! He thought Jopfer would stay his servant, but it's turned around on him!"

Helati was able to follow only some of what he said, but it was enough to make her hair stand straight. A servant of the circle was high priest? Jopfer? That name sounded familiar. She was almost certain he was an old friend of her brother.

"Well, we can discuss that later," Brogan concluded. He looked around. "The fire will burn down without any trouble, and I've nothing else to take care of. I suppose we can leave immediately, then. I won't bother with taking my axe, of course."

"All right, you walk in front of me."

He shifted around. "You should unsheathe your sword, just in case. I would."

Granting his point, Helati pulled her sword free and pointed it at his back. "Let's go."

"Where are we going?"

"Village center." The center was not far from her own dwelling, and it was where most of the minotaurs gathered to talk.

"Good. I'd prefer somewhere more crowded for the time being."

She did not ask what he meant by that. As they started out the door, however, Helati suddenly recalled something. If Brogan was a cleric, then by rights he had abilities that could make her sword useless. She had seen clerics, not only those of Sargas, who could stop a foe in their tracks with but a glance. It was like magic, and yet not. So far, though, Brogan had made no false moves.

They stepped out into the darkness, the one-horned male

scanning the area as he walked. Outside, he seemed a little on edge. That, in turn, made Helati more attentive. Did Brogan have allies? She hadn't considered that possibility.

Brogan took a few more steps, then paused. Helati readied herself, expecting him to turn and attack suddenly, but the other minotaur simply coughed and then continued ahead.

Helati took a step after him.

Suddenly the cleric turned and roared, "Get down!"

For some reason, Helati obeyed. As she did, a whistling sound caught her attention. She looked up from where she had dropped and saw Brogan, an arrow sticking out of his shoulder. He grunted, dropping to his knees.

A second arrow struck the earth just beyond her head. Then, figures, shadows with raised weapons, began to emerge from the foliage. She counted two, then a third.

"Helati!" hissed Brogan. "If you've got a dagger, I could use it, please!"

She would have been glad to oblige him, but the first of the three was almost upon her. Helati barely had time to rise before an axe blade swung past her face. Backing away, she slashed with her own weapon, but her attacker moved aside.

The second attacker raced past her. Brogan was the intended target. Helati reached for the blade on her belt, but found herself too harried to toss it to her companion. The third figure had joined the fray, and both it and the second attacked at once. She was driven back, effectively separated from Brogan.

Darkness had prevented her from immediately identifying her assailants, only that one was male and the other female. It was not until the female missed with her sword and uttered a curse that Helati recognized her.

It was Keeli. The other minotaurs Helati could not identify.

Why were they trying to kill Brogan? Did they know of his defection? It was the only reason that made sense.

"Surrender and we'll take you to your mate!" offered Keeli in a snide tone.

"I don't think so. I . . . just . . . don't trust you for some reason, Keeli."

The other female laughed, then lunged. Helati dodged, but was thrown into the path of the minotaur wielding an axe, which was probably what Keeli had planned. The axe came down, barely missing her foot. She swung her sword and, more out of luck than skill, grazed the axe-wielder's arm. He quickly pulled back.

"I thought you were supposed to be good," Keeli said mockingly. "They said that Kaz himself trained you. Maybe he's not as good as they say. Maybe he won't last that long in the circus."

She was trying to goad Helati. The thought that Kaz might be facing death in the circus threatened to wreck her concentration.

What was happening to Brogan, she could not say. Neither he nor the third attacker were within sight.

Now the axe-wielder returned to the fray, but his swing was a little off. The second swing was not as shaky, but he left a bigger opening. Leaping away from Keeli, Helati thrust at the male's upper leg, near the muscle.

The blade cut deeply. The assassin did not scream, but fell to one knee. His axe he kept gripped in one hand, but he was badly wounded. Helati backed away, focusing on Keeli.

Blade clashed against blade. Keeli was good, but her moves were traditional, the type taught for generation after generation by instructors. Against most opponents, she would have been almost unbeatable, but Kaz, though more proficient with an axe, knew sword tricks that were outside all the usual rules.

Helati let herself be pushed back. She sensed Keeli's growing confidence that Kaz's mate was about to fall. Twice the assassin struck, and each time Helati yielded a little more.

When next her opponent attacked, Helati brought her blade under and around. Keeli tried to counter, but Helati instantly withdrew her sword, causing the former to overreach herself. Kaz's mate immediately lunged, making utmost use of the opening. She hoped only to wound Keeli, but the younger female twisted wildly in an attempt to sidestep the blade.

Her maneuver had just the opposite effect. Keeli's sword missed Helati's hand by a scant half inch. The force with which Keeli swung her blade brought her forward more than she had anticipated. The tip of Helati's sword sank deep into the other minotaur's chest.

Gasping, Keeli slumped forward. Helati barely had time to pull her sword free before her adversary fell to the ground. Keeli's life had already seeped away.

Helati did not waste time dwelling on her triumph. She eyed the wounded male, but he was clearly no threat. Turning her gaze to the side, she searched for Brogan.

She spotted him standing over Zurgas, the latter crumpled to the ground. The cleric was breathing heavily, holding his wounded shoulder. Helati took a closer look at the dead minotaur. The shaft of an arrow rose from Zurgas's throat. Somehow, Brogan had turned the arrow into a makeshift dagger. It was a reminder of just how skilled he was.

A scuffling sound reminded her of the third assassin. He was trying to drag himself into a position where he could either throw or swing his axe.

"I suggest you drop that before I kill you," she informed him.

"Kill me, then," he grunted in a familiar voice.

"No, she won't kill you. Not yet." Brogan walked up to the pair, gripping the wound in his shoulder. "Not until I've finished with you."

The assassin cringed. Helati had to keep herself from shaking.

"Keep away from me! I have the high priest's favor! You've betrayed your master!"

"The high priest isn't here," Brogan pointed out. "And if you doubt that I still have the power granted by Sargas, then I can think of a dozen fascinating ways in which to resolve those doubts."

The prisoner lowered the axe. He glanced from Brogan

to Helati. "I yield to you! Not to him! I give my bond to you! I swear!"

"And how can she tell if you're a warrior of your word? You hunt us from the darkness, giving no warning, no challenge. That is not the way of honor, is it?"

All Brogan did was talk, yet each fierce word seemed to pierce the prisoner like the tip of a blade.

"I swear!"

Looking at Helati again, Brogan asked, "Do you accept his bond?"

She did by nodding. Brogan nodded back, then asked, "Will you allow me to question this one in your name?"

"I gave her my bond. I did not give it to you!"

"But I may act for her, if she desires."

Twisting around, the prisoner pleaded, "Mistress Helati! I've lived here for more than six months, acting as agent of the high priest, especially when he became suspicious of this one's information. I am Yestral."

Yestral. The name was familiar. "I know you. You helped build the storage house."

"Aye. My orders were to watch and report all. Then, when Keeli and her mate arrived, she informed me that the high priest wanted Brogan eliminated for his betrayal. Since your mate was known to be riding toward Nethosak, where it was assumed he would be captured or killed, she also commanded your execution. Keeli said she'd bring the pair of you together. Zurgas and I were to follow and await our chance. She would join us if able. I obeyed, but it wasn't to my liking."

"How many others?" asked Brogan. "How many other agents does His Holiness have here?"

"None! I swear!" Yestral's fear of the one-horned minotaur was palpable. "Mistress Helati! I'm your prisoner, not his!"

"All right, but you'll answer all questions when I ask them. Is that understood?"

"I swear by the horns of Sargas."

They were interrupted by the arrival of three other minotaurs. Helati tensed, then saw they were ones she was certain she could trust.

"You see?" said the foremost, a dark-furred, bulky male with wide eyes who acted as smith for the settlement. "I told you I heard weapon play."

The other two nodded. One of them looked at Helati. "Are you all right, Mistress?"

"I am, but Brogan is wounded."

He waved off assistance. "It'll heal right enough. Someone should take care of this one, though, Mistress Helati. We also need to dispose of these two carrion."

"Agreed." She pointed at one of the newcomers. "You. Get some help to drag these two back to the main part of the settlement. I want this one bound and locked up in the storage house."

They moved to obey. Brogan joined Helati.

"What of me?"

"I'll take a chance on you, but you have to tell me what you did that made him fear you so."

He smiled ruefully. "I've got something of a reputation. Much of it is exaggerated, but . . . some of it isn't." His tone darkened. "I don't make excuses for that. I'll tell you anything you want to know about my past, but I ask that you leave that for tomorrow. I think I'm going to collapse soon if I don't tend to this shoulder."

Helati had almost forgotten about his wound. "Let me help you."

"I can minister to it myself. You have enough to concern yourself with. Get some sleep, Mistress." He nodded farewell, then walked toward his dwelling.

"One more question," she suddenly called.

"What?"

"You seemed to know that something was going to happen. How did you?"

He looked somewhat guilty. "It seemed like the sort of ambush I might've planned once."

She made no attempt to stop him when he turned away. Perhaps there was reason to be suspicious of him, but Helati doubted that Brogan was lying.

What about Kaz? Yestral's words haunted her. Kaz had

ridden into a trap, after all. They knew he would ride to Nethosak and try to rescue her brother. What had happened to him?

I have to go rescue him, Helati thought. I have to go after him before it's too late . . . but what about the children?

Brogan had offered to organize an armed force. She knew that if she asked for aid, he and most of the others would offer themselves, but to take so many into what certainly had to be the maw of danger . . .

I have to go alone. There's no way around it. Ayasha will have to tend the children. She loves them as if they were her own.

She shivered, thinking about that. It was fortunate that her friend cared for the twins so much. It was all too likely that if Helati did not return from Nethosak, Ayasha might find herself acting as mother to the young pair for the rest of her life.

* * * * *

Delbin looked around the chamber. The chains holding him against the wall had so far defied his supreme lock-picking skills, which really impressed him. That left him with only sleep or staring at the wall, but he was too curious to sleep. Why did a minotaur cleric desire his presence? Maybe he had never seen a kender before and was just curious. More likely, the bad minotaurs wanted to use him against Kaz. Delbin hoped someone would come by soon before things got too boring. So far, the only visitor to his chamber had been a guard who had inspected his head for injuries.

His head still throbbed, but not nearly as much as earlier. At least now Delbin could see clearly, not that there was much to see in the room. It was nicer than he would have expected from a prison cell. The place was clean and orderly. There was even a bed to one side, though he certainly had no way to reach it at the moment. A table and two chairs stood not far from the bed, also out of his reach. The room was dim at the moment because the only light source came from a pair of torches in the hall beyond his cell door. But Delbin's night vision remained exceptional.

With nothing else to do, he occupied his thoughts with the memories of the dream he had experienced just before blacking out. The man in gray again. The kender wondered why he had dreamt of the strange figure yet another time. True, the dream had been interesting, even entertaining at times, but why the gray man? Why had he not dreamt of being rescued by Kaz instead?

It did not matter. What mattered was that the gray man had reassured him, saying there was still hope. Hope for what, Delbin could not say. What the gray man had said after that was a hazy memory, but the kender had no difficulty keeping his spirits up. Already he began wondering if, by using the pick he had secreted in his hand, he might be able to unlock the fascinating mechanism that kept the manacles sealed. . . .

A murmur from the hall distracted him. It was not one of the guards, but rather what sounded like a child shuffling down the outside corridor.

A moment later, a bedraggled-looking head popped up at the door. Actually, it looked more like the upper half of a face that belonged to a gully dwarf. He had seen a few of them running around, cleaning refuse off the streets, but this was the first one he had seen up close.

"Hello, my name's Delbin. What's yours?"

The gully dwarf blinked, then replied, "Galump. Galump is Galump's name. Delbin's a kender."

"Yes, I am. What're you doing down here? Are you a prisoner, too? Did you escape? They certainly have good chains here, so if you know how to unlock them, I'd sure like to know."

It took the raggedy figure some time to digest this before finally answering, "Galump's no prisoner. Galump does what minotaurs say he do."

Delbin recalled the collars he had seen the gully dwarves wearing. He did not think it was nice that the minotaurs made the poor creatures do such tasks and wear such nasty collars.

The gully dwarf suddenly dropped out of sight. Delbin recalled almost too late the short attention spans of these lowly creatures. "Wait, Galump!"

Galump popped back up into sight. He had to hang on to the door to be able to peer inside. "What Delbin want?"

"Can you help me get out of here?"

This seemed to sadden the gully dwarf. "Galump can't do that, no, he can't. If he could, he would help nice human girl, nice girl who mean bull who hits Galump keeps in cell."

Another prisoner? "If you help me, maybe I can help her. We could all escape together."

Even though all Delbin could see of Galump was the top half of his head, the gully dwarf's fearful reaction was evident. "No! Galump could not do! Disobey the high one and he'll eat us like he eats the others!"

"Eats the others?" People thought it was difficult to keep track of what kender said, but Delbin thought Galump's kind was the most baffling race. "What do you mean? You don't mean he actually *eats* them, because that's highly unlikely. What you probably mean is that he punishes them badly, but don't worry, because if we get the girl—a human girl?—out, then we can go to my friend Kaz and he'll protect us—"

"No!" The gully dwarf dropped out of sight, his disappearance followed a moment later by the sound of light, receding footfalls.

He sure is afraid of the high priest, Delbin thought. He really believes the high priest minotaur will eat him, but minotaurs don't eat other races, as far as I know, even though they're descended from ogres and long, long ago, like my friend Kaz told me, ogres sometimes . . ."

A human girl?

"Now what would a minotaur want with a human girl?" Delbin whispered to the emptiness. "Maybe she's a slave like poor Galump. Maybe she's a princess the high priest is holding hostage." Delbin cared very little for this high priest. He was not a nice minotaur, not if he was making gully dwarves and little human girls into slaves.

"Well, I'll just have to save her, and Galump . . . and all the other gully dwarves and prisoners the high priest has and deliver them to Kaz. He'll know what to do. He will."

With renewed gusto he went to work on the lock. Normally kender enjoyed the challenge of a good lock, but this time Delbin was impatient. He had to get going. He had to rescue this princess. She was probably a shy, helpless young lass who had never been outside in the real world, not like him. Maybe she would reward Kaz and him for rescuing her by showing them her kingdom.

Orderly footfalls in the corridor caused him to quickly hide the pick. The newcomers drew nearer and nearer until they finally paused before his cell. He made out two guards and one figure clad in the robes of the priesthood.

One of the guards opened the door. Both entered, to be followed by the most sinister minotaur Delbin had ever seen. The kender actually felt a twinge of fear, something rarely experienced by any of his kind.

"I am Jopfer, High Priest of the Temple of Sargas, the Soul of the State. I would like to speak to you about your friend Kaziganthi." He leaned forward and stared into the kender's eyes. "And you will answer me as I desire. Do you understand?"

The fear grew stronger . . . and the simple fact that it did frightened the kender more than the fear itself.

Chapter 13
The Red Dragon

Scurn was in a foul mood. Not only had he been humiliated in the circus again, but he was now out of favor with both the high priest and the Supreme Circle. His only hope was to recapture Kaz and his companions before someone else did, not an easy task, since there were search parties all over Nethosak. Of course, some of the parties had spent more time sparring with each other than searching, which was some consolation. The servants of the Supreme Circle had little love for the servants of the state priesthood, and vice versa. Neither cared for the members of the guard. Members of the guard, in turn, thought little of either group.

Scurn drank from his tankard, finding only the dregs of his ale remaining. Yet another thing to curse about. Still, it was probably good fortune that he had finished his drink. He was due back at guard quarters. Scurn had, through his rank, pulled the authority for yet another search party. This time, he swore, he would find Kaz and see to it that his rival was dragged before Jopfer himself.

As Scurn rose, he mulled over his latest humiliation. Truth to tell, he secretly admired Kaz's combat skills. Kaz had defeated him fairly, but leaving Scurn alive but unconscious was an insult. Kaz should have killed him, as such a combat demanded. By leaving the guard captain alive and relatively unharmed, he had belittled Scurn's skill.

You should have killed me, Kaz, he thought. An honorable death was preferable to a bloodless defeat. Scurn felt diminished in the eyes of his warriors. Only Kaz's capture or death would appease the disfigured captain.

Scurn exited the tavern, his mind on where to search next. He wanted to check back with his old clan. Orilg was hiding something. Even Dastrun, who was supposed to be a supporter of the emperor, had said nothing of value when questioned. Yet Scurn was certain the clan had harbored the fugitives for a short time. He had a witness who claimed to have observed members of Orilg behaving suspiciously outside the circus at the time of Kaz's disappearance.

I should go back and shake old Dastrun by the collar until he talks! He knows. He does.

The main quarters of the guard lay just ahead. Because of its importance, the headquarters was not all that far from the emperor and the circus. Scurn picked up his pace, growing more eager to renew the hunt. He recalled now that Ganth had many former comrades among the mariners. There were more than a few who might be willing to give him and his son shelter. He also needed to consider the sector where untried or failed minotaurs made their humble homes. One of these multiple dwellings could easily serve to hide Kaz, Ganth, and Hecar. That sector was overdue for a scouring anyway.

"Captain Scurn?" called a female voice.

He paused and turned. A female warrior several years younger than him ran up, breathing heavily. He did not recognize her, but pinned on her chest was the badge of the guard, a circle within which was depicted a watchful eye superimposed over an axe. "I'm Captain Scurn. What is it you want?"

She gave him a salute, then, gasping, said, "I was sent to find you. The sergeant on duty said you were at the Baleful Basilisk, but I couldn't find you there. So I decided to check this area."

"You must've just missed me. Now spit it out. What's got you running?"

"Captain, there is news that the fugitives have been spotted in the wharf district! Your second took the search party out, but I was left behind to inform you! If we hurry, we can meet them by the warship *Sea Lancer*."

"The *Sea Lancer*?" Scurn did not know that particular vessel. "Is Kaz there?"

"So the rumor goes. The captain is an old member of his father's crew."

"So I was right!" The captain seized her by the shoulders. "Quickly! How long ago? They aren't simply going to board the ship, are they?"

"No, Captain. Right now they're waiting for you. If I don't show up with you soon, though . . ."

"Then let's get going!" Scurn rushed past her in the direction of the docks.

She fell into step beside him, now silent. That suited Scurn, who was busy thinking. Kaz was familiar with the area, which meant the guard had to be doubly careful. Fortunately, Scurn himself was familiar with the docks, having worked there for quite some time.

The female hurried ahead of him, saying, "We should turn down this way. The other path is blocked by construction work."

"Construction work?" Scurn could not recall any work, and he had been down that street the previous day. "What work?"

"They've decided to expand the woodworks again. It started only this afternoon, but they're going to be working through the night, Captain."

"Hmmph." On the whole, the news was not that surprising. The woodworks were vital not only for shipbuilding, but in other areas of construction as well. They had been enlarged once before, but with activity at its highest since the peak of the war, Scurn could see why the circle would demand improvement.

He turned down the path, again pulling ahead of her in his impatience. The street here was much more narrow, almost an alley, but it did lead in the direction of the docks. Scurn paid his dark surroundings little heed. He saw the like often enough in his duties.

The shadowy form of a tall minotaur materialized before him, almost as if by magic. In one hand he wielded a sword that was pointed at Scurn. The newcomer's intention was clear even if his features were not.

"Stand where you are," the figure said in a gravelly voice.

"You're a fool—" Scurn began, but then a second figure wielding an axe appeared, settling into a fighting stance. Even without being able to see their features, Scurn knew who at least one of this pair had to be.

"Kaz—" he began, reaching for his weapon, but choking on his next words . . . this time because a sword point prodded his back.

"No sounds, no moves," his own companion said in his ear.

"Very well done, Lass," said a new voice. "Smooth as a morning breeze, you were."

"Thank you, Father."

Father? Scurn wanted to turn around and look at the female, but sensed that her warning was a serious one. It was one thing to die in combat, but another to die uselessly in a dark alley. He would wait. Kaz and the others wanted him for some reason, and he suspected it had to do with that blasted kender that had been captured at the circus.

The scarred warrior relaxed more. The opportunity for triumph still remained. Somehow he would turn this latest humiliation into victory.

* * * * *

Kaz eyed Scurn carefully, noting that his adversary was calmer than he would have expected. That bothered him somewhat, but he could not let it overwhelm his thoughts. The plan had to proceed at the prearranged pace if it was to succeed. They had to strike when the temple was at its most subdued.

There were those who would have called his plan insane, and Kaz was one of them. Still, if minotaur tendencies ran true, invading the citadel of Sargas might prove far easier than anyone could imagine. The minotaur clerics thought that no one would ever be so mad as to enter their domain without permission. That was the sort of attitude Kaz had made use of many times in the past against opponents who, while skilled, had grown too careless with their power.

"Greetings, Scurn."

The disfigured minotaur snorted, but said nothing. He was taking Fliara's sword very seriously, a wise thing to do. At a nod from Kaz, she removed Scurn's weapons, including the small dagger that most minotaurs wore on their kilts.

"Now then, Scurn, let's talk. I'm glad to see you're the creature of habit I remember, but we did have to wait a while longer than I wanted. Still the same taverns and inns. Still the same impetuous behavior." Scurn glared. Kaz lowered his voice. "You're an excellent warrior, Scurn. Never doubt that I respect your abilities and even, at times, your sense of honor and dedication. I never chose to make an enemy out of you."

"You—" the captain started, before Fliara reminded him of the blade in his back.

"Best to get on with it, Lad," recommended Ganth. "You'll never change his mind. Dedicated he is, to the point of obsession. He'll not see anything but the side he's already chosen, and that's that."

Kaz knew that was true. He said, "I'll offer you the chance to gain your life and freedom, Scurn. I want something from you, and in return I'll let you go. You'll be free to hunt me down again and challenge me to proper combat. That's what you really want, isn't it? The circus doesn't count. The situation there was awkward at best. You want me in formal combat, warrior against warrior, just as you did when you tracked me down three years ago."

Scurn saw that it was true. He might want Kaz captured, tossed into the arena, and killed there, but deep down, the captain's greatest pleasure would be to defeat Kaz in hand-to-hand combat once and for all. Of course, that did not mean that Scurn would work to see that dream come true. First and foremost, he wanted Kaz . . . period.

"What do you want from me?" Scurn finally asked. "It must be something important. It can't really be that kender, can it?"

Fliara did not remind him of her presence again. Scurn could be ignorant, but he was not stupid. However, Kaz also knew that by allowing his rival to think that he, Scurn, controlled some bit of the situation, the scarred minotaur was more likely to go along with their demands. Kaz was familiar with the way minotaurs such as Scurn thought. The captain would be working on the assumption that he would betray his captors at some point. He would, if things went as planned, agree to help them.

"You're our guide," Ganth informed the prisoner. "We are all going to see His Holiness."

"You expect me to take you into the temple?" Scurn started to laugh, then remembered Fliara's sword. "You might as well surrender to me now. At least you'll have a chance of dying honorably in the circus."

"Nobody needs to die, Scurn, not if we do this the way I ask. That includes you."

"So you say, but I'm more likely to get run through from behind when you don't need me anymore, aren't I?"

Kaz stepped closer, matching gazes with the other. "I

don't want that to happen. Do you?"

Scurn was the first to look away. "No, like you, I want to see the axe coming!"

"Your choice, Scurn. Your life and freedom. All you have to do is lead us inside and past the acolytes. What we do after that is up to us."

The captain straightened. "All right. Not that I've got much choice. You'll be walking to your deaths, though. The high priest is not as kind as I'd be."

"Aye," Ganth interjected, "you're kindness incarnate. Now turn around."

Scurn obeyed. Ganth reached into a pouch and from it removed badges identical to the ones Fliara and Scurn already wore. Despite himself, the prisoner could not help but grunt in surprise.

"Amazing how these things can be found lying around," Ganth commented. Members of the guard faced serious reprimand for lost badges, so they generally took care of them.

"Where did you get those?"

"No time for questions now," Kaz reminded him. Even he did not know where Ganth had found the old badges. The mariner had asked his son not to ask, and Kaz respected that wish.

"Are we leaving now?" asked Hecar.

"Yes, we're ready to leave." Kaz faced his companions. "We need to be in and out of there. You all know your tasks. Anyone who doesn't want to commit suicide with me can leave now."

"You gave that speech before, Brother," Fliara piped up. "None of us paid it any mind then, and none of us does now." She tapped Scurn on the back. "Except maybe this one here."

"Let's get going, Son," Ganth commented. "I've got a pair of new grandchildren I'm looking forward to meeting."

"Let's move, then."

The party started toward the temple. Scurn walked in front, with Ganth on one side and Fliara on the other. Kaz followed, with Hecar close behind. Everyone now had their weapons drawn except for Kaz, who had a role to play, and, of course, Scurn.

Nethosak never truly slept, especially these days, but few minotaurs roamed the streets at this hour. A few passed by the group, but other than a furtive glance, most looked quickly away. It was not healthy to bring oneself to the attention of the guard.

They neared the temple much too soon. Torches lit the entrance, and two sentries clad in the colors of the priesthood stood at attention. Kaz glanced at the windows of the edifice and saw that most of them were dark. By now, the high priest would have retired, along with most of his staff. There would be some guards on duty, and a few acolytes.

"You don't think this'll work, do you?" Scurn whispered.

"It'll work, or the last thing you'll feel is this blade running through your stomach," Fliara commented matter-of-factly.

"Amusing," replied Scurn. "But not as amusing as this little plan of yours."

They marched up with Scurn looking as if he were in full command of the situation. The guards looked poised to block their path, but Scurn showed his badge of rank and informed them, "I've got a prisoner that the high priest wants to question." He indicated Kaz. "A companion of the chief fugitive being hunted tonight. Let us pass."

The pair looked at one another, then the larger of the two nodded, at which point they stepped aside.

Expression set, Scurn led the group past. The doorway opened from within. Another pair of guards waited, but they were the only ones Kaz could see.

An acolyte met them when the doors were closed behind them. He looked slightly irritated, as if they had just disturbed him from his catnap. It was interesting, Kaz noted, but the higher the rank of a cleric in the temple of Sargas, the less devout they seemed to be. Oh, they performed all the same ceremonies, but their smug attitudes made them almost interchangeable with the staffs of the eight members of the Supreme Circle.

"What is it you want, Captain? His Holiness has retired for the evening."

"I've got a prisoner he'll want to see first thing in the morning," Scurn replied without prompting. "A companion of the chief fugitive, Kaz. He knows the kender, too."

The acolyte nodded approval, looking past Scurn. His mouth twisted in distaste. "Such betrayal to the cause is ever shameful. You are sure he is one of the traitors?"

"He's traveled with Kaziganthi for years. Knows him better than anyone. As I said, he is also acquainted with the kender."

"A kender. Can you believe it? A minotaur who travels with a kender. This Kaziganthi has fallen low."

"Captain," Hecar interjected. "Maybe we should get this honorless one in a cell before he slips free again." That there were cells in the temple was common knowledge. In the course of their duties, the clerics of Sargas were forced, so the high priests always insisted, to treat heretics as criminals. No emperor, however popular, had ever had the courage to question the existence of this private dungeon.

"A cell?" blurted the robed minotaur. "He should be thrown into the arena! Take him there."

Fliara casually tapped her sword against Scurn's side. He quickly spoke up. "I'd rather he were kept here, Brother. And the high priest would surely agree. He is too valuable to waste in the arena—not yet at least."

The acolyte weighed this seriously. "I am not accustomed to making such decisions. That was the duty of Brother Merriq."

"Then get him."

"Brother Merriq," the other said frostily, "is no more. He perished bravely, capturing . . . capturing the other prisoner. A fire of some sort, I understand."

Kaz could barely refrain from smiling. So Delbin had not been captured without a good fight. Kaz had no pity for Merriq. He had been the epitome of what was wrong with the minotaur homeland.

The robed figure was taking much too long to consider the matter. Hecar spoke again. "Captain, can't we just put the prisoner in the cell ourselves and take responsibility?"

Scurn frowned, but Hecar's words made the acolyte brighten. "Of course, if you want to take responsibility for the prisoner, you may go ahead. I cannot say how His Holiness will react, but as long as it is your responsibility . . ."

Even Scurn seemed disgusted with the robed minotaur's attitude. The acolyte was one of those middle-level subordinates who would do anything as long as it didn't threaten his own well-being. It was the type who never rose very high in the ranks, but seemed to last forever.

"We'll take responsibility for any taint he leaves in the holy temple," the scarred minotaur answered somewhat sarcastically. "Just tell us where the cells are and we'll take him there. You won't have to worry about a thing."

"I'll have to have someone lead you there."

The robed figure stepped away quickly before anyone could suggest that he himself lead the party to the cells. Scurn glanced at Kaz, who kept his expression neutral.

A couple of minutes later, the acolyte returned with what was obviously a novice. The novice, a shorter, muscular minotaur, seemed caught between fear and anger, most of it aimed at his superior.

"This one will take you to the cells. Be about your business, then depart this building. Make certain the prisoner is completely secure before you leave, or it'll be your heads. In the morning, someone will alert His Holiness."

He turned away again before there could be any objection. The novice watched him depart, then looked at the others with a scowl on his face. "Come this way. Walk quietly, for the high priest rests now."

"Will we be passing near his chambers?" Scurn asked on his own. Fliara shifted ever so slightly toward him.

"No, his private rooms are beyond the great audience chamber. The cells are below."

Kaz was relieved to hear that. The farther they were from Jopfer's rooms, the better.

The novice led them down one corridor after another, gradually descending into the bowels of the temple. All along their journey, the eyes of Sargas watched them.

Here was a relief of Sargas saving the first minotaurs. Over there was a tapestry showing him building the border mountains. One image showed Sargas raising ships from the sea. Artisans had worked diligently to create the illusion that Sargas watched the viewer even as he performed his miracles.

They descended deeper. Kaz counted the levels in his head, estimating distance and time. He hoped the cells would not be much farther. One fortunate thing was that they had passed only a few sentries and never more than a pair at one station.

"This level is where the traitor should go," the novice finally said, just when Kaz was beginning to think they were never going to reach the bottom. "We'll take him down—"

The entire party paused as four sentries blocked their path. Unlike the previous ones they had passed, these sentries were alert and bristling.

"No one comes down this way," commanded a dark minotaur who was the apparent leader. "By orders of the high priest."

"We have a prisoner—" the novice began.

"No one."

"The high priest'll want this one in a special place," Scurn interrupted. Fliara's weapon had suddenly found itself nudging his back. "He's a companion of the renegade we've been searching for."

"We've got our orders."

Scurn tried again. "He's also a friend of the kender you have prisoner. The high priest will be glad to have him nearby. He'll be able to make use of him. Leverage and that sort of thing."

For the first time, the sentries seemed uncertain. The leader looked at his companions, then at Kaz. "I don't know . . ."

Ganth glanced at his son. Kaz nodded slightly. Choosing a moment when the guards' attention was elsewhere, he stepped past Ganth and Scurn, in front of the guard leader and one of the other sentries. Raising his hands, he brought forth Honor's Face.

Startled, the guards looked up at the magical axe as if it were Sargas himself. Kaz quickly lowered the axe shaft with both hands and struck wide, hitting them both. The flat side of the axe head caught the second sentry squarely, knocking him completely over. The leader stumbled back, stunned but able to keep his footing.

Ganth reached out and shoved the novice's head back against the wall. The novice struck the wall hard and, with a grunt of astonishment, slid to the floor.

"Don't try anything!" Fliara commanded Scurn, who had started to reach for a weapon dropped by the guard leader.

Ganth seized the guard leader and threw him against the wall, just as he had done to the novice. Hecar and Kaz moved forward. The remaining pair of guards, suddenly outnumbered, backed away. They did not get far before Kaz and Helati's brother caught up to them.

Kaz made the most of his axe in the narrow passage, swinging it diagonally. This action forced one guard back, while leaving Kaz wide open to an attack from the other. Hecar filled the gap, however, countering the other minotaur's attempted thrust and bringing his blade up underneath, stabbing the guard in the stomach.

The death of Hecar's foe drained the fight from the remaining temple guard. He dropped his blade and fell to one knee, hands over his head. "I yield myself."

Hecar came up and took charge. Their foes had been too stunned to give an alarm. To Ganth, Kaz said, "We need to bind him and put them in another cell. The dead one, too."

"What about him?" Kaz's father asked, indicating Scurn.

"We still need him. Just make certain he knows what'll happen if he opens his mouth at the wrong time."

"I think Fliara's taught him about that already."

They gathered up the guards and located the nearest cell. From the pouches on their belts the party removed rope and cloth. Within a few minutes, the guards were secure. The only traces that remained in the hallway were some bloodstains, which they could do nothing to hide.

"I have the keys," Hecar said, holding them up and dangling them. "Now we just need to find him. Surprised he hasn't picked the locks himself and met us already."

Kaz brought the head of his axe to bear on the one guard still conscious. "I'm going to remove the cloth around your muzzle, and you're going to answer the question I'm about to ask. You get one chance, or you join your dead friend. Understand?"

The guard nodded.

"Good. Now where's the kender?"

The guard answered, "Third corridor, second cell, but you'll regret—"

Replacing the cloth over the prisoner's protests, Kaz joined the others. "Let's go."

With Fliara keeping an eye on a suspiciously docile Scurn, the group hurried in that direction. The halls were darker here, only an occasional torch illuminating the area. As they passed each cell, Kaz peered inside. He had had a notion to free the other prisoners, but not one cell was occupied.

"Jopfer must want a lot of privacy for the kender," Ganth remarked. "There should be at least a few poor heretics being retrained down here."

Kaz was the first to reach the third corridor. He peered inside, seeing little more than darkness. These cells were far larger. The torchlight barely illuminated part of a chair and possibly a small table.

He tugged on the door. It opened.

Delbin had escaped . . . but where was he now?

"Kaz! Look what I just found!" Hecar came toward him with a squirming bundle. It was a gully dwarf. "This is the same one I think helped capture me. He did something to my harness!" The minotaur raised the sorry figure up so he could look it in the face. The legs of the gully dwarf . . . a male, Kaz thought . . . kept spinning, though his feet were high off the floor. "Well, now we can talk about the lesson I'm going to teach you—"

"Hecar—"

"No hurt Galump!" the gully dwarf pleaded. "Galump is Delbin's friend! Good friend!"

"What's that?" Kaz moved forward, seizing Hecar's arm. He had his companion lower the creature called Galump to the ground. The creature tried to dash away, but Hecar maintained his grip. "Stop that!" Kaz commanded. In a softer tone, he asked, "You're a friend of Delbin's?"

"Yes! Galump is Delbin's friend! Yes!"

"Do you know where he is? It's important."

The gully dwarf hesitated, then murmured, "High one will eat us if I say . . . He shouldn't have gone after her." The gully dwarf leaned forward and hesitantly asked, "You Kaz?"

The minotaur blinked. "I am. How did—"

"Delbin's friend." Galump attempted to think. It was manifestly a strain. "Delbin's friend. Delbin wanted to help Galump. Galump help Delbin." He broke into a childlike smile. "I show you."

The gully dwarf twisted out of Hecar's grip and started down the hallway. After a moment's hesitation, the minotaurs followed.

Galump hurried deeper into the temple. Kaz was amazed and horrified at how many cells there actually were beneath the temple. Finally, Galump pointed at a cell door midway down a corridor. Kaz hurried past him and peered through the grill into the darkened cell. He could neither see nor hear anything within.

Then a chain rattled slightly. Kaz heard a short gasp that did not sound like the kender. In fact, it sounded like a female, but not really like a minotaur.

"Delbin!" He called, trying to keep his voice quiet enough so that it would not echo. "Delbin! It's Kaz!"

The chain rattled more. He heard someone rise.

"Delbin!"

"Kaz?" came the kender's hopeful voice. "Kaz!"

The chain dropped to the floor with a loud clash. Delbin burst out of the darkness from one side of the cell . . . followed, to Kaz's astonishment, by a human female in her early or mid-teens. The girl paused only when the chains she wore yanked her back.

Kaz snarled, studying the length of chain. More and more, he desired the high priest's neck between his hands. What right did Jopfer think he had to do this to a harmless, innocent child? She could not be any real threat to a minotaur. There was no honor in the cleric's actions, only evil.

He turned away from the door. "Where are those keys?"

Hecar raised the ring of keys, but Delbin was already at the door. Before any of the minotaurs could say anything, there was a click. A moment later, the kender pushed the door open. "The manacles are really hard, Kaz, but the doors are simple. I locked it when I heard someone coming, just in case."

"Amazing," grumbled Ganth. "Minotaur locks are some of the best in the world, and this little one flicks them open without a care."

They followed Delbin inside. The kender took the girl by the hand. She was staring at the minotaurs in open fear. "Don't worry. We're all going to rescue you."

"Who is she, Delbin?" Kaz studied the girl. She looked as if she had some elven blood, but was otherwise unassuming.

"She's—" The kender frowned. "She says she doesn't have a name, Kaz."

"Is that true, girl?"

"I don't think I've ever had a name."

"Why didn't your parents give you one?"

She looked down. "I don't remember them."

"She said she's been on her own as long as she can remember, but she doesn't seem to remember very far back, maybe a couple of years, I think—"

"Shouldn't we be leaving soon, Lad?" interrupted Ganth.

"We have to take her with us, Kaz!"

"A human girl?" Hecar shook his head. "She'll stick out worse than a kender!"

"Nevertheless, we will take her." He looked at the girl. For some reason, she reminded him of someone. "Don't worry—girl—you'll go with us. I wouldn't leave anyone here to wait for the high priest."

"I don't like him. He kept saying I'd be here for centuries."

"Jopfer's truly mad," Hecar retorted. "Becoming high priest has made him crazy."

"Can you get the manacles open, Delbin?" Kaz did not want to have to use the axe. Striking the chains would make more noise than they could afford. It was a wonder no one had heard them so far.

"I think so." The kender was already at work. "I think I almost have this one figured out." To the human he said, "Don't you worry! We'll get you out, and then you can come with us back to Kaz's home, and then we can come up with a name for you—"

"I think I've decided on one," she abruptly announced with much seriousness. "I think I found one I like."

"That's all very nice—" but Kaz got no farther.

"I want to be called Tiberia, or even just Ty." The girl smiled prettily at Kaz. "Delbin mentioned a dragon in a story he told me while he was trying to free me. About a dragon called Tiberion. I like that name."

"Tiberia it is then," snorted Ganth. "We can admire the choice later. If you can't get those manacles open in the next few seconds, Delbin, then we'd better—"

Scurn swung his elbow back, catching a momentarily distracted Fliara in the stomach. She bent over, the air pushed out of her, allowing the scarred minotaur to seize her by the arm and shove her. Fliara collided with Hecar.

The action caught the others off guard. Scurn turned and raced through the open doorway.

"Somebody stop him!" Ganth called, already chasing the scarred minotaur.

"Delbin!" Kaz called over his shoulder as he started after them. "Get that bracelet open and get her out of here without us if you have to! We'll meet where we stayed before this whole mess began, but don't wait long! Get her out of Nethosak!"

"But, Kaz! I haven't told you the biggest thing! You should hear what she's able to do!"

"Later, Delbin! Free her!"

The kender was already back at work on the chain as Kaz and the others rushed out after Scurn. Kaz trusted the kender's skills, at least where sneaking around was concerned. If anyone could get Tiberia out unnoticed, Delbin could.

Scurn and Ganth were out of sight as he turned the corridor, not a good sign. If Scurn made it up to the next level, he would be able to warn some of the temple guards.

Then he heard the sounds of a struggle. Kaz twisted around the corner and discovered Scurn and Ganth fighting hand-to-hand, the older minotaur's sword on the floor between them. It was a credit to the undiminished skills of Kaz's father that he had caught the escaping captain before Scurn could climb the steps.

Scurn saw Kaz coming. A dark glint appeared in the disfigured warrior's eyes. Scurn opened his mouth and shouted loudly, making as much noise as he could. The cry echoed throughout the hall and, no doubt, the floor above.

Ganth finally freed a hand and punched his adversary in the jaw. Scurn stumbled back, falling over the steps. The older warrior reached down to retrieve his sword.

"What's going on down here?" called a voice. Less than a breath later, three temple guards appeared on the steps, weapons drawn.

"He's a traitor!" Ganth quickly replied. "He tried to kill the high priest's prisoner!"

The guards looked at Scurn with surprise, then started down.

"You fools!" Scurn snarled in turn. "That's the fugitive, Kaz, back there! He forced me at sword point to bring them here! I was the one who just shouted!"

The foremost guard looked the trio over. "I think you'd all better come with us. We'll let one of the clerics hear this mess. Now turn your weapons over."

Scurn revealed that he had no weapon. Ganth glanced at his son, then turned the blade so that the hilt pointed at the guards. One of the other warriors reached for it.

The blade slipped from the mariner's hand. As the guard reached to retrieve it, Ganth seized his wrist and pulled him forward hard, knocking the shocked minotaur into Scurn. Both fell roughly to the floor.

As if by magic, Fliara and Hecar appeared behind Kaz. The three wasted no time before charging the remaining sentries. Ganth backed away, seizing his lost sword before rejoining his son and daughter.

Hecar struck the guard who had fallen, knocking him senseless. This gave Scurn the opportunity to grab the unconscious warrior's blade and bring it up against Helati's brother. The attack was weak, but it prevented Hecar from joining Kaz and the others.

For the first time, Kaz saw his youngest sibling in action. Fliara was swift, her smaller stature working for her in ways he would not have expected. Twice she got under the guard of an attacker, bleeding him. Fliara was versatile, using both orthodox and unorthodox moves to confuse her adversary.

Kaz's own opponent was no match and was quickly backed up, leaving Fliara's male alone. He tried to slash at her, but she shifted under him, running her blade into his chest. As he collapsed, Fliara joined her brother in pinioning the sole remaining guard.

All of a sudden, more guards appeared at the top of the steps. This time, there were at least seven. Kaz and his sister found themselves abruptly losing the ground they had gained. Soon they were pushed back near Hecar and Scurn, who were still battling.

"We're trapped down here!" Fliara informed Kaz needlessly. "There's nowhere but the cells behind us!"

Three more guards joined the squad. Although not all of the temple sentries could do battle, the small band was being continually pushed back down the steps. Ganth ran one through, but two more appeared. Kaz and his group retreated. Hecar was forced to abandon his duel with Scurn, lest he be isolated.

"The one with the axe!" the scarred warrior shouted. "The high priest will want him alive if possible, but kill the others!"

As Kaz backed even farther, he bumped into a small form. At first he thought it was Galump, but then he saw it was Delbin.

"Kaz! There's no other way out! I looked all around, but I couldn't find a path anywhere—"

Kaz deflected a sword thrust. "Where's Ty?"

"She's here, Kaz! Listen, she thinks she can get us out of here!"

"Don't talk nonsense! Get back!"

"But listen, Kaz! She can do magic! She can!"

He had no time for the kender's babble. "Well, then let her do it! Get us out of here! Take us anywhere!" Kaz succeeded in knocking away one minotaur's sword, but that minotaur immediately retreated, and one of his comrades renewed the press. Kaz cried, "Ty, if you can do it, get us out of here!"

"I don't know, Kaz! Delbin took off the chains, which the high priest said held back my power, but I've never tried it with so many people. Usually it's just myself!"

He had no idea what the young human was talking about. She talked like a kender. Perhaps there was some truth to the story. Perhaps Ty was a mage. If she was, then she was their only chance to escape. It certainly would not hurt for her to try.

"You have to do it, Ty!" Delbin insisted. "Just concentrate hard on getting us someplace else! You should be able to do it! I'll bet you've got a lot of power!"

A pair of guards prevented him from saying more. Kaz fought off their attack and prayed to Paladine that Delbin wasn't crazy this time.

"There's more of them coming!" Ganth cried. "We'll have to break—"

The corridor vanished . . . to be replaced by a huge, familiar room dimly lit by a few well-placed torches.

"—away and . . ." the old mariner's voice faded as he and the others realized the change in surroundings.

"What happened just now?" Fliara demanded. "Where are we?"

Kaz quickly surveyed the group. They were all there, his father, sister, Hecar, Delbin, and the human girl. Ty was pale and shivering, but seemed all right, especially considering the fact that she had just done what Kaz had assumed was impossible, . . . transported them all from one location to another.

"That was fun, Ty! How did you get all of us here? I didn't think you could do that!"

"Where are we?" repeated Fliara. "This looks like it's still part of the temple!"

"It is," Kaz responded. "It's the audience chamber of the high priest, a place we should definitely not be." He started toward the doors. "Come on!"

They had gone only a few steps when every unlit torch in the chamber burst into bright flames.

"Interesting," came the voice of Jopfer. "I found you just in time, didn't I, Young One? Your great powers begin to manifest themselves."

The band turned to see the high priest standing at the top of the dais, arms folded. A satisfied expression covered the tall figure's features.

"At last, this will come to an end."

"Jopfer!" shouted Hecar. "What's got into you? What's happened to you?" Helati's brother started forward, angry at his old friend. "You were never one with much love for the temple. You hated all they stood for, but now you've become the worst of them!"

"The truth would surprise you," the cleric returned, his tone one of mockery. It was almost as if he enjoyed some jest the others knew nothing about.

"Upon reflection, it would do to take a glance at the face of honor," someone said in Kaz's ear.

He looked around before realizing that the voice had sounded like the infernal figure in gray again. It was bad enough that they stood before Jopfer, but did the gray man have to haunt him just now? Still, Kaz turned slightly away from the others and held the mirrorlike finish of his battle-axe so he could see . . . or not see . . . the form of the high priest. The others he knew he could trust.

Kaz stared into the axe face, certain that he would see nothing but an empty dais.

What he saw, however briefly it appeared, nearly made him drop the axe. Honor's Face had revealed the truth about Jopfer, but Kaz had difficulty believing it.

Kaz wasted no more time. He had briefly contemplated using the high priest as a hostage, but now, with practiced aim and no warning whatsoever, he threw Honor's Face at the cleric.

The high priest glanced at the whirling weapon, then caught it by the handle when it was mere inches from his chest.

"Dwarven make," he hissed, as if the mere thought of the race disgusted him. His nostrils flared. "And elven taint. A foul but fascinating combination. I shall study it in more detail later."

To Kaz's horror, Honor's Face vanished. He tried to will it back, but the axe would not return.

"Your will is nothing compared to mine," the figure on the dais hissed. "All your wills combined are nothing to me. I am power itself. I am greater than all the race combined!"

"You're mad, Jopfer!" Hecar called. He took a step nearer to the platform. "And you might've been lucky with that axe, but you're still only one minotaur!"

"Aye, let's see how your tricks work against all of us," Ganth added.

The other three minotaurs started forward. Kaz gazed at them in dismay. They truly did not know the extent of the horror.

"Get back, all of you!" Kaz cried. "He's not what he appears!"

That made them pause. Even the high priest seemed momentarily startled.

"Mage or cleric, Lad," Ganth said, resuming his advance. "It's all the same to me."

"But he's neither! He's not even a minotaur!"

The last word was punctuated by mocking laughter that echoed so loudly in the chamber that every member of Kaz's band had to cover his or her ears. The robed figure continued to laugh for several seconds, sounding more bestial by the moment.

"Clever little warrior!" he cried, his toothy smile unnerving Kaz, who knew the truth. "Clever little minotaur! I will have to wring the secret of your cleverness from you just before I end your short, useless existence! You've guessed! You know me as I truly am, do you not?"

"I know you . . ."

"What're you talking about, Kaz?" asked Hecar. "What're you saying about Jopfer?"

"He's neither Jopfer nor even a minotaur! The high priest is a dragon!"

They looked at the cleric as if expecting him to refute the incredible claim, for dragons had disappeared at the end of the war. Not a single dragon, good or evil, had been seen since, as far as most knew.

Jopfer said nothing. He merely nodded, acknowledging Kaz's warning . . . then began to swell in size. His snout twisted; his teeth grew longer and sharper. The fur covering him became scales as red as fire. The robe fell away, revealing expanding wings and a long whip of a tail that had not been there a breath before.

His hands became claws with long talons, and his arms twisted. He was already ten times his original size.

It all happened in the blink of an eye. Where the minotaur had stood there now squatted a red dragon of immense proportions. Kaz noted how the huge chamber allowed the creature free movement and wondered if perhaps—and the thought was a chilling one—if perhaps the place had been built with him in mind.

"I am Infernus!" roared the dragon, looking down at them as if they were insects. "I have worked centuries to make you all what you are! I have guided you in guise after guise!" He raised his head high. "I am your true god . . . and you have been very, very naughty children indeed!"

They backed away suddenly as a fear washed over them. It was no normal fear, not even what one might expect to feel when confronted by such a leviathan. Kaz recognized it as dragonfear, a magic of the creatures he had not felt since the war.

The dragon, Infernus, lowered his head. "And as naughty children, it's time you were punished."

Chapter 14
The Emperor

"You shouldn't even be here!" insisted Kaz, fighting the dragonfear. "The dragons have all left Krynn! Since the end of the war!"

"The gods commanded that we depart, yes," agreed the red leviathan. "They compelled us! We served them well . . . on both sides . . . and for our reward we were to be cast out of this world! Yet I resisted! I fought against the pull! One by one, my brethren flew off into the air, unable to command their own wills, but still I managed to resist!"

The red dragon clambered down from the dais, eyes

darting from one minotaur to the next. Each time his gaze returned to Ty. Kaz noted that and began to wonder.

"My anger was my strength. I had served my lady well, working over the centuries to achieve her goal, and now I was supposed to abandon my work for her, all that I had strived for! It had become more mine than hers, and I was simply to leave it behind because of her failure! I, Infernus!"

Where were the clerics and the guards? Kaz had expected others to barge in by this point. Did they not hear the bellowing? He could not believe the minotaurs who worked in the temple knew the secret of their high priest. Perhaps a few high-ranking ones did, but even that was doubtful.

Again Kaz tried to will his axe to his hands. This time, he felt a slight tug, as if Honor's Face sought to return but was prevented. Yet it gave him a little hope. The dragon's will was not invincible. Kaz might be able to get the axe back if he could distract the dragon enough.

Providing he got the chance.

Infernus seemed glad to have an audience, albeit a captive one, for which to boast of his exploits. They were probably the first outsiders to know the truth . . . no doubt because the dragon intended to kill them all.

"You are my children, more than you are the offspring of either Sargas or his mistress, dark Takhisis! I have made you into the terrors that you are, guided you over generations for her, obeyed foolish edicts, and given you over to other masters so that you would be honed by the harshness of your lives. All so that you would become stronger, more defiant soldiers! Now, I can lead you to fulfill your glory, and mine! I will rule, and your kind will act as my talons, reaching out farther and farther until we have all of Krynn under control! You shall bow to no one, no god or goddess, but me!"

Infernus looked up to the ceiling. If Kaz had understood the dragon correctly, then the history of the minotaur race was a mockery—centuries of endless manipulation by forces without and within—the dragon the greatest manipulator of all. Every high priest for countless generations may have been this dragon in minotaur form.

The shiver that ran down his spine was not influenced by the dragonfear, but rather the realization of what had happened to all those minotaurs, many of them no doubt good, honest clerics. What had Jopfer thought when the offer was presented? Had he thought that here was a way for someone to correct the ills of the priesthood? Had he believed that he could work with his former masters and make the temple of Sargas an ally of the circle?

When had he finally discovered the truth? Just before Infernus stole his form and destroyed him?

The baleful gaze of the huge red creature suddenly focused on Kaz. "A shame you had to be so defiant, Kaziganthi de-Orilg. You and I share a kindred spirit, but that is why you could not obey me. You were useful for a time, though, spreading the glory of minotaur skills beyond the homeland. For a time I let those tales spread among your own kind, knowing such feats as were rumored could only encourage others to strive harder." He dipped his massive head in what Kaz supposed was a bow. "I am glad I decided to let you live after you departed the circus. It would have been a pity to rid myself of both you and your brother at the same time. Until you began to settle down and draw others from the homeland, you were more aid than hindrance to my plans. Had you accepted my offer, you would have redeemed yourself and become my greatest general. I hoped you would. Truly I had hoped so. You are what I have been striving to create, Kaziganthi. You are the minotaur warrior that knows no defeat, knows no challenge that cannot be overcome!" Infernus cocked his head. "You still have one last chance."

"You must be mad!" Kaz began, enraged. "After what you've done to me and mine you still have the arrogance to offer—"

"You!" The voice was Ganth's, as Kaz had never heard his father. The mariner, sword raised, stared wide-eyed at the leviathan. Despite his dragonfear, the older minotaur began edging forward. "You had Raud killed! And you had *Gladiator* sent out on that doomed mission, didn't you? I remember the high priest sanctioning it! By the Just One's beard, I remember the temple practically insisting we be sent out into those dark waters immediately . . . without a cleric aboard, which was standard practice back then! You knew we'd run into those ships, those marauders, and that storm as well, didn't you? You expected us all to perish, didn't you?"

Eyeing Ganth, the dragon coldly replied, "It was my duty to cull the weak, the unstable, and the unpredictable from the ranks. The race had to be tempered constantly if it was to be of use to my mistress." Infernus scowled, but not at them. "And what was done?" the dragon raged. "They were wasted, used as fodder by those who could not appreciate my efforts! I strained to create for her a perfect race through which she and her consort could take Ansalon. Then her insipid little mortal minions wasted so much effort! All the centuries of work, the strengthening through adversity and winnowing . . ."

"You killed Kyri, you slimy serpent . . ." Ganth growled. "You killed my crew. You killed hundreds . . . thousands . . . You killed my son. . . ."

Kaz moved too late to stop his father. The older minotaur bounded forward, rage overwhelming reason. He raised his sword high, calling out an old minotaur war cry.

Raising one limb, Infernus reached forward and batted Ganth away.

"Father!" Kaz and Fliara both cried. Ganth literally flew over their heads, his weapon clattering to the floor. The companions, save for Ty, forgot the dragon as Ganth crashed into the floor several yards away, his body sprawled.

Even before Kaz reached him, he knew that his father was dead.

He looked down at the lifeless body. From the marks on him, it was possible Ganth had died before he landed. A single blow from a dragon could easily kill most mortals.

In that moment, the accursed voice of the gray man murmured in his head, "I'm sorry, Kaz. I had no control."

"Get out of my head!" he muttered, turning on the dragon. Infernus was personally responsible for the deaths of his parents and his brother. He was, as Ganth had pointed out, responsible for the deaths of thousands, all in the name of some foul plan to create a perfect race of warriors to serve a sinister goddess. Kaz faced the murderous beast, again seeking to will Honor's Face to him. Briefly, he almost thought he would succeed, but the dragon's will was still too strong, even though Kaz was fueled by intense grief and anger.

As he abandoned his effort, he became aware of a lone figure standing before the fearsome behemoth.

Ty.

"I won't let you hurt them anymore!" the girl called.

"Ty! Get away from him!" Kaz yelled.

"You are young. I will forgive your foolishness," Infernus told the human. "But do not test my goodwill!"

"You killed Kaz's father!" shouted Ty, ignoring the dragon's words.

A fireball large enough to consume a minotaur burst from the human female's hands. It flew at Infernus, striking him in the chest. The dragon grunted, batting away the flames.

"Consider yourself fortunate that the balance must be maintained, young one. Now behave yourself."

A transparent shell of bright red fell over the girl. It sank down, first enveloping, then passing through its victim. The last traces disappeared into the floor, but the aftereffects were evident. Ty slumped to the floor, overcome with dizziness.

"This has gone on far too long," declared Hecar. "We have to take him or die trying. What other choice have we? Are you with me?"

"The girl must be freed," came the voice of the gray man again. "There must be balance in all things for you to succeed. Balance leads to balance."

"I said get out of my head!" Kaz growled. "Take your

advice and stuff it back into whatever dream you come from!"

Fliara touched his arm. "Kaz! What ails you? Who're you talking to?"

He had no time to answer, for Infernus refocused his attention. "You were not supposed to die in the circus, Kaziganthi, but your father would have, as an object lesson to you. That is rectified. Now, however, I see that I might as well have let you perish. You will never bow. Never. It would be efficient to simply eliminate you and your small band once and for all, but there would be little satisfaction in removing you in such a . . . draconian . . . fashion. Your deaths must be elaborate to excite the masses, something even more extravagant than the ritual executions I'd earlier planned. I shall have to think about it."

They started forward, but it was already too late. Emerald shells similar to the red one that had enveloped Ty covered each of them. Kaz felt his body stiffen, his mind grow distant. The shell passed through him and, by the time it sank into the floor, he could not move at all, save to breathe. Out of the corner of his eye, Kaz could see Hecar's hand, as pale and still as his own.

"Why are you doing this?" came Ty's voice. "Let them go and I'll do everything you say! I won't resist anymore!"

Infernus seemed impressed. "You need to be as helpless as the rest. I thought I took your true origin into account. You are stronger than you appear, Young One! Good! That means you will live a long, long life for me! Many, many centuries!"

"What do you mean?"

"You still do not understand?" The great red chuckled. "Ah, the naivete of youth! Do you not understand why you are so important to me? Do you not realize what happened?" Infernus leaned his head back. "All the dragons were called away. I knew I would be compelled to follow, but I resisted. You see, my young one and my statuesque friends, there is a balance that must be maintained at all times. For me to remain on Krynn past the calling, there must have been one of my opposite number also on the world! One of the dragons of foul Paladine, you see. Yet, for this one not to obey meant that there must be unusual circumstances. I searched Krynn, sought out the magic forces. Where was there another of my kind, and how had he or she also escaped the call?"

He leaned forward again, smiling. A new wave of dragonfear washed over the helpless group, though none could do anything about it. Infernus chuckled again.

"My agents discovered the fragments of a shell. A single egg had been left behind and had hatched." As he spoke, Infernus began to shrink back to his minotaur form. It was a slow process, a small degree with each breath.

Utilizing his magic, the dragon explained, he had taken the fragments of the shell and used them to seek the hiding place of the hatchling. As long as the other dragon existed, Infernus could remain on Krynn. However, if something happened to either one, the other would likely be forced out of the world.

"Then I found the young one. Or rather, my spell found a creature that appeared to be the hatchling." He grinned. "It found you . . . Ty. What an amusing name."

"I'm no dragon. If I was, you'd be sorry!"

Infernus found this amusing. Infernus seemed to find everything amusing. "I thought the same, but I observed you. I sensed. I thought. Then I saw that it was true. You are a dragon, Young One. You must be one of the accursed silvers, who shape themselves with more ease than most of us. A newborn especially, with no one to mind it, can shift without intending to. It can take on a form based on the inner knowledge our kind possesses, or from things it happens to see. A young dragon might take the form of humans, who might have been the first intelligent beings it remembered seeing."

"I am human!"

"It can only have been about eight years since the call, yet you are taller than you should be, older in appearance, too, when you wear that form. That fooled me for a time, but then, young dragons grow fast at first. Deny it all you like, but do you not feel your blood calling? Do you not dream of flying through the sky, soaring at undreamt of heights? We all dream of that from birth on. It is a part of our heritage, dark or light, hatchling."

"No . . ." but Ty's voice evinced uncertainty.

"Yes. You cannot deny it."

Kaz struggled to move, but the dragon's spell held him fast. A multitude of thoughts swirled within him. Ty was a dragon? As insane as that sounded, it made some sense. The girl's fantastic if erratic ability with magic was impossible for one so young and untrained . . . if she was human.

Infernus spoke of balance, just as the voice of the gray man had. What was the connection there? He was certain the figure in gray had some past significance. Something Huma of the Lance had once spoken about, but the memory was still hazy.

His thoughts scattered as Infernus, much smaller now, suddenly shifted form. The wings shriveled, drawing within his back. His savage maw reshaped into the more familiar muzzle of a minotaur.

The dragon's tail was the last item to vanish. Before them all stood the false Jopfer, his robes floating and wrapping around him.

"You and I will have a lot of time to talk about these things, Ty. You shall realize your destiny under my tutelage. As for these four . . ." The high priest returned to the desk, pulling a cord.

A moment or two passed, then the doors opened and two acolytes hurried inside. They froze at the sight of the figures standing before them.

"Summon the guards," commanded Infernus in his role of Jopfer. One of the acolytes did. When the guards arrived, the high priest ordered, "Remove these to cells on different levels from the one set aside for the girl. Be especially thorough when binding the kender. I want them all here for their ritual combats. Their deaths will mark the commencing of the day of destiny for the glorious minotaur race . . . and myself."

They were suddenly able to move again, though temple guards surrounded them. One of the sentries prodded Ganth's body. Kaz snarled and tried to push him away, but the other soldiers held him back.

"Remove that unsightly object and return it to the clan of Orilg. Inform their patriarch that the emperor and I will want to see him in a few days to explain his involvement in these activities. He will receive a summoning when I desire his presence."

"Yes, Holiness."

To Kaz's horror, his father's body was unceremoniously dragged away. Slowly it dawned on Kaz that none of the other minotaurs had evidently heard anything that had gone on in the chamber, including the high priest's revelations.

"You fools!" he dared shout. "You don't even know what happened here! You don't even know the truth about your high priest!"

They were all looking at him. He was about to say more when his eyes met those of Infernus. There was a knowing look in them, a gleam that invited Kaz to say whatever he wanted. The robed figure would not stop him from speaking the truth.

Kaz shut his mouth. The high priest had good reason for not caring whether Kaz informed the others about his true identity. If he had not seen the dragon for himself, he would not have believed his story either. Everyone knew the dragons were gone, and what minotaur would believe that every high priest for centuries past had been the self-same dragon in disguise? That was the beauty of the red dragon's plot. The truth was too outrageous.

The edges of the robed figure's mouth crept upward. "Take all of them away except the human."

The guards had just begun leading them away from the chamber when several more arrived, their leader none other than a severely shocked Scurn. He looked at Kaz and the other captives, then at the high priest.

"Holiness—" he started.

"Captain Scurn. I find these intruders in the temple and I find you also here. Is there a connection?"

Before the scarred minotaur could defend himself, one of the guards said, "Holiness, we saw him lead this group into the temple, claiming this warrior was a prisoner you would desire to question and the others a unit of the State Guard."

"Holiness, I can explain! I led them here, then alerted the guards to their trick!"

Infernus smiled, rubbing his jaw. "Then you are deserving of a special reward, something of your heart's desire, I think."

Scurn gave Kaz a triumphant smile, then dipped his head in gratitude to the robed figure.

"I'm going to grant you a personal combat against four of the present grand champions from the surrounding arenas. It will be one of the highlights of the circus in the coming days. I'm sorry that it cannot be Kaziganthi de-Orilg himself, but this should more than satisfy you, wouldn't you say? If you kill them, you will be returned to the guard with full honors and a ranking high enough to earn you a post of commanding officer. If you die, then . . ." Infernus shrugged. The scarred minotaur was a veteran of the circus, but he was no match for four grand champions.

Scurn's strained voice expressed his realization that he had just been more or less sentenced to death. "But . . . but, Holiness . . ."

"Guards, escort Captain Scurn along with the others. See to it that he has the proper accommodations. It will give him time to consider his choice of actions when confronted by enemies of the state."

"Holiness, I am a captain of the State Guard—"

"Which follows the dictates of the emperor, the circle, and, of course, the temple." Infernus waved a languid hand. "You are all dismissed. Prepare yourselves for the circus. There will be no interruption of the combats this time."

With a protesting Scurn in tow, the guards prodded Kaz and his companions out of the audience chamber. Kaz caught one last glimpse of Infernus descending the dais and walking toward a hapless Ty. Then the doors closed.

Kaz tried once more to summon Honor's Face, thinking that they might as well make a last stand here as in the circus, but his thoughts were too confused. He had failed them, Ganth most of all.

And Ty, a dragon? It did not sound so surprising, not after all Kaz had been through during the war. Huma's silver dragon had also been a beautiful human maiden. Kaz had also seen one or two other dragons take human forms.

Hecar walked up next to him. "Kaz, I grieve with you. I swear that each blow I strike in the arena will be in your father's honor. They'll see a battle like they've never seen."

"Be quiet!" snapped a guard.

They completed the journey in silence, even Scurn, who was still obviously befuddled by his downfall. Kaz almost felt sorry for him.

The guards separated the prisoners, putting each into a different cell. They were careful to search the kender beforehand, removing several items, including a tinder box belonging to one of the guards.

Kaz and Scurn were the last two to be incarcerated.

"Inside," one of the guards commanded Kaz. When he obeyed too slowly, both guards prodded him. Once inside the cell, which was lit only by a torch that one of the temple warriors held, Kaz was quickly chained to the far wall.

The lead guard looked over the chains to be sure they would hold, then said to the prisoner, with a grin, "You won't be going anywhere this time. I'll promise you that."

He received no response from Kaz, which made him scowl. A moment later, the guards exited, taking Scurn with them.

Darkness enveloped Kaz, the only illumination coming from a small, barred window in the door. His eyes adjusted slowly. What's the point? he asked himself discouragingly. Infernus had everything under control. The minotaur race was his tool, to direct as he pleased. No one would believe that the high priest was anything but one of their own. Few would likely cross the high priest, even if they knew his origins.

What a jest it was, the history of the noble minotaur race. All they had achieved, all the adversity they had suffered, was for the sake of a dark goddess and her servants. Warriors had lived and died for generation after generation in the mistaken belief that they fought for the future of their own kind.

Warriors like Ganth.

Kaz closed his eyes and tried not to think. He forced himself to ignore the streaks of moisture gliding down his face and waited for the oblivion of exhaustion to overcome him.

What he got instead, after some hours of fairly fruitless waiting, was a visit from the gray man.

* * * * *

Polik did not like being dragged from his bed before sunrise. Polik, in fact, did not like being dragged from his bed several hours after sunrise, but Jopfer had requested his presence and the emperor feared the high priest sufficiently to obey.

The acolytes spirited him to the temple with their usual efficiency. It did not do for others to see the emperor rushing to an audience; that was bad for the image Polik had worked hard to perfect. That was why he had lasted in the role for as long as he had. Both the warlords and the high priest had found him well-suited. Polik believed he would go down in the annals of minotaur history as the emperor who had led his people to their destiny, and all he had to do in return was follow the words of those like Jopfer.

"This way," indicated one of his guides as they entered a hidden doorway of the temple. "His Holiness is impatient."

One thing that did annoy him was that few of the high priest's people bothered to address him as emperor. He would bring it up with Jopfer, delicately reminding the high priest that appearances were important at all times.

What did that emaciated fiend want at this time of night? Had they finally located the damnable Kaz? The shame of that travesty in the circus still angered the emperor. How had Kaz been allowed to wear that medallion? Where had it come from? As far as he knew, his rival of old had thrown the thing to the ground after the death of his brother . . . Raum or something like that. It unnerved him to think that Kaz had kept it all these years. Had he always planned to come back to challenge Polik?

Kaz was not that big a fool, but . . .

Before he realized it, he was in one of the smaller rooms behind the great audience chamber of the high priest. These were Jopfer's private rooms, the place where the pair generally met.

The high priest himself was seated in a chair behind a wooden desk that was a perfect copy of the stone seat atop the dais. Jopfer seemed lost in thought. The acolyte in the lead respectfully cleared his throat.

"You are here," Jopfer said complacently. "I expected you sooner. We have an important matter to discuss."

"I came as soon as I could." The emperor made no move to sit. He never sat down, no matter how much he ached, unless the high priest indicated it was all right to do so.

Jopfer gave no such indication. He dismissed the acolytes, then, when they were gone, he said, "Kaziganthi de-Orilg and his associates are in the custody of the temple."

Polik brightened up. "You have them all?"

"All. The old one, Ganthirogani of the same clan, died during the capture. His body will be returned to the clan, which will have some explanations to make."

The minotaur did not envy Dastrun, but was glad it was the Orilg patriarch and not him who faced the high priest's displeasure. "Good news, indeed. My thanks for alerting me to this."

"You should not have been so careless in the circus, Polik, altering my orders. If not for the fact that someone had already confused the commands and placed Kazigan-thi in a certain deadly situation, I would be especially angry. He was to have fought a single ogre, a certain triumph for him. Then, with his confidence swollen, he would have seen his father killed by the gladiators. It would have shattered his spirit, I think, made him malleable." Jopfer idly scratched his chin. "Merriq has paid for not being able to properly transmit commands."

So, despite Polik's transgression at the circus, the high priest was willing to forgive and forget. Polik was not quite certain he understood, but he was willing to accept his good fortune. "Then if that is all—"

"There is more."

"More?"

"Certain plans have come to the fore. A missing component of my—of our—success is now within my hands. I think it is ready to use. I do not see why we need delay any longer. The fleet is ready, and our warriors chafe at the bit, desiring blood and glory. It is time we gave them free rein."

Polik almost sat down in astonishment. "The campaign is to begin? The Supreme Circle—"

"Will sanction everything, some of them because they are as bloodthirsty as their warriors and the others because they would look like cowards to the rest." Jopfer's eyes seemed to blaze with anticipation. "For the announcement, we must plan a special day in the circus, a showing of our might to the general population. The event will highlight the deaths of the rebellious minotaurs, your ultimate combat victory, ensuring your place at the head of our people, and the announcement of the impending campaign."

The campaign. Polik could scarcely believe what he had heard. The campaign was to begin at last. "Where do we attack?"

Leaning back, the high priest replied, "I've chosen the humans to the west of us. It will be a two-pronged attack, with the fleet sailing north and coming around to their shores up there. They will transport an army with them, of course. Meanwhile, the rest of our forces will come through the mountains and crush their eastern border."

"Such a two-pronged attack could work against us as well as for us," Polik dared to point out. "They're only humans, I grant you, but there is always the unexpected."

"The plan will succeed. I will give you details concerning it on the morrow. Rest easy, Emperor. We have tremendous power behind us, a force as great as any army. On the day of the attack, you will know the details. I can say nothing more for now, but it will be a sign to our people that their patience has been rewarded. It will be a sign that this is the beginning of our conquest of Krynn!"

"At last . . ." Polik rubbed his huge hands together in anticipation, then recalled something said earlier. "Did you say my 'combat victory'? In the circus?"

"You are overdue for a victory, Emperor. This incident with the heretics has further emphasized the need to renew the people's faith in you. A successful duel prior to the announcement will nudge them in the correct direction."

"Against Kaz?"

"The thought had occurred to me," replied the high priest. "He has become uncontrollable, no longer a trustworthy addition to our commanders. He will have to die, but I fear that for us to ensure success in such a duel as you suggest, we would have to drug him beyond what is feasible. This combat must look true to all. No, his fate will be different. For you, I can find a more suitable opponent. There are two or three candidates among the grand champions, one especially who considers himself a far better choice for emperor than you, Polik. As a matter of fact, he was encouraged to make a formal declaration . . . or rather, he will be. See to it that he gets his reply in time for the event."

"Of course, Holiness." Another victory under his belt. No one would be able to deny his destiny, save for Jopfer, of course. However, Polik saw no reason why he could not find a way to remove the one obstacle to his complete authority, sooner or later. It would not be too troublesome to eliminate Jopfer.

"You may return to your bed." The high priest turned away, his thoughts already elsewhere. The acolytes came up behind Polik.

The day of destiny was to begin. The emperor could scarcely believe his luck. He had begun to wonder if the day would ever come. Jopfer was correct; it would be good to prove his right to rule just before the announcement. An imperial combat was definitely called for.

As the acolytes led the emperor out of the temple, his thoughts turned again to how simple it would be to remove the one minotaur he feared . . . once the campaign was well underway, of course. There were those among the circle who would welcome Jopfer's demise. From among them he would be able to find a capable assassin. Then, it would simply be a matter of timing. For all his power, there were limits to the high priest's control. It would not be hard to kill him.

After all, under the cloak of authority, Jopfer was just a minotaur like the rest of them.

Chapter 15
The Gray Man

Ayasha did not like the reason Helati gave her for needing her to watch the children, but she understood. Helati did not want to spend time arguing. It was terrible enough pulling herself away from the infants. She felt like a negligent mother, but hoped that, if something happened to her, they would grow up understanding why. She had to try to bring their father back.

This was her quest. The other minotaurs could fend for themselves.

No one was in sight as, before dawn, she stepped out to saddle her mount. In a few minutes, she would be on her way, with no one but Ayasha and her mate knowing her secret. She had given Ayasha permission to let others know once she was far away.

"You can't be serious about riding there alone, can you?"

Helati whirled about to find Brogan, his shoulder bandaged, standing a few yards behind her. He had moved so silently that neither she nor her mount had taken any notice of him. "What're you doing here, Brogan? And why isn't your wound healed? You are a cleric."

"My faith in Sargas has been . . . weak . . . of late. This is the best I could do. That's not important, though." He shrugged, changing the subject. "It's strange. I had a dream a short bit ago, about a human. I've rarely seen humans, save in war, and certainly not one all dressed in gray . . . from top to bottom. It was a short, strange dream. He told me he could not stay long, but he wanted me to wake up and find you. The children needed you more since Kaz was gone. That was what he said. Then, I woke up."

His words were disconcerting, especially about this human in gray. "Just your own fears, Brogan. There's nothing to the dream."

"But you're leaving," he pointed out. "And dream or not, I think you need to stay here."

"You were the one who wanted to gather an armed force and storm Nethosak . . . or was that a ploy at the time to get most of us back in the grip of the emperor?"

His expression made her instantly regret the rash comment. "It was meant honestly. I've thought things over, Helati. Kaz was correct about a large force being more hindrance than help. That is even more true now. If we rode in to save Kaz, we'd be riding right into the high priest's hands. The high priest is the one to watch, not old Polik."

"I can't just sit and wait. Kaz may need help."

"He may be dead already," Brogan returned bluntly. "I'm sorry to say that, but it could be true. Riding to Nethosak would then accomplish nothing except that you would share the same fate. Would Kaz want you to abandon the children?"

"That's not fair! You know I'm not simply abandoning them!"

The one-horned minotaur dipped his head apologetically. "I said that badly, but you know what I mean. The children should be your primary concern now."

"And what about Kaz?"

"He may return with your brother and the kender, all of them none the worse for their experiences. He may be a prisoner of the high priest. He may be dead. The point is, you must stay here and wait."

"Who can I ask to go in my place? This concerns my mate and my brother. Should I be any less than Tremoc? He journeyed over Ansalon time and time again, tracking down the murderer of his own mate."

"Tremoc was Tremoc, and although his legend has much merit, it shouldn't be the basis for this decision. Besides, you don't have to go to Nethosak yourself. There is another way to find out what's going on, Mistress Helati."

"What do you mean?" She eyed the other minotaur. "What other method could there possibly be?"

Brogan looked away. He seemed ashamed. "I have . . . a swifter way to contact Nethosak, swifter even than if we had messenger birds to use. Something I brought with me as an emergency measure."

Her eyes narrowed. "What is it?"

"A small medallion. I purchased it from a black-robed mage during the war, when I often needed to go places where I could not use my own powers without being noticed by a cleric of Paladine. It can contact anyone in Nethosak, but only for a short time. It turned out I never used it. I brought it with me, though. It should still work."

"Can I use it?"

"It's attuned to me, but . . . perhaps. I'd rather not explain a lot about it. . . . It's not something I'm proud of now." He spread his hands. "You must believe me, Helati! I would not lie to you about this. I never thought to use it since I planned to abandon my former allegiances, but now the opportunity and the need demand it."

Helati thought over his words carefully, then nodded. "All right, but let us both try it together."

Brogan agreed. They returned to his dwelling, where he moved aside a small chest.

"I was looking at it when you came. You see, I was already contemplating contacting someone I know back there." The one-horned minotaur pulled out a small silver medallion with a blue crystal in the middle. There were markings on it, but Helati could not make them out. Brogan held the item cupped in one hand.

"How does it work? I've never seen anything like it before."

"It's simple. I merely have to put my thumb on the crystal and my index finger directly opposite it on the other side of the medallion. Then I think of the location or person and close my eyes." He gave Helati a grim smile. "It cost me quite a lot, but I felt a need for it at the time."

Indeed, there was much about his murky past that needed to be explained, but that was not important to her now. Helati moved nearer so that she could read the detail on the artifact. Her mind was racing. "Who did you plan to speak with earlier?"

"I think there might be a few friends of mine who would still give me aid. I will try for them now."

"No, let me try. I have a better idea."

He looked at her, uncertain. Then, shrugging, Brogan handed her the artifact. "As I said, originally it was attuned to me."

"I have to try." Thumb and index finger in place, Helati concentrated. She tried for Kaz, but for some reason, the great clan house of Orilg invaded her thoughts instead.

"—to me—" began a voice.

She was so startled, she broke contact.

"What is it?"

"You have no need to fear that it won't work for me, Brogan." Without waiting for his reply, Helati tried again.

"—agreed to by him! There will be no further word on the subject!"

Dastrun. She would know his voice anywhere. The spell was working.

All at once, the voices were accompanied by an image. It was the chamber where Dastrun and the other elders held court, and they seemed to be arguing about something amongst themselves.

"He knew the danger!" insisted Dastrun. "He made a pact! We abided by that, not even telling the guard where he had gone! That is the end of it!"

"They are scheduled to die in the arena during some contrived ceremony," pointed out an elder female. "They are to die for no good reason, Dastrun!"

"It has been decreed—"

"Decrees! We're talking about honor and justice, Patriarch!" called another voice.

"The high priest has declared them heretics and traitors," argued another, "especially Kaz!"

Kaz. They were talking about Kaz. She had thought so. Then the patriarch spoke again. "He made his agreement. We will abide by it. The clan can gain nothing by dragging itself down with Kaz and the others. They will die in the circus, and that will be the end of it. Kaz is dead from this moment on. I have made my—"

"No!" Everyone in the chamber looked up, seeking the source of the voice. Only after the echo had died away did Helati realize that she had spoken.

"What in the name of Sargas?" muttered Dastrun.

Recovering, she spoke again. "No, Dastrun, that won't do."

"Who is that? Where are you?"

"I'm Helati. Kaz's partner and mate."

Many of the elders whispered to one another. The patriarch looked disconcerted. "Where are you hiding?"

"I'm not hiding, Patriarch. I've been given a device that I used to find out what is happening to Kaz. Well, I've found out what I wanted to know, and I do not like it."

"Now, Helati—"

She braced herself. Orilg was going to listen to her, Dastrun or no Dastrun. She had some things to say about

loyalty and honor. She was going to make them listen—
and act.

Kaz had better not die, Helati thought. If Kaz died, she
would make the clan pay dearly for its failure. There was
a side to Helati she had never let her mate see . . . but Dastrun and the other elders were about to be reminded of
why she had been nicknamed "The Terror" as a young
warrior.

Thinking of two infants waiting for their father to
return, she started talking.

* * * * *

The tap-tap-tap of the staff against the stone floor was
the first thing that alerted Kaz to the presence of another
in the cell. He opened his eyes slowly, wondering why he
had not heard the door being unlocked or even being
swung open. When his gaze focused on a pair of gray
boots half-obscured by a robe of the same color, he tried to
jerk himself to his feet. Unfortunately for Kaz, the chains
did not allow him to move so freely. The only thing he
succeeded in doing was nearly losing his balance and
crashing back against the wall.

The human in gray watched him in silence. He looked
exactly as he had appeared in the dream, save that he was a
little taller than Kaz recalled. The robed figure was, in fact,
nearly as tall as the minotaur. It also occurred to Kaz that he
could see the gray man clearly even though the torchlight
from the hallway was still the only illumination available.

"Another dream?" Kaz asked.

"It is hard to tell sometimes, isn't it?" The gray man
smiled in sympathy. "Sometimes I find myself wondering
whether I am awake or sleeping when I do this. This time,
though, I would venture to say that it is the former. Yes,
the former, not a dream."

"If you've something to say, you'd better say it before
the guards come to drag you away."

The gray man glanced over his shoulders. "Oh, they
can't hear me, Kaz."

"Why am I not surprised? All right, then, what do you want this time?"

A sigh escaped the robed human. He leaned on his staff. There was sorrow, great sorrow in his eyes. "I grieve for your loss, Kaz. I tried to predict what would happen, but I could only guess in the end. If I could truly see the future, it would be a terrible danger to Krynn, for I'd be tempted to alter one thing after another despite the agreement I made. That would only make matters worse, not better."

Kaz snorted. "I've no idea what you're talking about, mage. You are a mage, aren't you? Or are you a cleric of Gilean?"

The questions seemed to amuse the gray figure. "You might say I'm the foremost mage in the world and perhaps, in my own way, an unofficial cleric of the God of Neutrality. I am certain my appearance makes you think the latter, though the color gray is more the mark of my agreement with the gods Solinari, Lunitari, and Nuitari. It is the way they assure that I will not forget my place, or my vow." He shook his head bemusedly. "And they say the gods have no sense of humor. They have one. We just do not think their jests very funny."

"You still haven't told me who you are or why you're here." Kaz was growing tired of the gray figure's vague and confusing comments. "Why've you been haunting us? What's all this talk of balance?"

The staff went tap-tap-tap again. "So many questions, and so little I can answer. Your friend Huma was not half as questioning."

The minotaur's eyes narrowed. "That's where I know you from. I remember now! Huma said he met you before discovering the dragonlances!"

"There was a world out of balance then. The dragonlances were needed to restore balance, and the knight Huma became the catalyst. He was the most worthy one we could find within the time still left to us, and he proved to be better than anyone could have hoped. There are similarities between the two of you, you know. That was why I decided to keep an eye on you. I knew that even with the war over, there was still a danger, an imbalance. It is a gift, or perhaps a curse, given to me. I can know what the threat is, but am limited as to what I can do."

"You knew the truth about our high priest?"

"I discovered it. You have no idea what the presence of the two dragons means to Krynn, Kaz. The dragons, good and evil, were supposed to depart as part of the peace created among the gods. It was a pact of the highest magnitude. Yet, because one egg, the egg of a silver dragon, was lost, the entire pact could unravel. The egg meant a dragon stayed behind. In an attempt to effect some sort of balance, the world allowed for another dragon, one of evil nature, also to remain on Krynn. Unfortunately, it was the red called Infernus, one of the deadliest of the Dark Queen's servants. You, already tied to this history, became our one hope."

"What do you mean, 'already tied to this history'?" Kaz shifted uneasily. For some reason, he felt the gray man spoke the truth.

The staff tapped against the floor again. "There was a mage who held a wounded dragon prisoner. He used threats to her eggs to force her to do his will . . ."

Kaz's head sank. "I remember. The dragons should've been gone. It was just after the war. She and her mate had not left because they wanted to get their eggs back, the ones Brenn the Black Robe had stolen." He raised his head again and glared at the robed figure. "But Brenn fell victim to his own magic and, although the dragon perished, I brought her eggs to a place where her mate took them from me. They should be safe now, wherever they are!"

"The male silver was also wounded. You recall that. Because of his wounds, Kaz, one slipped from him. It slipped when it began to hatch, although he could not have known that. He circled, but could not find it and assumed it had broken. That was not the case, however. Dragon young are hardier than other newborns. Dragon eggs are very sturdy, and the fall only cracked the egg and stunned the hatchling. When it finally woke and freed itself, it did not know where or what it was."

"Ty . . . ?" Fate was laughing at Kaz again. That was the name of the young female's father—the male silver.

The gray man nodded. "The first intelligent creatures she saw, only days later, were humans, families moving on to new homes. Wanting to join, she reshaped herself without thinking. Although she was never with anyone long, the shape became so much safer to use that she soon forgot her birth form."

"All right!" snarled Kaz, growing weary of all of this. "So I'm tied to her past. That's all. You didn't have to involve me in all of this! I'm not responsible for what happened later."

"No, you are not. You were chosen, by me. The Dark Queen will use this situation. Everything for which you fought side-by-side with Huma of the Lance will be lost. We will return to endless war, with the outcome this time questionable." The gray man sighed again. "Ansalon has not recovered sufficiently from the last war to suffer such another. I chose you because I believed you would understand that. I chose you because I believed you were the best hope there was of returning Ansalon . . . and your own people . . . to its proper path."

"My father is dead . . . and I never wanted to be a hero."

Tap-tap-tap. "Kaziganthi de-Orilg, if I could, I would take your place, but I swore a vow to all three gods of magic, who, having removed themselves from the affairs of the others, have a vested interest of their own in maintaining the balance of the world . . . regardless of what their mages do. My power does not wane no matter which moon is dominant, but in return I must use care and I must always strive to help Ansalon, all of Krynn, remain in balance. I must guide others, and am never allowed to be the one who acts. Always it must be another."

Kaz was not certain that he agreed with, or even understood, everything the gray man said, but, in truth, he agreed that Ansalon could not endure a return to war. "Have you come to offer me a chance, then? Are you going to set me free and give me the means of facing Infernus?"

"Do you wish it?"

"Given a choice . . . yes."

"I have spoken to the young dragon. She will abide for now, but only because she is lost in her own mind. If you desire to help, to restore the balance, Kaz, there is one thing you must do, whether you perish or not. You must awaken the dragon within her."

Kaz grunted. "I thought Infernus was trying to do that already."

The gray man shook his head. "No, he seeks only to release the form and power of the young one to do his bidding. He seeks to twist the silver into his servant. If you hope for victory, you must awaken the true dragon. You must stir Tiberia to be what a silver dragon is meant to be. Only then can you possibly defeat the creature Infernus."

"I won't be able to do anything as long as I'm like this," Kaz retorted, indicating his chains with a rattle. "Are you planning on releasing me?"

His ethereal companion looked away in what might have been outright embarrassment. "You will know when the time comes." The staff tapped against the floor again. "The guard is stirring."

The minotaur glanced at the door, hearing, in the distance, the movements of the sentry. He turned his gaze back to the gray man, but the human was no longer there.

"Typical mage," he snarled under his breath. "More damned trouble than help!" Still, his mood had lifted, his determination returned. He had battled ogres, mages, and even living statues, defeating all of them. He might fall to Infernus, but he was not going to go complacently to his death.

It would have eased his mind if he had been able to retrieve Honor's Face, but surely any strong minotaur axe could cut through the scaly hide of a dragon, couldn't it? There was one way to find out.

Something blotted out the light. The shadowed head of the guard covered most of the barred window as he glanced inside at the prisoner.

"Something the matter?" Kaz asked.

The sentry peered inside, then snorted. After one more quick glance, he shook his head and departed without a word.

Alone again, Kaz considered the gray man. From what little he now recalled of Huma's encounters with the figure, the gray man never said more than he needed to say. He did not promise that Kaz would succeed; nor did he promise that the minotaur would live, even if he somehow did garner victory. Huma had died even though he defeated the Dark Queen; the same might happen to Kaz. It was not a comforting thought, but it did not dissuade him. If he had one last opportunity even to slow down the dragon's machinations, then he would gladly take it.

He wished the others were not involved. They might all perish. Even if the gray man mourned them also, he would immediately start searching for someone else to restore the balance. In some ways, his methods seemed almost as heartless as those of the dragon. Yet it was the gods who forced the mage to act as he did, the gods who interfered whenever they felt like it.

That was not quite the truth, and Kaz knew it. Paladine was not like that, and Kaz supposed that even the hands of the most powerful gods were tied at times.

"Paladine," he whispered. "Kiri-Jolith . . . and you, too, Habbakuk." The three gods made up the pantheon honored by the three orders belonging to the Knights of Solamnia. Kaz respected these three the most for their sense of justice and honor. Especially now, it made more sense to honor the Solamnic gods rather than Sargas, who seemed to demand so much and give pitifully little. "Do you think you could make an exception and interfere just one time? For me?"

He received no answer, of course.

*   *   *   *   *

Infernus looked out over his city, his kingdom. His eyes allowed him to see everything in exceptional detail despite the darkness. He could make out the tall walls surrounding the northern reaches of Nethosak. Nethosak had become a marvel that any race could admire, and the damage done by the war was but a memory. He had molded the minotaurs well in that respect; they worked like bees in a hive, constantly building and rebuilding for the good of the race.

There were exceptions, however. The greatest of these would perish, though, and his taint would fade before the year was out. The new campaign, the red dragon's campaign, would demand the minotaurs' full attention.

The minotaurs were his by right. Infernus knew that. It was he who had worked so long to make them what they were now. When he had come, at his mistress's bidding, Nethosak had been a young city only a fraction of its present size. The temple of Sargas had been less of a power then, as had been the governing body of the race. Already a competitive people by nature, Infernus simply played on that aspect of the minotaur personality and busied himself creating what would become the Great Circus and the games.

With his ability to shift form, he had easily infiltrated their kind. A green dragon, often used for plans involving subtle cunning, might also have succeeded in influencing the minotaurs, but greens, Infernus thought with a snort of derision, were poor military beasts. They were good for little plots behind the scenes, but they failed to comprehend the intricacies involved in creating an armed force or fighting a strategic, large-scale battle.

He had thought first of assuming the role of emperor, but the temple and the role of high priest offered a more secluded, secret hierarchy. It provided him with the privacy he needed, plus its influence could be even greater than that of the other arms of the government, if played correctly.

So much work, Infernus thought with pride, returning to his chambers. Under the guise of the high priest Presir, whom he had, of course, been forced to eliminate, Infernus had caused the first temple to be built. Its grand scale had appealed to the populace, and he had known that, when completed, it would continue to impress future generations as well. The audience chamber and his own personal rooms he designed so that he would be able, at times, to return to his true shape. Infernus had directed the artisans to carve the dragon relief that now stood over the massive doorway to the audience chamber.

He had actually enjoyed revealing himself to the small, pathetic group that had attempted to rescue the hatchling. Only the minotaur supposedly chosen to be the next high priest ever saw his true form, and that just before the dragon dispatched the unfortunate and took on his corporeal shape. In some ways, it was a pity these heretics had to die. It would have been a pleasant respite for Infernus to, on occasion, speak to someone who knew the truth.

Of course, there was the hatchling. Given time, she would understand better than anyone else.

"You would be more comfortable if you would just give in to your destiny, Young One," Infernus informed the tiny figure standing in the middle of the chamber. "I could ease the restraints a little bit, then."

"I won't help you!" Ty was surrounded by a field of crimson that pulsated with each breath the young woman took. The strain of standing through the night was obvious in her tense expression, but she had not sat down since Infernus had moved her here from the great audience chamber.

"Your will is a credit to your heritage. A human, even a minotaur, would not be so strong. They are all weak, the little races. It is we, the dragons, who should have rightly come to rule Krynn." The high priest indicated the city outside. "We are everything they are not. Look at what little they have done during their existence. They spend so much time quarreling with one another that they fail to achieve much else. They need the guidance of an older, wiser race to show them how the world was meant to be. They need us, Young One. That is why you should be willing to help me. It is for their own good."

"You're lying! Kaz and Delbin would never want me to

help you!"

There was a fleet waiting to depart in a matter of a few days and a vast army poised to march around and through the mountains to the west. They were awaiting his command. He did not have the time to spend trying to convince this confused young silver dragon of what was the right thing to do. Infernus decided that once the minotaur Kaz was dead, he would resort to harsher methods of persuasion. She would change her mind when the minotaur's body was brought to her. The hatchling's defiance, too, was a credit to her race, but enough was enough. Infernus had a world to conquer.

"You are weak, Young One, not so much in power but in mind. I see I shall have to do what I can to educate you, to teach you. You will come to appreciate my efforts, believe me." Infernus steepled his hands. Centuries of role-playing had ingrained certain human habits in the dragon's mind and body. He talked to Ty as he would one of his faithful acolytes. "This is for the good of all. You will agree in the end, even if your friend Kaz understands too late. It is better that his life ends before the great campaign begins. He would not cooperate, and his continued presence would only confuse otherwise loyal soldiers."

Yes, Infernus thought. The death of . . . Tiberia's . . . champion and the threat to her tiny kender friend would be enough to break the young one's will. It was a pity he could not take the girl to the circus to watch the minotaur's death, but it was too soon to risk bringing the youngster out in the open. Still, the same spell that had allowed Infernus to first discover his counterpart could be used again. The female could watch the events unfolding in the circus from here, in the temple, alone and helpless.

His captive continued to stand, as if by this mere act of defiance she could hurt Infernus. Infernus shook his head. "You weaken only yourself with this act, Young One. The minotaur will still die, and you will eventually collapse. Why not conserve your strength? Perhaps, if you get some rest, you will see things as they truly are meant to be."

To his surprise and mild pleasure, Ty did just that. She

sat down resignedly and, with a sigh, rubbed her eyes.

Then she did something that confused even the red dragon. Ty looked up and stared, her expression a questioning one. It was almost as if she were asking if she had made the correct decision by at last sitting down. But Ty was not staring at him. She was staring over the high priest's shoulder.

Infernus turned quickly, wondering if the minotaur Kaz had somehow magically escaped again, but there was no sign of any other figure. Uneasy for some reason he could not fathom, the dragon crossed the chamber and peered around, seeking any shadowy area that might hide a watcher as small as the kender. Still there was nothing to see.

He turned back to Ty, but the young one had already closed her eyes, exhaustion having swiftly taken over. Finally Infernus dismissed the matter and departed the chamber. He still had a war to finish planning . . . once he made the final preparations for the minotaur's death spectacle.

Chapter 16
Clan Loyalty

The announcement that Emperor Polik was to answer a challenge
in the circus was not the most important reason for the
vast crowd that squeezed into the huge arena that day.
Polik had been winning his challenges for so long that
most assumed he would win again. There were, of course,
many who would have preferred to see him lose, especially a few select members of the Supreme Circle who
cared neither for him nor for the influence of the high
priest. Be that as it may, most of the crowd, both those
able to gain entrance and those forced to wait outside and
simply listen, had come for different reasons.

The short but unforgettable appearance by Kaz, a supreme champion still recalled by many—whose fame had reached a new zenith since his escape—had galvanized many minotaurs. There was something of a mystique about the infamous champion who had shunned his race at the height of his success. When it was announced that he had been recaptured and would appear in the circus again, anticipation had begun to build. Many in the audience actually sympathized with Kaz, realizing that it took bravery to step away after reaching such a plateau.

Aside from Kaz, there was another reason why the minotaurs flocked to the circus in even greater numbers than usual. That reason was the rumored announcement. No one knew just what that announcement was supposed to concern, but it was to take place immediately after the emperor's expected victory, and the majority opinion was that the day of destiny had finally arrived. Everyone knew that the fleet was ready to set sail. The armies had been training near the mountains and were, by this point, ready for battle. The work still continued on ships and weaponry, but the might of the minotaurs was ready to be let loose. So the general populace was ready to believe.

Some wondered if the race had sufficiently recovered from its years of war and bondage, but they kept their thoughts to themselves. The emperor, with the high priest's blessing, insisted that the minotaur race was ready. The Supreme Circle, while a little less enthusiastic, affirmed its confidence in the people.

At the moment, the elite legions were marching in full dress uniform around the floor of the circus. Armor gleamed in the sun as hundreds of minotaurs marched in perfect unison. Each unit carried high its standard, emblems depicting creatures of strength. There were those of the Bear Legion, the Lion, the Hawk, and, favored of the temple, the Dragon. The order of appearance was based on the battle records of each of these units, with Dragon inevitably first, but all were considered stalwarts of the cause. Horns blared as each unit passed the boxes where the rulership of the twin kingdoms sat. Cheers went up from the different sections when individual commanders paraded past. It was a glorious day for ceremony.

Polik contemplated all this as he prepared for the imperial combat. Everything was going as Jopfer had said it would. Oh, to be sure, there were those in the audience who resented his reign and protested the efforts he and the high priest had put into the new campaign, but their only choice was to join the war or be dishonored in the eyes of their fellows. The high priest had been exceptionally successful in his determination to undermine all resistance. Minotaurs were encouraged by the temple to inform on naysayers. The number of spies employed by the temple and the circle—not to mention his own private corps—had quadrupled in the past few months.

One of his aides entered the chamber. "Emperor, a cleric seeks permission for a private audience with you."

It was about time, the graying minotaur thought. The combat was only minutes away. He had begun to wonder. "Send him in." To his servants, he said, "You are all dismissed. Do not return until you are summoned."

They knew the routine almost as well as he did. Polik did not care what they thought. Their livelihoods depended on his whims.

A robed figure, who might or might not have been the same cleric who had come the last time Polik had fought, entered the room moments later. They all looked the same to Polik—tall, narrow fellows with little humor. The cleric gave the emperor a cursory bow, then remained silent until the aide had departed.

"Well? Is it done?"

"Your challenger has received the blessing of the temple, as is proscribed by law. He has drunk the ritual goblet of wine and even now awaits the summons to the field."

That was it, then. The cleric had given the fool the carefully drugged wine. The temple was adept at creating mixtures that did their work and later left no trace. In fact, someone drinking the same wine only half an hour later would feel no effects. His challenger would not even be affected until about the time he stood on the ten-foot-high, ten-yard-wide wooden platform and it began to rotate under the power of a dozen or so minotaur warriors. It was then that disorientation would strike him.

That was all the advantage Polik needed. Sometimes he felt he could have defeated a challenger undrugged. The clerics, however, had the process down to perfection and did not like any tampering. Jopfer was very much like his two predecessors, so much so that Polik, who also had collaborated with these two, sometimes felt as if he were dealing with the same cleric who had first crowned him emperor.

"And Kaz?" he finally asked. "What about Kaz?"

"At this time, he and his companions are being rounded up for their journey to the circus."

"They should've been dealt with before my combat. My combat should be the culmination of events."

The cleric's expression did not change. "His Holiness has decided they should be used as examples after the grand crusade is announced. Their deaths will be used to remind other heretics what it means to defy the destiny of our race."

Polik scratched his jaw. "Suppose so. Would've done it different, myself." He shrugged. "That's it, then. Time for the duel."

"Sargas be with you, Emperor Polik."

"Yes, yes . . ." The emperor turned away, seeking his helmet. As ruler of the empire, he was allowed to wear the ceremonial helmet in the hand-to-hand combat. "You're dismissed."

The robed figure gave Polik a brief look of contempt, but the emperor's back was to him. With a final, even more cursory bow, he departed. Almost immediately, the servants and the aide returned.

"Are we ready to begin, Emperor?"

"Just help me find my helmet. I know it was here a moment ago."

Sighing silently, the aide forced back the thoughts that sprang to mind—thoughts that, were they known, could have got him tossed into the arena alongside the rebel Kaz—and started to search for his master's missing helm.

* * * * *

Infernus sat in the booth set aside for him and his aides, four lesser clerics flanking him. He was clad in the most elegant robes of the high priest, gold trim and diamond sparkles making him glitter in the sunlight. It was all the dragon could do to suppress his eagerness and satisfaction, but he had to maintain the mask of quiet confidence, especially now.

Back in the temple, the hatchling, Tiberia, would be watching all of this. Infernus had decided it would be good for the young one's education to see just how well her captor's plans were progressing. The spell would give Ty a view of what went on in the arena based on the red dragon's own perspective. The young one would see everything, including the death of her would-be champion, through Infernus's eyes. It was a clever spell.

The day of destiny is upon us, Infernus thought, allowing himself a satisfied smile that brought shivers to the one cleric who happened to glance his way. My day . . .

* * * * *

They're coming, Kaz thought, fidgeting. They're coming, and the cursed gray human still hasn't given me any kind of sign! The day before had passed without any clue as to what Kaz was supposed to do to free himself and the others. He had expected some clue from the mage before this moment; after all, the human had more or less promised. From what little he could recall of Huma's experiences with the gray man, nothing indicated that the figure was a liar or a trickster. Still, he was beginning to wonder.

Ty, Hecar, Delbin, Fliara . . . their lives all depended on Kaz. He could not let them down, even if it turned out that the gray mage had let Kaz down. When the guards came for him, he would find some way to win.

Paladine watch over me . . . and Helati and the children, just in case.

"It's time."

The voice startled him, especially when Kaz realized whose voice it was.

"It's about time you got here, mage."

"It is all a matter of balance, Kaz," responded the gray figure standing near the minotaur. "I can act only when it is time. Too much interference, and things might be tilted even further out of balance. We would not want that, trust me."

Kaz shifted. "Someday, I hope to have a conversation with you that makes some sense. Meanwhile . . ." He shook the chains that held him. "Are you going to free me now?"

"This is the time for everything to come together, Kaz. This is when the potential to rebalance the scales is at its zenith."

With the last word, the minotaur's chains—empty, but still locked—suddenly clattered against the wall. Kaz looked at his free hands, then at the manacles. There were some advantages to being a mage.

"What happens now?" he asked as he tested his arms and legs.

"The path is open to you." The door swung open just enough to allow Kaz out. "The rest is up to you."

"What about the others? I can't just leave them."

"I will watch over them as best I can. The kender knows what I plan and will do his part. If it encourages you further, I will tell you that a certain stubborn catalyst has made her mind known in Nethosak despite my intentions. As is sometimes the way, this catalyst's presence has given me a new and unexpected path to use, a path that your friends must take rather than aid you." When Kaz still hesitated, the gray man added, "Trust me. This will not work if they are with you, Kaz. You know that."

He did, but it was difficult to admit it, even to himself. Alone, Kaz could slip through the halls to where Ty was being kept. With the others, he ran the greater risk of discovery.

Thinking of Ty, he started, "The female. Where—?"

"Look in the lair of the dragon," the mage returned. For the first time, a hint of impatience appeared on the gray human's face. "The guards have been delayed, Kaz, but not for long."

The minotaur started for the door, pausing just before stepping through. He turned one last time to the gray figure. "I don't suppose you have a weapon?"

In response, the mage suddenly tossed his staff toward Kaz. The warrior reached out and caught it in midair. Despite its thinness, it felt like a strong, sturdy piece of wood. It would have to do. "My thanks . . . Hecar and the others . . . you'll . . ."

"It is the least I can do for you, Kaz."

"Thank you."

As he hurried out the door, he thought he heard the gray man add, "Huma would have been proud of you, minotaur."

* * * * *

As the minotaur disappeared down the hall, the gray man walked calmly over to the empty chains and stood in front of them, his back to the wall. The manacles materialized about his wrists and ankles, securing him. The mage nodded, then smiled. In his place there suddenly stood a minotaur, a minotaur who looked exactly like Kaz.

He waited for the guards to come.

* * * * *

With the events of the arena captivating nearly all of Nethosak, even the temple was nearly bare of occupants. Kaz did not encounter a sentry until almost the ground level. The sentry, not expecting an assault from below, had grown lax. When Kaz discovered him, he was leaning against the wall, staring up at the ceiling.

A blow with the staff to the stomach, followed by a

solid punch in the jaw, was enough to deal quickly with the guard. Kaz dragged him into an empty cell and laid him to the side so he would not be visible. As he finished, however, the minotaur heard the sounds of an armed escort.

Keeping clear of the open door, Kaz waited until the sounds continued past him. It was the escort for him and his comrades. He prayed to Paladine that the gray man would indeed watch over his friends. He also hoped the mage had done something to prevent them from noticing his disappearance. Kaz needed some time to reach his goal.

In the lair of the dragon. That could be only the high priest's personal chambers. Ty must still be there. It made sense, since, if the female had been escorted back to her own cell, she would have had to pass Kaz's. That had not happened.

There were no apparent guards when he entered the ground level. That was not too surprising. The vast majority would be attending the circus, the better to emphasize the glory of the sons of Sargas. Kaz had some inkling of how Infernus's mind worked. The dragon was one for showmanship and flash. He reveled in power and wanted others to recognize the supremacy of that power. Now that tendency was working for Kaz.

He had made it halfway from the stairs to the high priest's chambers when he nearly ran headlong into Infernus's chief acolyte. The other minotaur was so stunned, he did not react until Kaz was already upon him. The staff caught the acolyte under the chin. Kaz dodged a reckless swing, then lowered the staff on his adversary's head.

The blow should have only stunned the robed figure, but to Kaz's surprise, his opponent slumped to the floor. Kaz glanced at the staff, recalling that it belonged to a mage, then shrugged. A meditation chamber provided him with an adequate place to hide the body. Kaz hesitated once he had the cleric in there, pondering the voluminous robes and the high hood.

A few moments later, clad in the same robe and with

the hood pulled up over his head, he continued on his way. There was no method by which he could hide the staff, so he kept it out and used it as a walking stick, pretending some leg injury.

Two clerics, obviously on their way to the circus, gave him perfunctory acknowledgments, then hurried on. A temple guard straightened as he walked past.

His good fortune faded as he reached the doors to the audience chamber. Two guards stood on duty, guards who stared intensely at him as he walked up to the doors.

"I'm on official business for the high priest. Let me pass."

They did not move. The one on the right announced, "We've orders not to admit anyone. That comes from His Holiness himself."

"My orders are new. His Holiness left important papers behind that I'm to retrieve. Do you want to face his displeasure after I tell him you wouldn't let me pass?"

The words were enough to cause the two sentries discomfort, but still they stood their ground. The same guard spoke again. "The orders were very clear. No one is to enter, save the high priest himself."

"Commendable," replied Kaz with a nod. He stepped closer to the two. Both sentries shifted stance ever so slightly, showing their weapons, in this case a pair of sturdy battle-axes. "But I think I have a way of resolving this problem."

He brought the staff up sideways and charged both guards. One raised his axe and managed to deflect his end of the staff, but the other was slower. The staff caught him in the throat, and he went down, coughing and struggling to breathe.

The other sentry fought back, pushing against Kaz's staff. Kaz slipped to the side and used his momentum to strike the gasping minotaur with the hard end of his weapon. Again, the blow, which should have only stunned the guard, sent him slumping to the floor.

The remaining guard was still off balance. He stumbled forward, and Kaz caught him on the back of the neck, just below the head. The second guard joined the first on the floor.

The battle had not gone unnoticed, however. From across the temple, several guards and clerics came running. Kaz cursed, pulling a door open. He slipped through even as the first of the guards threw a lance at him. The weapon bounced harmlessly off the door.

The doors were designed to be barred from the inside, something Kaz found very useful. Kaz had the entrance barred in seconds. That would certainly hold off the guards for a time. Now he had to find Ty.

The audience chamber was dark, but it was not difficult to locate the rooms in back. Kaz found the doors, but could not open them. They were either locked or possibly ensorcelled. He glanced at the doors, then at the staff the mage had given him. It was not Honor's Face, but he was certain it was imbued with magic.

Raising the staff, he aimed for the center of the door. Behind him he could hear the barred doors to the audience chamber rattle as the guards threw their weight against them, so he rammed the staff against the door.

It shattered, sending splinters flying everywhere. Kaz had to fall back immediately lest he be injured by the debris.

No magic had kept the door sealed, only a simple lock. Clearing the remnants with the aid of the staff, Kaz entered.

Tiberia sat in the midst of a chamber that seemed almost as huge as the one from which he had just departed. A pulsating shell of crimson light covered the small figure. Prior to the minotaur's appearance, Ty had evidently been staring at a greenish globe that floated at the young prisoner's eye level. Even from where he stood, Kaz could see faint images skimming along the globe's surface. It was just like the red dragon to make his captive watch the deaths of Kaz and the others.

Ty rose to her feet at the sight of the minotaur. Her eyes were tired. A smile broke across her features. "Kaz!"

"I've come to free you, Ty."

"I know. The gray man said to wait for you."

"Nice of him to do that." He wondered if the mage had said anything else, such as how to break the spell that surrounded Ty.

The staff had worked before. Perhaps it would work again.

"Ty, curl yourself up into as small a ball as you can."

The female did as Kaz requested.

"Ready yourself!"

Kaz brought one tip of the staff down on the crimson field.

The force unleashed by the dragon's spell when the staff hit burned the magic artifact to ash and threw the minotaur across the chamber.

* * * * *

The guards chosen to escort Hecar and the others gathered the party together. Scurn was among the prisoners. The guards placed Hecar next to an oddly contemplative Kaz, who obeyed their captors' orders without protest. He did not have an opportunity to do more than glance at Helati's mate, but when he did, Kaz smiled back at him. It was almost as if Kaz knew some jest, which he had not shared with the others.

What can he be thinking about? Hecar wondered. Does he have a plan of escape?

They reached the main level just as several guards and clerics went rushing toward the doorway leading to the high priest's audience chamber. The guard leader called a halt and started toward one of the clerics, but Kaz suddenly broke his silence.

"If you delay, we won't make the circus in time. They can handle the matter."

If Hecar and the other prisoners thought it odd for Kaz to speak these words, the guards and their commander seemed to find them completely sensible. The leader nodded, and the small band continued on, departing the temple moments later.

"Kaz!" whispered Hecar. "If you've got a plan, you'd—"

"Be silent!" snapped a temple soldier. He swatted Hecar on the shoulder with the flat of his blade. Hecar was tempted to forego the circus and end his life in a valiant but futile struggle with the guard.

"Rest easy, Hecar." Kaz gave him that same peculiar smile again.

"But, Kaz—"

Delbin abruptly giggled. Hecar glanced at him, wondering what even a kender could find so humorous at this moment. Delbin glanced at Hecar, then barely forced back another giggle after looking at Kaz.

"Just a little longer, Delbin. It's almost time for the surprise."

None of the guards seemed to take notice of what Kaz was saying, which further perplexed Hecar. It was as if they knew Kaz was there, but paid no mind to anything he said or did.

There were ten guards besides the leader, which was something of a compliment to the four minotaurs and one kender they guarded. Given weapons and free hands, Hecar was fairly certain he and the others could have fought their way to freedom . . . at some cost, of course. Still, that was not likely to happen.

The streets were nearly deserted, most of the city's population having gathered in or near the Great Circus. Now and then a minotaur passed within sight of them, but, compared with the normal traffic in the busy city, Nethosak was a ghost land.

Then the attack came. Hecar likely would have chosen the same location, for it was narrower than most of the path, and the street was deserted, with many hiding places for armed warriors.

The band and their captors were suddenly surrounded by roughly a dozen or so minotaurs bearing swords and axes. Some of the newcomers were vaguely familiar to Hecar, but he had no time to consider that, for the guards formed a defensive position, some of them concentrating their weapons on the captives.

"Stand aside," commanded the guard leader. "These warriors are destined to redeem themselves in the Great Circus."

"You mean they're supposed to die there," said one of the strangers, a tall, dark-furred minotaur with a streak of white between his horns that ran all the way to the back of his head. Hecar was certain he knew him, but from where, he could not recall. "For daring to defy the high priest's desires and nothing more. I had another brother who died for reasons something like that. There's no honor in such a death."

"This is treason. You defy the will of your lords."

The leader of the newcomers smiled. It was a smile that Hecar had seen on only one other minotaur. Kaz. "We've got a history of defiance in our clan."

Beside him, Hecar heard Kaz quietly say, "All right, Delbin. It's time."

The temple guards did not seem to hear or notice the kender suddenly touch his manacles, which slipped off a moment later without a sound. Only belatedly did Hecar note the tiny lockpick in Delbin's hands, a lockpick that the kender put to use with astonishing speed on Hecar's own manacles. In the space of seconds, he had the chains off Fliara as well.

It was not until Delbin reached Scurn that one of the guards blinked and noticed what was happening. He turned to stop the kender's efforts, shouting, "The prisoners—!"

His outburst was all that was needed to send the two groups into battle. Three guards turned on the prisoners. Hecar, using his chains like a flail, swung at a soldier. His blow struck the minotaur's sword hand, causing him to drop his weapon. Delbin was instantly there, seizing the sword and handing it to Fliara, who was closest.

The minotaur with the streak in his hair laughed as he fought back both the escort leader and another temple guard. He wielded a sword large even by minotaur standards, a sword that whipped in and out and around with such speed and daring that it confounded the pair who fought him. Neither could get past his blade. The escort leader fell seconds later to a thrust.

Two more guards fell, one of them wounded in the leg, but one of their rescuers also died. Hecar swung the chains at any guard who came within range. One soldier managed to press Fliara back, but Hecar pulled his chains around the attacker's neck and did not loosen his grip until the guard ceased to move.

Someone bumped into Hecar from behind. He turned, expecting another attacker, and found Scurn, one hand still manacled, struggling with a guard who had evidently tried to run Hecar through the back. The guard was strong, but Scurn was stronger. The scarred minotaur pushed his opponent to his knees, then raised his knee into the guard's chin. Scurn's adversary collapsed.

Circumstance makes for strange shield-brothers, Hecar thought as he turned to fight some more. Never thought I'd owe that one my life.

"Give yourselves up!" demanded the leader of the rescuers. "You can't win this battle!"

The remaining soldiers lowered their weapons. Four of their number were dead, including the escort commander, with at least three others injured. Of the rescuers, only one had fallen and another had a wounded arm. All in all, a good battle, at least from Hecar's point of view.

"Toron!" Fliara ran over to the minotaur with the streak in his fur, hugging him. For no reason he could fathom, Hecar felt a twinge of jealousy. He was certainly not attracted to Kaz's sister. Certainly not.

"This is hardly the situation I'd expected you to get into, little sister!" roared the one called Toron. "You were always the strict, rule-abiding one in the family!"

"Toron?" The name was more than familiar, but as with Fliara, many years had passed since Hecar had seen this same minotaur. Toron, like Fliara, had been much younger. Hecar turned to where Kaz had last been standing. "Kaz! Your brother is—"

Kaz, however, was nowhere to be seen.

Hecar quickly scanned the street, fearing that somewhere he would find the fallen body of Helati's mate.

However, it almost immediately became apparent that Kaz was not among the dead and wounded.

Delbin tugged on his hand. Hecar looked down at the kender, who was trying to hold back a giggle. "He fooled you really good, but then he looked exactly like Kaz, which is what he told me he had to do in order to give Kaz the time to get where he had to, and, besides, it would have been harder for Kaz to do certain things if we were still prisoners in the temple—"

"What the blazes are you talking about, Delbin? Are you saying that wasn't Kaz with us?"

"No, it was the gray man from my dreams, and he said Kaz had the best chance to rescue Ty if we were out and safe, and, besides, Helati's been talking to your clan, which is why—"

"Which is why we decided to show the temple it can't push around Orilg, especially my own family." Toron walked up and patted Hecar on the shoulder. "And that includes you, Hecar! I missed the rest of what this little creature said! Where's Kaz?"

Hecar shook his head. "Delbin says he was never here, that some mage was here, disguised as him. That much I think I understand. Kaz went to rescue a . . . human female"—it would not do to tell Toron the truth just yet—"who is a prisoner of the high priest. The female's important for some reason."

"Then we should go back and help him! The others can handle these prisoners!"

"No!" piped up Delbin. "The mage said we should go to the circus!"

Hecar paused. On the one hand, he wanted to go back and help Kaz, but on the other hand, their interference might make it more difficult for Kaz to slip out with Ty.

"I wish Helati were here," he muttered. Her advice had always been sound.

"She's done enough as it is," replied Toron, "considering all she helped plan!"

"Helati's here? How is that possible? Where is she?"

"Not here, at least not in the flesh, but—"

Fliara joined them, cutting off her brother's explanation. Her expression was one of great concern. "Where's Kaz?"

"Not here," her brother replied, "that's all I understand. He might be back at the temple, if what Hecar here said is true."

"Then we've got trouble."

"Why's that?" asked Hecar.

She looked around, verifying something. "Scurn's missing, too."

* * * * *

As the ceremony announcing the imperial duel began, Infernus felt a tug of warning in his mind. The tug was something he had added to the hatchling's prison spell; it warned him if, say, the young one's power grew sufficient to disrupt or destroy the crimson cage. It also, as a matter of function, warned the dragon if some outside force attempted the same thing.

Infernus did not think the hatchling was sufficiently schooled yet to free herself. That left only outside influence and that, to the disguised leviathan, meant, impossible as it seemed, only one audacious creature.

"Kaz . . ." he whispered.

One of his subordinates, hearing the high priest mutter, immediately turned to see if his master desired something.

The chair of the high priest was empty.

Chapter 17
The Silver Hatchling

The fall, if not the shock, should have killed Kaz. He knew that very well. He should have struck the wall or the floor with the force necessary to crack his hard head open or snap his neck. It would have been appropriate. It would have been almost exactly like the death of his father.

Yet, while Kaz's head throbbed as if every drum in the homeland were being beaten, he was far from dead. His muscles ached, but that was fine compared with broken bones and a battered body.

"Kaz! Don't die! Don't!"

"I'm—" The minotaur tried to rise too swiftly and

encountered throbbing pain. "I'm alive, Ty, but I think I might regret that good fortune for the next several minutes."

"I thought you were going to die! I tried my best to keep you from falling so hard!"

Kaz's head began to clear. Finally he could see well enough to observe that Ty was still a prisoner, but the spell that held her had grown pale now, almost pink, and did not pulsate every time its captive breathed. The girl's words started to make some sense . . . he thought. "Are you saying . . . are you saying *you* kept me from breaking my neck?"

"I couldn't let that happen! Not after . . . not after . . ." Ty fought back tears. "Not after I couldn't save Ganth!"

"It's all right, Ty." Kaz slowly rose. The throbbing lessened, but his arm, the same one that had been injured in the woods, now hurt intolerably. "You can't be blamed for not saving him. Blame Infernus, if anyone."

"I hate him! I wish I could do something!"

Kaz rubbed his chin, more to take his mind off his pain than because he was thinking. "You might be able to, Ty. You remember the gray man from your dreams? He spoke to me. He told me you have a power within you. All you have to do is remember what it means to be a dragon, a silver dragon."

Ty closed her eyes, visibly concentrating. Precious seconds passed, but there was no sign of success. After a few more seconds, the young woman opened her eyes and shook her head. "I'm sorry, Kaz. I've been trying. I've been trying ever since he put me in here. I tried harder when the man in gray said you'd be coming for me, but I still can't do it! I only remember being human!"

From what Kaz recalled of dragons, they were born with an intelligence that was already exceptional, by minotaur standards. They understood innately how to use their wings and their most basic skills, physical and magical. Magic was so natural to them that they picked up the most simple tricks only days after hatching. They were adaptable when young, growing set in their ways only after reaching adulthood.

"It's in you, Ty. It's the only way you'll be able to defy Infernus. He wants you to be a dragon in form, but not in mind. He wants you to be a frightened child, obedient to him. He also needs you alive, so remember that you have some hold over him."

Ty tried again. For a moment it seemed as if she might succeed, then she fell back, gasping. The female shook her head again, saying nothing.

"Maybe if I can get you out of there first." Kaz searched around for the staff, then, noting a trail of ash, recalled what had happened to it. He wondered if anything had happened to the gray mage at the same time. Magic-users' staffs were supposed to be important to them, often containing spells that the mages spent years creating. Sometimes the staffs were even tied to the lives of their owners. Had he injured the gray man?

That could not concern him now. If he had no wizard's staff, then he needed to find something else magical, something to make headway.

Something magical?

The globe that depicted the events of the circus still floated in the same place it had prior to Kaz's rescue attempt. Its magic came from the same source: Infernus. It was risky, mostly to the minotaur, since Ty's power protected her better, but he could see no other possible tool.

"Ty, I'm going to try something. Do you think you can protect both of us from some magic?" He indicated the globe.

The young captive understood immediately what Kaz intended. "I'll do my best. I think I can, Kaz."

"Good. Now let's hope I can touch this."

"Infernus touched it a lot."

"That's encouraging, at least." Kaz gingerly reached for the globe, hoping the red dragon's ability to grasp it without harm was not due simply to his having created it.

His hands tingled as they closed on the magical sphere. Touching it was like touching something soft and malleable, yet solid. It was slightly warm. Encouraged, he held it tighter, raising it to chest level.

Kaz raised the globe over his head. "Get ready, Ty."

He threw the magical artifact at Ty's prison, at the same time backing away as quickly as he could.

Nothing happened, for just before it would have touched the magical cage, the globe suddenly vanished.

"You are a very tenacious pest, minotaur."

Infernus stood near the window. His eyes were a fiery red. The artifact floated above one hand. Without his gaze leaving Kaz, the red dragon dismissed his device.

"Others have said that about me before," Kaz returned, wishing he had Honor's Face in his grip. At least with the magical axe he would have stood a good chance of leaving Infernus with a permanent souvenir of this encounter. "Most of those are dead."

The false minotaur laughed. "Do you seriously think those words unnerve me, Kaziganthi de-Orilg? Do you imagine me shivering in fear at your implied threat? You are no more a threat to me than a bee's sting or a drop of rain. I am Infernus! I am the embodiment of power! I am a dragon!"

"Careful, your loyal followers out there might hear you."

"These rooms are proofed against sounds, minotaur. I have, on occasion, dealt with those who have failed me or attempted to cross my will. The hunters who failed to capture you. A cleric who protested my methods, calling them dishonorable. A fool of a general who thought he could bully a newly ordained high priest into being his servant." The robed figure indicated his domain. "They all challenged me in here in one way or another and paid for their folly . . . as you shall now."

Infernus pointed at the minotaur.

A wave of molten rock poured over Kaz before he could even move. At first the heat was searing. The rock flowed over him from all sides. Kaz fully expected to die there and then.

He did not. The rock cooled as it touched him, turning so brittle that all he had to do was move to shatter it and free himself.

"Impossible!" roared the red dragon. "Impossible . . . or your doing!"

His last words were directed at Ty, who stood defiantly even though still a prisoner. The damage the staff had done to her crimson cell had given her some respite. Ty had been able to regain some of her strength.

"I won't let you hurt him!"

"You will not? You who are less of a threat than he is? Little One, if you bore a will as strong as the minotaur's, I might consider your words of some import, but you are nothing. You are an infant not yet familiar with much more than breathing and eating. You know a few basics of magic and think you can stand against me! I am centuries old, far older than most and far more dangerous than any. Do not interfere again, Little One. I need you alive, but not necessarily whole. Simply alive."

Ty glared.

A wind buffeted the disguised dragon, but did little more. Infernus smiled and waved a hand. The wind died away. The dragon glared back at the defiant young female.

The cage began to crackle with renewed energy. Ty's legs buckled, but to her credit, she did not scream.

Angered by the high priest's assault on Ty and knowing it would be his best chance to strike, Kaz leapt for Infernus. Unfortunately, Infernus was far swifter than any minotaur could ever have been. He reacted even as Kaz was in the air, turning his burning eyes on the flying figure. Kaz found himself floating in midair, helpless. The high priest stalked toward him, his expression less and less like that of a minotaur and more and more like what would appear on the reptilian visage of a dragon.

"Enough! It is time we ended this! Emperor Polik is no doubt just beginning his duel, the one that will reaffirm his right to lead the race in the grand campaign. He will win, of course, though the duel is planned to take several minutes simply for the sake of drama. My presence will be required then for the announcement." His mouth stretched in a way that was impossible, showing far too many teeth. "Consider yourself fortunate. That means I shall make your death a quick one. Not a painless one, but a quick one."

Kaz barely bit back a cry as his arms, legs, and head stretched in different directions. His muscles strained, and it felt as if his bones were about to be torn apart. He fought against the strain, but his efforts were for naught. Slowly but surely, he was going to be dismembered, one piece at a time.

"Let him go!" he heard Ty call. "Let him go!"

Infernus only laughed.

"I said let him go!"

A cry coursed through the chamber, but it had not come from Kaz. The minotaur fell without warning to the hard floor, only a last-minute turn preventing him from breaking his arm. As it was, his left leg felt numb.

"You . . . hurt . . . me . . . you . . . little . . ." Infernus sprawled against a column, his chest heaving rapidly and his eyes wide in both anger and surprise. There was no physical evidence of what Ty had done to the red dragon, but the robed figure's reaction was enough to indicate that it had been a mighty blow, indeed.

Rising from the floor, Kaz quietly stalked toward Infernus. Every muscle in the minotaur's body cried out in pain.

"I can see . . . that your education is going . . . to require some rethinking."

The minotaur was close enough. "Infernus?"

The red dragon turned, still not quite recovered.

Kaz punched him.

He had the satisfaction of watching Infernus fall back, the blow so sudden that the high priest did not possess the wherewithal to brace himself. The robed figure tumbled to the floor, rolling several feet.

If I only had Honor's Face, Kaz wished. I could probably end this now.

It was not until he had completed the thought that he realized the axe was somehow in his hand. The dragon's will had been shattered to the point where his hold over the magical weapon had vanished. Once more Honor's Face obeyed its master's command.

Kaz grinned, starting toward the sprawled figure. Infernus was just rising to his hands and knees as Kaz reached him. The minotaur stopped, raised the axe, and said, "This is for my father and every other minotaur, dragon!"

A blood-red serpent knocked him off his feet. Kaz fell back, still somehow managing to maintain his grip on his weapon, and saw that his first observation had been inaccurate. It was not a serpent that had attacked him, but rather a long, scaly tail.

A dragon's tail.

Infernus was shifting, throwing off the form of a minotaur. The robe tore to shreds, unable to contain the swelling form. Folded wings burst through the back of the garment, then opened and stretched. The last vestiges of the high priest's clothing scattered as the red dragon expanded. He was nearly full-grown before Kaz could even rise.

The draconian visage twisted toward him. "Insufferable creature! Audacious gnat! You dare strike me! You dare to think you can destroy me!"

"You like to hear yourself talk, don't you?" Kaz challenged, trying to throw the dragon off. "You do a lot of talking, Infernus."

His words further enraged the leviathan, which was what Kaz had hoped for. The more enraged the dragon got, the less thinking Infernus would do. Red dragons, the minotaur recalled from the war, had terrible tempers that often led to their downfall in combat.

"I will crush you!" Infernus raised a massive paw and brought it down.

Kaz jumped aside. It was a clean miss. He adjusted his grip on Honor's Face and waited. If Infernus did that again, Kaz would be ready.

"Your race was nothing until I came along, minotaur!" the immense dragon cried. "Beasts no better than the cows you resemble! I made you into the master race! You yourself are the product of my careful culling of the weak!

You should be grateful to me! Without my touch, this race would have died out long ago!" Infernus hissed. "Now all I demand is my due."

"Your due is waiting for you in my hands," Kaz replied calmly, hefting the axe.

Infernus raised a paw and brought it down again. The strike was nearer, but again Kaz managed to leap out of the way. As he moved, he counterattacked, swinging Honor's Face up in a vicious arc. The gleaming head buried itself deep in the dragon's paw.

With a roar of rage, Infernus pulled the injured appendage away, tossing Kaz and the axe aside in the process. Blood splattered both the floor and the minotaur as the red dragon shook his paw. The minotaur scrambled to his feet, retrieving his weapon. Without hesitation he advanced toward the crimson leviathan's other forepaw, axe up and ready to strike.

His monstrous adversary saw him too late. Infernus had time only to register the small figure's new position before Kaz brought the deadly axe down again.

If the first cry had been deafening, the second threatened to make Kaz's head burst. It seemed impossible that those outside could not hear the dragon's roars despite whatever spell or handiwork was designed to block the sound.

"Gnat! I will eat you instead of killing you outright! First a hand, then a foot, using my magic to keep you alive and conscious until I snap your head off your limbless torso! I will wreak such pain on you as you have never imagined!"

"You're talking again," Kaz pointed out. "All you ever seem to do is talk."

"Ha!" The eyes of Infernus gleamed. His mouth opened. A great burst of flame shot toward the minotaur. It was too wide to avoid. Kaz rolled to the floor, praying the flame would go over his head.

Instead, the length of flame turned upward at an impossible angle just before it reached Kaz. Tapestries caught fire, and the ceiling began to smolder.

The dragon turned back to his captive. "You again! You are becoming more trouble than you are worth! I can see that before I can remove the minotaur from my sight, I must first deal with you!"

To the minotaur's horror, Ty and the magical cage started to fade away.

"Kaz!"

"Ty! Fight it, Ty! You're a dragon, same as him! Your powers are every bit as strong! You've seen that! Don't let him send you away, Lass!"

"Ka—" The last faint image of Ty dissipated.

"Now, then!" roared Infernus, swinging his head around so he could again concentrate on the minotaur. "Now, then. This has taken long enough, gnat. Emperor Polik should have begun the duel by now. I am needed by my people. It is time you died."

"You think so?" Kaz held Honor's Face before him. It had served him well in the past, but he doubted it was strong enough to turn away the dragon's magical might.

Infernus chuckled. "Oh, yes, gnat. I do."

The dragon raised his head. There was no hope that the axe, even with its powers, could stop dragon flame from such a huge and savage creature.

All of a sudden, the floor began to rumble. The red dragon rocked back and forth, stunned by the unexpected quake. He roared his anger, but Infernus could do nothing, his balance already lost. His wings flapped, but in the chamber he did not have the room to rise aloft. In the end he merely tipped over, fortunately not in the direction of Kaz.

The minotaur rolled away from the center of the quake. Kaz had no idea what could be causing the natural occurrence, but thanked Paladine, Kiri-Jolith, Habbakuk, and any other god that might have had a hand in it.

From within the rising, cracking floor came a roar of challenge. Stone fragments flew in every direction as the swelling floor rose higher. Infernus struggled to roll over so he could right himself, but the vibrations shook him loose each time he almost gained a talonhold.

Then the cause of the quake burst through the floor, rising swiftly and pulling itself free. Its silver head gleamed, and wings as smooth as ice stretched for the first time ever. Despite the physical similarities between the two reptilian visages, there was something noble in the face of the second dragon, a sense of honor. That alone was the great contrast between the two behemoths.

The silver dragon looked around, finally locating Kaz, who could only stare in awe.

"Kaaazzz! I couldn't let him hurt you!"

"Ty . . . Tiberia."

"So the hatchling has found herself!" mocked Infernus, righting his massive form. "Not the most opportune time, but I will make do. This means I may start your education even sooner."

"No!" Tiberia whirled about to face her counterpart. "No! You don't care about anyone but yourself! You hurt others and expect everyone to obey you!" The silver dragon raised her head so she could almost look Infernus in the eyes. "I don't have to! I don't have to, and I'm going to make sure no one else will ever have to, either!"

As powerful as the young dragon was, Kaz doubted that Tiberia alone was a match for Infernus. She might have the raw power, but she lacked the red's guile and experience. Infernus would deal with her swiftly unless someone could direct the hatchling, someone with more experience in combat involving dragons.

Why always me? Kaz silently grumbled. Why always me?

Infernus leaned back as he spoke, possibly due to his injured forepaws. "You challenge me, do you, Little One? You think you have the might? My kills, especially of your kind, number high. I've not had a good struggle in many years. I won't kill you, of course, since I have need of you, but you will not fly for decades and you will always move with a limp, perhaps because one of your limbs will have been bitten off."

His words were having an effect on the silver dragon, who had never fought before. Kaz saw uncertainty grow in Tiberia's eyes, and the glittering wings began to twitch nervously.

Infernus was not paying any mind to the minotaur, the red considering the other dragon a more serious threat. Kaz waited until the larger creature's head swayed away from him, then ran as fast as he could.

"Give up now, Little One," Infernus was saying. "There is a place for you, too, if only you will see the way. There is—"

It was at that moment that Kaz leapt onto Tiberia's back. The silver dragon jerked, but, fortunately, did not whip around to remove the sudden weight. What she did do, however, was back away abruptly from Infernus, the spell of fear broken by the minotaur's action.

"Tiberia . . . Ty . . . back away farther, but let me get to your neck so I can sit there!"

The dragon obeyed, albeit a bit awkwardly.

"A dragon rider are we?" Infernus unleashed a throaty chuckle. "And where is your dragonlance, minotaur?"

"The axe and my friend will do just as well, Infernus!" Kaz's words were meant more to instill some degree of confidence in his companion than to frighten the red dragon.

As he expected, Infernus did not take his threat seriously. "I will remember your sense of humor after you are gone, gnat!"

A whirlwind filled the chamber, tossing loose rubble directly at Kaz and Tiberia. The dragon managed to bash away the first few large pieces, but several easily flew past her guard. Kaz pulled himself behind Tiberia's head and neck as much as he could, but stone after stone pelted him, marking his arms and legs with small nicks and cuts. Tiberia roared as stones struck her with considerable force.

"Surrender him, hatchling, and I will cease!"

"I won't!" cried the silver dragon in a small voice. "I won't!"

Kaz struggled upward. He needed to be high enough for Tiberia, and only Tiberia, to hear him. "A fireball! If you can make a fireball, aim at his—"

Tiberia unleashed a fireball, a good-sized one, at Infernus's chest. The flames licked at the red dragon for several seconds, but the monstrous creature seemed barely affected by it.

"Fire? You send fire against me? I am a red dragon! Fire is my element more than yours!"

A ring of flame burst to life around the pair, causing the silver dragon to back up. The ring was so tight that Tiberia could move only a few steps. Infernus laughed.

Again he spoke so that only the silver could hear. "Listen to everything I say first, Tiberia! I want you to make another fireball! I—"

"It won't hurt him!"

"Don't worry about hurting him that way! Listen! I want a fireball in his eyes! The biggest and strongest fireball you can create! Do it now!"

Kaz held his breath, hoping Tiberia would do as he said. They needed to reverse the course of battle.

He felt the silver leviathan shudder. A sphere of flame larger than the red dragon's head flew unerringly into Infernus's visage. The smile of mockery twisted into astonishment.

"Now, Tiberia! While he can't see! Jump and attack! It's our best hope!"

The massive silver form leapt forward, crossing over the flames without hesitation. The young dragon trusted Kaz that much. Smaller than Infernus, Tiberia was still an enormous projectile. Infernus, still fighting to restore his vision, was unprepared for the force of a half-grown dragon falling upon him. The injured paws scratched at Tiberia, but there was no stopping the silver's descent. The two leviathans crashed together, Kaz desperately hanging on and hoping Tiberia would not be forced onto her back.

"Again, in his eyes!" the minotaur cried.

To her credit, Tiberia managed a third, though smaller, fireball even while tangled up with the red dragon. Infernus roared as he sought again to protect his eyes.

"Hold him fast!" Kaz leaned to one side and, using his better arm, swung his battle-axe in the direction of the red dragon's neck. Infernus twisted, however, and instead of the neck, the axe bit into his shoulder.

The red roared, throwing Kaz and Tiberia to one side. The silver's great form crashed through the wall dividing the room from the audience chamber. Tiberia's momentum was such that she ended up almost on top of the raised dais Infernus used when acting as high priest.

Kaz was astonished to find himself still holding on to his companion. Tiberia's body had knocked a clean hole. The warrior felt as if he had just survived the hailstorm of all hailstorms unprotected.

"I will chew you slowly, minotaur!" Infernus barged through the hole without pause, causing still more masonry to fly and creating huge cracks that ran up to the ceiling. "I will shred your wings, hatchling!"

Kaz wondered just how much more damage this part of the temple could take before the ceiling caved in. While both Tiberia and Infernus were likely to survive such an incident with little more than a few bruises, Kaz was not so well armored.

The silver dragon stared at her foe. Another fireball formed before Infernus, but this time the red dragon reacted quickly enough to disperse it.

"No more of that trick, hatchling," snarled the crimson terror. "No more tricks at all."

Infernus charged. Tiberia tried to back up, but fell over the desk and the dais. The collision between the dragon and the dais was enough to shake Kaz loose. He fell over the front end of the dais and rolled down the steps just as the two dragons met.

The minotaur took one look at the two gigantic forms descending in his direction and scurried away toward the barred doorway as fast as he could. He had no plans to abandon Tiberia, but he would be little good to his friend if he were crushed.

Under the combined mass of the two dragons, the desk and dais were quickly reduced to rubble. Kaz gave thanks that the red dragon had seen fit to have the audience chamber built so vast; as it was, he was only a few yards away when the dragons' heads finally struck the floor.

The pair fought with tooth and claw now, Infernus trying to tear out Tiberia's throat with his talons, and the younger dragon simply trying to shield herself. There was no good target for Kaz, not yet, but he did have an idea.

"Tiberia! The injuries! Bite them!" Honor's Face always struck deeper than a normal axe and always dealt more damage. Even now, it was clear the red dragon was experiencing spasms of pain.

Tiberia tried to snap at the injured appendages, but her position would not allow her to get close enough. In desperation, she sank talons into one of the red dragon's injuries. Infernus hissed and backed away, the paw now covered in blood.

Using the respite to save herself, Tiberia pulled her silver form toward Kaz and the doorway. Kaz turned and tried to open the doors, but realized almost immediately that there was no way he could do so in time.

Infernus raised a paw and roared, "No! You will remain in here! I command it!"

It took Kaz a moment to understand why Infernus suddenly seemed so anxious. If Tiberia crashed through the doorway, the presence of dragons would be revealed. Infernus clearly did not desire that information known to anyone, not even the clerics.

The crimson behemoth started a spell, but there was not enough time for him to complete it. Kaz threw himself to the side. The doorway and the surrounding walls gave way easily under the weight of the retreating giant. Kaz wondered if the clerics and guards still waited outside. If so, he almost pitied them.

The moment a gap appeared, the minotaur rose and darted through it. Tiberia was halfway out into the temple's front hall with Infernus following close behind. Whether it was his rage or the thought that the silver dragon had already revealed the truth about what was happening behind the doors, the high priest moved as if he did not care who saw him.

The scene in the hallway was one of chaos. A number of bodies were scattered here and there, victims of the collapsing doors and walls. Infernus had spoken true when he had said that his chambers were proofed against sound. Kaz found he had no sympathy for the servants of the high priest. There were still several alive, but they were doing little at the moment, save gawking at what had burst out of their master's chambers. Some of the more intelligent quickly turned and fled. There were some challenges even too great for minotaurs.

Kaz was caught up in conflicting choices. He wanted to get Tiberia out of here. The silver dragon could not maneuver well, and at close quarters the advantage would continue to belong to her larger, more experienced foe. Yet, fighting Infernus in the sky was not something Kaz wanted Tiberia to face, either.

As he tried to get nearer to the silver, who had by this time made it out into the somewhat cramped hallway, Infernus burst through what was left of the wall. Pieces of marble rained down on those nearby. One cleric died screaming as he was crushed. Kaz dodged the first two pieces that slammed into the floor near him, then tripped over rubble just as he was almost out of range. Twisting helplessly, he fell onto his back. His sudden upward view revealed yet another enormous fragment bearing down on him.

Before he could react, strong hands gripped his shoulders and pulled him up. Honor's Face skittered away. Kaz finally pulled free of his rescuer's grip and glanced over to where he had been lying. The fragment had embedded itself deep into the floor. He would have been crushed. Grateful to his rescuer, Kaz looked next to him and discovered a wide-eyed Scurn.

"You vanished during the rescue, Kaz!" shouted the scarred minotaur, finally looking down at him. "I knew you'd come here! I knew you'd try to rescue the damned human whelp, and I want to help, for what the cleric did to me!"

"Scurn! Never mind that! Just get out of here! Only a fool would stay here!" Which means me, Kaz silently added.

"What's happened here? Where's the female? Why're there dragons, Kaz?"

He saw no use in lying to Scurn. "The girl's the silver one, and your precious high priest is the red! They're both dragons, Scurn! They've always been dragons!"

"Dragons? The high priest is a dragon? What nonsense is this?" Nonetheless, the other minotaur eyed the red differently.

"He's always been a dragon, you fool! Every high priest has been *him* for centuries! He killed them and then made himself look like them! Just listen to him!"

Perhaps Scurn might have disbelieved what, even to Kaz, sounded like nothing more than a fantastic tale, but at that moment Infernus caught sight of them.

"Gnat . . . and the unfortunate captain as well! How appropriate this is! You will get to die together after all!"

The voice was not exactly Jopfer's, but, from Scurn's horrified expression, he clearly recognized the high priest.

A silver form again blocked the red one's path. "I said leave them alone!" demanded Tiberia. "Kaz is my friend! You can't hurt him!"

"As stubborn as a red you are, hatchling, but more repetitious, it seems." Infernus eyed the younger dragon again. "I see I must still beat that stubbornness out of you. You and your little friend have cost me dearly as it is!"

The two dragons faced off once more, their huge bodies wreaking havoc with the building each time they even moved a few paces. A portion of the ceiling caved in behind Infernus. Most of the remaining clerics and guards had retreated from sight.

"That's . . . that is the high priest?" whispered Scurn.

"That's a dragon, too, Scurn, one that thinks it should control our lives, our destinies! It thinks it has the right to be our master!"

"Our master?" The other minotaur's expression grew grim. Kaz had touched the one point of agreement among

285

all minotaurs. No one but a minotaur had the right to rule the race. Anyone else, anything else, was an enemy of the people. "He wants to be our master?"

The dragons snapped at one another. "That's right, Scurn. Our master, body, mind, and soul."

"Never . . . our master . . . Sargas take me for a fool!"

"Then we have to help the silver dragon! She's our only hope! We have to do what we can!"

Scurn nodded absently, his eyes still fixed on the red form. Kaz wondered if he was thinking of all he had done in an attempt to ingratiate himself to the high priest. "You're right, Kaz. You're right."

To the other minotaur's surprise, Scurn abandoned him, fleeing through the temple entrance and losing himself in the streets beyond. The action was so sudden, it left Kaz stunned. He had not expected much aid from Scurn— what could the other minotaur do against a dragon?—but he had not thought Scurn capable of such outright cowardice, regardless of his flaws or their past enmity.

Scurn's flight did not go unnoticed by Infernus. "So much for your ally, minotaur! A sensible coward, that one!"

"But I'm still here, Infernus."

"As if that makes a difference, gnat!"

With his tail the red dragon battered the wall to his side, sending fragments flying toward both Tiberia and Kaz. Tiberia swatted away what she could and actually used one wing to deflect others from the minotaur.

"Be ready for me, Tiberia!" the minotaur called. Fortunately, the silver understood what he wanted, for Tiberia lowered her back end, making it simpler for Kaz to leap aboard again. Kaz hooked both feet into areas where the scales gave way a little, effectively creating stirrups.

Infernus moved forward only a breath after Kaz had gained his mount. Talon struggled against talon. Then, while the two behemoths battled, Kaz extended his good arm and opened his hand. Once more, Honor's Face returned to him.

The red dragon had attempted no further spells, perhaps preserving his strength for physical combat. It might even have been the result of Infernus having lived so long among the minotaurs. While they did not completely eschew sorcery, they preferred physical strength over the power of magic. A dragon who had worn the guise of a minotaur for centuries may have picked up some of the same tendencies.

Of course, even without magic, Infernus stood a good chance of defeating them.

Tiberia and the red snapped at one another, Infernus ever gaining advantage. Kaz struck whenever he could. Only one of his attacks had any effect on Infernus, a gouge in one paw. Anger fueled the red's attack, though, and almost immediately the ground gained was lost again.

The minotaur felt truly ineffective. With a dragonlance, he might have had a chance to spear Infernus and end this with his life still intact, but, despite the power of his axe, he lacked the reach to do more than harry his foe. If he hoped to be at all effective, he had to be able to reach Infernus's neck or strike his torso with the hope of piercing deep. Only then could he hope to do grave injury to the beast.

Kaz glanced at his favored weapon, wishing, for once, that it was one of the legendary lances of the war. With the lance, they could win.

Honor's Face shivered in his grip and stretched. The mirror blade sank into the shaft, which grew longer and longer yet felt as if it weighed no more. A swelling near the minotaur's hand became a protective guard. Another outgrowth stretched to the neck and shoulders of Tiberia, gently wrapping around her throat.

In the blink of an eye, before the gaping minotaur's astonished gaze, Honor's Face had become the very thing he needed for victory. Kaz now held a dragonlance, secured for battle.

He had always wondered about the origin of his axe and now he realized that it had always been linked to the lances. The dwarf craftsman who had given it to Sardal

Crystalthorn might have been one of the same group who had presented Huma with the first dragonlances.

Kaz shifted the lance. Whatever the reason, he had what they needed. "Tiberia! Back away!"

His companion did. Infernus did not at first realize why Kaz had given the command until his fiery eyes caught sight of the long, majestic weapon trained on him.

"We have a knight among us," he mocked.

"No knight," Kaz returned, fixing the point on the dragon's chest, "but a knight's dragonlance. Forward, Tiberia!"

It was a sign of the young one's faith that she obeyed this latest command without hesitation. Tiberia charged forward. Infernus roared contemptuously, attempting to swat the lance aside, but somehow it shifted, moving away from its original target almost of its own accord. The point dug into the red dragon's wing, tearing through the tough membrane with as much ease as a burning knife in soft snow.

Infernus roared in pain, glancing at the huge tear. The lance bit again while his attention was diverted. Kaz barely had to make sure of his aim. The dragonlance moved like a creature with a mission of its own . . . which perhaps it was. There had always seemed to be something lifelike about the weapons. Kaz recalled how they rarely seemed to miss their targets, even if inflicting only minor damage.

Twice more the dragonlance nicked an increasingly baffled Infernus. None of the wounds was serious alone, but the total of the dragon's injuries could not help but begin to take a toll, even on such a massive beast as the red.

Infernus backed up, destroying more wall and causing yet another segment of the ceiling to collapse. His eyes fixed on the dire weapon wielded by the minotaur. Kaz could almost sense the magic being deployed.

The dragonlance suddenly glowed. A crimson aura surrounded it, slowly turning it as black as pitch. Kaz felt the dragonlance stiffen, grow cold.

No! Not now! the minotaur desperately thought. We

have him! Incredibly, the dragonlance seemed to react. The blackness faded and the weapon grew pleasantly warm. The aura vanished.

"Not possible!" hissed Infernus. "Not possible!"

Perhaps if the red dragon had been at full strength and concentration, he would have succeeded, but now his magic was not strong enough. The lance struck twice again in rapid succession, piercing the same wing again and, on the second attack, nicking the side of the dragon's neck just above the shoulders.

Infernus pressed himself against what remained of the wall, his breath a little ragged. There was a hint of surprise in the fiery orbs, a hint of surprise and the first glimpses of fear. Nonetheless, he was not beaten. "I have worked hard and planned long! You will not deny me my destiny! You will not deny me my minotaurs!"

Kaz's retort went unspoken, for the floor was suddenly aswarm with other minotaurs. They raced about, some carrying lances, others swords, and one group in particular carrying what looked like long, thick ropes ending in grappling hooks. They quickly cordoned off the dragons, those with grappling hooks beginning to spin them around and around.

Leading the group was Scurn. Each man with him, Kaz realized, was a member of the State Guard, whose headquarters was not far away. Even with news of the coming announcement, the guard did not leave the city unprotected.

Neither dragon paid the minotaurs much notice until the first of the grappling hooks went flying. One caught Infernus on a leg, another on his stomach. A third snagged the dragon on the long, sinewy throat. The lancers moved in, their long weapons balanced against the ground so that if a paw or tail tried to land on them, it would first encounter a very sturdy, pointed lance. They avoided Tiberia entirely, though many eyed her with some wariness.

"What jest is this?" bellowed Infernus, affronted by the audacity of the small creatures. "Cease this!"

He got one of the grappling hooks off, but in that time

three others snagged him, two on one of his forelegs and another on his torso.

The scene threw Kaz back a decade. He recalled the same techniques used by the minotaurs and others under rare circumstances when the enemy's dragon allies were caught on the ground. Grappling hooks to catch on to the scaled hide of the dragon, so great a number that even a leviathan would not be able to pull free.

Scurn had evidently remembered the technique.

"Kaz!" called Tiberia. "What do I do?"

It was tempting to retreat and hope that the enterprising Scurn and the guard could pull Infernus down, but Kaz suspected this was one dragon that would not be caught for very long. He doubted that Scurn thought otherwise. The guard captain was doing what he could to give Kaz and Tiberia some advantage.

"Back a step!" he called. "Watch your footing! We charge for the chest. Let the lance do the final work!"

The silver dragon obeyed, carefully avoiding the minotaurs near her feet. Kaz lowered and aimed the dragonlance. One swift thrust and Infernus would be but a bad memory.

As Tiberia steadied herself, Infernus ceased his attempts to pry away the hooks and stared at the younger dragon and his rider. His fiery orbs narrowed, and a knowing look crossed his visage.

All of a sudden, Infernus leapt skyward, his head striking the ceiling hard. The dragon's skull was thick, and the ceiling broke, raining destruction and death down upon the guard. Most of the ropes from the hooks fell loose as the red dragon burst free of the temple, but one minotaur was carried aloft to a point just above the ceiling before he lost his grip and plummeted to his death.

Only when the battered corpse struck the floor did Kaz recognize that it had been Scurn, tenacious to the end. Kaz doubted he would ever fully understand the other minotaur, a warrior who had been rival, foe, and, finally, ally. Honor's Face had once revealed Scurn to have had little honor of his own, but Kaz wondered if, had he taken a second look minutes ago, the reflection would have been strong.

Scurn was only one of many who had died because of Infernus, however, and now the dragon was in the air and flying, revealed to all. There was only one choice left to the minotaur and the silver dragon. They had to follow.

"Stand back!" he commanded the remaining members of the guard. They obeyed without further encouragement. Kaz waited, then leaned close to Tiberia. In a quieter voice he said, "We have to go after him, if you think you can fly."

"I think I can, Kaz. I know I can," Tiberia answered, sounding much older than when the battle had started. A dragon's instincts, perhaps. Kaz held on tight as the silver flexed her wings for the first time . . . and leapt through the hole in the ceiling.

Somewhere above them, they both knew, Infernus waited.

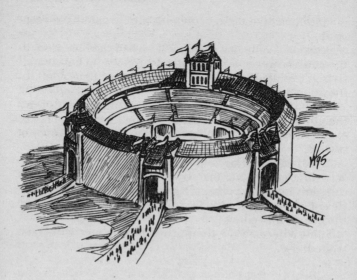

Chapter 18
Aerial Combat

At Toron's and, surprisingly enough, Delbin's insistence, Hecar and the others headed for the circus instead of returning to the temple. Surrounded by the other minotaurs of the Orilg clan, they looked like simply one more group of interested warriors late for the grand announcement.

"I still don't like it!" Fliara muttered to Hecar. "I don't care what Toron says we should do . . . and I certainly do not care what that little monster insists, either! We should go back! There's Scurn to consider, if nothing else. That one has hated my brother for years."

"Toron's words aside," Hecar returned, "Delbin was

as serious about us not going back as I've ever seen him serious about anything. I know a kender's word generally doesn't count for much, but I know this one enough to understand that his insistence means a great deal. I was also next to Kaz . . . or what seemed to be Kaz, if I understand Delbin . . . before the rescue. He was acting strangely. I don't know. I can't say why. But I think we should go to the circus."

"And what can we solve there? We're just a few among many!"

"Is that what you think?" asked Toron, suddenly nearby. Taller than even Kaz, he moved stealthily for a minotaur. He grinned. "Wait until you hear what Helati had planned . . ." His grin grew wider. "Too bad we might not need it, what with Kaz not coming here after all and the rest of you free. Your sister's quite a speaker, from what I understand, Hecar. She gave Dastrun a good scolding."

"But I thought she wasn't here at all. What do you mean?"

"I'll explain later—" was as far as Toron got when the entire party heard the crash.

The sound reminded Hecar of the war, when siege weapons could level half a city in the name of Takhisis. As part of the advance force, he had watched many a rock crash down on buildings and walls, killing defenders and civilians alike. Hecar had never liked siege warfare; it made no distinctions between worthy opponents and innocent children.

"By the horns of Kiri-Jolith, what is that?" roared Toron, suddenly gazing skyward. "It can't be a—"

But it was. Hecar and the others knew what word Kaz's brother could not bring himself to utter. They knew the word, but could no more speak it than the dark-furred warrior, so stunned were they by the sight.

A dragon. A red dragon soaring high into the sky, burying itself in the clouds above.

They stood there, trying to make sense of it, but just as the first shock finally passed, they heard a smaller but no less significant crash.

This time a smaller, sleeker dragon, gleaming silver, raced skyward. There was something on its back, something that Hecar was fairly certain was a rider.

"Silver and red," he whispered. He could never forget the battles he had watched in the sky during the war. "Deadly foes. They'll fight to the death. The rider . . ." It seemed a voice spoke in his head. He nodded to himself, not caring whether the others heard or not. "Yes, it is Kaz. It would have to be."

Belatedly he realized that both dragons flew in the general direction of the circus.

* * * * *

Clouds had gathered over some parts of Nethosak, and Kaz knew that among them hid Infernus. Not for a moment did he think the red dragon was hiding in fear. Rather, Infernus was simply using the heavens to his best advantage, counting on Tiberia's inexperience. This was the first time the silver had flown and, although flight was natural to dragons, Tiberia's unsteady journey so far was an indication of just how much practice she needed.

"What do I do, Kaz?" the silver dragon gasped, pushing hard to gain more altitude. She was clearly frightened, but trusted Kaz to guide her along. "I don't see him!"

"He's in the clouds just above that tower." Infernus might be a master of aerial combat, but the minotaur had picked up a few things during his time as a dragon rider. A creature as large as a red dragon could not hide forever. "Go up! Do it now!"

Arcing awkwardly, the silver dragon rose. Kaz gripped Tiberia and the lance tightly, hoping they would break through the clouds without being attacked. Infernus would not flee. He had to defeat the pair if he hoped to salvage his plan. Fortunately for Tiberia, the red suffered the disadvantage of needing the silver alive. That did not mean Infernus had any intention of sparing Kaz. The minotaur was certain that his death was a priority.

They broke through the clouds . . . and found nothing.

Kaz craned his neck, searching. "Move ahead, but slowly."

"Should I go higher?"

"No, we—" It suddenly occurred to him what Infernus had probably done. "Yes, higher! Higher! Now!"

Startled, the young dragon was slow to react.

Infernus burst from the clouds just below them, colliding into Tiberia's underside. As soon as they touched, the red dragon twisted so that he could sink his claws into his younger counterpart's sides.

Only by sheer luck did Kaz hold on. He cursed himself for being a fool. Infernus had flown back down and come up under them. It was a simple tactic he should have predicted. Evidently he had been away from war much too long.

"I will shake you loose, gnat!" roared Infernus, twisting both dragons around and around. His greater wingspan gave him more control. Tiberia sought to counter his weight, but could not. "I will watch you plummet to your death as Captain Scurn did so nicely!"

It was impossible to get the dragonlance into position. A long tentacle nearly swatted him from his already precarious angle. The minotaur looked around and saw that what had nearly hit him was not a tentacle but rather one of the ropes left over from the guards' attempt to drag Infernus down. At least two of them whipped about as if alive.

Again the rope flew by. Kaz glanced at it, then he pulled himself tighter against Tiberia and shouted, "The rope! Grab the rope with your mouth and pull back!"

Tiberia did not understand at first. Then, as Infernus increased their spinning, the silver dragon snapped at the tether. She missed, but it hovered within range. Tiberia timed her next attempt better, catching hold of a long length of the rope. Immediately she followed the rest of Kaz's instructions.

The grappling hook was lodged deep in the lower scales of the red's neck. As Tiberia pulled, the hook tore deeper. The sudden pull by the other dragon caused Infernus to lose his momentum and, in part, his grip. He shifted his position to regain his advantage.

Kaz stared at the wings, now closer. He made an estimate of Tiberia's jaws and neck. "The wing! Let the rope loose and bite!"

Below them, the red dragon had obviously decided on the same tactic, but Tiberia was small, and her wings, flapping somewhat erratically, made for a more difficult target than the red dragon's much larger ones. Infernus could not stretch his wings back far enough. The silver stretched as far as she could, opened her maw wide, and bit.

Her foe shuddered and, for a moment, the three simply dropped. Tiberia's jaw remained clamped on the wing.

With a snarl, Infernus brought his lower paws up and, using the incredible strength of his legs, pushed the two leviathans apart. By doing so, he further damaged his wing, for Tiberia did not let go willingly. The red dragon fluttered awkwardly around, trying to compensate for the terrible injury.

Less injured, the silver dragon regained control almost immediately. Kaz shifted. They had to strike now before Infernus was able to adjust. He lowered the dragonlance, aimed, and called out, "Fly at him, Tiberia! Fly at him with every ounce of speed you can muster!"

Her companion nodded, spread her wings to their fullest, and pushed herself toward her foe.

They were too near one another for the silver to pick up much speed, but likewise were they too near for the red to maneuver away in any direction without his younger counterpart compensating.

Kaz gritted his teeth for the collision.

The dragonlance pierced its target in the left side of the chest. Infernus roared in agony and, out of sheer reflex, seized hold of Tiberia. Unable to concentrate fully on flying, the red dragon began to drop . . . taking his adversaries with him.

Around and around they spun as they dropped through the clouds. Tiberia flapped her wings as hard as she could, trying to slow if not stop their descent. Kaz realized there was no way the silver dragon could support the three of them, and that Infernus had no intention of releasing his grip. The minotaur tried to pry the dragonlance from the red's chest in the hopes that Infernus might then let them loose, but the lance would not pull free. It was as determined to remain impaled in its target as its target was determined to hold on to Tiberia.

We're going to die! Kaz thought as the first tower tops came into sight below them. We're going to die. Damn you, gray man, we're going to die. I hope you and your balance are happy.

"I . . . won't . . . let you . . . get . . . hurt . . . Kaz!" bellowed the silver dragon. "I won't!"

In desperation, Tiberia stretched her neck down as far as she could, focusing on her target. A fireball barely half as large as Kaz struck one of the red dragon's injured paws. Under other circumstances, Infernus might have shrugged it off. Wounded as he was, however, the crimson leviathan reacted with a shriek of agony.

Tiberia flapped her wings with all the strength she could muster, at the same time pushing away from her dark counterpart with her legs and tail. Infernus tried to grab hold again, but the other injured forepaw could not maintain its grip.

The red dragon fell below, backside down. Infernus might have righted himself had he had more time, but they were already too close to the ground.

Only then did Kaz see that they were over the circus.

The streets and stands were already filled with running and milling figures, all trying to avoid the massive forms plummeting down at them. Tiberia could regain control before they reached the circus, but Kaz saw that Infernus was going to land half in the field and half on the stands, crushing hundreds.

"Tiberia! Knock him into the field!" The field was large enough to contain four beasts the size of Infernus if only they could shove him to the side.

He could have saved his breath, for the young silver dragon was already swooping down, evidently having come to the same realization as the minotaur. Tiberia strained with her talons, trying to gain some hold on the hapless, writhing red. Infernus no longer seemed aware of what was happening to him. He merely snapped at the smaller dragon and tried to slash one of Tiberia's legs with his own claws.

The silver dragon seized the one limb. Infernus dug into her paw. Tiberia did not cry out. Her wings shifted.

Infernus crashed into the ground, Tiberia landing on him, then rolling away. Kaz was thrown toward the red dragon.

He bounced against Infernus, then slid helplessly down the crimson terror's side. Belatedly Kaz realized that Tiberia had prevented a major disaster. Both dragons had managed to land on the field.

But what had happened to the silver dragon? Kaz stumbled to his feet and looked around, trying to orient himself at the same time. His left leg seemed on the verge of collapse, his wounded arm was half numb, and his ribs hurt, but he refused to allow the pain to overwhelm him as he searched. Kaz could not see the silver dragon's immense form, though.

Then he saw the small, very human shape lying against one wall of the field. So accustomed to the human form, Tiberia had reverted to it upon unconsciousness.

Kaz prayed the young female was only unconscious.

Then movement behind him reminded the minotaur there was another dragon to consider. Infernus had taken the brunt of the fall and was gravely injured, but the red leviathan was remarkably strong . . . strong enough still to grasp victory from defeat.

There was only Kaz to stop him. Minotaurs filled the stands, but they stood uncertainly, clearly stunned and confused by the spectacle. By the time they chose to act, it might be too late.

Kaz looked around for some sort of weapon, something he could use to finish off the dragon. To his surprise, he found just what he needed not far from him. It was a godsend, especially considering the shape it had worn when last he had seen it.

Honor's Face, no longer a dragonlance, lay not more than a few feet away. It could not have arrived there of its own accord, yet, there it was. Kaz did not question how it came to be there. He seized it with renewed hope, took one last look at the still form of Ty, then charged toward Infernus.

The dragon suddenly succeeded in righting himself, flipping over and nearly crushing Kaz in the process. But Infernus was not yet recovered enough to rise, much less fly. Still, it wouldn't be long, and Kaz had to move swiftly.

He leapt. The dragon saw him, but too late. The minotaur landed on the upper edge of one wing, then scrambled up to the red dragon's shoulder. Savage jaws snapped at him, but Infernus could not twist his neck enough to reach the minotaur. The red dragon tried to shift enough so that he could bring a paw up, but his injuries and twisted position made it difficult.

Kaz reached the neck. Infernus tried to shake him off, but Kaz hooked his feet into the scales and held fast. He gripped his axe.

"Leave me, gnat, or I will crush you! I command it!"

"No more commands, Infernus, not as high priest or dragon! It's time we were allowed to make our own way in the world!"

"Ungrateful fool!" bellowed the injured dragon, sounding much like the high priest. His voice echoed throughout the circus. "I have guided your race to the glory it has attained! I have molded you into the finest warriors! I sent you into slavery time and again, the better to cull the weak and bring to the forefront the stubbornness, the pride, and the strength you now display! All I ask in return is your allegiance! We will rule the world!"

"You mean *you'll* rule the world . . . we'll just do the dying for you." Kaz raised his battle-axe.

"Your kind was nothing before me and will be nothing without me!" Infernus punctuated the statement by snapping at Kaz. The red dragon was clearly weak, thankfully too weak to cast any spell, it seemed.

"We'll take that chance." Kaz aimed.

Infernus suddenly began to push up. Even as the minotaur brought the axe down with all his might, the red leviathan tried to roll over toward him. Infernus intended to crush Kaz beneath him.

"I am your master!" the red terror roared. "I am your destiny!"

Kaz's footing started to fail, but he did not let up. Honor's Face struck the dragon's neck, sinking deep. Infernus, hissing in agony, pushed harder. Kaz raised the weapon again, knowing he might not complete another swing.

"Paladine, let this blow swing true!" he snarled through clenched teeth. His world was tilting, and only one secured foot prevented him from toppling off the spinning beast.

Once again, Kaz brought the magical axe down.

Once again, the axe changed. It seemed larger, longer, the blades growing as huge as Kaz himself. Yet it was no harder to hold the oversized axe and was no more difficult to guide toward its target. In fact, it was almost as if Honor's Face directed his hand toward the most vital spot on the dragon's neck.

The mirrorlike blade struck deep into Infernus . . . and continued to bite. Incredibly, the cut spread, penetrating the entire neck. Infernus bellowed, and his whole body shook. Kaz lost his grip on the axe and, finally, his footing. He slid backward and would have fallen headfirst to the ground if not for the grappling hook still caught in the dragon's neck. More out of luck than skill, the minotaur caught hold of the rope. He was flung around, but his drop slowed.

The red's shaking ceased.

Still dangling, Kaz waited. Infernus shuddered again, but the motion ended after only a few seconds. Kaz waited a little longer, then began to climb back.

The first thing he saw was Honor's Face. The axe lay on the upper part of the dragon's shoulder. It was back to normal size. Its mirror finish was as pristine as ever.

The second thing he saw was that Infernus's head and neck had been cleanly severed from the body.

Too exhausted to cheer much about the red leviathan's death, Kaz dragged himself over to the axe and picked it up. His battered reflection stared back at him.

"Wish I'd known before that you could do that," he muttered. "It would've come in handy now and then."

All around him, the air filled with thunder. No, Kaz corrected himself, it was not thunder, but the stomping of hundreds of minotaur feet.

Applause and cheers added to the stomping. Kaz heard someone call his name, someone whose voice was familiar to him. Others in the audience, either taking their lead from that voice or recognizing him on their own, also called his name. It quickly grew into a chant that he had no doubt could be heard throughout all of Nethosak.

Then the guards arrived. They started toward the area where Kaz and the dragon were, but before they could get very far, minotaurs began to pour from the stands. They came from all sides. Kaz readied the axe, thinking he could take a few of his enemies with him, when he suddenly noticed that the newcomers were not attacking. They were forming a defensive ring around both the massive corpse and the minotaur, weapons displayed against the guard.

Only then did Kaz recognize several of them as members of Clan Orilg.

"Kaz!" called one warrior. He fought his way through the others and clambered up the dragon as if it were something he did every day. The crowd continued to chant and applaud.

"Hecar? How did all this come about?"

"You can thank Helati and Brogan for it."

It looked as if more than simply Orilg had come to his aid. It was not possible for the entire clan to be here, since many members lived far from Nethosak, which meant that a number of the minotaurs defending his position had to hail from other clans.

"Helati had a little talk with Dastrun and the clan. . . . I'll tell you later how she did that. Not even certain I understand myself. She found out what you'd been up to and what you'd been fool enough to agree to. Then she heard you were supposed to die in the circus today, so she reminded the clan of what its honor meant. It finally agreed to help." Hecar glanced at the crowd and grinned. He clearly enjoyed the moment. "We were supposed to charge the field when they brought you out . . . but no one expected this sort of entrance! That's something I'll have to tell you about in detail later." His eyes widened. "Fliara and the others—"

"Are there." Kaz pointed at one of the entrances. Fliara, Delbin . . . and, if Kaz was not mistaken, his brother Toron, whom he had not seen in longer a time than Fliara. There was no mistaking that streak of hair or that face.

He wondered if Toron knew about their father.

"I think they want to make you emperor, Kaz."

"Polik might have something to say about that."

"I doubt it. He was on the platform taking his victory bows when you and the dragons fell." Hecar shook his head in disgust. "And never have I seen a more pathetic combat. Anyone who did not wonder at his challenger's sluggishness already knew that the combat had been rigged. The longer it went—and it seemed even Polik thought it went too long—the more pitiful it became. It was more a slow slaughter than a battle."

Blinking, Kaz looked down the field. Toward the back end of the great beast he made out a portion of the splintered and exceedingly flattened platform used for imperial challenges. There was no sign of a body on what little of the platform could be seen, and he had no desire to go and verify his friend's words. What was left of the late emperor would be something that would appeal to neither his stomach nor his eyes.

"So you see, they have no qualms about making you emperor. After all, how many minotaurs fight and slay a dragon, especially one of such size, and especially one everyone heard claim it was their master and destiny?" The other minotaur snorted. "As if we would ever accept such a beast as our master!"

Kaz scanned the throng. Hecar was probably correct about the crowd wanting to crown him. Even among those of the circle, there was obvious sentiment for Kaz. One or two members scowled or pretended indifference, but with the exception of those few and a handful of clerics, everyone was saluting the slayer of the dragon.

Dragon? In the aftermath of the red terror's death, Kaz had momentarily forgotten the other dragon, the brave youngster that Kaz considered more responsible for the red's destruction than he.

Abandoning Hecar, he leapt off the massive corpse and went directly toward where he had last seen the young female.

Ty was still there, still unmoving. Kaz broke through the defensive ring and hurried to her side. He knelt down, turning Ty over. The female was breathing. Giving thanks to Paladine, Kaz raised her in his arms. As he did, Ty opened her eyes.

"Kaz?"

"Hush, Ty. It's all right. We beat him. Infernus is dead."

"Did I do good?"

The minotaur snorted. "You did the best anyone could've done under the circumstances. I'm proud of you. Your parents would've been proud of you, too."

Ty smiled, then closed her eyes again.

"The balance is almost restored. You have the gratitude of many, Kaz."

Still carrying the transformed Ty, Kaz turned. The gray

man, staff in hand, stood behind him.

"I thought I broke that," the minotaur commented, referring to the staff. "And what's that you're saying about the balance *almost* being restored? Infernus is dead. The danger is past. When the smoke clears, they'll see that this invasion is going to drive us only to ruin."

"The invasion does not matter without Infernus, Kaz. If they launch it, the minotaurs will fail. This is not their time . . . if such a time is ever to come. I can promise you that." The mage glanced down at his staff. "As for this, it is more durable than it appears."

"What about the balance, then? What do you mean?"

His hooded companion sighed. "The red dragon is dead, but the silver remains. If she remains too long, one of the Dark Lady's draconian creatures will awaken. Although it might be hard to believe, there are worse dragons than Infernus. Should both dragons remain in the world for very long, the compact made at the end of the war will crumble. It has been crumbling these past eight years. I have been busy, very busy, but for a long time even I did not know the truth. Still, Takhisis will be allowed to renew her drive for conquest much too soon if the hatchling is not dealt with immediately."

"I think you told me that before, but what can I do?"

"There are two choices, Kaz." The gray man studied Ty. "I may take her to where she must go. However, I can take her only if she truly wants to leave."

"And the other choice?"

"She must die, minotaur. You will have to kill her, since I am forbidden to do so. She must die or the world returns to imbalance, and thousands of others must die in the ensuing conflicts."

"I won't kill her! You're mad, mage!" Kaz backed away from the gray figure.

"Then she must leave. She must come with me."

"To what? To where? She obviously knows nothing about where you want to take her! She knows only this world." It seemed unfair to the minotaur that Ty had to be taken from everything and everyone she knew because some gods had made a deal. Ty belonged here. Kaz would be more than happy to allow her to stay in the settlement. In the short time since he had met her, she had proven a brave, honorable companion.

"Kaz?"

He looked down to see that Ty had opened her eyes again. By the looks of her, the young woman had heard everything that had been said. "Ty, I—"

"Kaz, I'll go with him."

"Listen! The gods don't have to have their way! They—"

Ty slipped out of his grip. Her stance was unsteady, but she refused help from the minotaur. She gazed at both Kaz and the gray man. "I know I don't have a choice, really, Kaz. I have to leave." Ty steadied herself. "I don't want another war like the one you've talked about, Kaz. It sounds awful. Fighting Infernus showed me how terrible another war would be."

"Do you mean that?" It still seemed unfair to Kaz, but the female sounded determined.

"I do. If I stay much longer, another dragon will awake. I couldn't face that. Too many people would get hurt or die, including maybe you and Delbin."

"The decision is made, then," announced the gray man. His expression softened. "For what it is worth, Tiberia, I regret it must be so. You deserve to live as you desire. I can say only that you shall at least join your sire and your siblings where you are going."

Ty brightened. "I'll see them?"

"I promise." The gray mage smiled. "Then you all shall have a pleasant sleep."

Sleep was one thing Ty definitely needed. The female required time for her injuries to heal. She closed her eyes, then asked, "Is it far? I don't think I can fly far."

"You will not need to fly." Raising his staff, the gray man looked behind him. A hole appeared, a hole that glowed brightly from within. "We will walk. It is not so far that way." He extended his free hand to the transformed dragon. "If you are ready, we should leave very

305

soon."

Ty turned to Kaz. "Could—could you say good-bye to Delbin for me? I wish there were more time, but . . . I don't want another dragon like Infernus coming."

"I'll say good-bye to Delbin for you."

She leapt forward, wrapping her arms around the minotaur. Kaz froze, then slowly hugged Ty back. "I won't forget you, Kaz! Thank you for everything."

Kaz lifted her chin, meeting Ty's eyes. "You are an honorable warrior, Tiberia, and a good lass, as my father would have said."

Ty lowered her gaze. "I'm sorry about Ganth, Kaz. If it hadn't been for me—"

"Don't think that. Infernus was responsible. Ganth would thank you. You avenged not only him and my mother, but all those minotaurs who died so that Infernus could mold us to his and the Dark Queen's damnable vision."

From behind Ty, the gray man called, "Tiberia. It must be soon. Already there is stirring."

Breaking away, the young human dragon joined the mage. Ty looked back at Kaz and smiled.

"Paladine watch over you, Ty," the minotaur called.

"Thank you again, Kaz. . . . I'll think of you."

"And I you."

"You have my gratitude, too, Kaz," added the gray figure, somewhat sadly. "And my apologies for what I had to do. Know that your father . . . and mother . . . watch over you."

"I understand . . . and thank you, mage."

With that, the pair walked into the hole. As they entered, Ty waved one last time. The hole vanished as she lowered her hand.

It was over, just like that. Kaz felt cheated. The female had hardly time to recover and enjoy some peace with her newfound friends. She had hardly time to see the world. Then again, as a dragon, she might someday see a world that existed long after Kaz was gone.

"Kaz!" There was no mistaking Delbin's voice. "Kaz!

Is Ty all right? Where is she? I thought she was over here, but—"

"Take a breath, Delbin," said Hecar.

Kaz turned to face his friends and family. Hecar stood there with Delbin and Kaz's brother and sister. They were not alone, either. There was an entire contingent of minotaurs, not all of them from the clan of Orilg. One group in particular simultaneously interested and worried him. They were members of the Supreme Circle. There also was a handful of clerics.

"I'll tell you about Ty later, Delbin," he said, warily watching the others close in on him. "I promise."

The circle paid little mind to Kaz's friends and relations, barging through the gathering without comment. Kaz looked them over and saw that all eight members were there, their identities marked by the clasps of their cloaks. Three he recognized personally, but the others not at all.

"Hail, Kaziganthi de-Orilg!" called a scarred warrior with gray fur on top and one eye covered with a patch. His name was Athus, and Kaz recalled him from the war. Athus had never struck him as someone who would bow to the high priest's dictates, but it was difficult to say how the old warrior had changed over the years.

"Hail, Athus." Kaz surveyed the gathering. "Come to personally arrest me this time?"

"His Holiness—" began one cleric.

"There is your high priest." Athus pointed at the red dragon's huge form. "We all heard the voice. We all know that voice and that tone even if the form is different. Am I right, Kaziganthi?"

"You are."

"It is a lie!" The same cleric pushed forward. "When the high priest comes—"

Kaz snorted. "You should begin thinking more about which of you is going to be the new high priest, rather than wasting time on empty protests. Jopfer, as you knew him anyway, is dead. That leaves a vacancy that must be filled, don't you think?"

The cleric shut up. Kaz watched with amusement as the robed figures began to eye one another. These were some of the red dragon's highest-ranking servants. Any one of them could claim the right of succession. There would be some duels before the week was out, which did not sadden Kaz in the least.

Athus also seemed to enjoy the clerics' sudden realization. He finally shook his head, responding to Kaz's earlier question. "No, Kaziganthi, we've not come to arrest you. Far from it. If anything, I think the majority of us are quite pleased to see you."

That was exactly as he had feared. Kaz remained quiet, waiting.

"Emperor Polik is dead." A trace of a smile again escaped Athus. "Definitely dead. As his challenger died before him, there is a void that must be filled, a void even more important than that which the priesthood faces." The graying minotaur ignored dark looks from more than one cleric. "I think we've all seen and heard enough today to know who exemplifies what we most seek in an emperor. Honor, bravery, determination to face all odds in the course of one's duty, and, of course, the cunning and strength needed to attain victory in combat."

"Listen all around you, Kaziganthi," spoke one of the other members, a shorter, wider minotaur with one crooked horn and, for one of their kind, what would be called a flat snout. "They are still chanting your name. They want you, Kaziganthi! We want you!"

Athus nodded. "We salute you, Emperor Kaziganthi, slayer of dragons and champion of the people!"

The clansmen of Orilg who stood nearby cheered, especially Kaz's siblings. But Hecar seemed less enthusiastic. He was proud of his sister's mate, but he knew Kaz better than the rest. He was probably the only one here who truly knew what Kaz thought of becoming emperor.

Kaz faced the circle and the clerics. He could not deny feeling pride that he had been so chosen. It was the greatest accolade his people could have given him.

"I prefer Kaz as a name," he responded, standing as tall as he could. His body wanted to lie down and sleep for a month, but he did not listen to it, not yet. "And I prefer to decline your offer. I'm not the kind of emperor you want, and I never will be. You'll have to fight that out among yourselves."

As soon as he was finished speaking, Kaz walked past the stunned and gaping minotaur leaders, joined his family and friends, and headed for the circus's nearest exit.

Chapter 19
The Future

Kaz could not help but admire Nethosak as the ship carrying him and the others departed for the south. His people had indeed accomplished much in a few short years, yet if they could forego their historic drive for power and spend more time on improving their lives, he believed they would accomplish much, much more. The minotaur race was indeed destined for glory. However, one did not necessarily need to achieve glory through conquest.

He hoped some of what he had said to the Supreme Circle and the rest had sunk in, but only time would tell.

"I can't believe how much you got out of them, considering you threw the throne back in their faces," Hecar remarked, standing next to him. "This ship, calling off the invasion, the funeral pyre for your father . . . a magnificent, touching sight that was, too."

Kaz nodded. He, Fliara, and Toron's family had represented the children of Ganth and Kyri, the others being far off in other parts of the homeland. They would be notified, however, along with other relations. The pyre had rivaled those of great emperors of the past. Dastrun, much to Kaz's pleasure, had been forced to give a great speech extolling the old mariner's accomplishments. He had done an excellent job of it, too, perhaps hoping he would be able to maintain his position as patriarch even though both of his patrons were now dead.

There had been other pyres, too: one for Scurn, who Kaz made certain was honored for his bravery, and one, not very well attended, for the late emperor. The burning of Infernus's body had taken a great deal more effort, considering both the dragon's size and its natural resistance to fire. A variety of flammable oils had helped that effort.

Kaz turned to his friend. "Should I have accepted?"

"No. I, like the others, was proud that they wanted you, but it's not right for you. You want something different. You don't want to conquer a world. Besides, Helati would have killed both of us if you had accepted."

Kaz chuckled. "There is that. As for conquest, hopefully the Supreme Circle and the new emperor will think long before they embark on rash adventures. The gray man said that if they continued with the invasion, they would fail."

"I'd like to meet this gray man . . . and give him a piece of my mind. I still haven't forgiven him for using you, maybe all of us, like that. No, I've changed my mind. I'd rather give him a piece of my fist."

Now that things were calmer and Kaz could think, he felt he understood the mage better. There was always a hint of sorrow in those eyes, sorrow and, most of all, frustration.

Thinking of the mage made him think of Ty. Most of

the minotaurs had taken his word that the silver dragon had vanished because her work had been done, but Hecar and the kender had wanted to know a little more, especially Delbin. It had taken some effort to explain to the kender, but when Kaz had finished, Delbin had been so impressed by what had happened, he had immediately sought his notebook . . . at which point the kender had discovered one or two objects that belonged to Athus, as it turned out.

"Forget the mage," Kaz told his companion. "He did what had to be done." After another pause, he asked, "Do you think they really listened?"

Kaz had been forced to make a speech rejecting the crown for the benefit of the crowd, while trying to keep from offending them. He knew, he told them, that he would not be a good emperor. He had enough trouble leading his own small settlement. He recommended some immediate changes concerning one or two members of the circle, who saved themselves further dishonor by resigning there and then. As for the clerics, they needed to spend some time working themselves back into the good graces of the people.

Toward the end of the speech, after telling everyone what Infernus had done, Kaz reminded the minotaurs of what mattered most. They were their own leaders now, possibly for the first time in their nation's existence. If they made mistakes, they could blame only themselves.

"Remember that life without truth or honor is nothing," he had concluded. "If we are the children of destiny, we must act suitably."

"Are you two going to stand by that rail through the entire trip?" bellowed Toron from behind Hecar and Kaz. Kaz's brother had decided to join the settlement, taking his family—his mate and three small children—with him. They evidently were still below, possibly with Fliara, whose company Hecar seemed to enjoy.

In fact, there were more than a hundred minotaurs aboard the ship, dubbed *Dragonslayer* in Kaz's honor, and even the crew included new additions to the settlement. Several were from his old clan, but many had come from others. There would be more coming as the weeks went on. Kaz might have rejected the role of emperor, but he still had found no way around turning his back on the village that had grown around his dwelling. With a hundred more minotaurs, it would be more like a town from now on.

He hoped he would not be calling it a city before long.

At least there were not any gully dwarves aboard. Clan Orilg and the circle had taken it upon themselves to escort the creatures back to their home, such as it was. Galump had become unelected leader of the newly released slaves, who had nearly forgotten their enslavement already; such was the benefit of a limited memory span.

"We were taking one last look at Nethosak," Hecar finally responded to Toron.

"I can do without the entire homeland! There are better adventures than fighting one worthless war after another. I would rather my children explore when they grow older."

Coming from Toron, who had always played warrior even as a very young child, that was something. Kaz nodded his agreement. "Exploration would be good. There's another continent. Why should Nethosak be the only one sending ships to chart it?"

Hecar looked both of them over. "First you're going to take some time to raise your children, Kaz, or Helati will have both of our hides . . . and you would do well to do the same with your own mate, Toron. She seems the strong-minded type when it comes to family."

Kaz's brother laughed heartily. "Perhaps I'll go down even now and see if my mate needs me. I'll leave you two alone to admire Nethosak."

As he departed, Hecar mumbled, "It's going to take me a while to get used to him, Kaz."

"Think of him as a younger me."

"I'd rather not. You couldn't ever have been like that."

Kaz laughed. The two of them returned their gazes to the shore. Kaz knew that the bulk of minotaur history to come would always emanate from Mithas and Kothas, especially from Nethosak. Good or ill, though, the future would be determined by the minotaurs themselves. Kaz suspected their basic nature would not change much.

The dream of destiny would, of course, continue without Infernus. Deep inside, Kaz suspected that most of his people needed the dream, if only because they felt too unlike the other races to comfortably live with them.

"We have been enslaved, but have always thrown off our shackles," Kaz found himself whispering. "We have been driven back, but always returned to the fray stronger than before. We have risen to new heights when all other races have fallen into decay. We are the future of Krynn, the masters of the entire world. We are the children of destiny."

Hecar grunted in disgust. "Are we really?"

He shrugged. Nethosak was tiny in the distance now, seemingly inconsequential. Kaz squinted and thought he could still make out what might have been the ruined roof of the temple.

"I don't know," the minotaur murmured more to himself than to his companion. "I don't know. We'll just have to wait and see, won't we?"

They watched Nethosak continue to shrink, thinking no more about its future. After all, Kaz and the others, including Helati and the rest of those already at the settlement, had their own to consider . . . and that was more pressing at the moment.